DAMASCUS REDEMPTION

Richard C. Pendry

WORDCATCHER publishing

First Edition, 2016, published by Octavo Publishing Ltd .

Second Edition, 2017.

Published by Wordcatcher Publishing, Cardiff.
02921 888321
www.wordcatcher.com

Paperback ISBN: 9781912056309

Dedicated to my father.

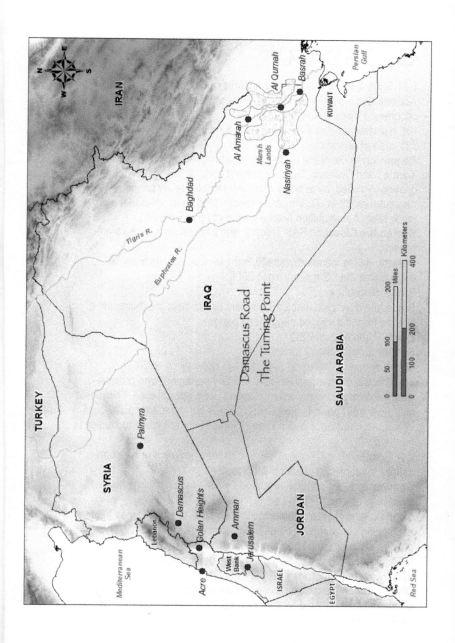

GLOSSARY

5.11 Shirt: tactical shirt used by security operators

Actions On: a set of predetermined steps taken when an identified occurrence takes place.

AK: Kalashnikov Assault Rifle, model number AK47.

AO: area of operation.

B6 armour: most of the armoured vehicles used in hostile areas are Toyota Land Cruisers. These armoured cars, or B6s as they are commonly called, have been fitted with the necessary protection to rate them as B6 III. This means they can stop small arms that use conventional ammunition (with a calibre of up to 7.62mm).

Beaten the Clock: an SAS Trooper who has returned alive from a mission.

Beretta: Italian manufactured M9 9mm semi-automatic pistol, in service with the US military since 2006.

Binos: binoculars.

Blade: the nickname that SAS troopers use to describe themselves, derived from the winged dagger cap badge.

Braai: South African BBQ.

Brit Mil: British Military forces.

C 130: Hercules Transport Aircraft, also known as a HERC.

The Circuit: the name given to ex-military personnel who provide close protection security within a limited geographical area. The oldest and most well known is the London Circuit, but there are now circuits in Iraq, Afghanistan, Libya and any location in which close protection is required.

CO: Commanding Officer of a British military regiment or battalion, usually the rank of a Lieutenant Colonel.

Comms: all types of communication device - ranging from phones through to elaborate radio sets.

Connex: easily transportable accommodation. It usually takes the form of shipping containers or other prefabricated dwellings configured to provide office or living accommodation.

CPA: Coalition Provisional Authority, the government set up to run Iraq directly after the invasion in 2003.

Dhow / Badan: a small boat used throughout the Persian Gulf. It may be motorized, propelled by sails or oars.

DFAC: military dining facility

ECM: Electric Counter Measures - devices that block electronic signals used to initiate IEDs.

EFP: Explosively Formed Penetrator, also known as an explosively formed projectile, also known as a roadside bomb or IED. It is a shaped-charge designed to penetrate armour effectively from a distance. This deadly bomb uses high explosives to melt a copper or brass slug, and to project it at high speed towards an unsuspecting target.

FCO: Foreign and Commonwealth Office, the British government's overseas directorate.

FNG: fucking new guy.

Full Screw: army slang for a full corporal, a junior NCO.

H: Hereford.

Helo: abbreviation for helicopter.

IED: Improvised Explosive Device often called a roadside bomb.

IDF: indirect fire, mortar or rocket fire that is aimed indiscriminately, as opposed to direct fire, which is aimed accurately at a specific target.

IPS: Iraqi Police Service, the organisation set up by the Coalition to police Iraq.

KIA: killed in action.

LA85A2: standard issue Brit Mil rifle.

LS: landing site.

Ma'dan: name given to those that live in the Marshes

MIA: missing in action.

MI: Military Intelligence.

Military Medal: military decoration (known as 'the MM') awarded for acts of bravery among those below the rank of commissioned officer.

Minimi: a Belgian machine gun developed by Frabique Nationale that fires 5.56mm ammunition. Also called a Section Attack Weapon' (or SAW) by the US military.

MP: Military Police.

NAAFI: Navy, Army and Air Force Institute which provides welfare for British military personnel.

NATO Coffee: coffee with milk and two sugars.

OC: officer commanding a Brit Mil unit up to the size of a squadron or company, usually the rank of a Major.

OP: operation.

Para: serving or ex-member of The Parachute Regiment

Presel Switch: switch device on a radio that when pressed allows the operator to send a message.

PSC: Private Security Company.

RAMC: Royal Army Medical Corps.

RAR: Royal Australian Regiment.

Recce: reconnaissance.

RMP: Royal Military Police

RPG: Rocket Propelled Grenade.

RQMS: Regimental Quarter Master Sergeant.

RSM: Regimental Sergeant Major, appointment held by a Warrant Officer First Class, the senior enlisted man in a Brit Mil formation.

RUF: Revolutionary United Front, the rebel group in Sierra Leone that tried to overthrow the government during the civil war (1991-2002.)

SAS: 22 Special Air Service Regiment, based at Hereford, part of the British Army's Special Forces Group.

Scoff: Para slang for food.

SF Club: Special Forces Club.

Snatch Land Rover: A vehicle based on a Land Rover chassis, initially used in Northern Ireland. The vehicle is armoured with a fibreglass composite.

SNCO: Senior Non Commissioned Officer.

SOPs: standing operational procedures.

Sunray: the callsign used by the commander of a Brit Mil formation.

TAB: tactical advance to battle, speed marching.

Vauxhall: Vauxhall Cross – the building located on the South Bank of the River Thames in London. It houses the Secret Intelligence Service / MI6.

Wellhead: engineering component at the surface of an oil or gas well that provides the necessary structural and pressure-containing interface for the drilling and production equipment to operate.

Zero: the base/HQ location within the communication network.

PROLOGUE

The two children stood at the entrance of the temple, their silhouettes lost against the backdrop of the large wooden door that the youngest now closed behind them. 'Sshh,' the girl whispered in annoyance with her brother as the *click* of the lock engaged, breaking the silence.

Determined not to utter another sound, they both stood perfectly still, trying to control their breathing, their small chests heaving from boisterous play. They watched as the robed figure at the other end of the temple conducted the ceremony. A ritual they had seen performed many times.

The sword was held aloft in praise. The sun's rays, finding their way through the building's reed walls, glinted on its highly polished surface, as the robed figure - uttering words that neither child understood - offered the ancient weapon to the stone box set in the centre of the small, crimson-dressed altar.

As the silence settled once more, the girl grabbed her brother's shoulder. She pushed an index finger to her lips in an attempt to control his bubbling energy. The boy, annoyed at the interruption, brushed her hand aside and continued to watch. He replicated the actions of the priest with his own wooden, toy sword, observing, enthralled, as the ceremony drew to a close. The priest placed the sword on a bed of lambskin, the soft leather sheet covering the cold steel as more unknown words filled the silent void.

The robed figure turned, his face agitated at having been disturbed. But, at the moment he recognised the two intruders, their innocence framed so perfectly against the heavy wooden door at the end of the nave, his scowl vanished, replaced by a loving smile. 'Come,' he said, as he dropped to one knee and stretched out his arms, 'Come, Rachel. Come, John. Come to Papa.'

John, now exempted from the usual protocol of the holy place, needed no second invitation. He rushed forward, the noise of his bare feet slapping on the cool stone slabs. His footfall amplified by the vaulted ceiling which was held in place by a row of woven reed columns, their thickness supporting the arched ceiling many metres above his head. Rachel took a little longer to reach her father, her progress more dignified, the extra two years conferring on her a consciousness yet to appear in her younger brother.

'How are my two special people?' he said as he embraced them both. 'What have you been up to today?'

'We went out into the Marshes,' John answered, unable to curb his excitement. 'In Uncle Peter's boat. I caught a fish, didn't I, Rachel?'

'Yes, Papa, he caught a fish,' replied Rachel. 'And he wants Mama to cook it for supper.'

'Can we, Papa? Can we have it for supper?' asked John.

'We will have to check with your mother first. But.... I can't see why not,' he said, as he stood up, taking their small hands in his. 'Come, let's go and ask her.'

The three stepped out into the late afternoon sunlight, the midday heat waning, dissipated by the cooling breeze that blew in from the Marshes, making the abundant reeds bend and their baggy clothes billow. 'When will I start to do the ceremonies?' John asked as he skipped alongside his father, wooden sword in hand.

'When you're bigger,' replied his father.

'How much bigger?' John continued. 'Will I know the words by then?'

'I didn't know the words at your age either. But don't worry; I will teach you, like my father taught me.'

The village was coming to life as the Iraqi sun ebbed, the more strenuous chores of the day easier to accomplish at this enabling time. The animals knew what was to come, now became restless, their calls more frequent as their expectations grew, signalled by the fading light. This was the time of the day that John loved. His work done, he could return home, spend time with the children and help his wife as she prepared the evening meal. He loved the village; it was his world, and as its Elder, he was in charge of it. He had no additional privileges for being their leader; his house was of the same ancient design, with the same adobe walls and thatched roof as all the rest; it was no bigger. There were no trinkets on display, for these were simple people.

There was however a reward, a prize that he never mentioned, but which he was reminded of every time he looked at his two children. They were his bloodline, the direct descendants of the knight who had come from the West over 800 years previously. They were the future of the Masahuin.

'So, was *your* father called John?' asked the child as he looked up with large, inquisitive blue eyes.

'Yes, he was. And he named me John. And you will name your son John also. It is our tradition. The eldest boy in our family is always named after Sir John, the knight that came and delivered our people, the Masahuin, to Jesus.'

The boy nodded in answer, his six-year-old brain absorbing the information as best it could.

Rachel stopped dead in her tracks and pointed at a dark speck which, although low on the horizon, was clearly visible. Its shape struck against the clear blue sky as it skimmed across the reeds in the foreground. 'What is it, Papa?'

He knew what it was. There had been more and more of them, their presence increasing above the sea of marshes that surrounded the Masahuin village. They had been there since Saddam had begun his fight with the Americans, after the invasion of Kuwait. Some of the young Masahuin had gone to fight in the uprising in Basrah, their youthful enthusiasm uncurbed even by their pleading mothers, who now waited in anguish for their offspring's homecoming. Some had already returned among the flotsam of men who had dared to stand up against the Iraqi President. He knew that no good would come of it. He knew that the ancient tradition of letting the marshes protect them was diminishing. He acknowledged that the outsiders they'd already sheltered would now tell of the mysterious people living deep in the marshes, and of their strange customs. But what could he do? The code of chivalry given to them by the knight said that they must comfort those who are in need and protect them until they are able to protect themselves. They had fulfilled this instruction, but he knew that his community was made vulnerable by it. These aircraft could hover like birds of prey over locations to which formerly only the skilled Masahuin had been able to navigate.

'RUN,' he shouted as the solitary speck turned into a swarm, the low drone of engines clearly audible, as several aircraft headed directly for them. 'RUN. Run to the house. Tell your mother to stay there until I return.'

'Where are you going, Papa?' Rachel cried, looking back at her father.

'I must go to the temple. I have to protect the Secret. You'll be safe. Now, GO!'

He watched as the two figures disappeared into the house, then turned, and ran. Horrified, as the ground all around him began to erupt with plumes of dust, as bullets struck the loose surface, he stumbled, his legs unable to keep up with the adrenalin being pumped through his body, his mass skidding to an ungainly halt as the dark belly of the helicopter passed over him. He watched as what appeared to be an oil drum was jettisoned from the fuselage. The cylinder tumbled through an awkward trajectory, hanging in the air for what seemed like minutes before it gave in to gravity and smashed into a house fifty metres ahead of him. For a second, there was nothing except the stink of petrol. The explosion was huge.

I am in hell, he thought, as he watched the fireball devour everything in its path, the power of the inferno even sucking the air out of his lungs. *Lord, what have we done to deserve this?* he mouthed as he fell, unconscious.

PART ONE

CHAPTER ONE

Belgrave Square, London,
May 5, 2007.

The call on his mobile phone the previous evening had come up as 'number withheld.' He hadn't answered - he didn't like surprises - and had let it ring out. Minutes later, his phone had registered a message. The caller hadn't left his name. There was no need; although this was a voice he hadn't heard in over six years, there was no mistaking the thick Glaswegian accent. 'Mason,' it said, 'I need to see you tomorrow. Come to my office first thing. Fifty-One Belgrave Square. It's urgent.'

His finger had hovered above the *delete* button. And, on any other night, annoyed at the intrusion, he would have pressed it. But, for some reason – maybe only curiosity - he didn't delete it. He'd known this man all his adult life, but couldn't guess what 'urgent' might mean. *He's up to something.*

Mason had been on his own for years - got used to his own company. Was he feeling lonely now? Craving his past life? What was it about this message that intrigued him? It would have been so easy to let it go – as easy as sleeping

1

in when you could hear the rain lashing against the window – as easy as dodging the early morning run you'd promised yourself. In the end, he decided to leave it to fate. *'First thing?' Well, if I wake up in time, that's the sign*, he said, as he pulled the covers over.

Mason counted off the numbers of the plush stuccoed houses that fronted onto the affluent West London street. Recognising the number in front of him as the one in the message, he climbed the small flight of marbled steps and paused, staring at his faceless reflection in the highly polished black Georgian panelled door that stood between two ornate pillars.

He took the note from his pocket and checked its details with those of the brass plaque to the right of the door, its well-attended finish gleaming in the early morning sunshine. He let out a long sigh. The black enamelled letters on the plaque were clearly visible: 'Target Security, 51 Belgrave Square'. *This is the place*, he said to himself, looking around, taking in the location. On either side of the Target building were other grand Georgian structures, their ornate balconies draped with flags that fluttered in the light morning breeze. He recognised one of the flags straight away: the pale blue and white stripes of Argentina. The dark green flag on the building to the right took longer to identify, a gust of wind finally revealing the white crescent moon and star of Pakistan.

This is about as respectable you can get. So JJ O'Hare is rubbing shoulders with ambassadors in one of the most prestigious areas in London. This property must be costing him a fortune. I knew he'd gone out on his own. I heard he's doing well. But this is...unbelievable.

He was rooted to the spot as the anger grew inside him. He felt like he was back in school, summoned by the headmaster. *Who the hell does he think he is?* he said to himself. He made a fist with his right hand, crushing the note into a ball, throwing it at the door before storming off.

At the road junction he was still consumed by his feelings. He walked straight out into the busy morning traffic, only coming to his senses when a cab was forced to swerve, giving him a long piercing blast of its horn.

Mason jumped back onto the pavement, his anger now directed at the cab driver, who he could see driving off into the distance, his arm out of the window, right middle finger pointing skyward.

He stood at the kerb and watched the surge of black cabs, red buses and four-by-fours pass in front of him, looking for a gap to dash into. There was none. As he waited, he was engulfed by diesel fumes, the acrid smell from the countless exhausts bringing him to his senses, his anger subsiding.

So where are you going in such a hurry, anyway? Okay, you haven't seen him for ages. Sure, you didn't like him then, and it's doubtful you will like him now. But you're not exactly spoilt for options at the moment, are you? Why don't you see what he has to say? There's no harm in that. Calmed, he retraced his steps.

He walked back up the marble steps and onto the portico and pressed the intercom. 'Target Security,' answered a metallic voice, 'How can I help you?'

'I have a meeting with JJ O'Hare.'

'And your name, please...?'

'Mason'.

'Ah yes, Mr Mason. Mr O'Hare is expecting you. Please come in.'

The buzzer sounded. Mason pushed the door, stepped over the crushed note, and entered JJ's world.

As the door closed behind him, he realised that he could go no further, his way blocked by a Perspex screen. A polite but authoritative voice spoke: 'Mr Mason, please empty your pockets and place the contents in the tray to your right. Then step forward into the cubicle.' As he entered the transparent chamber, the door closed behind him with a click. The nozzles that lined the confined area began to hiss as they

3

analysed the air within.

Checking for explosive residue. This is advanced. I bet even MI5 doesn't have this yet.

'Okay, Mr Mason. You can step through now. Collect your belongings and make your way over to the reception desk,' the guard continued, pointing to Mason's left, where three ladies wearing headsets were chatting away with polished accents.

One of the receptionists looked up at him. 'Hello, Mr Mason,' she said, with a smile, as he approached.

'It's just Mason, thanks,' he said, returning her pleasantry.

'Yes... Mr O'Hare will see you shortly. Please take a seat.'

The waiting area was to the left of the reception desk. It had three black leather chrome legged sofas laid out in a hollow square. In the middle was a coffee table, adorned with the obligatory waiting room magazines. On the sofas sat five men, so busy filling out forms that they were unaware of Mason as he sat down.

He reached over and picked up the nearest magazine from the glass-topped table, checking out his waiting companions as he did so. They were all wearing badges, the black felt-tip scrawl displaying their first names. Four of them had shaved heads and were dressed in badly fitting suits, each man unknowingly tugging at his shirt collar in an attempt to gain comfort. *Bought in a hurry, especially for the interview, I bet... These are no businessmen.*

He continued to scan the room, his eyes resting on the man who sat on the end of the sofa to his left. It was difficult to gauge his height, but he was big: over six feet tall, with dark skin - the type that came from sun beds - and wore his blonde hair long, over the collar, with an earring in his right lobe. Mason estimated he was in his late twenties. He was dressed casually - the only one of the five not in a suit - and his clothing seemed to have been bought a size too small. His jeans and T shirt struggled to cover an expanse of

4

muscle he seemed eager to flex at every opportunity. His jaw, large and over-pronounced, tensed as he pondered over the form. *Steroids... has to be. The other guys are ex-military, but this one... I don't know.*

Mason's bemusement was turning to intrigue. He threw the magazine hard onto the table and waited, ready to gauge the men's reactions. Only one of them looked up. The rest were so engrossed in their clerical task that they remained oblivious to his test. He was in his forties, with 'Steve' written neatly in capitals on the white patch of his lapel. His skin was pink and heavy, telling of a life of over-indulgence, the coloured stripes on his tie alluding to a military past. He looked at Mason, the two men exchanging a nod before his concentration returned to his form.

Mason's eyes shifted to the young suntanned man. As he studied him further the man looked up and caught his eye. 'Rob, mate,' the man said, offering his hand, 'but everyone calls me Thor.' As they shook, Mason noticed that he had a Viking's helmet tattoo on his right bicep, with the name 'THOR' above it.

'You Scandinavian, then?' asked Mason.

'No, mate. I'm from Watford

Mason nodded, as he let go of the powerful grip. 'Yes... yes... of course,' he said, turning away in an attempt to end the conversation.

None of the other men in the waiting area had given Thor much attention. He had tried to be polite, but each one had given him the cold shoulder. Mason's brief acknowledgment of him had been welcome. Thor was the type who needed to talk when he was nervous, and boy was he nervous.

'You here for a job in Iraq then?' asked Thor, desperately trying to keep the conversation alive.

'Maybe.'

'I saw the advert in a body guard magazine,' he continued. 'Didn't realise that people would be taking it so seriously, you know, suits and all,' he said, nodding towards the four men who were still writing away.

5

'Iraq is a serious place' replied Mason.

'Yeah...yeah, I know that. My mate is out there now, he tells me everything. The bombs, the shootings, everything. He's a good guy. We were doormen together.'

Mason held up his hand in a sign to stop the conversation. 'Did you just say doormen?'

'Yeah, we both are. Work the clubs in Watford.'

'So, not military?'

'Naaah... nearest I've been to a gun is the army cadets when I was fourteen.'

Mason sat back. He could see it now. It made sense. 'You look like a doorman,' he said.

'Thanks,' replied Thor, tensing a bicep in gratitude.

'So, let me get this straight,' Mason said as he sat forward. 'You're here because you answered an ad in a magazine. And if you pass the interview, you're going to join your doorman friend in Iraq?'

'Yeah. That's it.'

Mason sat back into the leather sofa, looked at the ceiling and exhaled. He looked again at the men who were still grappling with the written forms. He was out of practice; he knew that. While constantly on operations, the men of the SAS developed an additional sense: instinct, intuition: call it what you will. The outcome was the same; Mason and the men he worked with could *read* a room, or any other environment for that matter. Situational awareness, they called it. It was the ability to pick up on things virtually hidden from the untrained eye.

He looked again at the four men still struggling away with the biro pens. They were ex-military. That was a given. But they were well into their forties. And, from the way the buttons were straining on their newly bought suits, it was apparent they hadn't seen the inside of a gym in a decade. *These guys are well past their sell by date*, he mused, as his eyes came back to rest on the prize of the bunch: Thor. *What the hell is JJ playing at?*

'Are you okay, mate?' asked Thor, noticing that Mason

had put his hands over his face.

Thor's question broke the spell. Curiosity had led Mason here. But it wasn't doing very much for him now. *Fuck this, I'm off*, he thought, as he got up and headed for the exit.

The receptionists gave a puzzled look as he strode by their desk. But he didn't even give them a second glance; he wasn't playing their game anymore. Stopping at the exit, he motioned to the guard to open the door, the curved Perspex barrier taking what seemed like an age before producing enough of a gap to allow his departure.

As he neared the heavy polished external doors, a booming voice from behind stopped him in his tracks. 'Hey, Mason, where you going?' The words hung in the air, as the whole office paused at their labour and looked at the two men.

JJ closed on Mason with measured steps. He could read the body language and sense the tension. He noted Mason's stance: his left shoulder pointed directly at the *threat*, a telltale sign of his annoyance, of his willingness to fight. As JJ got closer, he held up both his hands, a disarming gesture that humans have used since primordial times. It worked. They shook hands, the tension eased.

'Where you off to? I was looking forward to a chat,' said JJ as he took in the appearance of the man he hadn't seen for over six years. He noted how Mason's sandy-blond hair was going grey at the edges. And that he was carrying a few more pounds over his six-foot frame. But the nose was still crooked - broken in a long forgotten fight - and the steel blue eyes were still as intense as the first time he had seen them, when they had looked up at him from beneath a layer of blood and dirt, on a God-forsaken hill in the South Atlantic.

'You know me, JJ. Can't sit still for a minute.'

'Hey... now you're here, why don't we have a chat? Come on... for old time's sake. What ya say?' JJ had stopped his prey from bolting, but he wasn't home yet. 'Not here, of course,' JJ said as he slipped his left arm around Mason's back and ushered him forward. 'Upstairs in my office. You fancy a coffee?'

Mason took a step forward, allowing JJ the impression that he had successfully placated him. They were playing a game; he knew that; he wasn't stupid. Why not let JJ think that he had won?

The first floor office was large, its width spanning the whole of the front of the building. In front of the glass-panelled French doors that opened onto a balcony, with a magnificent view of Belgrave Square, stood an antique desk, its red leather top and gold-inlay, a perfect match for the heavy red carpet and the thick velvet curtains whose swags and tails cascaded down the Georgian frescoed walls.

'What do you think of my office, then? I've just had it refurbished,' JJ said as he closed the oak panelled doors behind them, 'and the desk is an antique. Some French King used to sit behind it,' he continued in his thick Glaswegian accent.

JJ was five years older than Mason. But, unlike the other SAS soldier, he had never been known for his good looks. His DNA - and too many street brawls as a kid - had scuppered any chance of him growing handsome, the long scar on his forehead an obvious testament to his harsh upbringing. He was not a vain man, but he was justifiably proud of his shock of fiery red hair, which matched his temper. His legendary fury had been unleashed on many occasions in the quiet agricultural city of Hereford, the SAS's home. He was shorter than Mason – five-foot-eight, to Mason's six-foot - and his barrel chest gave him a disproportioned appearance. But it allowed him a strength that few men possessed - a strength Mason was reminded of with his vice-like grip.

Mason put his hands on his hips and took in the surroundings. 'Yes, very nice, JJ. A tad austere for my liking, but I can see where you're coming from,' Mason said, aiming to dent the Glaswegian's bravado.

The comment had the desired effect; the wind slightly blown out of his sails, JJ offered 'I've been rude... Sorry'.

Eager to change the subject, he continued. 'Let me introduce you guys. Mason, this is James.'

James stood behind the desk, looking out onto Belgrave Square, a ring binder in his hands, his back towards the two men. Mason had noticed him as he had walked in, and found it odd that he had not turned around. *Deep in thought? No. More likely a superiority complex with a large helping of arrogance,* Mason mused, as he analysed the man, who even now only half turned his body in acknowledgment. *Tall, six foot, pin-striped suit – pressed to perfection. Black brogues you could see your face in. Well ordered hair and moustache. Holds himself well. Ex-officer.* He had come across this type on many an occasion, the choice of cap badge known before he had even seen the red and blue diagonal stripes on his tie.

'Guards?' Mason asked.

'1st Foot Guards... Grenadiers,' James replied.

'James is my overseas advisor. He knows everyone. Isn't that right, Jimmy boy?' added JJ.

'I try, John,' James replied with a detached tone, shifting his gaze from Mason and back to his paperwork.

Mason had been his own man since leaving the military, discovering that he could cope pretty well without the orders that had dictated his life for over twenty years. Only now, he found himself being lorded over by a man with whom he'd had a tense relationship for most of his military career. He was uncomfortable, and just wanted to get the meeting over with. 'It's good to see you, JJ, but I'm pretty sure you didn't get me here to talk about interior design. You mentioned last night that it was urgent?'

'Don't you just love this guy?' JJ motioned to James as he sat down behind his regal desk. 'Straight down to business. That's always been one of the things I've liked that about you, Mason. Okay, let's cut to the chase: I need a *Blade* in Basra. I heard that you weren't working, and I thought you might want to help out? It's good money: a thousand bucks per day.'

'What? Working with guys like those downstairs?'

'Look… we're expanding. I know that Target's no SAS Squadron. But, with guys like you on board, we can take it in the right direction, yeah? Come on. Sit down. Let's discuss it.'

'One guy downstairs is a fucking doorman, JJ. How can you justify that?'

JJ sat back in his chair, his anger growing. He had built up Target from nothing into a multi-million pound company. He'd done it his way, and he didn't have to justify anything - not to anyone. 'You're right,' he answered, using all his willpower to control the Celtic rage now building within him. 'That's exactly why I want you onboard. You'd be the head of training. By passing on your knowledge and experience, you'd actually be helping them survive.'

Mason knew that JJ wanted something different from him; that was the whole idea behind this meeting. He'd always been the same. Whenever he spoke to guys in the regiment, they all knew he was after something; there was always an agenda. There was no way Mason would consider going out on the ground with a bunch of wannabes. That was out of the question. But training? He hadn't seen this one coming; it was a curveball.

'Look, pal… I know it's a big ask. But, in the end, you might end up saving lives,' JJ said as he sat back in his chair, his rage replaced by the poise of a man about to win the hand.

'When do you need to know by?' asked Mason.

I've got him, JJ thought, as he picked up an expensive fountain pen from the leather bound desk, and slowly unscrewed the top. 'Today… in fact…' he paused, glancing at his wristwatch. 'I need to know now… The plane leaves this afty.'

'I need to make a few phone calls,' Mason lied. 'Can you give me an hour?'

'Aye. No problem… but can you do me a favour: let the wee girls downstairs know. James and I have a ton of stuff to go through.'

'That's very magnanimous of you, John,' James said as he dropped the file on top of the desk. 'For a second there, I thought you were going to lose it. There are plenty of ex-SAS guys out there. Why bend over for this one?'

'He's different,' JJ answered, screwing the top back onto the fountain pen. 'We called him 'Lucky'… Did over twenty years in 22 SAS. He survived all sorts of dodgy operations.' He hesitated, his mind wandering. 'Do you know there is a clock up in 'H' with a load of names carved on it for guys that never made it back?' He didn't wait for the answer; his ramble was intended mostly for himself anyway. 'The guys that came back 'beat the clock'. But Lucky? He never got a bloody scratch. There was a pipe bomb in Armagh: Crossmaglen, I think it was. Landed right in the middle of a group of the lads. Thing went off, killed one, seriously injured two. Mason had a chunk out of his Kevlar helmet. That was it. Unbelievable, like some sort of divine bloody intervention.'

'So, what's he been up to lately, then?'

'Ah well, that's a sad story. He had some bad luck a few years ago… lost his family. Word is he held himself responsible. Wheels fell off. Climbed into a bottle to try to forget.'

'Is this wise, JJ?' James asked as he sat on the corner of the desk. 'Do you want to risk getting a drunk involved when you're so close to selling Target? You've done really well so far. MI6 are mightily impressed. As you well know, there were serious doubts at first. But you're proving them all wrong; Target's services have been a good investment for everyone involved.'

'We need to find that bloody wellhead before any sale. That's the deal, remember? And, with our friend Lucky on board, that has just become a lot more likely.'

'But I thought he was just doing the training?'

'Jimmy... Jimmy... Jimmy, you need to trust me. I'm good at reading people: finding out what motivates them, makes them tick. I've known Mason for ages; I know exactly what buttons to press. Today, he thinks he's in charge of training. But give him a couple of weeks... And he'll be end up running the whole show. He won't be able to stop himself.'

JJ nodded at the photograph that stood proudly on the desk: a black and white picture of a bunch of dishevelled soldiers, all with beaming smiles, 'Mount Longdon. That morning, after the battle, we were all just glad to be alive,' he said, picking up the picture. 'It was Mason's first action. He got the Military Medal,' JJ said, in grudging admiration, his voice tailing off to a whisper. 'Christ, it should have been a Victoria Cross'.

Mason gripped the handrail, taking the steps one at a time, allowing his brain to mull over the last twenty minutes of his life. *I can stay here and drink myself slowly to death... probably end up a drunk, stinking of piss in some gutter somewhere, or, I can go to Iraq. And if I die, at least I can do it with some dignity - die like a soldier after all. What have I got left anyway?.Nothing.*

By the time he reached the bottom step, he had his answer ready.

He walked towards the front desk, the receptionist again looking up, giving the same rehearsed smile.

'Can I help you?'

He took a deep breath. 'Tell JJ I'll take the job,' he answered.

'Yes. Mr O'Hare said you would. Here are your tickets,' she said, handing him a sealed brown envelope. 'There is a cash advance in there also. Mr O'Hare said you would need it. The bus for the airport leaves from this office at seventeen-hundred hours sharp.'

Mason walked towards the exit and was soon outside in the morning sun. He slid a finger under the flap of the envelope and revealed the contents: a one-way ticket to Amman, Jordan and a thousand pounds in crisp fifty pound notes. His head was spinning. *I need to gather my thoughts. Where's the nearest pub?*

He didn't have to go far the doors of the Plumbers Arms had just opened, the staff busy arranging the outside furniture, ready for a new day's trade. He sat down at the end of the bar, facing the door. *Controlling the room as always. Old habits* he thought as he scanned the shelves of the heavy dark wooden bar, its mirrored alcoves crammed with every type of spirit imaginable. 'What can I get you?' asked the barman as he closed on his first customer of the day.

'I'll have the Oban,' he said, pointing at the bottle of single malt whisky, 'make it a double.' He picked up the tumbler and knocked back the straw colour liquid. 'Another' he asked, before the barman could replace the bottle. 'Best leave it out, eh' he said, placing a handful of fifties on the bar.

With the shot of alcohol satisfying his initial craving, he paused, cupped both his hands around the tumbler and brought it slowly up to his lips, savouring the bouquet of smoky peat and heather, his mind beginning to wander.

Mount Longdon, Falkland Islands,
08.04 hrs, June 12, 1982.

'That's the best brew I have ever had, Taff,' Mason said as he took another sip of the brown liquid from the thin, steel mug. The heat radiating into his fingers offering a small but welcome relief from the numbing cold that gripped his exhausted body.

'Thanks, Mace. Any time for you, butt. My pleasure.'

Mason smiled and huddled closer to the Welshman. Both Paras, desperate to shield themselves from the biting wind, had pushed their bodies into the small hollow at the base of a heavy rock outcrop, the aperture worn away by generations of sheep attempting the same practice against the unforgiving South Atlantic wind.

'That was a bloody hard night, mate. I thought I was never going to get through it,' Taff said, as Mason passed the mug back to him.

'Well, you did - which is more than I can say for those poor sods,' Mason said, as he gestured towards the bodies that lay in a neat row thirty metres or so to their left. Their lifelessness starkly cast by the sun as it climbed into the bitterly cold morning sky.

'How many are ours?' asked Taff, pulling up the collar of his para smock.

'Three. The ones on the right. The stiffs on the left are Argies,' replied Mason, watching two Argentinian prisoners place another of their fallen comrades in the growing line. The gaping wounds of each cadaver covered with a camouflaged shroud - the final use for the men's waterproof ponchos, held in place against the buffeting wind with heavy rocks.

'What the fuck is going on here?' the figure shouted, his outline obscuring the macabre scene as he squared up to the two young Paras.

'We're havin' a brew,' answered Taff.

'I can see that, you fucking idiot. I'm on about over there,' the man gestured with his thumb towards the prisoners. 'And it's fucking sergeant to you.'

'They're sorting out the dead,' Mason answered, staring into the mug in an effort to escape the gory picture.

'Are some of those our dead?' the Sergeant asked.

'Yeah. Three,' replied Taff. 'All got the good news from a machine gun that was in the trench over there. That's right, innit, Mace,' he said, pointing at the fighting position that had once commanded the approach to the summit, but which now lay torn apart, its interior smouldering from the blasts of high explosive and white phosphorus grenades used to breech its defences.

'Did you two take the trench out?' the Sergeant asked.

'No. I'm A Company, Sarge,' replied the Welshman, ' I got lost. This was a B Company show: Mason's lot. I got here about an hour ago.'

The Sergeant turned and gestured to the two figures in the distance that were picking their way through the jagged rocks and stunted grass that made up the steep slope in front of the trench. The Sergeant's outstretched hand, placed on top of his helmet – the signal for 'on me'- offering a far better means of communication on the windswept hillside.

'What's happening, Sarge?' one of them panted, as they approached.

'Payback,' answered the Sergeant, through clenched teeth. 'Follow me.'

The three paras closed in on the burial party, the butt of the Sergeant's rifle smashing into the prisoner's head as he knelt placing rocks on the poncho of his fallen comrade, the blow sending him forward, the blood pouring from the gaping wound.

'Get him!' shouted the Sergeant as the second prisoner bolted, his escape thwarted by another bone-cracking blow.

'He's going to waste them,' said Taff, watching the prisoners being made to kneel with their hands behind their heads. 'He fucking is! Look, Mace... The crazy Jock bastard.'

Mason was watching in disbelief as the execution party organised itself. The Sergeant was standing behind the two cowering prisoners, rifle cocked and ready, while the other two Paras stood protection on either flank.

'What the hell are you doin'?' Mason shouted as he ran towards the group.

'None of your business, boy. Just sit down and enjoy

your brew,' the Sergeant snapped.

'You're wrong, Sarge; this *is* my business,' Mason said as he drew the heavy Argentinian .45 Colt pistol from his belt. 'These prisoners surrendered to me. So that makes me responsible for them.'

'Surrendered to you? You little shit,' said the Sergeant, placing the butt of the rifle into his shoulder. 'You'll be telling me next that it was you that took the position and killed all these.'

Mason raised the pistol, his right thumb pulling back the thick hammer as the gun drew level with the Sergeant's face. 'That's right, Sarge. It was me. The machine gun took my section out with one burst. I was the only one left.'

'Put that gun down. I'm a fucking Sergeant.'

'The guy I took this pistol off is over there,' Mason gestured to the line of bodies. 'I think he was a Captain or maybe a Major...' said Mason, lining the sights up with the Sergeant's face. 'I guess rank doesn't count for much up here on this fucking hill.'

The Sergeant looked directly at the young paratrooper, measuring up the man who had dared to stand in his way. His uniform was caked in mud from weeks on the march, his hair matted, his face obscured by the blood and grime of battle. But he held himself with a bearing beyond his youth, the conduit for his confidence a pair of steel blue eyes that drilled deep into the Sergeant's skull.

'They're not worth a bullet,' the Sergeant said as he kicked over the prisoner in front of him. 'Come on. Let's go,' he said, turning to his henchmen.

Mason watched the three men disappear behind a rocky outcrop, gesturing to the prisoners to carry on as he walked back to his shelter. 'Let's have another brew, Taff,' he said as he sat back down.

'Who the hell were they?' Mason asked as he watched Taff pour chocolate powder into the boiling water.

'Mortar Platoon, I think. Crazy bunch, if you ask me. I saw the Sergeant on the way down - on the Canberra. I'll

16

remember his name now in a minute...'

Mason was taking the first sip when he heard a spine-chilling scream carried on the icy wind. The cry - in Spanish – was muffled, but unmistakable. He had heard it for the first time in his life the night before. It made the hairs on the back of his neck stand on end. It was the cry of someone about to die. As he jumped up to find out the source, the tell-tale crack of a 7.62 round echoed around the rocks.

'I remember now,' said Taff, taking a big gulp of hot chocolate. 'JJ O'Hare, that's him.'

Plumbers Arms, London,
May 5, 2007.

Mason's daydream was interrupted by the barman, whose attention was drawn to the expanding pool of blood on his freshly polished oak surface. 'Are you okay, sir?' he asked as he collected the remains of the glass tumbler from between Mason's hands. 'Must have been a crack in it,' he said as he handed over a napkin to his bleeding customer. 'It's virtually impossible to break one of these otherwise,' he continued, mopping up the remnants of the spillage. 'They're toughened.'

'Nothing's impossible', Mason mumbled, as he wrapped the napkin around the gash in his hand just at the base of his thumb. 'Just remember that. Nothing.'

The coach was already in front of the office when he got there, a fifty two-seater more than adequate for the six passengers. He recognised the occupants from the form-filling session earlier that day. They had swapped their suits for sand-coloured trousers and   short-sleeved check shirts, but their awkwardness still hung on them, as obvious as the sweat stains on their new clothing. He nodded to them as he walked up the aisle, while looking for the emergency exit. Old habits die hard, his training compelled him to ensure that he always had an alternative escape route - even in the most innocent of settings.

The traffic was surprisingly light for the time of day, and they were soon on the M4, heading west for Heathrow Airport. Ahead of them lay some ominous-looking clouds, heralding a storm. Sure enough, it was just minutes before the rain began to fall. As the bus drove further into the dark clouds, Mason put his forehead against the cool glass, watching as the rivulets of rainwater streaked across the window. Lulled by the rhythm of the bus and the day's Oban, he was soon asleep.

Hereford,
Six Years Earlier.

Katie opened the bottle of wine while Mason was upstairs enjoying his first bath in over a month. Isabella had been carefully put to bed, finally dozing off in her daddy's arms after a marathon reading of her favourite story: Cinderella.

He had arrived earlier that day, unannounced, after an equally unannounced mission. Katie didn't ask him where he had been, but from his deep sun tan she knew it must have been somewhere hot. She used to quiz him when they were first married, trying to draw from him even the smallest clue. But she had given up when the answers weren't forthcoming. Only after talking to the other wives did she find any comfort on this score; she realised that none of the SAS men were ever talkative about their clandestine work. Now, she was just grateful that he was home and safe.

As the cork popped out of the bottle, Katie tried to control the butterflies in her tummy. She hated him going away, but she loved the homecomings. The candles were on the dining table and the glasses were ready. When she heard the footsteps coming down the stairs, she started to pour the wine. She was so happy; her man was back.

'What's for dinner?' he asked as Katie handed him a glass of wine.

'Your favourite: fillet steak - just the way you like it.'

'And for dessert?' he said, as he grabbed her, his excitement getting the better of him. 'God, I've missed you,' he said as their lips met in a passionate embrace. He pulled her onto the sofa.

'What's that?' she said as the cushion beneath them began to vibrate.

'It's the bloody work phone,' he answered.

'Ignore it, baby. Please,' she whispered. He picked the phone up with two fingers - as if it was contaminated.

'But... it's the work phone. You know I have to.'

Katie watched as the happiness drained from his weathered face, replaced by a look of disbelief, 'What are they playing at?' he rasped as he read the message. 'I don't fucking believe it. It's a squadron scramble!'

'But you've just got back. Isn't there anyone else in the bloody SAS besides you?' Katie shouted. Mason put his arms around her and pulled her close. She buried her head in his chest as her eyes hazed with emotion, the full consequences of the phone call hitting home, her self-control vanishing in a flood of tears. 'Please don't go. I miss you so much. Isabella will be devastated if you're not here in the morning.'

She's right. It is me. Always me. I've been flat out for the last six months. I've only seen Katie and Isabella for a handful of days. I'll ignore it. To hell with them. Someone else can lead the mission.

'Please don't cry,' he whispered. He stroked her long auburn hair in an attempt to stop the tears he could feel soaking through his shirt.

'If you don't acknowledge the message, they'll send

someone to the house,' she said, looking up at him. 'I don't want Izzy woken. If you're going to go, you'd better do it now.'

22 Special Air Service had the worst divorce rate of any unit in the British Army. The time that the soldiers spent away from home had a dire effect on their relationships. Nearly everyone within the unit was on their second or third marriage. Mason and Katie were the exception.

They had met on a night out in Hereford. Katie had reluctantly agreed to accompany a girlfriend who was on the lookout for a new *blade*. It was August - selection time - and the town was full of untested, wannabe SAS recruits. It had become a phenomenon - almost a mating ritual - as hundreds of young females flocked into the cathedral city during those weekends, looking to snag a Special Forces guy.

Katie's friend soon achieved her aim, leaving her to fend for herself in the pheromone-filled atmosphere of a nightclub. Mason spotted her from across the bar, revelling in the way she dismissed the men drawn to her good looks.

He was smitten at first sight, watching her every move with delight, thinking that she was the most beautiful woman he had ever seen. Katie soon became aware of the man with rugged good looks looking at her, and flirted with him from a distance, giving him an occasional glance, a smile and a flick of her long flowing hair. When he moved closer, he could see how amazingly pretty she was, and was totally taken by the sparkle in her dark brown eyes. She made him feel like a schoolboy. He was hooked.

They courted for the rest of the year, and he proposed on New Year's Eve. She refused. She knew that being a military wife was tough; her father had served in the RAF, and she was only too aware of how lonely her mother had been. But Mason was determined, and it took another six months before the woman of his dreams finally succumbed to his charm. They were married the following autumn.

Isabella was born a year later and was the image of her mother. His 'two girls', filled the hole that had previously existed in his life. His own mother had died when he was eight. His father, a successful barrister, had reacted to the loss in the only way he knew how: by throwing himself headlong into his work. And in an attempt to rid himself of the anguish – for the memories of his beloved wife rekindled every time he looked at his son, the remarkable resemblance to his mother simply too painful – he took the selfish option, and packed his son off to boarding school. Mason's father had tried to make things as normal as possible during the school holidays. But things were never the same. Mason's innocence had died with his mother. Immediately, he knew that he was no longer a child; he realised that he was out on his own, and that nobody was going to look after him. He excelled at school and learned to love it. The masters liked him and the other boys looked up to him. But he would have given it all up in a heartbeat to get his mother back.

None of that mattered anymore. He had his own family now, and there was no way he was going to let anyone take them away from him.

When he arrived at the camp, the MOD policeman quickly checked his ID and instructed him to go straight to the operations room. The whole place was throbbing with activity, men running from building to building, their arms full of weapons and other heavy paraphernalia of war, the air thick with diesel fumes as engines raced with excitement. 'Get a move on, Mason, or you're going to miss this one,' shouted an anonymous voice over the noise of a revving Land Rover. The remark didn't land well. Mason's sense of humour - his 'ha ha tank' - had run empty. He wasn't in the mood for smart comments.

'Evening, Sergeant Major,' said the OC of B Squadron, as Mason entered the operations room. The rest of the squadron were already assembled, and were standing around casually, waiting for his arrival. As soon as the men saw him enter, the banter started.

'Glad you could make it.'

'About time, wanker!'

It had taken all Mason's will to pull himself from his family, and he hated himself for doing it, but that was behind him. *Best get my soldier's head on,* he said to himself as he looked around the room. He had served for the last twenty years with these guys. They truly were his brothers-in-arms, each one prepared to follow him anywhere and obey his orders no matter what. He knew everything about them, as they did about him. They were a unit forged on the anvil of war, tried and tested in every environment and on every continent. They were without a doubt the most professional, meanest, most heroic and ugliest bunch of reprobates ever to don camouflaged suits. 'Good evening, gentlemen,' Mason said, walking amongst them with his legendary smile. The guy to his left gave him a bear hug, while those close by ruffled his hair and jostled him.

'If you're all done with the male bonding thing, we'll start,' barked the RSM as he called the men to order.

Mason sat in the middle of the front row, the other noise in the room diminishing. When they were all seated, the OC began. 'The British Embassy in Sierra Leone has come under fire from rebel forces, and is in danger of being overrun. B Squadron's mission is to deny the embassy compound to the enemy, and ensure extraction of all embassy personnel,' said the Major with a calm, measured tone.

The briefing continued for a further two hours, and covered every contingency that the men could expect. The long and short of it was that, directly after the meeting, they would be flown by helicopter directly to RAF Lyneham, where they would pick up the Special Forces C130 that would take them onwards to Sierra Leone. In-flight refuelling would take place over Algeria. The first boots would be on the ground in seven hours and thirty-four minutes' time. Everything they needed for the op was already on the Herc. The briefing concluded and the men were dismissed. They filed out of the room, the sound of rotor blades clearly audible as the door was opened.

'Sergeant Major, a quick word,' said the OC, as Mason walked past. 'Look... this isn't my idea,' he said, with his usual calmness, 'I tried to get you off this one, but I was overruled. You were asked for by Downing Street, no less. My hands were tied. I know you only got back this morning, and you were expecting a month off. And I know that Katie is going to be pissed. Who can blame her? But you have my word: set this up and I will have you back in 'H' by this time next week. Okay?'

Mason looked at the man who had been his direct superior for over two years. He knew that if he said it, he meant it. 'I appreciate that, Sir. Thanks,' he replied.

The plan went like clockwork; they had the embassy secure within thirteen hours of receiving the brief. It turned out that the intelligence they had received from local sources was highly inaccurate, the capability of the rebel forces greatly exaggerated.

Having accomplished their mission, B Squadron, for their remaining time in-country, sat around the embassy pool and topped up their tans in the West African sunshine until a company of paras arrived to relieve them. The OC was as good as his word; a week after their deployment, B SQN were back on the C 130, on their way home. Morale was good, and the banter was fierce.

Danny, a good looking lad from 9 Squadron Royal Engineers, was the most junior member of the squadron and, as the new guy, was the current target for much of the ridicule. He had been caught chatting up a very young looking Thai woman while on an exercise in South East Asia a few months earlier, and had been given the nickname 'Paedo Danny'. The name fitted really well into the chorus of the Queen Song, *Living on My Own*, and whenever he entered the room, the guys would mercilessly launch into an enthusiastic rendition. Danny was the last to get on the Herc, and as he walked up the ramp of the aircraft, the whole of B SQN 22 SAS erupted with a rousing chorus of 'Paedo Danny, Paedo Danny.' Danny just took it. He had to. Any sign of weakness or anger would mean that he would receive even more abuse. He just had to suck it up and play along until someone else did something to attract the mockery of the group and become the next target. He smiled and shrugged his shoulders at the bewildered RAF Loadmaster.

'It is pretty catchy though, don't you think?' said the Loadmaster as he hummed away.

Mason was happy; he was on his way home to his girls, and had a month off to look forward to. But his joyful reveries were interrupted as one of his Sergeants sat down next to him. 'I bet there's no choppers at the other end to take us back to 'H',' chuntered the Sergeant.

'You know the score. They only love us on the way out. With all the defence cuts, I wouldn't be surprised if they make us TAB back to 'H'. But stop moaning; you're getting paid, aren't you?' said Mason with a grin.

When they arrived in Hereford, Mason was met off the coach by a grave-looking RSM. 'You need to come with me. The boss wants to see you,' he said, turning and walking off in the direction of the OC's office. Mason shouldered his kit bag and followed, his mind frantically trying to grasp what this break with protocol could mean.

This is strange, he thought, as the pair approached the office block. *It's never happened this way before. The debrief has already been completed in-country with MI6, and the report has been approved.* A thought occurred to him and his stomach sank. *I hope he's not going to mess with my leave again.*

The OC was busy watering his plants on the windowsill when they entered. He looked distracted. 'Come in, Mason. Take a seat,' he said, putting down the watering can.

'Is there a problem, sir?'

'Look Mason, there is no easy way to say this,' the OC began. 'Katie and Isabella were at her parents while you were away. When they were coming back this morning, they were involved in a crash with an articulated lorry. I'm sorry, Mason. They are both dead.'

London Heathrow Airport,
Terminal Three,
May 5, 2007.

The bus lurched to a stop. 'Terminal Three. Everyone off,' shouted the driver.

'Next stop: Iraq,' laughed one of the guys at the front.

CHAPTER TWO

All Saints College, Oxford.

'Good afternoon, ladies and gentleman. And welcome to All Saints,' the Dean said, calling the meeting of esteemed academics to order as he adjusted the microphone on the lectern to the correct height. The noise of the excited crowd died away, and the last of the guests took their seats. The head of faculty was a slight man, whose appearance and small stature were now amplified by the large academic gown and position centre–stage, under the portraits of the famous alumni lining the oak-panelled walls. He waited until there was quiet before he continued. 'We have a wonderful line-up of speakers for you today, and I'm sure that you're as eager as I am to hear them. I would therefore like to introduce our first speaker in today's set of lectures on ancient history: Professor Cornelius Gregory of All Saints.'

Cornelius rose to the applause and shook the Dean's hand as he moved towards the lectern, adjusting the settings on his computer so that the first slide of his presentation filled the large screen that served as the backdrop. 'Thanks very much for that warm reception,' he said. His right hand nervously pushed back his spectacles, his fingers carrying on, brushing through the head of jet black, unkempt hair that hung just above the collar of his favourite tweed jacket. He was not a striking man: pale skin, tall, wiry, with very little dress sense. But none of that mattered to this committed bachelor. His work was the important thing. It consumed him. There was no room for distractions. *I hate lectures*, he thought as he looked at the crowd. His nerves getting the better of him as he scanned an audience comprising his peers, their faces staring back, eager for him to bare his passion.

'Today's topic is entitled *The Third Crusades - also called the Kings Crusade - (1189-1192) and its Impact on Mesopotamia*,' he said as he picked up a book from behind the lectern. 'And for those who have read my hardback *In Search of Saladin's Secret*,' he continued, holding it up for all to see. 'You will notice some common themes.'

'My aim today is to examine the important events that took place after the besieged city of Acre fell to the crusading forces in 1191. But, to chronicle the events fully, I must first start in Damascus, 1894.' Cornelius looked around the room. Complete silence. He had them. His nerves had vanished. *God, I love this job.*

'In 1894, the Archduke Franz Ferdinand of Austria was on an official tour to Damascus. Whilst there, he paid homage at the tomb of Saladin, the First Sultan of Egypt and Syria, and the emphatic General who recaptured Jerusalem and led the Muslim opposition against the Crusaders in the Levant. But what he saw disappointed him,' he said, flashing up a picture of the great General's tomb. 'It was dilapidated, and, to the Archduke's mind, not a fitting resting place for such an iconic and exceptional leader. Moved to action, he approached the Ottoman Governor of Damascus and offered to pay to have Saladin's remains placed in a casket more befitting of his rank and status as a general. During the disinterment, however, a very interesting discovery was made,' he said holding up a small piece of yellowed paper, no bigger than that from a small notebook.

'This is the original transcript from a document that was found in Saladin's sarcophagus,' he said, flashing up a copy of the text up on the screen. 'Unfortunately, the original parchment, written in Arabic, was lost. But this one, transcribed and translated by one of the Archduke's men, who was supervising the works, has survived. For those that don't speak German, I will translate.'

Almighty God, I have been your servant and have done your bidding. I have driven the infidels out of the Holy City and have carried out my duty as best I could. But I come to you with a heart full of sorrow, as it is I who destroyed the great Treasure at Palmyra. I did it to save further death and bloodshed. But I know it was not mine to take. I have carried the shame with me, but as I now stand before you at my time of judgement, I plead for your forgiveness.

'Those of you instructed in the rituals of Islam will know that at the time of burial, the deceased is wrapped in a simple cloth shroud or *kafan*, and takes no personal belongings with them.' The Professor gave a theatrical pause to ensure that the audience was with him. Seeing the nods of acknowledgment, he continued. 'So the parchment must have been immensely important to the great General - important enough for him to break this religious protocol.'

The Professor walked back to the lectern and flashed up a picture of a modern city built on a peninsular, its coastline surrounded by a blue animated sea. 'This is the modern day city of Acre in Israel,' he said to his captivated audience. 'But it would have looked rather different in the late 1180s. In 1189, it was besieged by the Crusaders, who were themselves then besieged by Saladin - a siege within a siege, as it were. Baha al-Din, Saladin's servant and biographer, wrote a good account of the blockade up until the final surrender of the city to Richard I - who arrived with the French King Philip, and Leopold V of Austria in the spring of 1191. But Baha al–Din also left us something else.'

To reinforce his statement, Cornelius flashed up another document onto the screen. 'This is Baha's account of an incident which occurred when the city had finally fallen. It's in Arabic. I will again translate.'

My master, knowing that the city had fallen, its treasures and possessions no longer under his protection, dispatched a force of Saracens to destroy the Secret that was hidden in the

28

east, rather than let it fall into the hands of the bloodthirsty Crusaders...

'So it appears that Saladin's parchment has been corroborated by an existing twelfth century account. But there is a third and final piece of evidence that I must show you ladies and gentlemen.'

For someone who hated lecturing, it had to be said that Cornelius was damn good at it. He'd worked the crowd, fuelling their excitement, building them up. Now he was going to deliver the finale.

'Some of you might be familiar with the squire Ernoul's Chronicle,' he said, trying to gauge his audience's recognition. 'Well... for those of you that aren't, he was an important historian, who was in the service of one Balian of Ibelin, an important figure in the Kingdom of Jerusalem at the time of the third Crusade. In one of his manuscripts - which can now be found in the Laurentian Library in Florence - he records the events after the siege of Acre. The full transcript is in my book,' he said, holding up the hardback for the second time. 'It's written in some very longwinded Latin, so, if you will excuse me on this occasion, I will paraphrase.'

'On the eve of the fall of Acre, the three sovereigns met to discuss the apportionment of the spoils. In order to secure the treasury from the pillaging that would no doubt start when the defenders had capitulated, King Philip offered the services of his most trusted knight. On the morning of the final battle, he was to take a small group of trusted men and rush to the city's treasury in order to secure it from looters. Ernoul tells us that, when the knight got to the treasury, he found that all the gold and silver had been removed. But a number of important documents and records had been left behind. In amongst these papers, the knight found evidence of a treasure that was far more valuable to the Crusaders than any gold or silver, and which had been hidden in the ancient city of Palmyra.'

Cornelius moved to the centre of the stage and gripped his hands in enthusiasm. 'Ernoul goes on to tell us that Richard and Leopold were not interested in pursuing any quest for treasure, it being a distraction and drain on resources. So it was Philip who sent the knight in search of Saladin's Secret.'

'There we have it, ladies and gentlemen: Three independent sources – which...' he said with a clap, to emphasise his next word, 'gives us TRIANGULATION.'

'Ah... Professor,' said a bearded man in the second row. 'You have covered the third Crusade. But where does 'the impact on Mesopotamia' come into this? After all, the Land of the Two Rivers is some way from the Holy Land.'

'I was just coming to that,' said Cornelius as he sipped at a glass of water. 'Ernoul mentions in a later chronicle that nothing is ever heard from the knight; he vanishes. But there are rumours that he escaped to the east with Saladin's Secret.'

'Do you know where he went?' asked the man in the second row again.

'I'm glad you have asked that question,' Cornelius smiled, 'as it leads me on to the second half of my lecture. 'Let's look at Syria,' he said as he flashed a map onto the screen. 'If the knight wanted to go east, he would at some stage have crossed this,' he said, pointing at a blue line that diagonally intersected across the chart from left to right, 'The river Euphrates. Its source is in South East Turkey, and it runs through Syria and Iraq until it joins with the Tigris - here,' he said pointing at the map, 'The Marsh Land, just above Basrah.'

My hypothesis, ladies and gentlemen, is that the knight went to Palmyra and from there travelled east to the Euphrates. He then sailed down the great river and ended up in the Marshes.

'Can you prove this?' asked the man in the second row.

'The Marsh Lands are very inhospitable to outsiders,' answered Cornelius. 'But Gertrude Bell, the famous Arabic

30

scholar, in one of her journal entries, speaks of a mysterious tribe, with pale skin and blue eyes, that live deep in the marshes. There was also an account, from 1942, in which a downed pilot was rescued by a mysterious group that cared for him until he was well enough to be moved. He was then taken to Basrah. In his account, the men had fair skin and blue eyes, and spoke an unusual type of Arabic not associated with the area.'

'Sheer speculation,' heckled a vocal attendee.

'It's a hypothesis, Sir. And I am working on evidence to prove it.'

'What about Saladin's Secret?' asked a lady in the front row. 'Do you have a theory as to what that is?'

'And what about the knight? Do we know who he was?' asked someone else.

The harrumph from the Dean was clearly audible as Cornelius readied his answer. 'Let me answer the second question first,' he said, taking another sip. 'Through extensive research, I have narrowed the knight down to several possible candidates. But unfortunately, unless any other evidence comes to light, I cannot be more specific now. Regarding the first question,' he said, giving a sideways glance at the Dean, 'my hypothesis on what I think the Secret is… is quite controversial.'

The Dean was on his feet before the words had settled. 'Ladies and gentlemen, I know this is a tad unusual, but I need to speak to the professor. Please avail yourselves of the tea and coffee. I'll only be a minute,' he said, as the audience stirred. 'But don't worry. The Professor will be here to answer any of your questions after the break.'

'Listen, Gregory,' the Dean whispered to the Professor, as the crowd made their way to the beverage table at the end of the hall. 'When I agreed to you delivering this lecture, you promised me that you would steer clear of the Saladin Secret and your theory. There is simply no evidence to back up this flight of fancy. As far as I am concerned, it's an infatuation that's gone too far. I'm not prepared to have the name of this

31

college sullied on the back of a half-baked idea... So unless you've found new evidence since yesterday, I don't want to hear any more of it. Do you understand?

Cornelius knew that his theory was correct. Every bone in his body told him so. It screamed acknowledgment of the hypotheses that had devoured him. But he still lacked the evidence. He knew that the Dean was correct; to bare himself in front of such a prestigious audience would only lead to ridicule. Dejected he looked at his shoes and mumbled his reply. 'Yes Dean...I'm sorry...it's just that I...'

'It's okay old boy,' the Dean said, reading hid discomfort. 'Tell them more about the marsh tribe that no one has ever seen. That should fill up the last twenty minutes. What are they called again?'

'Masahuin,' he murmured looking straight at the Dean, his dejection dissolving as he took hold of the hardback edition of his new book. 'The tribe in the Marshes,' he repeated, with a more defiant tone, pulling his shoulders back and straightening his body. 'The tribe in the arshes is called the Masahuin.'

Masahuin Village, Iraq.

It's coming on well, she thought, standing back to admire the rockery, the vibrant colours of the cultivated flowers an intense contrast to the bland beige of the ubiquitous reed surroundings. *Perhaps some more white? Yes. Mama loves the Rose of Jericho. The white petals are her favourite.*

'I will do it for you tomorrow, Mama,' she said aloud as she sat on the small seat that her father had made, her voice breaking the calmness. The only other noise was the

32

call of a moorhen, and the mass of reeds as they crashed together, obeying the dry afternoon wind. And then there was something else: another sound. Not harsh. Distant. Carried by the breeze. She stood, waiting for the noise again. Listening hard, she recognised the call. It was her name. 'Rachel, Rachel.'

'I must go now, Mama,' she said, as she straightened the small wooden sword that lay on top of the earthen mound. 'And John... You be a good boy.'

The village wasn't far. She used to enjoy the walk when she was younger. The significance of this place – the parcel of land located on the outskirts of the village, the place where they put the dead people - had been lost on her during her youth. But now, it had become a daily journey. The tears that had streaked her face every time she visited after the burial were now appearing less and less often.

As she walked past the derelict houses, their former inhabitants either dead or moved away, she spoke their names out loud. 'Hello, Joshua and Sarah,' she said, in an attempt to rekindle in her mind the image of the once-vibrant village that had existed for millennia but which was now in ruins.

'Where have you been?' her aunt Miriam asked her when she entered the house. 'The animals need feeding. Can you not hear them?' she said over the calls of the hungry beasts. 'And then go to get your father. It is nearly time for supper. The poor man must be exhausted.'

Rachel stepped outside, her arms heavy from the leather bucket of fodder that she began to tip evenly onto the feeding tray, the hungry calls of the goats and sheep abating as they began to chomp down. Walking back to the house to continue her chores, her eye caught the glint of metal high above her in the cloudless sky. A vapour trail thinly brushed against the blue canvas. It indicated the passage of the silver aircraft. *I wonder where it is going. Who's on it? What adventures will they have?* She thought this as she placed the bucket down by the back door.

'Rachel! Your father,' called Miriam from the kitchen.

Queen Alia Airport, Amman, Jordan, 00.42hrs, May 6, 2007.

Abdulla, Target's fixer in Jordan, met the six tired men off the plane as they arrived at Queen Alia International Airport in the early hours of the morning. Before leaving London, the men had been told it would be necessary to stay overnight in Amman while the visa arrangements were completed for the onward journey to Basrah. Abdulla was the guy responsible for ferrying the men from the airport to the hotel. He also had the unenviable task of navigating Jordan's bureaucratic minefield to ensure each man had a visa and the correct paperwork to enter Iraq. 'We have problem,' he told the group as he corralled them together in the arrival lounge.

'What's the problem, Abdulla?' asked Mason.

'No visa tomorrow. Holiday in Jordan. Embassy closed,' replied the short, scrawny man as he pulled at his baseball hat.

'Okay, so when can we get them?' quizzed Mason.

'Two, maybe three days. When office open, Abdulla get. Give me passport,' he said, holding out his hand to collect the documents.

'So what do we do until then?' asked one of the tired crowd.

Abdulla smiled broadly, revealing a mouth bereft of teeth. 'Get pissed... British good at getting pissed. If you want woman, I get. Good price. Plenty jiggy jiggy.'

The tired men suddenly came to life at the prospect of a three-day furlough. 'Lead on, Abdulla,' they shouted, patting the back of their new best friend, as Abdulla, grinning, led them to the transport.

The hotel lobby was quiet at this time of night, the check-in process short and sweet. Mason, his head splitting from dehydration, dispensed with the pleasantries and headed straight for his room. Once inside, he dropped his bag on the bed and headed straight to the minibar. *Haven't drunk enough water,* he said aloud as he opened the fridge door, the miniature bottles inside presenting themselves with a chink, chink, chink as the door came to a stop. He rubbed the bristle on his chin and went through his options: water or whisky? He took the small bottle of Johnnie Walker from its position next to the peanuts and turned the gold-coloured cap, the fastenings breaking under the pressure, the aroma filling his nostrils, his mouth watering with anticipation. The glass, cold against his lips, was itself refreshing. He stopped.

NO! The voice screamed in his head. *You've never drunk on an operation and you're not going to start NOW!*

He replaced the cap, his fingers shaking as he willed himself to put the bottle back in the space from which it had come.

The next few days were tough, as his body ridded itself of the emotional crutch that he'd used so freely since the accident. The day after they had arrived, Thor, worried at Mason's disappearance and his failure to answer the door, had sent for room service to open up. 'I'm okay,' Mason had shouted as Thor had entered. 'Just tell the guys I have a virus or something.' But Thor had seen it all before. As a boy, he'd watched as his father had tried to kick the habit on many occasions. Thor emptied the mini bar, made sure there was a plentiful supply of water, and had meals sent to the room. By the time that Abdulla pulled up, three days later, with their visas, Mason still looked and felt like shit. But he was over the worst of it.

The Jordanian Air Embraer jetliner was parked just about as far from the terminal as it could be, the reason dawning on

Mason as he and his fellow passengers spilled out onto the baking tarmac. *If this plane is back and forth to Iraq, they want it as far from the terminal building as possible*, he thought as he made his way up the steps. *Probably because they think there is a chance there could be a bomb on board. Great start to a journey, to think that I could be sitting on a pile of explosives.*

'Ladies and gentlemen, this is the Captain speaking. I would like to welcome you aboard the Royal Jordanian Airline flight J213 to Basrah International,' the captain said as the passengers readied themselves. 'Flight time is one hour and fifty minutes, weather is good, and there are no delays. Please ensure that when you are seated you keep your seat belt fastened in case we have to take evasive action against surface-to-air missiles. Enjoy your flight.'

Thor, who was sitting on his right, gripped the arm rests with a jerk, the veins on his massive hands bulging from the effort. 'Did he just say surface-to-air missiles?' he said with a squeaking voice.

'It sounded like it,' Mason replied. 'But remember... If your number's up, your number's up,' he said with a broad grin.

Mason had flown this route on a few occasions, but always in the belly of an RAF C130 Hercules. He had never had the luxury of a window, and was amazed at the sight that unfolded beneath him as the plane soared high above the Syrian Desert. Mason likened it to pictures he had seen of the surface of the moon. There were no mountains, just the occasional ridge that sprouted up and then disappeared back into the desert's vast expanse - a mixture of sand and rock, barren and dry. But water had once fallen in these parts, long ago. The proof was there to see in the form of innumerable wadis and gulleys that criss-crossed the desolate plain. *Beautiful*, he thought, as he watched the desert stretch out towards the horizon.

The plane banked to the right, setting a course to the south-east. And, as it did so, it revealed in the far distance a vast, glistening snake that seemed to be basking in the morning sun. *The Euphrates. It has to be,* he thought. He saw the serpentine form meander through the featureless terrain, its colour a striking mercury - a complete contrast to the bland, sandy backdrop. The river's banks were covered with thick vegetation, spreading in both directions inland from its shores - an indication of the ancient river's life-giving properties - properties that had enabled many a civilisation to survive in this ancient landscape. *Magnificent,* he thought in appreciation of the beauty and majesty of the river. Then a slightly less profound but equally interesting thought occurred to him as the aircraft banked to starboard, the prehistoric river disappearing under the wing, *I wonder what it would be like to sail on?*

The pressure inside the cabin began to alter, a sure indication that the plane was descending. In response Mason held his nose and blew, equalising the pressure in his ears, just as the 'fasten seat belt' pinged into life. *Iraq,* he thought. *Shit. The last time I was here was 1991. I never thought I would come back to this God-forsaken place.*

Basrah International Airport, Iraq,
11.17hrs, 9 May 2007.

The aircraft door opened, the temperature within the cabin rising as the cool air in the cramped cabin gave way to the true heat of the Iraqi summer. The passengers clambered to get their belongings together, eager to free themselves from the plane which was fast turning into a sauna. Mason didn't rush. He knew what to expect outside. This was the lesser of two evils. 'I thought Amman was hot,' said Thor, as Mason climbed down the aircraft steps. 'But this is ridiculous.'

'This is quite cool,' Mason replied, as they walked across the shimmering tarmac towards the arrivals lounge. 'Wait until next month. It gets really roasting then,' he said with a wry smile. Thor just shook his head and increased his pace, his body craving the cooler environment he anticipated in the immigration hall.

The airport building was a straight-sided affair set off from the taxiway, the two-storey construction following the custom of departure on the first floor and arrivals on the ground. It had been built in the '80s by a German company whose brief from the Iraqis was clearly *make it work, but keep it cheap*. The result of this approach was a practical but boring array of brick and reinforced concrete, the drab colour of which blended effortlessly into the parched surroundings.

Before he entered the door to immigration, Mason looked back at the aerodrome. It might have been short on civilian aircraft, but there was no mistaking the extent of military activity, the constant whirr of helicopter rotors and taxiing transport aircraft, creating a backdrop in which one had to shout to be heard.

As Mason stood in line in the large reception hall, waiting for his passport to be stamped, his eye caught a familiar-looking man in the waiting crowd. He was dressed in a khaki shirt and trousers, was in his mid-forties, of average height, medium build, and sporting what Mason quickly established was the obligatory haircut of the security industry: a shaved head. His facial hair was trimmed to perfection, the man's stubble was cultivated with pride, with every line of the gringo-style moustache and handlebar sideburns standing out on his suntanned face. Mason smiled as he realised his identity.

Warrant Officer Second Class, Billy Toy - affectionately known to his comrades as Tonka - had been Mason's opposite number in D Squadron, 22 SAS. The Regiment were a close-knit bunch, consisting of only 250 soldiers in total, with each of the four 'sabre squadrons' numbering around 50 men. When they weren't engaged on operational tours, each squadron was either training or on leave, so it was quite common for members of the SAS not to see their friends in other squadrons for months, even years at a time. But if you were in the Regiment for long enough, you got to know everyone, friendships being regularly resumed in the many watering holes around Hereford. Old comrades took great pleasure in meeting up, getting drunk and sharing war stories way into the early hours, the stories becoming more and more elaborate and heroic the later in the evening and the more the beer consumed. The SAS was one of the most exclusive clubs in the world. And once you were in, you were a member for life.

'It's been a long time,' said Mason, as he walked towards his old friend.

'It has. Remember the last time we were here?' asked Tonka with a knowing grin – and his chirpy London accent.

Virtually the whole of the SAS had been deployed to Iraq during the First Gulf War. Tonka and Mason had been in a combined unit that had rushed from the Kuwaiti Border to Basrah Airport in the first days of the invasion. Their mission was to secure the airport and use it as a landing site so that the Paras could bring in more men and equipment in readiness for the impending battle for Basrah. When they'd arrived at the airport, they found that the local population had beaten them to it.

'Who could forget that day?' replied Mason, his mind wandering back to the humorous scene. 'They looted everything!'

'Yep. Everything. Toilets, sinks, even the bloody water pipes! Do you remember the state of the poor donkeys?' replied Tonka as both men laughed and shook hands. 'The carts were overloaded beyond belief. Those poor animals must have had coronaries getting the stuff back to the city.'

'That was a good day, my friend,' Mason replied, warmly, the men's reminiscing taking them back to a place sixteen years earlier, when their lives were simpler and their bodies in better shape.

'A lot easier back then,' Tonka added.

'They were good days, Tonka,' Mason agreed.

'Anyway, let's get down to business. I've come to pick you up. Where's the rest of your band of merry men?' Tonka asked, Mason pointing them out one by one as they cleared immigration.

'Over here, you lot. We haven't got all day,' Tonka shouted.

Tonka ticked the names off his list as the men arrived, the group forming a semi-circle in front of the two SAS men. 'Welcome to Basrah. My name is Bill Toy,' he said, happy to see that the group was complete. 'I'm the Regional Director. For those of you who are ... slowww...' he said, looking around the group, making eye contact, exposing his authority, 'that means I'm the boss.' There was a further pause as Tonka let the information sink in. 'Now... if you ladies can grab your kit, there are vehicles outside that will take you to HQ where you'll get an in-depth brief, and will be issued with your weapons and equipment. Are there any questions?' he said, with a clear firmness.

'I have one,' said Thor.

'You have my undivided attention,' replied Tonka, his tone apparently softer, but with a sprinkling of sarcasm that was plain for all to hear - all except the young Thor.

'The food on the plane wasn't very good; I couldn't eat it. Do you think we could stop off somewhere for a bite to eat? I'm starving.'

Tonka looked at Thor and then at Mason in disbelief. Mason shrugged his shoulders in response.

'What's your name, then?' Tonka asked with fake concern.

'My name is Rob. But everyone calls me Thor.'

'Okay, Thor, did you have anything in mind?'

'An omelette would be nice.'

Tonka turned around and looked over to where the three Target Security drivers were stood by their vehicles. 'Take him and the rest of the FNGs via the NAAFI, would you?

See if you can get him a pie or something before he passes out from hunger.'

'Thanks. That would be great, sir,' answered Thor.

'Sir? I'm not a 'sir'. I work for a living,' scowled Tonka, his patience now wearing thin. 'Come on, Mason. You're with me. Let's go.'

Mason grabbed the door handle of the Toyota Land Cruiser and pulled, feeling the weight of the steel plate and thick bullet-resistant glass. 'Armoured?' he asked, climbing into the passenger seat.

'Yeah... B-6,' replied Tonka, stating the protection level of the vehicle. 'Will take 7.62 and 5.56 millimetres,' he said, putting on his aviator sunglasses. 'Not cheap... Two-hundred K's worth. No expense spared on this contract though, geezer. We've got loads of them.'

The airport at Basrah was split into two: civilian and military. Mason had landed on the civvy side, the newly installed chain link fences with guard towers serving as the demarcation. As they drove along the single lane metalled road towards the military checkpoint – the main entrance to the military camp - Tonka began his brief. The heads-up was normal SAS procedure for anyone arriving in-country.

'The only weapon system I have is my *short*,' began Tonka, using the abbreviation for a short-barrelled weapon or pistol, 'which is here,' he said, pointing at the weapon tucked into a small leather holster on his belt. 'There's a medical kit on the back seat, if required. Field dressings are on top.' He then covered the comms: their frequencies, individual call-signs and the call-sign they were reporting to. 'Hello, Zero. This is Sunray,' he said into the handset of the Motorola UHF radio, 'Leaving the obvious now. Heading back to your location. Over.'

The radio speaker crackled in response, 'Hello Sunray, this is Zero. Leaving the obvious and moving to my location,' Zero said in acknowledgement.

'Roger that. OUT,' replied Tonka, replacing the handset onto the clip on the dashboard.

The SAS use the radio term 'the obvious' as often as they can. A typical message could sound something like this: 'Off to the obvious location by the obvious route to pick up the obvious.' To the outsider this seems like utter nonsense, but that is the whole idea. Most radio transmissions get intercepted by the bad guys, so by talking in *clear* - naming locations, routes, timings - you are giving your plan away. The Special Forces use veiled speech, and because of their level of training and the intensive briefing before each mission, they all know exactly what their job is, as well as everyone else's.

These standard operating procedures, or SOPs, had been infused into the new private security companies that had sprung up overnight after the invasions of Afghanistan and Iraq - hardly surprising when the new companies were either run, managed or owned by ex-SAS soldiers.

As they approached the first checkpoint on the road to the military side of the airport, or Basrah Air Station (BAS, to use its acronym), Tonka ran through a quick set of actions.

'Okay, this is a Brit Mil checkpoint. Get your passport ready,' he said, slowing down the five tonne four-by-four. 'We're going to stop. I can't wind the window down, so I'm going to open the door. Don't make any sudden moves,' he said, looking over the top of his gold rimmed sunglasses. 'These guys have itchy fingers... They lost two guys at a checkpoint last week.'

Tonka slowed the Land-Cruiser to a snail's pace as he covered the last twenty metres. 'There are two soldiers on the gate, and another two in-depth with automatic weapons. Sangar to our one o'clock.'

'Seen,' acknowledged Mason as he identified the sandbag construction behind the boom gate, the gun barrels of the machine guns clearly pointing directly at them.

Tonka was right; the young British soldier at the gate was as nervous as hell. As Tonka opened the door, the sentry brought his L85 assault rifle to bear on the two men. 'Hello, mate,' said Tonka, jovially while showing his ID, trying his best to put the soldier at ease. 'Target Security. Just picking up from the airport. There are another three white Land Cruisers behind me.'

'Okay, sir. Just keep on moving. Not good to hang around here. This place is an IED magnet,' said the young soldier, waving him through as the other sentry lifted the red and white barrier.

Mason took hold of the handle above the door and braced for the impending acceleration. 'This place is getting a lot of bad press recently, Tonka. There seems to be a constant stream of coffins returning to the UK. What the fuck is going on?' Mason asked as the vehicle lurched forward.

Tonka was taking the young soldier's advice and had his foot down hard on the accelerator. 'They daren't let the real truth out,' he shouted over the noise of the straining engine. 'The fact is that Brit Mil is getting hammered. The poor sods are getting killed, left, right and centre.'

'It's like this,' he continued, releasing the pressure from the pedal, slowing the vehicle to the twenty-five kilometres an hour speed limit. 'Brit Mil is fighting a war that it's ill-equipped for, and can never win with the current strategy'

'That's crazy,' replied Mason.

'I know it; you know it; and the soldiers out on the ground know it... but it is what it is. Whitehall jumped at the chance of a scrap... 'It will all be over before Christmas... Tea and medals at four o'clock...' he said with a mock posh accent. 'You know what they're like. But the truth is that the invasion was the easy part. This bit - the *reconstruction phase*, as they call it - is killing us. Or should I say *them*,' he said, nodding at a passing Brit Mil convoy.

'Let's face it. How many times were we deployed without adequate equipment?' said Tonka.

'Yeah, you're right; we never had enough. We were always scrounging off the Yanks,' Mason acknowledged.

'Exactly. And things haven't changed,' added Tonka.

'We always thought that, in time of war, the top brass would break out the war supplies. Truth is, there aren't any. It's always the same with Brit Mil. What you see is what you get.' Tonka pulled off the road to let a convoy of vehicles pass. 'Thing is, we're fighting with one hand tied behind our backs. The troops want to do it, but they just haven't got the resources or manpower. And the result is they've stopped dominating the ground.' Tonka pulled back onto the tarmac. 'And, in losing that, they've lost control. The insurgents can virtually move around anywhere unhindered. We have the airport, Basrah Palace and a few other places in the city. But every night we have to put up with a constant rain of rockets and mortars. The death toll from the explosions is increasing every week. Brit Mil has a few islands in a sea of hatred. The Iranians have seen to that.'

'What have the Iranians got to do with all this?' asked Mason.

'The Iranians,' Tonka scoffed. 'That's another thing the politicians don't want to get out. They've been after Iraqi oil for years, and with Saddam out of the way it's game on. The post-invasion Iraq Coalition have done more for the Iranian cause in the last couple of years than they managed to achieve themselves in decades. Ahmadinejad's boys are all over this place like stink on shit,' he said picking his way through the busy military camp that had been constructed behind the high fences on the perfectly flat desert plain.

'I mean, whose crazy idea was it to dismantle the whole of the Iraqi security services anyway? Let's face it, Iran is only twenty kilometres from Basrah; this is their back yard. It's in their interests to stir up a shit storm. And what our politicians are keeping secret is that it's the Iranians that are funding the Iraqi insurgents,' he said as he pulled out of the way of an oncoming tank.

'It sounds like a real cluster fuck.' Mason shouted over the roaring 62-ton Challenger tank as it rumbled past them.

'Absolutely,' agreed Tonka, 'but the sad thing is that it's our troops who are paying the price. The EFPs that the

Iranians have introduced are taking a heavy toll on our guys.'

'EFP?' asked Mason.

Don't you keep up with any of this stuff?' Tonka asked.

'Nah… not since I got out. I've been off the radar.

'No worries,' replied Tonka, remembering the reason for Mason's exit from the Regiment. 'EFP stands for explosively formed penetrator. It's like an IED on steroids.'

'What... like a shaped charge?'

'Exactly… nothing new, they've been around since WWII,' Tonka said as he slowed the Land Cruiser, threading it through a hole in a concrete blast wall just big enough for a vehicle. 'But the Iranians have taken it to a whole new level. The explosives are wrapped around a solid slug of copper. When it explodes the metal turns into a molten mass that hurtles towards the target at warp-factor-ten. You know the score. But get this,' he said, as he brought the vehicle to a slow stop. 'You can buy these killing machines in Basrah for a thousand bucks. The Iranians have set up a regular cottage industry; it's employing loads of locals. The aid and development people would be proud if they had thought it up,' he said, while cranking up the handbrake.

'But why would the locals want to buy them?' Mason asked.

'Investment, mate. Shell out a grand... and if you kill a Brit or American... you get your money back plus five grand on top.

'No shit!'

'Exactly,' replied Tonka as he opened the door. 'It's a no brainer for them; these B6s don't stand a bloody chance,' he said, hitting the door with the palm of his hand. 'Like a hot knife through butter. They will even go through the armour on a main battle tank.

'But don't worry,' Tonka said with a grin. 'Uncle Tonka will give you all the info you need to stay alive. Fancy a brew?'

The Target office was located in a corner of the military compound at BAS, close to the runway, and in constant earshot of the drone of helicopter rotor blades. For its protection, it was corralled behind a ring of concrete blast walls. The four-metre tall, twenty-ton reinforced concrete monstrosities christened 'T' walls, that were invented out of necessity during the Iraq Campaign, and were designed to dissipate the shock waves from the high explosive blasts that were frequently concealed in cars, trucks, motorbikes and, of course, humans.

Inside the concrete compound was a small car park and two forty-foot porta-cabins joined together to provide a workplace, every nook and cranny filled with the usual office paraphernalia. Tonka led Mason down a narrow corridor and into what was the biggest room within the office complex. 'Welcome to the Operations Room' he said as he opened the door.

'This is Ronda. She's the most important of all our HQ staff,' said Tonka as he introduced a buxom woman in her early thirties. 'You need to keep her sweet, 'cos she's the one that sorts out your pay and leave. Mess her about and you get neither,' Tonka laughed.

'Pleased to meet you, Mason,' she said, looking up at the face of the man towering above her as she shook his hand. She stood at five-feet, her green eyes - strikingly large at the best of times – were now huge as they devoured the man that stood before her.

'So this is where the whole thing is run from,' Tonka explained. 'We have nine security teams, each consisting of ten expats, with a rotation of four men out on leave at any one time – two months on, one month off - giving each team six men in country. Each team has three armoured vehicles that they use to transport the client pretty much anywhere within the Area of Operations - from the Kuwait border in the south, to Saudi in the west, and Iran in the east. Ronda, be a love and get us a brew.'

'Of course, boss. How do you take it, Mason?' She said,

her face bright with excitement.

'NATO, thanks.'

Tonka's small office led off from the operations room. It was only big enough for a desk and two chairs - which were pushed up into the corner - and a filing cabinet. The walls were adorned with maps covered with pins in a variety of different colours. The only part of the walls not covered was where the AC unit was. There was no window.

'Nice office, mate,' Mason said, sarcastically. 'The maps mean anything? Or are they just bluff?'

'What do you think?' retorted Tonka, sitting down behind the desk and reaching for the bottom drawer of the filing cabinet.

'Bluff,' answered Mason sitting down on the chair on the opposite side of the desk.

'Bullshit baffles brains,' declared Tonka. 'You know that. It makes me look like I know what I'm doing... and anyway, it makes up for the lack of a window,' Tonka said as he picked a bottle of Johnny Walker out of his desk drawer.

'Yeah. No window. That's a bit heartless,' replied Mason.

'I'm not bothered, mate. What would I see if I had one? A twelve-foot concrete wall? Anyway, natural sunlight is overrated. We've always lived like mushrooms: kept in the dark and fed on shit. Why change the habit of a lifetime? A wee dram?' Tonka asked, holding out the bottle towards Mason. 'Goes well with a coffee.'

The aroma of the whisky spread instantly throughout the small office as Tonka splashed a measure into his coffee. Mason was transfixed. He couldn't take his eyes off the bottle. It took all his strength to break the stare. He tried to swallow, but the saliva in his mouth had disappeared, his mouth parched. 'Water would be good,' he mumbled as he reached for one of the several bottles that were neatly paraded on Tonka's' desk, 'I've got a mouth like an Arab's flip flop.' He took hold of the bottle, unscrewed the blue cap and drained it, crushing the plastic container in his hand when it had run dry. 'I've spent the last few years living in a bottle, mate. I'm not going back,' Mason said, as he tossed the flattened plastic in the bin.

Tonka nodded and replaced the cap on the whisky bottle. 'Perhaps later, eh? Better then.'

Mason nodded, 'Yeah... later is best.'

So, what you been up to since you left the Regiment?' asked Tonka. 'Oh. Sorry about the accident, by the way. Kate was a lovely woman.'

'That she was.' Mason replied, not wishing to dwell. 'Well... Let's see? After the accident, they kept me on in Hereford. They didn't deploy me anymore - they could see my heart wasn't in it - so they gave me a place on the training team. But I began to drink more and more. It was just too easy... I found it was the only thing that would numb the pain.'

Tonka nodded in sympathy.

'But it began to take a heavy toll. I started to turn up late, smelling of booze. They cut me as much slack as they could, hoping I would get over it. But eventually The CO called me in and told me to take early retirement,' he said, picking up a pencil. 'I jumped before I was pushed... they gave me a full pension, and that was that.'

'Their loss, mate,' Tonka chipped in, trying to lighten the atmosphere.

'Some of the guys gave me a few scraps off the table... London... the circuit, body-guarding and that,' Mason continued with a lighter tone, 'but the phones stopped ringing after I dropped a client'.

'You did what?' Tonka butted in with amazement.

Mason repeated it. 'I dropped the client.'

'You have my undivided attention, me old son,' Tonka said, the new topic changing the mood in the office in an instant, as an impish grin started to spread across his tanned face.

'Well... we were staying in the Dorchester... all expenses

paid. It would have been a cushy gig. But the client - a wealthy Russian - turned out to be a right prick.'

Tonka leaned forward, hanging on Mason's every word.

'He wanted us to take turns at sitting outside his door. I think he was on a power trip or something. But anyway, we were getting paid good money, so me and the other two guys on the security team just soaked it up.

The one night, I was sitting outside while the Rusky was banging away on a five-thousand-pound-a-night hooker. We'd been on the go all day, and I am ashamed to say it,' he said with a large grin, 'but I fell asleep. So the Rusky blew his beans, right...'

Tonka's grin by this point had taken over his whole face, and he had started to giggle, in expectation of what was to come.

'The prick opens the door to let the hooker out.... Sees me sleeping and prods me in the shoulder,' Mason continued. 'I wake up and shoot straight to my feet... all startled and that... you know,' he said, looking at Tonka for confirmation '...and he starts giving me a hard time. I don't know why but I start to laugh. He then goes ballistic, and starts jumping up and down, ranting and raving in Russian.

The hooker is standing behind him; she doesn't know where to look. I look at her and she looks back at me... and then I just smacked him. He goes flying back, hits the wall and collapses in a heap.'

Tonka, by this time, was in a fit of uncontrollable laughter. 'So what happened then?' he managed to get out between spasms of belly laughs.

'Me and the hooker walk arm-in-arm out of the hotel. She gives me a handful of fifty pound notes and a peck on the cheek. She says it's the funniest thing she's ever seen'.

'So I can understand why the phone stopped ringing,' Tonka said, finally calming down. 'Was there a shit storm?'

'Not half... It was horrendous' said Mason. 'The guy I was working for lost the contract... He said I would never work in the industry again, and he was right. I was treated like a leper. How the police never charged me, I don't know... but they didn't.'

'Services rendered, mate,' Tonka said, touching his nose and winking. 'Someone made it go away... that's the old boy's network.'

'Yeah, you're right... Must have been, mate. I thought for deffo that I was off to do some male bonding with 'mister big' in the prison shower. But that was a few years ago. I've just been living off my pension since... It's not much, but it pays the bills,' he said as he sat back. 'So, what about you... What you been up to?'

Tonka sat back in his chair, his actions unconsciously copying that of his friend. He picked up a bottle of water. 'I did my full term: twenty two years,' he said as he undid the bottle's cap and looked at the ceiling. 'The last two were as RQMS, 21 SAS in London. Cushy gig. They just left me alone. Nice way to end up,' he said, with what seemed to be a smile under his large moustache. 'While I was there, I bumped into JJ at the SF Club and he offered me a job. So, when I was on my termination leave, I cross-decked over. It was great; I was working with Target and getting paid by the army. I was rolling in it.'

'So, you been here since the beginning then?' asked Mason.

'Yeah... I started the whole thing,' Tonka said as he took a swig of water. 'JJ put a bid in for the contract. He was the only Brit. Everyone thought that one of the big American security companies would get it, but he won. Even JJ was surprised,' he said as he wiped the water off his lip. 'When news of the award came, there was nothing in place; we were all running round like headless chickens... 2004... it was all new... we were making it up as we went along. No right or wrong; as long as we got the job done, everyone was happy. I enjoyed it.'

Mason noticed that Tonka's demeanour had changed, his body taking on an awkwardness. 'But to be honest, mate... I need a hand. Things have gone from bad to worse; the client is making my life miserable. When they told me that you were coming, I was over the moon,' said Tonka in a more sombre tone.

'Who is the client?' Mason asked

'Navaro Oil. They are a Texas-based oil company. They do all the ground work - you know, exploration and that... 'Dirty work,' they call it. When it's all done, the big boys - like BP and Shell - move in.'

'So, what's the problem?'

'Washington... Congress is ramping up the pressure. The thing is,' Tonka said, as he placed the half empty bottle of water on his desk, 'what people don't realise is that the revenue from selling Iraqi oil is being used to pay for the War. But production is way down; there's far less pumped now than there ever was during the Saddam days. It's costing the US billions for the war. And, although they keep throwing money into initiatives aimed at getting oil production up, it's just not getting any better.

'Navaro and the other companies have been told to sort it out. They have to show results. Washington puts the squeeze on them, and they pass it on to us... which basically means that our job becomes far more dangerous.'

Mason was good at reading body language. It wasn't something they taught at Hereford; it was something he had learned the hard way. But it had saved his life on a number of occasions. As Tonka spoke, Mason could see a bodily transformation, as if a physical wave of sadness had hit him. He looked vulnerable, naked.

'Are you okay, Tonka?' Mason asked.

'I am going through a bottle of this stuff a day,' Tonka replied as he kicked the desk drawer. 'Does that answer your question?' he answered, unable to maintain eye contact.

'Steady, tiger. I'm here to help you. Remember 'Who Dares Wins'? Yeah?' said Mason.

'The way I feel right now, mate, it's more like... who cares who wins?'

51

'They're bringing it forward' JJ snarled, slamming a copy of the email on to the desk.

'Sorry, John? Bringing what forward?' James inquired.

'Read it for yourself,' he said, pushing the sheet towards him.

James eased his way out of the Chesterfield and edged his way around the ornate desk, picking up the paper with his normal, casual indifference. Like most officers in the Guards Division, James came from a privileged background. His career had been mapped out for him well before he had been packed off to boarding school aged six: school, Cambridge and then the regiment of his ancestors. His life ambition had been to become the Regimental Colonel. But that was not to be. He stumbled at Major, and was told that he would go no further, even with his family's connections. Devastated, he had left and, opting for a change in career, joined MI6.

He was their man inside Target, his brief: to monitor the day-to-day activities and to make sure that JJ O'Hare didn't get into trouble. JJ was aware of this. Of course he was. And he hated having his every move scrutinised. But it was a small price to pay. Such was the importance of Target's recent activities that the British Security Services needed to know exactly what was going on within the company. After all, it was thanks to the British Government that JJ had got the contract in the first place. To everyone else, James was Target's overseas advisor.

'Diamond Four? Is that the wellhead near Al Amarah - the one that's causing all the fuss?' James asked.

'Aye, that's the one... the one that the whole bloody thing is riding on.'

'Well, you have everything in place now. You just need to get on and finish the game,' James said, as he fed the paper into the shredder.

Target Complex, BAS, Iraq,
15.31hrs, 9 May 2007.

The two men stepped out from the office and into the gaze of the unrelenting sun. From every direction, their senses were assaulted: the cacophony of noise from the military hardware took away their hearing; the sunlight blinded them; the scorching air dried their mouths and burnt their throats. 'Come on,' said Tonka, pointing at the Toyota they'd just arrived in, 'I'll show you to the accommodation.'

BAS was busy, there was no mistaking that. The empty space he remembered from his last visit in 1991 was nothing compared to this sprawling military town that had grown alongside the huge runway - the concrete ribbon, the runway's surface - an island in a desert sea. The camp was ravenous for supplies, its appetite fed by a constant stream of transport aircraft that allowed the beleaguered troops to carry on their fight for survival.

But there's no getting away from it, Mason thought as they drove through the heat. *Military camps look the same the world over; the only difference is the colour of the camouflage.*

On either side of the road were row upon row of beige tents. And, if it wasn't tents, it was vehicles - all shapes and sizes, the common theme being sand-coloured paint and the regimental straight lines always compulsory in military settings.

They arrived at the edge of a sea of connexes, the grey portable accommodation spread out in front of them in the ubiquitous neat rows. 'This is our accommodation,' declared Tonka. 'I know it doesn't look like one, but this is actually a hotel. It's run by a Lebanese company that got straight in after the war. Very entrepreneurial, the Lebanese.'

Tonka picked his way through the lines of well-ordered containers that seemed to stretch on into infinity. 'This place is massive.' exclaimed Mason. 'How many connexes are there?'

'I've never counted them. But they tell me there are well over two hundred. Target has sixty five. We're their biggest customer.'

Right next to the hotel complex, soaring over a hundred feet above it into the clear blue sky, was the air traffic control tower. This iconic building - a symbol of the glory days of the fifth President of Iraq, Saddam Hussein Abd al-Majid al-Tikriti - was the main feature of Iraq's second biggest airport. It could be seen for well over twenty miles on the flat desert plane that surrounded it. When Mason and Tonka's SAS unit had rushed from the Kuwait border to the airport in 1991, they found it a welcome friend. It had rendered their maps and compasses obsolete; their only requirement was to 'head for the concrete column'. But they were not the only ones to use it to their advantage.

'The guy who sited this complex wasn't very security-minded, was he?' said Mason, gesturing towards the tower.

'That's a deffo' replied Tonka. 'The bad guys use it as a marker. They just aim their rockets and mortars at it and hope for the best. The IDF hasn't been too accurate, but the word is that the Iranians have given the insurgents some lessons to up the ante. We are getting hit four or five times a day now, and it's getting more and more accurate. Best head for the bunkers if you hear the siren.'

Tonka stopped in front of a connex, 74A writ large in felt tip letters on the door. He searched in the pocket of his 5-11 tactical trousers and pulled out the key. 'This is your room' he said, unlocking the door.

The inside temperature was a complete contrast to the heat outside. 'That's good,' said Mason, gulping down the cool air. 'It's as good as drinking an ice cold beer.'

'What do you think?' Tonka asked, like an estate agent with a prospective customer.

Mason nodded as he checked out the room's contents: a double bed, easy chair, cupboard, chest of drawers and a flat screen TV sitting proudly on top of a satellite box. 'That's your en-suite' Tonka said, pointing to the door next to the bed, 'Toilet and shower. The TV has cable. You get Sky News, HBO, TCM and all that sort of stuff. The room's cleaned every day, and the laundry is twice a week.'

'Wow' Mason said, feasting his eyes. 'I'm impressed.'

'We try our best' Tonka said with a smirk.

'But, let me get this right...' Mason said as he sat on the end of the bed. 'The poor squaddies are living in tents in the hundred and thirty degree heat, and we're living in the lap of luxury?'

'Yep... We live like kings, and we get paid four times as much as them. No wonder they hate us.'

'Who the hell pays for all this, Tonka?'

'It's all kosher, geezer, don't worry,' Tonka said as he sat in the easy chair. 'It's called a 'cost plus' contract. 'It works like this: we pay for everything we need - vehicles, wages, weapons, food, accommodation - all the overheads. We then get paid a percentage of our expenditure as profit. So, the more we spend, the more money we make. The client doesn't ask questions; they just want the job done. We bill the client, the client bills the US Government,' he said, smiling. 'So, in answer to your question, the US tax-payer is paying for your double bed, cable TV, en suite and your three squares a day.'

'That's unbelievable,' said Mason, reclining backwards and propping himself up with a pillow.

'No. That's a cost plus contract.'

'So, what you're saying is that this contract is just like a licence to print money?'

'If you put it like that, yeah. I suppose it's just like having a massive blank cheque,' continued Tonka. 'Anyway,' he said, pointing at the cupboard in the corner of the room. 'Your body armour and helmet is in there. There's also a pistol and few rounds to go on with. You can get the rest of your kit tomorrow. There is nothing else happening today, so you might as well get your head down.

I'll catch you in the morning' he said, opening the door to leave.

'Do you want to talk about anything?' asked Mason.

Tonka paused and rubbed his chin, uneasily, 'No... No... It's okay.'

'I can sense something's up, mate. Are you sure?

Tonka hesitated at the door, his shoulders and back hunched as though he was carrying an unseen load. 'Maybe a quick chat,' he said as he and sat back into the chair, his anxiety clear, his body stiff, like a boxer waiting for a punch that he knows is going to hurt but can't avoid.

'So, what's the beef?' asked Mason.

Tonka took a few deep breaths. 'It's just not the same anymore,' he said, sitting back into the chair. 'Do you remember what it was like? If we had problems, we sorted them out amongst ourselves. There was no wingeing, no need for shrinks, no blabbering off to the wife. You could talk to the guys. They were the only ones that understood, 'cos they'd been there and done it with you.'

Mason nodded, seeing the turmoil etched into Tonka's face.

'I suppose it's Palitoy's fault,' Tonka said, looking at the floor.

'What? Palitoy the toy company?' asked Mason.

'Yeah... Palitoy. They made Action Man. Remember him?'

'Yeah, I know Action Man! We all had one when we were kids. But what's that got to do with us now in Iraq?'

'Look... You asked me, so I'm telling you. So just shut up and let me talk. Christ, it's hard enough as it is. I was nine, and my dad got me an Action Man for Christmas. I loved it. It started me off. I was army barmy from then on. I couldn't get enough of it. When I was twelve, I joined the Army Cadets. I lied about my age; you had to be fourteen so I forged my dad's signature. It was a shit signature, but they didn't care. The more the merrier as far as they were concerned. Do you remember when the Iranian Embassy siege came on the TV?' he asked, looking over at Mason who nodded. His friend's face registered a smile as the iconic pictures of the SAS men blowing their way into the building flashed into his brain.

'It was unbelievable. I nearly wet my pants with excitement. I went into school the next day and told them I wanted out. I think they were glad to see the back of me, so they sent me to the Army careers office. The fat Colour Sergeant in the recruiting office asked me what regiment I wanted to join. SAS of course I said. He laughed at me. Prick! Said I was the second kid that day that wanted to join the SAS. I didn't know - I was a young lad - keen but naive... very naive. Anyway, he signed me up for the Royal Green Jackets. No surprise there - that was his Regiment - and I was soon packed off as a boy soldier.'

Tonka's shoulders loosened, and his arms, which he had held defensively across his chest, dropped down to his side. He looked much more relaxed. *It's as if talking about his youth is acting like a tonic*, Mason thought as he listened.

'They kept me there for three years before letting me try for the SAS. I wanted to go straight away but they said it would be an embarrassment for the RGJ if I failed. When I finally went on selection, I passed first time. Straight in! I remember seeing that fat Colour Sergeant in the mess not long after. I was going to go over and give him what for, but he bought me a pint and patted me on the back. I was so proud. I had achieved what I set out to do. Being badged as a member of 22 SAS was the proudest day of my life.'

As a senior non-commissioned officer in the SAS, part of Mason's job was to ensure that his men were fit for duty - not just physically but also mentally. He was used to being a shoulder to cry on, and had taken care of a number of guys through many traumatic events. He looked over at Tonka and watched as the smile that had started to appear on his face receded. 'I see their faces when I close my eyes,' said Tonka, looking directly at him.

'Whose faces?' Mason asked.

'The faces of the people I've killed. When I close my eyes and try to sleep, they barge in. I can't stop them. Their faces, full of life at first, and then their blood-streaked contorted faces after. How many people have you killed, Mason?'

'I never kept count. I didn't think it was appropriate.'

'How could we just kill like that?'

'The people that we killed were our enemies. That's all there was to it. We just followed orders.'

'Orders? Yeah. That's what the Nazi soldiers said about the concentration camps. You can't hide behind orders all the time. Orders never pulled the trigger; we did,' said Tonka, sitting forward and putting his head in his hands.

'How long have you been feeling like this?' asked Mason.

'For years now,' Tonka continued, without looking up. 'But it's got worse since I've been out here. It started when I was in Sierra Leone. That turned out to be my last operational job. I asked to be reassigned after that, so they packed me off to London.'

'What happened in Sierra Leone?' asked Mason.

'We were patrolling with local government forces, looking for a band of RUF paramilitaries. They'd raided a village. Our job was to track them down. At nightfall on the sixth day in the bush, we cornered them on a piece of high ground. I had the local troops secure the area, and planned to go in with a dawn attack. We put in sporadic fire into their encampment all night, to keep them on their toes. They actually helped us out by lighting...' he paused to take a breath, 'lighting a camp-fire. Easy to spot. And at first they fired back at us. But eventually they stopped.

'At first light, we attacked. There was no fight; they'd gone - disappeared into the night like ghosts. What we didn't know was that they had taken hostages - three girls from a local village. They had all been tied up and gagged and made to sit around the camp fire. They were all dead from gunshot wounds. Two had died where they sat. But the other one...'

Tonka looked directly at Mason as he relived the nightmare, his eyes welling with tears.

'...She'd crawled off. We didn't see her at first, but one of the locals followed a blood trail from the fire. She had been hit in the guts and had tried to get away from our gunfire. We found her hiding under a fallen tree. It would have taken her hours to die. A gut wound is the worst. You know that?' he said, looking at Mason, who nodded his answer.

'Hours to die... All alone and in agony. Her face... her face...'

The horrific picture that had been burned into his soul now acted as the trigger that released his tears. As they flowed, he slumped back into the chair.

'It's not your fault. You don't know who pulled the trigger; it could have been anyone,' said Mason.

'That's true. In, fact I didn't shoot any rounds... so it couldn't have been me. But that's not the point. I gave the orders. I'd laughed at the RUF, thinking how stupid they were to light a fire. And I ate, drank and joked while the girl died. All alone. Frightened. Wracked with pain, and all because of me.'

Both men were silent as Tonka's words hung in the air.

'Do you believe in God, Mason?' Tonka said, as he sat forward in the chair. 'Because I do, and I don't think he likes people like us.'

Mason didn't answer. The room went silent once more as Tonka took control of his emotions. After a few minutes, the only visible evidence of his outburst was the tear tracks on his cheeks. As he calmed down, he wiped the moisture away with the palms of his hands. Now nothing remained in their shared consciousness except the inner turmoil that both men battled with every day.

All men had a breaking point, and it looked to Mason like Billy Toy had reached his. He had served with distinction and courage in his time with the SAS. He was a soldier. He had accepted his responsibilities, and had taken the rough with the smooth. When the men were in the regiment, it was straightforward; they had no need for outside help; they looked after themselves. After a difficult operation, everyone got together and got drunk. They talked it through. The guys that hadn't *beaten the clock* were toasted in the mess, and it was finished; everyone moved on. It was counselling of the best kind; you were with your mates, and they supported you.

When they retired, they were suddenly left to fend for themselves. Taken away from their comrades. Becoming once again ordinary citizens, trying to live out their lives like everyone else. But most still carried around the baggage of war. Stress at that level just didn't go away - it festered like cancer, often appearing when least expected, and ensuring that the SAS stayed at the top of the table when it came to suicide rates amongst ex-British Army soldiers. The two men sat in silence.

Some soldiers would have given their right arm to be in the SAS, but there were others who wished they had never joined. It was the job that had the ultimate kudos, they were the best of the best: an SAS Trooper; a superman; someone who had had everything thrown at him, and had shaken it all off to pass the test. Other men, lesser men, looked up to them. But the accolade of having the right to wear the winged dagger on the beige beret had to be paid for with sacrifices - sacrifices that to some became unbearable, prices to be paid over the rest of their lives.

'I'm sorry. I didn't mean to unload on you like that' said Tonka as he stood up. 'You must think I'm a right nutter?'

'You're out of your tree,' said Mason with a smile, trying to defuse the tense atmosphere. 'But you always have been. I still remember the story about you when you were knocking off that guy's wife. Let me see if I can get it right,' Mason paused as he tried to get the story straight. 'He was away, and you were taking advantage of his absence by slipping her the one-eyed bed snake. Roger, so far?' he asked, wanting to confirm that he had it correct.

'Roger' said Tonka, his smile returning.

'So... you'd been out on the piss all day, and you go back to hers. She goes upstairs to get her slut gear on, whilst you're having another can on the sofa. The phone goes, and you answer it. It's her husband. He says 'Who the fuck is this?' And you say...'

At this point Tonka joins in: 'I'm the bloke that's sitting on your sofa, drinking your beer, patting your dog, and about to go upstairs and fuck your wife.' They both laughed uncontrollably, the tension now forgotten.

'It wasn't funny. I nearly got the sack over that one,' Tonka laughed. 'They had to post me out of H. Her husband was looking for me for months.

'It's good to see you again, Mason. I missed all this shit,' Tonka said as he opened the door.

'Me too, mate. Don't worry. We're going to sort it, okay? Now fuck off; you're boring me.'

Tonka smiled 'Roger that, big guy. See you tomorrow at zero seven hundred for scoff' he said, stepping out of the room. 'I tell you what,' he added. 'Some things never change. You're still a wanker.'

Mason unzipped his small travel bag and started to unpack. He picked up his spare trousers, bought in London only a few days earlier. *It seems like months, not days*, he thought as he opened the cupboard. As he put them on the shelf, he noticed two boxes at the bottom of the cupboard. The larger of the two was hard black plastic. The second, placed on top of the first, was made from cardboard. There was no mistaking the contents; no need to read the label.

In the SAS, troopers didn't call it a pistol; they called it a short, referring to its short barrel - as distinct from a rifle, whose longer barrel made it a *long*. Unlike the regular army, SAS men were able to pick the *short* weapon systems they carried. Some men opted for Smith and Wessons, others for Sig Hausers. Mason had always carried the Ceska Zbrojovka

75, commonly known as the CZ - the Czech-made 9mm. *Please*, he thought, peeping inside the box, like someone opening a surprise present. Disappointment. 'Shit! A Glock 17' he said out loud.

The Glock was an Austrian pistol that had been adopted by the Americans in a big way. Nearly all the US law enforcement agencies, and even the military had been equipped with this strange, plastic gun.

It was different from other pistols because it didn't have a safety catch. The manufacturer's claim that it didn't need one - because of the relatively 'safe' action of the stiff trigger mechanism - didn't really cut it with the guys in Hereford. The SAS used them only as a last resort. New recruits that picked them as their primary weapon system were usually taken to one side and enlightened before anyone else saw and ridiculed them.

The trigger's in-built 'safety catch' made for a very hard pull before the firing pin was released and the bullet fired. Novices found this action difficult to master, making their aim inaccurate to say the least. And it was only after shooting thousands of rounds that proficiency was gained. The lack of a safety catch seemed like 'shooting made easy' for novices lacking the dexterity to flick off a safety catch before firing.

Mason took the weapon out of the box, his big hand wrapping comfortably around the plastic moulded pistol grip. With his left thumb, he instinctively searched for the magazine release button. He pressed it, the empty magazine dropping away from its housing and onto the bed.

He put the gun down and picked up the box of 9x19mm Luger ammunition. The magazine was designed to take seventeen of these rounds, hence: Glock 17. But only the uninitiated used seventeen. In carrying out the manufacturer's instructions, undue pressure would be put on the spring inside the magazine, eventually causing 'stoppages', which meant the weapon wouldn't fire. The SAS left nothing to chance: sixteen rounds was the magic number.

He picked up the first bullet and rolled it between his thumb and forefinger. It was over six years since he had touched a weapon, the feel of the bullet instantly bringing back memories. He held it to his nose, taking in the distinctive aroma of brass and cordite, as one might smell a blooming flower.

He could strip and assemble any weapon in the world. He could do it blindfolded, upside down, with one hand, you name it. In the SAS, the men had held competitions where they raced each other at stripping and assembling weapons and filling magazines. One of his favourites - a game he himself had invented - entailed filling magazines while submerged underwater. It was Mason's party piece, and quickly became popular.

They had once held a competition filling magazines; the rules on that occasion were that it had to be performed while drunk, naked, and of course at the bottom of a swimming pool. Mason won. But his challenger nearly drowned. They had to drag him up from the bottom of the pool, unconscious, and give him mouth to mouth. SAS men would never give in, even if they ran out of air.

Mason looked down. He had filled the magazine in seconds, not even realising it. He placed it at the opening of the magazine housing, at the bottom of the pistol grip, and pushed it home. He made sure it was in correctly, hitting it with the palm of his left hand. The click that resonated told him that it was secure. His left hand now moved to the stop slide, his forefinger and thumb immediately finding the grooves cut into its side. He jerked it to the rear and released it, allowing the mechanism to pick up a bright, shiny bullet from the top of the magazine, and feed it into the chamber.

He placed the loaded gun on the bed in front of him. *If I want to end this, I can do it now*, he thought as he looked at the pistol. *Get it over with, nice and clean.* As he picked up the gun and held it to his head, a vision of Katie - in the summer dress that he loved - burst into his mind. He pressed the gun barrel against his temple, and placed the pad of his right index finger on the trigger. *Perfect. A squeeze and it would all be over. I can be with them.*

'No, baby, not like this,' Katie spoke to him. 'You're a soldier; you deserve better. Not like this... please.'

The silence was broken by the siren signalling a rocket attack, its shrill scream cutting into his brain. Reality. His finger relaxed and the gun fell away from his head.

CHAPTER THREE

All Saints College, Oxford,
09.05hrs, 10 May 2007.

'Late again,' the professor muttered as he opened the cupboard to look for a clean shirt. 'Damn.' The cupboard was empty. He walked over to the laundry basket in the corner and pulled out yesterday's crumpled shirt. *No problem,* he thought as he shook the creased material and smelled the armpits. He picked up a can of deodorant and sprayed liberally at the offending patch. *A smell to hide a smell.* With the rest of his clothes thrown on, he was just finishing tying his laces when the phone rang.

'Professor?' an agitated voice asked before Cornelius had time to speak. 'The Dean is waiting. He would very much appreciate your attendance.'

'I'm on my way,' Cornelius answered, not waiting to hear the response.

The Professor hurried down the oak-lined stairwell, cursing the flights of stairs that led to his third floor apartment. Gown in hand, he burst into the quad, breaking its serenity as the door crashed against its frame. He rushed along the stone path, framed by immaculate lawns and manicured flowerbeds, connecting the college's many quads. He tried frantically to pull on his gown, his efforts interrupting the undergrads lying casually on the lawns.

Cornelius was the son of a successful British diplomat. His father had travelled the world with his gin-soaked mother at the taxpayer's expense, dropping their eight-year-old son in a private school as if depositing a piece of luggage. The young Cornelius had hated school; his one wish at the time had been to make himself invisible, so that he could avoid the regular punishment given out by the bigger boys. He would often hide in the attic for hours, if not days, coming down only when everyone was asleep, to raid the fridge.

As a child, he spent most of his time reading books. They were his friends. They didn't hurt him or make him cry. History books were his favourite; he loved the stories of ancient Greece and Rome. And while the other boys played sports, he immersed himself in the ancient world - a world he found alien yet familiar. He became obsessed with the stories of combat and glory, and aspired to the lofty ideals he found amongst the pages of history books. He took inspiration from heroes like Hercules, Odysseus and Perseus, whose noble feats belonged to a world rather different - and much more interesting - than his own. He longed to learn everything there was to learn about their world.

When the time came to leave school, he already knew that he wanted to devote his life to delving deeper into the ancient world. He tried the entrance exam for Ancient History at All Saints, drawn to the college by its strong reputation in his subject and by the renown of the college fellows. He passed it with the highest-ever result.

His life changed when he got to university. He was still a geek, but now, for the first time, he was a geek amongst a herd of other geeks. And the best thing was that, at university, instead of being beaten up and taunted, he was rewarded for his geekiness. He loved it - so much so that he never wanted to leave.

And he never had to leave. His Bachelors degree immediately led onto a Masters and then a Doctorate. At every stage of his academic career, his achievements had been astounding, and when offered a senior lectureship by the Dean, his dream was complete. He could now spend the rest of his life in the cocoon that All Saints represented, secure within its walls.

'Please take a seat, Professor. The Dean is expecting you,' said the secretary - a balding man with a pugnacious personality, who looked over the short-of-breath Professor with contempt.

You only get summoned to the Dean's office for one of two things, Cornelius thought, as he waited: *praise or punishment. I haven't done anything to warrant praise, recently, so it must be...*

'Ah... Cornelius, thank you for coming,' said the Dean checking his watch, as Cornelius and his escort entered the book-lined office. 'We'll have to keep this brief, as I have another engagement,' he continued motioning for the still-panting professor to sit opposite him.

'I am sorry, sir,' Cornelius began, in an attempt to avert the inevitable.

'Don't worry, my dear boy,' the Dean answered in a calm voice, his tone matching the peaceful scene that was framed through the bay window behind him. 'You have a brilliant mind, Cornelius,' the Dean continued, gesturing for the nervous academic to listen rather than interrupt. 'I've always admired your passion. But I'm afraid that your energies are... are... being misdirected. I've received complaints, allegations, that you've been neglecting your students. This hypothesis of yours - The Saladin thing...'

'The *Secret*' interrupted the secretary.

'Yes. The Saladin Secret. I'm afraid it's become an... obsession. It's affecting your work.'

'I know... I know,' Cornelius said as he lowered his head.

'I've protected you, Cornelius. This is not the first time I've received such information. But now, the Governing Body is involved. I understand you're due to depart on another dig. Is that correct?' the Dean said as he swivelled his chair to look out of the window.

'Yes, Dean. I leave soon for Palmyra. The Italian archaeological mission there has found another early Christian church - the biggest yet.'

'Well, I hope for your sake that it gives you what you need,' the Dean said as he swivelled back to face Cornelius, 'because I can't cover for you anymore. As I say, this obsession of yours is taking up far too much of your time and energy. It's been years since you published anything of any value, and your standing as a historian is suffering as a consequence. Look...' he said, placing his elbows on his desk, 'The Governing Body has to consider the reputation of the college and the university. In order to remain a world-class institution, we can only afford to employ world-class academics. Unfortunately, at the moment, you are falling short of that mark. You've been hard at this topic for how many years without a result?'

'Four years, Dean.'

'Four years with nothing to show,' the secretary interrupted.

'Yes... yes. Four years. Well, Cornelius. I hope for your sake that this dig is successful. But remember this: if you don't come up with something soon, you're out.'

BAS, Iraq,
06.45hrs, 10 May 2007.

Mason stared at his image in the mirror. The face that looked back at him was haggard from lack of sleep. There had been a total of four IDF attacks on the compound during the night. The siren heralding the impending impact of the rockets, and the inaudible message announcing the *all clear* when the threat was past, had done a great job in robbing him of any sleep. For the first three attacks – as ordered – he'd donned his body armour and helmet, and ran to the bomb shelter. But, by the fourth time, he'd had enough, opting instead to pull the duvet over his head and cross his fingers.

At 0700 hours precisely, there was a knock on his door. 'Come on, sleepy head. Hands off cock and on with socks,' said the encouraging thick Cockney accent. 'Let's go and get some breakfast.'

On the short walk to the building containing the DFAC they passed a tired-looking punch bag, swinging under a shaded lean-to. 'You used to box,' said Tonka, throwing a fake punch towards Mason.

'Yeah... did a bit,' he replied, with an exaggerated duck away from the punch.

'Might want to give it a go later... I've got some gloves in my room.

'You trying to say something?' Mason asked, suddenly reminded of the image he'd seen in the mirror earlier.

'No, mate... All good. In fact, you can have the gloves... I don't do phys any more... All that exercise has got to be bad for you... Come on. I'm starving.'

The DFAC had the same grey, external appearance as the other buildings, but its internal dimensions were far greater, allowing it to seat a hundred diners comfortably.

Both men joined the small queue at the hot plate, and selected their breakfast. Mason was amazed at the amount of fried food that Tonka piled onto his plate. *That's enough cholesterol to kill a horse*, he thought, watching the mound of sausages, bacon and egg grow bigger.

'You not hungry, then?' asked Tonka, as Mason sat down at the table with only a cup of tea. 'Most important meal of the day, breakfast, ya know.'

'My stomach takes a few days to acclimatise. I find it better if I ease myself in. I'm OK with the tea, thanks,' Mason lied. The truth was that he had taken a long look in the mirror that morning, and he hadn't liked what he'd seen. Six years of neglect. His once daily routine of running and gym had lapsed, and the result: a body he barely recognised, the *tat* of a set of para wings on his right upper arm being just about the only thing that hadn't altered.

'Yeah, Whatever' said Tonka, with a sideways glance and a mouth full of greasy breakfast. 'See what we spoke about yesterday?' he said, taking a slurp of tea, 'you know...

my stuff… that's just between us, right?' he asked.

'Yes, of course. Strictly confidential. Why wouldn't it be?'

'You know. It's a bit personal and that,' said Tonka, looking slightly embarrassed.

Mason looked at him, his face serious. 'What the hell makes you think that people would be interested in an old has-been like you?'

Tonka grinned. He'd got the message. 'Yeah. You're right. Sorry, mate.'

'At any rate,' Mason added, 'the way you're stuffing your face, you're going to be dead pretty soon.

Tonka swallowed the last mouthful. 'Come on,' he said, swallowing, 'We need to go and see Rick.'

Rick's office was a stark contrast to the cramped environment that was Target. Spacious, with windows so thick with blast film that they threw a yellowed light on the cheap grey carpet. Below the ceiling fan was a large desk. The man sitting behind it took a Cuban from a box as the two men entered. Lighting the cigar, he blew a long line of smoke into the air, his eyes never leaving Mason. 'Is this the new guy?' he asked.

'Yes. This is Mason,' said Tonka as both men shook hands. 'Mason, let me introduce Rick. He is the Navaro lead in country.'

'Yeah… I'm the client,' said Rick, sucking again on the large cigar, 'and I guess that makes me the boss… uhhh, Toy?'

He didn't need Tonka's endorsement; there was no mistaking Rick's confidence, his air of authority. He had been in the oil exploration business all his life; his gaunt, weathered face and lean frame testament to the harsh existence that he had chosen in his relentless search for black gold.

'Diamond Four?' he queried with his North-American

drawl, 'Show me.'

'From the information that's been provided, I'm making it to be around here', Tonka said as he placed a yellow dot on the map that covered the office wall.

Rick pushed back from the desk and stood in front of the map. He placed his finger on the yellow dot and mumbled as he studied the surrounding area. 'Al Amarah, Al Nasiriyah, Al Qurna. Looks about right,' he said, as he looked at his watch – a hunk of Swiss gold that dangled on his skinny wrist. 'May 12,' he said, as he turned his attention to Mason. 'So, you're the SAS guy they've been talking about'. Rick checked Mason out from head to toe, as if he was a prize bull at an auction. 'I hope you're as good as O'Hare says you are. We're paying your company good money for shit at the moment.' He turned and looked back at the map. 'I wanna see some results. Are you hearing me, Toy?'

'Yes. Rick. No problem. Now that Mason is here, it's full steam ahead.'

'It wants to be,' said Rick, giving Tonka a menacing look. He popped the cigar back into his mouth, squeezing out the words 'Now, if you will excuse me.'

Mason and Tonka stepped outside. 'Diamond Four: What's the beef?' asked Mason as they headed for the operations room.

'It's a wellhead,' replied Tonka. 'Come into my office and I will give you the lowdown,' he said, opening the door to the Target complex.

'Navaro have been in Iraq for ages' said Tonka as he made himself comfortable back in his cramped office. 'Diamond Four is the name of an exploratory shaft that they drilled back in 2002. It gave some incredible results... really special. They were about to open it up when the shit hit the fan and Iraq got invaded. Navaro - or whatever they were called back then - had to pull out in a hurry, and they lost all their records.'

'So that's why Rick only has a rough idea where it is?' asked Mason.

'Exactly,' replied Tonka. 'But, with the added pressure from Washington, Navaro are desperate to get in the game.'

'So what's so special about it?'

Tonka unfolded a map and put it on his desk. 'Remember this?' he said, circling the area to the west of Basrah City with a pencil. 'Az Zubair - one of the largest oilfields in the world. Total production at present: two hundred thousand barrels of oil per day. It is expected to produce over a million when running at full capacity. Now, this area' Tonka said, circling a large area north-west of Basrah 'is where the new oil field is. They're calling it Halfaya. Rick reckons that the reserves are huge. We're talking forty maybe fifty years at three million barrels a day.'

Mason whistled as he sat back in his chair, 'That's a shit load of oil.'

'You're not wrong, geezer' replied Tonka, 'That will make it by far the biggest oil field in the world, and Navaro - first in - will get the lion's share.'

'But there's a catch, right? There's always a catch,' asked Mason.

'Yeah, there's a catch,' Tonka said, referring back to the map. 'Rick reckons that most of the new oil field is underwater. It's in the area where the Tigris and Euphrates Rivers meet. The whole area is covered by marshes. It's all very historical. They reckon it's where the Garden of Eden was. You know: Adam and Eve and all that.'

'Yes, mate. I get it' said Mason as he studied the map, 'I went to Sunday school.'

'The Marshlands cover a huge area. But it used to be a lot bigger - nine times bigger, to be exact.'

'So what happened?' asked Mason.

'Saddam wanted to get rid of the Marshlands after the First Gulf War,' explained Tonka. 'Do you remember the uprising that happened after we pulled out?

'Yeah, I remember. It was bad,' answered Mason. 'The people in the South rose up against Saddam, thinking we were going to help them. But we just buggered off, and he took them to the cleaners.'

'Correct,' Tonka confirmed, with a scholarly tone. 'Now, these marsh Arabs, or Ma'dan as they call themselves, took part in the uprising with the Shias from Basrah. Saddam crushed the uprising and then decided that he wanted payback. He started draining the marshes. He actually diverted the great Euphrates River away from the Marshes. As the water receded, he put in roads. And in went the troops. The Ma'dan had used the reeds and water as a natural defence system for a millennium. But, without it, they were helpless. Saddam systematically wiped them out, using helicopter gunships and chemical weapons. Do you remember the no-fly zones in Iraq?'

'Yeah... after we left,' answered Mason.

'That's right. They were put in place to stop Saddam from killing the Ma'dan with his helicopters. He tried to bomb them back into the Stone Age. The UN reckons there was a quarter of a million Ma'dan before he started. Now there are a few thousand.'

'Okay, so that's the location,' Mason said as he sat back in his chair, 'but from what you're telling me, there's nothing stopping them from drilling, except for the water. And that's not much of a problem, surely? Look at the North Sea: There are oil rigs all over that.'

'But the North Sea doesn't have bandits, fanatics and general crazies,' Tonka said, opening a bottle of water. 'It was a Brit Mil area... And they had to pull out 'cos it was too hot for them. The whole area is controlled by some pretty nasty tribes, and they're basically not having any of it.'

'So, what are you saying?'

'Look... It's a bad area, and chances are that anything that goes on up there will get hit. It's like this: the war has always been about oil. Bush and Blair used weapons of mass destruction as an excuse to get involved. The real motivation is pretty obvious. This is one of the most oil-rich nations on earth. Everyone's trying to get their hands on it.'

Target HQ, London,
11.02hrs, 10 May 2007.

'So, when Diamond Four's been located, the deal's complete, and the sale can go ahead?' asked James.

'Aye... That's what Navaro have said,' answered JJ.

'They're going to ask me at Vauxhall for the details and figures,' James said, taking out his notebook.

'I get $20 million for Target, and an option on Navaro shares.'

'Any idea what the shares will add up to?' James asked, with his usual detached tone.

'At the moment, with the current share price, it's $5 million. But who knows, when the Halfaya field is up and running... eh?'

James jotted down the figures onto the smooth paper of his moleskin notebook. The line of zeros testing his composure to its limit. It was an effort to maintain his customary coldness, even though he'd practiced and played it like a hand of bridge. His face was creaking under the strain as he completed his notes.

'Not bad for a kid from the Gorbals?' added JJ as he picked up the picture of himself alongside Tony Blair.

JJ O'Hare had left 22 SAS under a shadow. Nobody in the Regiment talked about it; they were a close knit bunch that didn't say much at the best of times. But when one of their own was involved, there was a definite stonewall. Rumour had it that, after the First Gulf War, a lorry load of captured weapons went missing, thought to have disappeared over the Kuwait border. JJ was the guy in charge, and the buck stopped with him but there was no direct proof. It rolled on for a while but he could see that his career had been blocked. And so eventually he *pulled the pin* and resigned.

Unemployed, he'd set up a security company in London. It had bumbled along for several years, but after the attack on the Twin Towers things started to get interesting. He made his way to Baghdad. And, using his skills and contacts, had made sure that when the security contracts started to flow, he was ready.

He soon capitalised on the tremendous demand for security - which was in short supply - allowing him to charge $2,500 per day for each of his men, some of whom had been guarding building sites in London only weeks before. In his first year, he turned a profit well into seven figures. And, when in 2004 the big contracts started to emerge, he was perfectly placed.

No one had expected this small, unknown British company to win the biggest ever security contract awarded in Iraq. The American security companies were amazed and furious when it happened. But there was no surprise in Washington nor Westminster, for that matter. The deal was the outcome of negotiations and scheming at the highest political level.

The reality was that Washington had thrown the Brits a bone. They wanted them involved in the post-war security and reconstruction effort in Iraq. Giving a British company a high profile contract was a useful way of sending a message to the global community that this was a cooperative effort. On Capitol Hill, they knew very well that the tender would be hotly contested among the powerful American security companies. In fact, those companies' efforts to have the Target contract overturned resulted in a large amount of publicity - which was of course welcomed by both sets of politicians. The US could now point to Britain as a key ally in Iraq's reconstruction effort, at a time when America was noticeably short of friends. The 'coalition' arrangement also allowed an apportionment of blame should things go wrong.

However, the only negativity surrounding JJ's bid was that stemming from his chequered past. Although the FCO supported him - using his military background as justification - some within Westminster balked at the idea of a man with such a *colourful* history attaining such a high profile - and, of course, such a lucrative contract. Ultimately, the decision was made for them - Target's proposal was the only British bid. It was JJ O'Hare or nothing.

The rest was history. The award accorded JJ O'Hare a degree of respectability that he had never thought achievable. It soon offered him the ultimate accolade of respectability: dinner at No.10 with the Prime Minister.

'Okay, James,' he said, as he carefully positioned the picture in the centre of his desk. 'It's time to start pushing the buttons.'

Target Complex, BAS, Iraq,
09.20hrs, 10 May 2007.

Adjacent to the Target office, but hidden from view by more four-metre-high concrete T-walls, were two forty-foot ISO containers. 'This way,' Tonka said, as he led Mason through the access doorway. 'This is where we keep all our stores,' he explained, both men entering the first metal container.

'Stan, this is Mason. Kit him out and let him pick his weapon,' Tonka said, winking at the store man.

There was no mistaking the design of this compact storeroom; it was military through and through. Mason had been inside hundreds of such quarters in his time. And, no matter where they were - a tent in the Arctic or under a tarpaulin in the jungle - they all looked the same: row upon row of perfectly lined clothing and equipment.

Mason remembered a time not long after he had joined the paras when he'd been sent to the stores as punishment for a deed he could no longer remember. In readiness for an inspection, the Colour Sergeant in charge had made him line up row after row of screws, all in neat lines, like toy soldiers. It had taken him hours. But, when the inspecting officer came in, he hadn't even looked at the fruit of Mason's labour; why would he? Mason was just made to tip them back into the box from whence they came. *That's the Army for you,* he thought. *I suppose you don't have to have obsessive compulsive disorder to be a store man, but it would certainly be an advantage.*

Stan sat behind a desk that was covered with a blanket pulled as tight as the skin on a drum. There were two receptacles: one for pens and the other pencils, all of the latter being perfectly sharpened. The brass nameplate that sat between the writing receptacles was inscribed 'Roger 'Stan' Matthews'. *Boy, this guy has got OCD bad,* he thought. *I bet he's brilliant at his job!*

Stan was in his mid-fifties, and was evidently fighting a losing battle against middle-aged spread - the buttons on his 5.11 shirt pulled tight as they fought against his ever-expanding midriff. Mason remembered his reflection in the mirror from that morning, and pulled in his own stomach as Stan greeted him.

'It's a pleasure to meet you, Mason' said Stan, offering his hand.

'The pleasure is all mine,' said Mason, charmingly, remembering the golden military rule that you should never piss off store men or cooks.

'I met you in Hereford one time,' Stan continued.

'Ah, yes. I thought I recognised you,' Mason lied.

'You've got a good memory,' replied Stan, smiling. 'I was attached to the SAS for a few months. I'm a *Hat.*'

Mason laughed, but quickly tried to stifle his merriment. 'Sorry. I'm not being rude. But I haven't heard that expression in a while,' he replied.

A *Hat* was the name that the Parachute Regiment called everyone who was non Airborne. It was probably the biggest cause of fights in Aldershot. Members of the Parachute Regiment even used the term when referring to their opposite numbers in the other Airborne units, such as the Engineers and Artillery. Of course, they were Paras too. But, to the purists in The Parachute Regiment they would always be *Hats*, as they had been transferred into the regiment rather than joined directly. Even in the SAS, guys who hadn't come from the Parachute Regiment were called *Hats*. It was a derogatory term. And, to call yourself that was like calling yourself a 'wanker'.

'Attached?' queried Mason.

'Yes. I was in the Ordnance Corps.'

Figures, thought Mason, as Stan led him along the rows of neat shelving. 'Help yourself to anything you want' he said. 'There's shirts, boots, gloves. Pick up anything that takes your fancy. Just put it into this,' he said, handing Mason a big blue mail sack. 'You can sign for it later.'

'This is like Crimbo,' Mason said, as he handed Stan the full sack, his shopping complete. 'What next?'

'Weapons, now,' he said, reaching for a bunch of keys. 'Let's go next door and take a look.'

Stan unlocked the two massive padlocks and pulled back the metal door. The unconditioned air from the metal box container hit them both like a brick wall as they stepped into the confined space.

'Holy shit!' said Mason, as Stan flipped the light switch. 'You've got enough stuff here to start a small war.'

Just like the other container, everything was laid out in military fashion. But this time, it wasn't uniforms; it was weapons - loads of them. Mason left Stan and walked down the neat line, the uncomfortable heat forgotten as he checked out the different weapon systems: AKs, M4s, GPMGs, Heckler Kochs, MP5s... the list went on and on. As he passed them, he said their names aloud, touching each one with the index finger of his right hand, like a kid strumming a stick against a picket fence.

'Tonka said to take your pick' shouted Stan.

Mason nodded and carried on, memories flooding back to him of the jobs he'd been on, and the weapons he'd used. Half way up the second aisle, he stopped; he'd found what he was looking for. He reached out and picked it from the shelf. It felt good. This was his favourite: the M4 Colt Commando rifle, with an attached M203 40mm grenade launcher. *Happiness is*, he thought.

'He said you would pick that' said Stan from behind, with a grimace. 'We had two of those. Tonka has the other one'.

'Is it okay? asked Mason. 'You don't seem too happy.'

'No. It's fine,' answered Stan. 'It's just that I have lost a hundred bucks. I had a bet with Tonka: he said the M4 203, and I said an MP5. He obviously knows you better!

'Great!' replied Mason. 'It's been good doing business with you. Do I get Nectar points?' he asked with a grin.

'So, which one did you pick?' asked Tonka as Mason entered the office.

'Stan wasn't very happy with my choice; put it that way,' Mason replied.

'He reckoned that you'd go for the MP5,' Tonka said, laughing, 'but I knew you better. I remember that time in the First Gulf, when you engaged that armoured column. How many vehicles did you take out with the 203?... Six?'

'Nah... it was only four.'

'If you had been killed, they would have given you a VC.' Tonka said as he slapped the desk. 'But not even a scratch. Good ol' Lucky Mason, eh? I'm sure you're being kept around for a higher purpose, eh, Lucky?'

'Have you got those bag gloves?' Mason interrupted, deliberately changing the subject.

'Bottom drawer, mate. At the back... I think,' Tonka said, throwing him a bunch of keys. 'Swing by when you've finished. I'm waiting for some stuff from London. Should have it in a couple of hours.'

Mason went back to his room, and put on an old pair of shorts. He didn't bother with a top; *it would be drenched in seconds*, he thought, as he wound the protective hand wraps around his knuckles.

He loved to box. He was good at it - the energy of moving around the ring, the physical challenge, but - most of all - the tactics needed to defeat a good opponent; these disciplines had always excited him.

As he walked to the bag, his memory wandered back to his schooldays and the first time he had discovered boxing. After being left at the boarding school by his grieving father, he remembered looking in the mirror. He had looked the same, but felt different. Something inside him had changed. He was on his own. His mother and her love were already a fading memory. He had no one he could turn to - no one that could explain the new feeling lodged in the pit of his stomach - the feeling that made him aggressive, quick to act. But he would never forget the day that he found out.

Sports afternoon at school took place every Wednesday, with each boy choosing what sport he wanted to take part in. Most picked football, rugby or tennis, but Mason had decided on something else.

As part of his induction on his first day, he was shown around the school's facilities, with one building leaving the most lasting memory. It was the old gym by the river. A solid, redbrick structure, its unyielding design offered a good indication of its purpose. He remembered the austere interior like it was yesterday: the smell of sweat; the polished chevrons of the herringbone floor, its sheen so great that the slightest touch of a gym shoe produced a violent screech; the lattice of the climbing bars outlined against the high windows; the coarse hair of the hanging ropes and, of course, the boxing ring.

After a few weeks, he plucked up enough courage to ask the sports master if he could try boxing. At first, the answer had been 'No,' his age counting against him. Boxing was for the older boys. But his persistence paid off, and the sports master eventually agreed to pair the nine-year-old *new boy* with the smallest opponent he could find.

He was shown how to stand, how to throw a punch, how to defend. And, when the sports master was satisfied, the first bout was arranged. Word quickly spread about the fight:

the *new boy* against an opponent three years his senior.

When Mason arrived at the boxing gym the following week, he was met by a crowd of masters and classmates who, impressed by the pluckiness of the school's newest member, had come to see the David and Goliath spectacle.

The bout was spread out over three rounds of two-minute duration, in the amateur tradition: the sports master acting as referee, and the head-boy the time-keeper.

'Ding, ding,' the bell sounded. 'Round One.'

Fifteen seconds into the fight, he was already thinking he had made a big mistake. The bigger boy just stood there and threw punches that, because of his long reach, all connected with Mason's head. By the end of the first round, he was dazed. As he walked giddily back to his corner, the referee put a hand on his head and told him there was no embarrassment in quitting. Mason gritted his teeth and shook his head.

'Ding, ding.' Round Two.

This was a replay of the first, the bigger boy just standing back and punching. Mason was trying, trying really hard. But he just couldn't get close enough to land any blows. At the end of the second round, the referee announced that he was going to stop the fight. The news was met with a chorus of booing from the spectators. Mason was having none of it; he pleaded with the referee to let it continue. Against his better judgement, the sports master agreed.

'Ding, ding.' Round Three.

Mason hadn't cried when his mother had died. Nor had he cried when his father had left him at the school. But now, tears were running down his face. He was angry. So, so angry. He was angry at his mother for dying, and at his father for leaving him. But most of all, he was angry at this boy who would not stop punching him.

In that instance, he found out what the new feeling was inside him; it was rage - pure, unadulterated rage. It was foreign to him. He had had no need for the emotion before. His mother and father had loved him. He had always been happy. But all that had gone. *And why is this boy hitting me?*

The crowd had started to ebb away as the fight had taken on the same predictable pattern. It was clear who the winner would be. It was no contest; the bigger boy was just cruising to the finish. But what happened next no one could have predicted. With less than a minute to go, Mason went berserk.

What was left of the crowd cheered as the underdog fought back, their cries causing the early leavers to run back. All were astonished at the sight of Mason sitting on the older boy's chest as he rained punches onto his opponent's head, the referee and time-keeper trying desperately to pull him off.

The sports master checked the dazed and confused opponent for injuries, while the victor was helped out of the ring, hailed a hero by his classmates. They congratulated him with pats on his back, ruffling his hair, before carrying him back to the dormitory, aloft on their shoulders.

From then on, everyone at the school knew his name. He got served first in the 'tuck queue', and always had the best bed in the dorm. The Headmaster had put Mason's unethical boxing behaviour down to high spirits, and gave instructions to the games master that Mason's energy was to be channelled into physical education. He relished the attention and recognition his sporting prowess had brought him, and never looked back.

This older Mason now squared up to the bag, its leather cracked and faded, the maker's name 'Champion' barely visible under the layers of black gaffer tape holding it all together. He gave it a soft tap, a cloud of dust filling the air. The plaited parachute cord attaching it to the beam creaked with strain.

The thermometer on the wall read 112°F. *Just a few rounds*, he thought as he readied the gloves. He couldn't remember the last time he had done any physical activity. *Nice and easy*, he thought, as he began moving his feet. *Don't want to overdo it.*

He started to punch. It felt good.

His blows were light at first, then gradually harder, as his muscles loosened. The punches came to his hands effortlessly, without thought, the combinations etched into muscle memory. Jab, right cross, combination, left hook, jab, jab, on and on, and on, and on. *Why had he taken that job? He should have said no, stayed with his girls. Why had the lorry driver fallen asleep?* He was angry, so angry. The salt from his sweat stung his eyes. He was crying, the tears lost in the stream of sweat that dripped onto the baked sand. Jab, right cross, combination, left hook, jab, jab, on and on, and on, and on.

He came round when the pitcher of water crashed into his sweating mass.

'Are you okay, mate?' a voice said from the small crowd that had gathered around him.

'What's happened? Where am I?' stammered Mason, as he tried to get up.

'Steady!' said one of the onlookers, placing a hand on Mason's shoulder to stop him.

'Just take it easy. You passed out. Too much work on the bag. It's the heat - you haven't acclimatised yet, mate.'

'Yeah… You're right' replied Mason. 'Just help me up, will you? I feel a bit faint… Hey, it's lucky you found me'.

'Not luck,' said one of the crowd, laughing. 'The camp manager came rushing into the DFAC, saying there was a madman outside!'

'Ah. Okay. Just do me a favour, will you. Help me back to my room.'

'Of course, mate. But you might want to get them checked out first,' said the onlooker, pointing at Mason's hands.

'Get what checked out?' asked Mason.

'Those. Look at the state of them!'

Mason looked down at his hands. The bag gloves had

gone, disintegrated, his knuckles a bloody mess of torn skin and leather.

'Shit. I think you're right,' Mason said as he got up on one knee. 'I must have got carried away.'

'Well, you got off lightly,' said another of the crowd, pointing back at the lean-to, 'Have you seen the state of the bag?'

Mason turned and looked at where the punch bag, or rather what was left of it, dangled from the beam. The leather outer skin was ripped away, the bag's innards strewn all over the floor like the guts of a butchered animal.

'Did I do that?' he said, looking at his hands. 'Stupid question.'

Target Complex, BAS, Iraq,
07.44hrs, 11 May 2007.

'Glad you could make it,' Rick said sarcastically as Mason entered the ops room. He took a big pull on his cigar and gathered his thoughts. 'Forty-eight hours, is that what you're saying?' he asked Tonka, returning to the prior conversation.

'That's the minimum amount of time' Tonka answered. 'There is a lot of planning and preparation that needs to take place first.'

'What's so hard?' Rick asked, stabbing the map with his index finger, pointing at Diamond Four. 'You just get in those little white trucks of yours and drive up the road for a couple of hours, then the guys get out and have a look around and find my wellhead. Simple.'

'We have to liaise with the military, get some up-to-date intelligence, get properly equipped, do some rehearsals…'

'STOP! STOP! STOP!' shouted Rick. 'I don't give a fuck what you have to do. O'Hare told me forty-eight hours. And that's it.' He took another pull on the oversize cigar.

'I'm not going to argue this with you, Toy. You know why?' he said.

Tonka shook his head.

''Cos you're going to lose every time,' he retorted. 'Just make it happen.'

Rick had left, but the smoke hung in the air, the acrid odour perpetuating the impression of the man's arrogance.

'Do us a favour, Ronda,' Mason asked the clerk, who was trying to make herself as small as possible behind her computer. 'Be a love and make us a cup of tea.'

'Sorry, mate,' he continued. 'I got your message and came straight away.'

'It's not a problem. The meeting wasn't scheduled. Rick just came in and decided to stamp his authority,' replied Tonka.

'Yeah, I saw that. So it's this bloody Diamond Four again?'

'Yep. JJ has told him that we can do it 48 hours from now. But you heard that.'

Mason nodded. 'So, how you going to play it?'

Tonka looked at a white board that hung on the wall next to his office door, the allocation of forthcoming jobs for the various security teams and their call signs listed neatly with differently coloured ink. 'Lima One hasn't got anything on for the next few days,' he said, deciding on his options. 'I'll give it them. No time like the present, I'd better go and break the news. Wanna come along?'

'I need to give you a *heads up* on this team,' Tonka said to Mason, as they drove towards the Target accommodation blocks. 'They're a bit of a mixed bunch, but, as an operational callsign, they're about the best we have. The six guys in country at present are... let me check...' he said, flicking open his notebook while keeping an eye on the road.

'Billy Ten Cocks,' he said with a smile. 'He's ex-45 Commando. A sexual deviant but a good lad. Smudge Smith, ex 1 Para. Another good operator. Been doing this game for years. He was out in Africa before this gig.'

'What's his vice? I take it he has one?' interrupted Mason.

'He's into big women. The bigger the better. Picked up the habit in Africa,' laughed Tonka. 'There's another Para: Tommo. Can't remember what battalion he was with. Hasn't got a lot going on upstairs.'

'Stupid?' asked Mason.

'You could put it like that. He's into bodybuilding... Been on the 'roids for so long that his brain is frazzled. He got so big that he got sacked from his last job,' smirked Tonka. 'He couldn't fit through the turret of the armoured vehicle he was using.'

'Serious?'

'I shit you not. Wait till you see him. He's huge. Then there's Paddy. He's from one of the 'fish and chips regiments'. Irish Rangers, I think?'

'Paddy? That's original,' replied Mason. 'So, what's his story, then?'

'He's a nice bloke. Very quiet. Doesn't say much. He is one of those survival guys. Into guns. Goes into the mountains, lives off the land and that. You know the type?'

'Yeah... Odd.'

'Come to think of it, he doesn't really talk. I think he's only said half a dozen words to me in as many months. He loves his weapons though.'

'He sounds like the type that has a list of people he wants to kill - guys that bullied him in school, and that,' added Mason.

'Stop. You're scaring me now. Shit, I hadn't thought of that. I'll be nice to him in future,' replied Tonka.

'Is there anyone normal on the team?' asked Mason.

'All depends what you class as 'normal'. I suppose the Australian is pretty down to earth. Not aware of any perversions. But there's something about him… I can't put my finger on it.'

'What's his background?'

'Aussie SAS. But I have my doubts. I made some inquiries on the old boy network, and no one had heard of him. I think he's lying,' answered Tonka.

'So, why don't you confront him?' Mason asked. 'I hate fucking liars. They know they'll get found out in the end. Why do it?'

'It's the money. Some guys will just lie through their teeth to get hold of it. They can put a CV together - Special Forces this, Special Forces that. It looks great to the HR people in London. But it's bullshit. I've had a few that have lied about their past - I've sent two or three packing already. It just takes a few phone calls to find out if they're genuine or not. But Dusty has done an okay job of holding the team together, so I've turned a blind eye.'

'Okay. So let me get this right,' said Mason, weighing up what he had heard about the team. 'They're a bunch of lying, perverted, steroid abusers who will kill if upset?'

Tonka laughed. 'Yeah. That about sums up the team. 'Oh, and I forgot to mention: You get the FNG. You know? Pie boy. I think he calls himself 'Thor.''

'What about the other four guys I came out here with?' asked Mason.

'I've split them amongst the other security teams' answered Tonka, bringing the vehicle to a halt. 'Right… Come on. Let's get this over with. They're not going to like this one little bit.'

The noise from the connex was boisterous, waves of laughter escaping through the thin insulated walls. 'Has that got anything to do with the team?' Mason asked, as he closed the passenger door.

'Yep,' replied Tonka as he banged on the wall. 'Are you decent in there ladies? Can we come in?' he shouted.

The team were all crammed into the small room, the air inside thick with cigarette smoke, the smell of sweaty feet and farts. To Mason, it was a cocktail that he was sadly used to. It smelled like a barrack room.

'This is Mason,' Tonka announced. 'He's come to give us a hand. These miscreants are Lima One. Go ahead and introduce yourselves.'

'I'm Tommo,' said the guy that was sitting nearest the door as he got out of his chair to shake Mason's hand. Mason watched him as he stood up. This guy just seemed to go on forever. *He is indeed massive; Tonka wasn't exaggerating*, he thought. His age was difficult to judge because of the teenage pimples on his face. Mid-thirties was about right, his height gauged at six-foot-six to eight. The head on top of his enormous shoulders was equally large, its stubbled finish matching his unshaved jaw, accentuating the mandible. Mason knew that among the long term symptoms of steroid abuse was the enlargement of the chin area. The man's enormous jawbone, combined with the other symptom - acne - was a dead giveaway that he was a regular user.. *Him and Thor are going to get on fine,* he thought.

'Jesus Christ! What are they feeding you on?' asked Mason.

'Roids' the reclining figure on the bed interrupted.

'Shut up, Billy, you *Hat* bastard' shouted Tommo, offering Mason his hand. 'It's a pleasure to meet you. Ignore my colleague. *This* is all natural,' he said, pointing to a set of huge pecs.

'Wouldn't doubt it for a second,' Mason replied.

The big fella sat down. The man on the chair next to him stood up and introduced himself. He was about a foot shorter than Tommo, and in his late twenties. His was a wiry build - like that of a distance runner, and he wore mousey-brown hair that was long and scraggy.

'Paddy. Pleased to meet you,' said the young man with an Irish brogue.

The man lying on the bed was next. He stood up, leaving

his cigarette in the ashtray, while transferring a can of Heineken from his right to left hand. His wavy black mane was thick with hair gel, a muscular physique and deep suntan exposed under a cut off T shirt and shorts.

'You must be Billy Ten Cocks,' Mason got in before the man could speak.

'That's right. How did you know that then?' asked Billy.

'You're a legend in your own lunch time, Ten Cocks!' shouted Tommo, trying to get one back. Billy laughed. His deep guffaw tangoed around the small room. It was contagious, and soon everyone was laughing, but none louder than Billy himself.

'He's sussed you, Billy' said Paddy, as the laughter subsided.

'Fucking Hell, lads! Paddy just said something, and I think he's even smiling? Might be wind, though. Quick! Someone take a photo,' Billy said, the laughter erupting again.

'Well, Billy. Have you got ten cocks or what?' asked Mason.

'Nah. Just got the one. But I use it like ten men. It's massive, and I can't keep it in my pants,' answered Billy, as yet another wave of laughter crashed around the room.

'He mentions the size of his cock at every opportunity,' said the man sitting next to Billy. 'You'll have to forgive him. He's a Boot Neck with an inferiority complex. I think it's because his mother didn't breast-feed him or something. I'm Smudge, by the way.'

Mason looked thoughtfully at the man who was now shaking his hand. 'Have we met? Your face is familiar,' he asked.

'Yeah. We have. It was way back in the Eighties. We did a course together. I was the instructor,' Smudge answered.

'That's right, in Aldershot. I remember... you were a full-screw then. I have no recollection what the course was, but I remember the piss up when we'd finished. Somebody called naked bar. 'Fifty paratroopers, bollock naked in the middle of Aldershot. Brilliant. What a night.'

'Yeah, that was me. I was the one that called "naked bar"; there was hell to pay afterwards; I got busted for that.'

The man was in his late forties, but looked older. He had shaved his head to hide his receding hairline. But, in doing so, had exposed a hideous pair of ears - probably damaged while playing rugby in his youth. These cauliflower lobes, combined with his brown teeth - stained from years of tobacco use – were doing nothing for his looks.

'Great to see you again, Smudge,' said Mason.

'Thanks, mate, same here. Oh, by the way,' Smudge said, pointing a thumb over his shoulder at a nervous-looking Thor. 'This is our FNG.'

'Yes. Thor and I have already met. We came over on the same flight,' he said, smiling at the bouncer from Watford.

Thor wasn't happy. It was obvious his ability to adapt to the environment was greatly hampered by his lack of similar prior experience. No doubt he had read all the books, done the courses, bought all the kit and spent enough time in the gym to look the part. But that didn't equate to being an *operator*. As the banter swirled around the room, Mason studied the young man. He looked awkward, unable to relax, constantly moving his hands and arms; across his chest, in his pockets. Unsure. His whole appearance seemed to suggest the word *stumbling*. Mason felt like an observer on a natural history show, torn between helping out a struggling animal or following the protocol and letting nature take its course.

'Glad to see you again, Mr Mason,' he said, happy to see a friendly face.

'It's just Mason, remember?'

'Yeah... yeah... Sorry, boss,' he stammered.

'You okay, Thor? You seem a bit on edge.'

'Yeah. A little bit. I'm worried about the job I have to do tomorrow,' Thor confessed.

'Oh yeah? What's that then?'

'It's my turn to go into Basrah and get the team beer.

Billy has given me the location, and I've got a local driver to help,' he said, unfolding a piece of paper. 'I've got to meet this guy. He's an Arab. His name is.. um... Osama Bin Laden?' he said, looking at the ex-Royal Marine for reassurance.

'Yes, mate. He's got a beard and wears a turban. You can't miss him,' Billy answered, with all seriousness.

'It will be okay, Thor. Just make sure you don't ask him for a long wait,' added Mason

'Long wait,' repeated Thor, as he wrote it down on his piece of paper, much to the delight of Billy, who took a sip from his can to disguise his amusement.

Throughout the exchange, Mason noticed one man in the corner of the room. This man was silent, detached, observing Mason's every move. Their eyes locked.

'G'day. I'm Dusty... Dusty Miller,' he said, stepping forward, taking Mason's hand in a vice-like grip. Dusty sported a scruffy beard, which made his age difficult to pin down. *Late thirties, early forties?* Mason wondered, holding onto a handshake that was *way over the top*. Dusty was wearing shorts that exposed his skinny white legs. He also wore a cut-off blue faded sweatshirt that showed off a well-defined set of chest and arm muscles - an anatomical configuration mockingly known in the military as a *top half Charlie*.

'Pleased to meet you, Mason. I'm looking forward to working with you,' he said with intensity. 'I'm sure you can teach me a lot.'

Tonka was right, Mason thought. *I am going to watch myself with this guy.* 'Tonka tells me you were Aussie SAS. When did you finish?' quizzed Mason.

'A few years ago now,' answered Dusty.

'I was attached to them for a while,' lied Mason. ''I'm sure we will have some mutual friends,' he added, watching for a reaction.

'Maybe,' replied Dusty as he broke eye contact. 'But, to be honest, I don't like to talk about it. I'm trying to put it behind me.'

'That's a pity,' Mason replied. 'You know where I am, though. If ever the mood takes you...' *That's 1-0,* he thought as he watched Dusty sit down. *He's going to be a handful, but nothing I can't manage. I've dealt with a lot bigger, hairier and uglier guys than him.*

'Now that you guys are all nice and introduced,' Tonka butted in, 'we can get down to business.'

'So this is not a social call?' asked Billy.

'No. Sorry to be the harbinger of bad tidings,' replied Tonka, unrolling a map. 'But you ladies have a mission.'

'I thought we were off for a few days?' asked Tommo.

'Things have changed,' Tonka said with a sombre tone as he placed the map on the bed and weighted the corners with the next round of Heineken cans. 'Gather round so that you can all see this.'

'Is that Al Amarah?' Dusty said, as he familiarised himself with the map. 'That can't be right? We don't work there.'

'Yes, Dusty, it is Al Amarah,' replied Tonka, 'and we didn't work there, but we do now.'

The room went silent, the previous laughter now defeated by a name synonymous with death and destruction. The only sound was that of the air conditioner as it struggled to cool these sweating men.

'Lima One has been tasked with finding the wellhead, 'Diamond Four', which is somewhere in this area,' Tonka said, pointing to the locale south of the infamous Iraqi town.

'Have we got a grid for it?' asked Smudge.

'Not exactly.' replied Tonka. 'Just an approximate area.'

'You're 'avin' a fucking laugh!' exploded Billy. 'So, let me get this right... You want us to go into an area which Brit Mil has pulled out of - 'cos it was too dangerous - and drive around, looking for stuff?'

'Steady on, Billy,' Mason said, coming to Tonka's aid. 'It's not going to be easy. But it can be done.'

'Do you know this area, Mason?' asked Smudge.

'I've never worked that far north. But, from what I've heard, the intelligence indicates it's a bad area,' he replied.

'Tommo's worked there,' revealed Smudge. 'Ain't that right, Tommo?'

'Yeah… back in 2003,' he said, taking a lock knife out of his pocket and flicking open the blade. '1 Para were based here,' he said, using the knife as a pointer. 'It was a right mess. We saw more action up there after the war had finished than we did fighting our way up from Kuwait. Is this the target location?' he asked, pointing at the circle on the map.

'Yeah… it's in that area,' replied Mason.

'Well, just to the south of that is Majar Al Kabir. Do you remember the six Military Policemen that were murdered by an Iraqi mob back in 2003? Well, that's where they *got the good news*. Up here' he said, pointing to another built-up area, 'is where Johnson Beharry from the Princess of Wales's Regiment won his Victoria Cross. He saved members of his unit in two separate ambushes.

'What Tommo's saying is that this place is a death-trap,' Smudge summarised. 'But that's not all,' he said, taking a pencil out of his pocket. 'This is the town of Al Qurna. It's situated where the Tigris and Euphrates meet. It has a road bridge that spans the water feature. See this?' he said, pointing at the black coloured ribbon connecting the two towns. 'This road runs for eighty kilometres - from the bridge all the way to Al Amarah. Once you've gone past the police checkpoint, that's it.'

'Aren't there any side tracks that can be used - rather than staying on the main road?' asked Mason.

'Nope,' replied Smudge, emphatically. 'All this area used to be underwater. The road is built on a causeway, and is elevated for its entire length from Al Qurna to Al Amarah. There are tracks that lead off to villages… yeah… you can see them,' he said, pointing to the fainter lines on the map. 'They go off left and right… but eventually, they all loop back onto the main road.'

Mason stared at the map, taking in all the detail. Before any operation, the SAS conducted a full appreciation of the ground 'in general' and the ground 'in detail' to see if the mission was viable. *This mission screams insanity.*

Mason looked up at Tonka, who, despite briefly catching his eye, turned away.

'It's the checkpoint at the bridge' emphasised Smudge, 'that's the killer. Once you've gone past it, you're committed. You either go all the way to Al Amarah or turn around. But, either way, those robbing, killing, Iraqi police bastards know where you are.'

'It's breaking every rule in the book. The element of surprise is lost when you hit the police checkpoint. Twenty minutes on target - the maximum you're allowed - is out the window 'cos you don't even know where the target is. And it's the same route back as used to go in. What the fuck?' said Mason, dropping into the chair in Tonka's office. 'Rick can't be serious?'

'Oh, he's serious alright,' said Tonka, as he closed the door. 'This is all on a 'need to know' basis,' he said, sitting down. 'It doesn't go any further. Understood?'

'Of course.'

'When Rick has a few beers, he starts to loosen up. He told me that he'd been back and forth to Iraq for over twenty years, working with the Saddam Regime, way before the First Gulf War. He comes over as an obnoxious prick, but I tell you: he's a shrewd operator... I overheard him talking Arabic the one day... He's bloody fluent. So, anyway... he tells me that he's been looking at the Halfaya field for years - knew the oil was there, but could never find it. He was so confident that he told Saddam: the best way to find it would be to drain the marshes. Apparently, the President loved the idea; he could kill two birds with one stone: he would secure the biggest oil field in the world, and he could get rid of the Marsh Arabs.'

'Fuck! Are you serious?'

'Why would I doubt him? Only a crazy man would want to brag about facilitating genocide.'

'Fair one.'

'But that's not all. A few weeks ago, I was sent an email by mistake. It looks like Rick must have pressed *reply all* inadvertently. Anyway... from what I can gather, if everything goes to plan and Target finds and secures Diamond Four, it looks like Navaro Oil is going to buy Target outright. Our friend JJ is set to make a great deal of money.'

Mason sat in silence, digesting the bombshell that had been dropped. 'So, what you're saying, then,' he picked up, after a long pause, 'is that we are being squeezed from both ends. Both Rick and JJ want this, and to hell with the consequences?'

'Exactly. I knew this was coming off. And I've already spoken to JJ about it. But I was told to wind my neck in, and just get on with it. Let's face it - if Rick is prepared to wipe out a whole tribe, a few security guys is nothing.'

'There's only one way this mission has a chance of succeeding,' Tonka said, breaking the silence.

'Go on. Enlighten me.'

'You lead it.'

'Hang on a minute, mate. I was brought on to do the training.'

'Do you really think that they stand a chance with Dusty?'

'I dunno. I mean... with a bit of luck and some good drills, it could be done.'

'So what d'ya think?'

'This isn't the army. You can't order these guys. I tell you what... If they wanna do it, and if they want me along for the ride, then, what the hell?'

'Okay. It's on then,' Tonka said, with an air of relief.

'They're not under orders. It's their choice, right?'

'Absolutely.'

'Okay, I'll go and ask the team,' replied Mason.

'Yeah. Of course. But there's not a great deal of time. It goes in forty eight hours.'

Mason stood up and took his cellphone out of his shirt pocket. He hit the speed dial button. 'Dusty. Get the guys together. We need to talk.'

Target HQ, London,
10.47hrs, 11 May 2007.

'WHAT THE FUCK DO YOU MEAN THEY WON'T DO IT?' The words boomed as James opened the office door.

'YOU TELL THEM THAT I FUCKING...'

He didn't wait to hear the rest. He hated it when the vulgar Scot lost his temper. *So negative.* He closed the door and retraced his steps onto the landing. He would wait for the tirade to stop. Leaning back against the ornate balustrade, he looked at the portrait of the Duke of Wellington standing in pride of place outside JJ's office. James devoured the scene: crimson tunic, gold braid, decorations. Every schoolboy's dream. And he had been there. He had served in the same Regiment as Wellington; he had carried the same aspirations: service to his country and, of course, glory. He had tried hard, put in the hours. But he'd never received the accolades that he thought he deserved. *Where have all my dreams gone?*

His money had gone the same way as his career. His elder brother had received the lion's share of the family wealth, only to squander it on outlandish business ideas. And, when their father had died, the taxman had taken the rest. James had had the equivalent to a couple of years' salary, but that had soon been soaked up with school fees and a wife keeping up with wealthy friends.

He thought of the rude, vulgar man in the office who was

already spending his money, boasting on the extravagant purchases that he was going to make. *It's just not fair. It's so unjust.*

'Hello, James,' said one of the secretaries as she knocked on JJ's door, 'You look deep in thought. Are you coming in?'

'Problem solved?' he asked JJ as he checked out the papers left by the secretary.

'Nah, it's not a problem. I'm just pressing more buttons.'

Target Complex, BAS, Iraq,
06.49hrs, 12 May 2007.

'Morning, guys,' said Mason cheerfully to Smudge and Billy, sitting down for breakfast with a cup of tea. 'Kit packed? I suppose this is a bit like standing in the door with the green on and refusing to jump,' he continued. 'Us Paras would know about that… eh, Smudge?'

'He hasn't told you, has he?' Smudge asked.

'Told me what?' said Mason as he sipped his drink

'Did Dusty come to see you last night?

'No-one came to see me,' answered Mason, as he placed his mug back on the table. 'You'd better start talking. What's going on?'

'Tonka called Dusty last night. Said he wanted a meeting with the whole team,' Smudge continued uncomfortably, looking at Billy for support.

'And what happened?' asked Mason. 'Come on. Spit it out.'

'Tonka told us that if we didn't do the mission, we wouldn't get paid for the last month. And we'd have to make our own way back home. No flight tickets,' Billy blurted.

'He also said that JJ would make sure that we would never work in the security industry again, and that the only

job we would get would be as security guards in Tesco's…
or something like that,' said Smudge.

'So, let me guess what happened,' Mason said as he
looked at the two men opposite him. 'You gave in, didn't
you? You're going to do the mission?'

Neither man spoke. They both looked down at the table,
avoiding Mason's glare. 'Have the facts changed?'
demanded Mason.

'No. Nothing has changed,' answered Smudge.

'I don't fucking believe it,' ranted Mason 'What are you
lot thinking about?'

'We're not happy either. But what can we do?' protested
Billy.

'I'll tell you what you can do,' Mason said, taking hold of
his mug, 'Tell Tonka to ram it! Go home and work in Tesco.
That's got to be better than ending up dead, surely?'

There was no answer. Both men looked sheepishly at
each other.

'And who is leading Operation Certain Death, if you
don't mind me asking?'

'Dusty' they replied in unison.

Mason slammed his mug down on the table with such
force that it smashed, the two men jumping backwards as
they were showered with the mug's contents. The silence
returned as all three men solemnly watched the pool of tea
run off the table and onto the floor.

What are you playing at?' Mason shouted at Tonka,
marching into his office.

Tonka reeled back in his chair. He knew this was coming.
'Steady, big fella,' he said, as he recovered and got to his
feet. 'I'm just the messenger. Remember?'

'What happened to the Tonka I knew back in Hereford?
That guy that had a set of balls.'

'I told JJ what had happened. I tried to sugar-coat it as
much as I could. But he was having none of it. You know

what he's like?'

'I know what's he's like. But you, Tonka? You're not like this. 'Are you really going to shaft them for their wages and flights home? Why are you letting him act this way?'

Tonka sat down, and reached for the bottom drawer. 'This is all I've got,' he answered, taking out the bottle of whisky. 'At least I am someone here. It's not the regiment, I know. But at least I have respect. Without this, I am no one. My wife left me and took the kids. What am I going to do? Go back home, sit in a pub, get drunk every day, and tell war stories for the rest of my life?' he said, staring at his old friend. 'I have nothing.'

Mason looked directly into the man's eyes. Was it Tonka? He looked and sounded like him, but he wasn't sure. Mason stared deep into his pupils. The black circles were enlarged to compensate for the lack of natural sunlight. The dilation made them more reflective. Mason saw in them the silhouette of a man against a bright doorframe. It was him. He was looking at himself. He was Tonka. They were one and the same: running away, hiding from the pain, using whisky as an anaesthetic.

'This industry is cutthroat,' Tonka continued, taking a slug from the bottle. 'I've had to repatriate six blokes' bodies back to their families so far. But, you know what? For everyone that dies, London receives a hundred CVs from guys wanting to take their place. It's all fucked up. But as long as there are men out there that will do this shit, it will just go on and on.'

'I want to lead the mission,' said Mason, sitting down.

'No chance. JJ said you were finished.'

'Look, mate,' Mason continued, his anger well under control, 'You know as well as I do that if Dusty takes the mission, you're going to be sending more men home in body bags.'

'That might well be. But it's not my call.'

'Oh, but it is. You're the guy on the ground. You call the shots here, not JJ,' he said as he got up and sat on the corner of the desk. 'Look... I died inside a long time ago, but these guys have their whole lives ahead of them. You know as well as I do that they stand a better chance with me.'

It made sense - a sense Tonka recognised. 'What are you suggesting, then?' he asked after a long pause.

'Let me lead this mission tomorrow. And then I will walk. I will go quietly, I promise.'

Tonka looked up from the bottle. 'It will cost me my job, but I have gone past caring. Do it. To hell with JJ,' he said, shaking on the deal.

CHAPTER FOUR

Target Complex, BAS, Iraq,
05.55hrs, 13 May 2007.

The silence at the car park was broken by three revving engines as each of the Lima One drivers checked over their vehicles. Oil and water levels were confirmed, as was the diesel - the preferred choice of fuel for armoured vehicles, because of its lower flammability. The fuel was safely stored away in the pair of anti-ballistic fuel tanks carried on the Land Cruisers.

As the chaste orange disk cleared the horizon, throwing back the darkness, the rest of the men, laden with the gear of war, struggled towards the waiting vehicles. Each was dressed in a tan Nomex flight suit. This fire retardant material was an essential accompaniment for any security operator travelling in a vehicle that could potentially become a Molotov cocktail. The Target operators loved the Nomex gear. It was big time. Every arm and leg was fitted with pockets of all shapes and sizes, and covered with Velcro strips. But the benefit that they appreciated more than anything was that the uninitiated took them as aircrew – a profession that with their limited education few could enter.

Mason took the map from his thigh pocket and unfolded it onto the bonnet of the middle vehicle, using four full magazines of 5.56mm ammunition in each corner to hold it in place against the light morning breeze.

'Gather round, gentlemen,' he shouted, over of the idling engines. 'I am going to run through this one more time.'

Each man heeded the order and jostled for position, their efforts to find a vantage spot hampered by their grossly exaggerated torsos. Over their flight suits they wore their body armour, a vest consisting of a weave of bullet resistant material and metal or ceramic plates, used to protect the vital organs in the chest and abdomen. Over that, they wore their *chest rig*, a system of pouches used to store everything a security operator needed when he was out doing a mission. As well as ammunition, the various pouches contained a medical kit, grenades, torches, radios and anything else one might think useful when operating in the most dangerous place in the world.

The result: these security men now resembled the Michelin Man, their inflated bodies almost double their normal size. There was an on-going competition amongst the men of Lima One to see who could carry the most ammunition. And there was clearly only one winner: Tommo - who was able to pack sixteen magazines into his abundant pouches. This equated to nearly five hundred 5.56 rounds. 'Not even Rambo can carry this much,' Tommo would say as he heaved the monstrous equipment onto his back.

Mason had worked them hard the day before. He'd got them to check all the weapons, equipment and vehicles. He'd held rehearsals, and after gathering what intelligence was available, held a full set of orders, covering every contingency. Everyone knew the plan; they each knew what they had to do, as well as knowing everyone else's part. What Mason was going to do now - with *the bonnet brief* - was a final pep talk, to make sure that everyone was switched on, and give them reassurance and self-belief.

His delivery came with an authority gained through countless prior missions.

Ground in general: the overall area that they were working. The road from Basrah to Al Qurna and onwards to Al Amarah, with the all-important police checkpoint at Red 10, and the junction at Red 11.

Ground in detail: the area in which they were going to look for the wellhead: yellow one.

Situation: *enemy forces*: intelligence was scant. There had been no attacks north of Al Qurna for the simple reason that no military callsigns ventured that far.

Situation: friendly forces: there were no green callsigns (military units) north of the Al Qurna Bridge. If anything goes on, we're on our own.

Mission: repeated twice: 'Lima One's mission is to locate the wellhead in the vicinity of the grid square, first the northings 2545 and then the eastings 5098'.

Next, the *phases* and the *actions on*.

Eye contact was essential to Mason's approach, as he asked each man in turn his role in a particular scenario. And finally *command and sigs,* the frequencies, the callsigns, the nicknames given to the various locations and the arrangement of the vehicles.

'Lima One Alpha: the lead vehicle will consist of Paddy driving and Billy navigating. I want you 50–100 metres ahead of us in urban and 100 plus when we're in the open. Understood?' he asked, the answer arriving from both men in the form of a thumbs up.

'Lima One Bravo: middle vehicle, will consist of Thor driving and me as team leader, command and control.' He looked over at Thor for confirmation. Thor gave a nervous nod in return.

'Lima One Charlie: third vehicle, will consist of Smudge driving, Tommo as rear gunner and Dusty as Vehicle Commander.'

Satisfied, he looked at his watch.

'Are there any questions, gentlemen?' Silence. 'Good. Then in five seconds it will be 06.15 hours... three... two... one... mark. Mount up. Let's rock 'n' roll!'

The three white Land Cruisers sped down the two-mile stretch of perfectly straight road that connected BAS to the front gate and the outside world. Mason looked over at the speedometer. 120km. 'You're doing a good job,' he said to Thor. 'You ever driven an armoured vehicle before?'

'No, boss,' came the curt reply, the concentration evident

on the man's face. The veins in his hands bulged as he gripped tightly at the steering wheel.

'You're doing great. Just relax,' Mason said, as he adjusted his seat. 'They're great in a straight line. It's on the corners you have to watch them. The centre of gravity is way high... they corner like a brick on wheels,' he said, smiling. There was no reaction. If anything, the veins looked bigger.

The brake lights on the lead vehicle blinked on. It was slowing. 'Main gate,' stated Mason, 'Slow down... keep your spacing.'

The main gate was the point where the Western Coalition Forces met the local Iraqi people. Behind them was the relative safety of BAS. In front: unknown danger.

BAS, like all urban areas, needed workers to ensure that it ran smoothly. The labourers, cleaners, interpreters and other tradesmen came in from the local communities. But, in order to enter into the British camp, they had to be strictly screened. This screening location led to an inevitable scrum of hundreds of waiting workers. They mobbed the area on a daily basis, their thirst and hunger being serviced by entrepreneurs who set up shacks by the side of the road, creating even more chaos. The bad guys were willing to exploit any opportunity, using the crowds, if necessary, as cover, laying in ambush for the military convoys that they knew would inevitably materialise.

'When we get clear of the Hesco chicane, I want you to floor it. Understood?' Mason said as he fastened his safety belt. 'It's not good to hang around this area. Keep up with the lead vehicle.'

'Yes, boss,' Thor nodded in agreement, the blue Kevlar helmet that he was wearing beginning to rock back and forth on top of his massive head.

'What size is that helmet?' Mason asked.

'Small' answered Thor as he dropped a gear in anticipation of the speedy getaway. 'They said that was the biggest they had.'

'Who told you that?'

'Billy. He said I looked good in it though... he took a picture and everything.'

'When we get back, I'll see if I can get you a bigger one. Remind me, okay?' Mason said, smiling, '...You know, I think Billy likes you.'

'Do you think so?' grinned Thor, relaxing his grip.

Mason unclipped the radio handset from the dashboard with his left hand, his right grabbing the handle above the passenger door in readiness. 'All Lima One callsigns,' he said into the black mouthpiece as he engaged the presel switch, 'STAND BY, STAND BY.' As Billy's vehicle cleared the final Hesco, he looked over at Thor. 'Are you ready?' he said as the adrenalin began to course through his bloodstream. He'd forgotten the feeling of excitement, the dry mouth, the nervousness before a parachute jump, the terror of bursting into a room full of villains, the exhilaration when you don't have to reason. Your body just does, the endless drills burnt into the muscle memory so deep that thinking is irrelevant. *God, I've missed this.* 'GO, GO GO!'

Paddy in the lead vehicle blew his horn and flashed his lights. The Land Cruiser, like the bow of a ship, parted the mass of pedestrians that filled the road, their numbers quickly thinning as their speed increased.

'Keep the spacing' Mason warned, as Paddy's four-by-four began to slow. 'Remember, if the lead vehicle gets blown up and we're too close, we'll get it as well.'

'Ok, boss,' nodded Thor, as he took his foot off the pedal, the three-vehicle convoy settling down into a cruising speed.

'Is this your first time in the desert?' Mason asked.

'Yeah,' Thor snapped, without his eyes leaving the road.

'Sand as far as the eye can see,' Mason mused as he made himself comfortable for the long ride, his comments made more for himself than for the benefit of his driver. 'It has a bland simplicity. You either love or hate it. I remember my first time. Spent six weeks living with the Bedouin. Sleeping under the stars, living off dates and coffee. I felt like Lawrence of Arabia,' he laughed. 'You get so used to the monochrome landscape that your eyes almost explode with the vibrancy from the vegetation when you get back home. It's amazing... You'll see.'

Thor wasn't listening. He was preoccupied. 'What types of tank are those?' he asked.

'T62s. Russian. They're left over from the last war.'

'I did start to count them, but I lost count.'

The tank hulks were everywhere, their carcases lying by the roadside like some sort of bizarre roadkill. Their thick armour, their metal protection, had been twisted and deformed into curious shapes by some deadly force.

'This area was really important to Saddam,' Mason explained. 'This is where the majority of the Iraqi oil comes from. He tried his best to defend it, but his army was no match for the Americans and the Brits. These tanks were just sitting targets for the A-10s.'

'What are A-10s, Mason?'

'Ground attack aircraft - tank busters.' Mason paused. 'You got kids?'

Thor gave Mason a puzzled glance. 'No, not yet but we want some. Why?'

'Well, here's some good advice then: don't go anywhere near these tank hulks. They're all radioactive - they virtually glow in the dark. The A-10s use depleted uranium in their ammunition. If your sperm gets anywhere near them, it will shrivel up and die.'

As they approached another hulk, Mason smiled as Thor quietly took his right hand off the steering wheel and covered his crotch.

The silence was interrupted as the radio crackled into life. 'Next junction, going left, left,' Billy relayed to the team.

'Going left, left,' Mason acknowledged as the three vehicles changed direction.

Ahead of them, in the far distance, across the sea of dunes, were three chimneys, rising up like dirty fingers into the cloudless sky. A thick black cloud of smoke spewed from each, streaking across the blue expanse as it was caught by the wind.

'What's that?' Thor asked.

'Oil refinery.'

'Are they on fire?'

'Nah, that's the *gosp* burn off,' replied Mason. 'It's natural gas. Normally, they would syphon it off to power turbines. But they've got so much oil here that they don't care; they just let it burn.'

'You know a lot about oil and stuff. Where did you pick that up from?'

'You need to know how they work, so you can blow them up,' Mason laughed.

The three white vehicles thundered north. Ahead of them was Al Qurna, behind them Basrah. And, fifteen kilometres east was the Shatt Al Arab - the huge waterway resulting from the merger of the Tigris and Euphrates, which also marks the boundary with Iran.

The whole area was a floodplain, the silt deposited by the overflowing river creating a vast fertile level that had existed from time immemorial, and which featured so significantly in the Bible. But the palm trees that had once grown in their thousands had now all disappeared. Felled, under the orders of Saddam Hussein during the Iran-Iraq War of 1980 to 1988, their presence had been considered inappropriate on a modern battlefield. The only crop now harvested from this rich, dark soil was unexploded ordnance - left over from a war that neither country had won, but which had destroyed many families.

Mason watched, impressed, as Paddy weaved the Land Cruiser from one side of the road to the other. Billy was keeping everyone informed with a running commentary over the radio. They were the team's eyes and ears, *and they were bloody good.*

'Parked car: right,' Billy advised - as he identified locations where the bad guys most regularly planted their roadside bombs. Paddy swerved left to mitigate the threat. 'Dead dog, central reservation… push right.' All three white four-by-fours, copying the lead, moved in unison in a dance of survival.

Mason sat with his map and Silva compass outstretched on his lap, his right index finger hovering over their present location. In his left hand was a Garmin global positioning system (GPS). The GPS was an excellent piece of kit, the triangle on the small screen showing exactly where they were, how fast they were travelling and the distance to the objective. The only potential issue was that it relied on an uninterrupted satellite communication to do its job. Mason wasn't taking any chances. His finger, map and compass were as non-technical as you could get. They didn't need batteries or satellites; they'd never let him down.

Mason knew exactly where they were, and it was his job to relay the information back to Tonka in the ops room. To facilitate the quick passage of info, they used colour-coded spots, each of which were pre-assigned and referenced to a specific location like a road junction, bridge or other significant feature. When they reached a spot, Mason informed Tonka in the ops room.

'Hello, Zero. This is Lima One, now showing Red Nine,' Mason said into the handset.

'Lima One, this is Zero. Now showing Red Nine. Roger that,' answered Tonka in acknowledgement.

'Where are they now, Tonka?' asked Ronda, looking over his shoulder.

'They're just approaching the bridge at Al Qurna' he said, as he moved the yellow pin on the map to the relevant spot. 'After the bridge, it's the police checkpoint: Red Ten.'

'So far so good, then…' she said, biting her lip.

'Yeah… So far so good. But this is the easy part. Red ten is when the fun and games start.'

The black ribbon of baking tarmac climbed up onto the bridge. Beneath them was the ancient waterway, sparkling as it reflected the intense sunlight. 'This is Al Qurna,' Mason said, turning to Thor. 'It means *corner* in Arabic. It's where the Tigris and Euphrates Rivers join together. From here on, they merge and become the Shatt Al Arab. I never thought I would get to see this place.'

Mason might as well have been talking to himself. Thor was so engrossed in driving he had heard nothing. 'Mesopotamia,' Mason continued. 'That's what Iraq used to be called. It means land of the two rivers.' He looked over at Thor again. 'You're not getting any of this, are you?' he asked.

'Not really,' answered Thor. 'I'm trying to concentrate. I can't think and drive... Sorry.'

'Check point ahead,' announced Billy over the radio.

'Check point. Roger that,' said Mason. 'Red Ten.'

The Iraqi Tricolour, hanging from the scaffolding pole way above the single story police checkpoint, fluttered lethargically in the hot dry air. The building had seen better days, the glass in its windows replaced by sandbags, its once smooth exterior marked by countless bullet holes.

It was here that the men of Iraqi Police Service (IPS) laboured through their twelve-hour shift, the monotony broken only by the trickle of traffic that passed their way. They knew most of the vehicles by sight, but they still stopped them, unable to pass up an opportunity to line their pockets or supplement their rations.

After the Second Gulf War, the Sunni-led Iraqi Army and Police Force was disbanded by the invading Coalition, leaving the country without any security. The US, Britain and other Coalition partners then went about spending billions of tax dollars putting right their huge mistake. In double-quick time, they had to reconstruct the whole Iraqi security framework. For it was only on completion of this task that the Coalition could pass on the security mantle and leave. The politicians and generals patted themselves on the back at how quickly they'd achieved this feat, but it was all smoke and mirrors. What they couldn't let out was that, rather than solving the situation, they'd made it worse. The IPS wasn't the solution… it *was* the problem.

'Look!' shouted the policeman, pointing at the approaching three white Land Cruisers. 'It's a PSD team… Quick… get the Sergeant.'

Security guys didn't like being stopped - especially not at checkpoints - because when you are stationary you are vulnerable. That's when people get killed or taken hostage.

'How's it looking, Billy?' Mason asked as he stopped the convoy 50 metres short of the checkpoint, allowing the lead vehicle go forward on a recce.

'They look friendly enough,' Billy said over the radio as his four-by-four edged forward. 'I am getting smiles and waves.'

'Don't stop them,' shouted the Sergeant, as he quickly took up a position in the doorway overlooking the road. 'Let them through… yalla, yalla,' he urged, emphasising the demand by waving his arms. As the first Land Cruiser drew level with him, he smiled and returned the thumbs up to the tan-dressed figure in the front seat.

As the second vehicle passed through the check-point, Thor looked nervously out of the window at the police officers. 'I don't trust these guys,' he said.

'You should never trust them,' replied Mason.

'Do you think that they have anything to do with the insurgents?'

'They *are* insurgents' Mason replied. 'Everyone knows that. But no one will ever admit to it.'

'But if people know this, why can't they do something about it?' asked Thor. 'Surely the police are there to protect - like the police back home?'

'The politicians and generals can't admit to mistakes,' added Mason, 'Too much time, effort and money has gone into this war and the reconstruction efforts. For them to admit a mistake would be political suicide. But if the truth got out that so much money has been wasted… they'd all be out of a job.'

'That's unbelievable,' answered Thor.

'That's reality.'

As they drove through, no one saw the Police Sergeant take the phone from his pocket; and even if they had, it wouldn't have looked untoward. What *would* have drawn their attention, however, was the commotion that ensued when they were out of sight. The police sergeant started shouting frantically at his men. The motorbike hidden in the shade revved into life, the two IPS men hanging on for dear life as the motorcycle sped off after the Land Cruisers.

'How long now to the road junction at Red Eleven?' asked Thor.

'It's forty kilometres,' Mason answered. 'If we can maintain a speed of 120 kilometres an hour, it will take us twenty minutes.'

'That's doable,' smiled Thor confidently. 'No problems.'

Mason smiled and nodded his head in agreement. But he wasn't happy. The SAS frequently referred to an acronym corresponding to their Regiment's initials. And it wasn't 'Special Air Service'; it was: surprise, aggression and speed. Mason mused that they'd now lost surprise. *They know our location. Chances are: they will be trying to put some sort of ambush together. If we can just get to that road junction in under twenty minutes, we stand a chance.*

The GPS handset that was stuck to the vehicle dashboard with Velcro was reading 122 km/h. The road was clear. It was 10:05. *We're down to just speed and aggression now. Twenty minutes... I just need twenty minutes.*

'Gentlemen,' said the Police Commander, placing his Nokia phone back into the breast pocket of his starched, blue uniformed shirt. 'It appears that Allah has sent us a present this morning. Assemble the men immediately.'

The Commander was tall for an Iraqi and carried his half-century of years well. He wore a large moustache on his dark-skinned face, the type very much in vogue with the *old regime*, made popular by Iraq's late president. Many of his peers had shaved theirs off in a move to distance themselves from those days, but not him; he wore his with pride - a badge of allegiance.

He was a proud man, having fought for his country in three wars, his loyalty to his President undented. His unit had been on the receiving end of the 'shock and awe' campaign in the Second Gulf War. The explosions that rained down on his troops - the coloured lights reminiscent of a firework display, broadcast so enthusiastically into Western living rooms - to him and his men hiding in their trenches had brought disfigurement and death.

He didn't know how many men he had lost. He had had to leave his soldiers where they lay, their number too great to bury during the unrelenting bombardment from the aircraft. Nor had the Coalition troops even bothered to count them; they had just used their bulldozers to cover over the trenches where the Iraqi soldiers had been slaughtered. What was left of the Commander's unit had walked back to their homes, melting away into the countryside.

The Coalition was jubilant after their swift victory. They had destroyed the enemy. But what they didn't realise was that the Iraqi military commanders and their men, although defeated, would continue the fight. They owed it to their fallen comrades. They owed it to their country. They would continue the war. And this time, they would win. It would just take longer than they had thought.

When the Iraqi army was disbanded, the Commander had joined the new police force, ensuring that his former soldiers were recruited also. His police rank was much lower than his army one, but it didn't matter what badge he wore; all who knew him treated him with respect, and it was because of his status that he was of interest to the Iranians.

He had agonised over the decision whether or not to accept the Iranian pay-cheque - to side with the old enemy - but what choice did he have? He couldn't live on the derisory sum the Iraqi Government paid him. And at least, with Iranian support, he could continue to fight the men who had disgraced his honour, murdered his men and humiliated his country. Thus the enemy of his enemy had become his friend.

'Al Amarah,' he said, as he lit a Marlboro cigarette. 'That must be their destination.' He took a long pull and placed his finger on the map. 'Here,' he said, pointing at a road junction that was ten kilometres south of their current position. 'This is where we will hit them. It will take less than fifteen minutes to get there. Mobilise the men immediately.

He watched as his men held on precariously to the sides of their Ford Ranger pickups, the vehicles gathering speed as their wheels took traction in the dry dirt, clouds of dust filling the courtyard of the police HQ.

He looked at his watch: 10:17.

The road after the checkpoint was straight for the most part. Built by Saddam in the eighties, its linear construction enabled his troops to deploy at quick notice during the Iran-Iraq war. The two lane road stood several metres above the plain, its elevation protecting it from seasonal flooding. But the road did nothing to help conceal movement; anyone off to either side would have had a perfect view of the three white four-by-fours as they sped along the metalled surface. But that was Mason's least concern; his main worry was the obstructions up ahead.

The GPS was reading 128 km/h, the distance to the road junction at Red 11: 25kms. He did the calculation. *Distance over speed*. 'Hello all stations, this is Lima One Bravo. ETA at Red Eleven. Twelve minutes, repeat, twelve minutes. Keep it tight... well-done.' He looked at his watch: 10:18.

'It's a walk in the park,' Thor said as he glanced over at Mason.

'So far so good... but we're not there yet,' Mason replied as he glanced ahead to check on the lead vehicle's progress.

'How far is the wellhead area from Red 11?' asked Thor.

'It's in the area down the track, past the bridge at Yellow One… maybe twenty Ks,' replied Mason as he glanced in the rear view mirror, the words sticking is his throat as he watched Dusty's Land Cruiser getting smaller. 'What's going on, Dusty?' he barked into the handset.

'STOP, STOP, STOP,' shouted back an Australian accent. Mason turned round, only to see Dusty's vehicle pulling off to the side of the road.

'Dusty! Why are you stopping?' Mason yelled into the radio.

'We hit a pot hole. My tyre blew.'

'Drive on it. We need to get off this road… Keep moving,' Mason urged.

'Negative,' Dusty replied. 'I can't go onto tracks with a flat. I will get bogged down.'

'I am telling you to drive on. We can fix it later. DRIVE, DRIVE, DRIVE!'

There was no reply. The answer was obvious as Mason turned to see Dusty open the door of his now-stationary Land Cruiser.

'Are you getting this, Billy?' Mason asked the lead vehicle.

'Yeah. Roger. Eyes on,' Billy confirmed.

'Reverse back and take up a covering position.' demanded Mason.

'Moving now,' replied Billy as Paddy slammed the gearstick into reverse, the five ton dead weight of the vehicle making the tyres screech as it carried out the driver's demands.

As Billy reversed back, so did Thor. Following Mason's instructions, he drove past the immobilised rear vehicle, parking his Land Cruiser across both lanes, blocking traffic from the rear. Paddy - in a similar and well-rehearsed move - had done the same from the front.

Without further instruction, the team went into a well-choreographed set of actions. The drivers stayed in their vehicles with the engines running. Billy jumped out of his seat and took up a position on the white line, his M4 Colt Commando in his right hand, his left fist clenched and raised towards the oncoming traffic - the signal to stop. This was a gesture that all Iraqis knew, and disobeyed at their peril. Tommo had taken a similar position at the rear, the small machine gun called the Minimi, with its belt of 5.56mm ammunition glinting in the morning sun, lost in his huge arms.

Dusty was already hard at work loosening the wheel nuts by the time Mason got to him. Mason was furious at being ignored, but now wasn't the time for fury; they had to work together. He went straight to the back and opened up the rear door. The boot space was crammed with all the team kit: first aid bag, vehicle tools, spare tyre and the thing he needed now: the trolley jack. He hit the quick release handle on the straps holding down the lifting device. The heavy metal object working free as he manhandled it. Within seconds it was under the Land Cruiser, Mason pumping hard on the handle. The jack picked up the Toyota four-by-four effortlessly, even with its added armoured weight. The damaged wheel was off, the replacement given to Dusty. And, as Mason re-secured the flat in the back compartment, Dusty tightened the nuts and hit the jack handle, releasing the vehicle from its support, the four-by-four bouncing on its now functioning set of tyres. Job done, Mason ran back to his vehicle, the last part of the drill being for Dusty to replace and secure the trolley jack.

'How long did that take?' asked Mason in between gasps as Thor pulled off.

'Just over four minutes.'

'Not bad,' said Mason, wiping the sweat from his brow. 'The F1 boys couldn't do much better.' He looked at his watch. 10:24. The GPS was showing five and a half kilometres to the junction. *I need five minutes of clear road and no more shit and we've cracked it.*

'Where are they now?' Ronda asked as she made that day's umpteenth cup of tea.

'They should have reached RED 11 by now,' responded Tonka. 'They need to get off the bloody road; they stand a much better chance on the side roads. Where the hell are they?'

'Can you see the junction, Billy?' asked Mason. 'No. Not yet... it's just around the next bend... 200 metres.'

'Start slowing down. I don't want you overshooting it.'

'Roger that. I should have eyes on it shortly.'

'Slow down a bit,' Mason said as he touched Thor on the forearm. 'Give Billy a bit more room.'

'No problems,' Thor said, smiling. 'I knew we could do it.'

Billy's vehicle was a hundred metres out in front. Mason watched as it rounded the sweeping left hand bend. As it hit the apex, Mason could see the brake lights engage. The radio crackled. It was Billy. 'All stations, STOP, STOP, STOP!'

The IPS officers could have done with more time to reach the *killing zone* – the area designated in an ambush where the enemy are engaged. The current position made it tighter. But, considering the factors, it was good enough. The Commander had instructed them to block the main road to Al Amarah at the junction, using two vehicles. Unable to go forward, and with his men encircling them from the rear - cutting off their escape route - the only other alternative was for them to go down the track to the left. But of course, that's what he wanted. There were to be no witnesses for what he had planned.

Paddy had stopped the lead vehicle fifty metres in front of two police pickup trucks that were across the road. 'It's a police road block,' shouted Billy over the radio.

'Stay calm, Billy,' Mason replied, the tone in his voice no different than if he was ordering a round of beers. 'Now... Tell me what you see in front of you.'

'Two police pickups. Range fifty metres, with a third behind them in depth,' informed Billy, his voice calmer. 'I am counting: five... six... seven police, out in the open with AKs. There is a man in the back of the left hand pickup with an RPG.'

Mason directed Thor to slowly drive onto the bend until they could see the roadblock. Now looking through his pocket-size binoculars, he took in the scene for himself. 'Can you see any obstructions down the track, Billy?' he asked.

'They've pulled up short of it. Can't see anyone down there,' Billy replied. 'They just seem to be on the road.'

I don't want to go forward, Mason thought. *So the only alternative is back the way we came. Fingers crossed, there's no one behind us. We will have to deal with the police checkpoint at Al Qurna, but we can sort that out when we get there.*

He took a deep breath. 'All stations, listen in,' he said into the radio. 'There is a police roadblock fifty metres to our front. They have automatic weapons and at least one RPG. We are going to reverse at speed, and head south the way we came. Does everyone understand the plan?'

'Alpha Roger,' Billy acknowledged.

There was a pause while Mason waited for Dusty's response. 'Dusty, acknowledge my last. Over.'

'Yes. I understand,' Dusty replied. 'But it's not a good idea. There are police behind me. There are at least five, with automatic weapons, and they are pointing an RPG straight at me.'

Mason's mind was racing. He knew that the longer they did nothing, the more vulnerable they were. If they stopped, they would all be taken prisoner. If he gave the order to crash the roadblock - front and rear - the RPGs at such close range would have a devastating effect. The IPS had set up a perfect ambush, so why then had they left the door open? 'Billy, can you confirm that there is no one down the track?' he asked.

'I can't see any movement,' Billy replied.

'All stations. Reference my last transmission, cancel. We will now head for the roadblock, and turn off left down the track, nice and easy. Understood?' He was being corralled; he knew it; but what other option was there?

Billy slowly moved his vehicle forward, turning left in front of the roadblock, heading down the dirt track. He waved at the police as he passed. But, unlike earlier, the only thing he received back was icy stares. As Mason turned the corner, following in precession, he saw another police vehicle pull up at the road block, a tall man with a Saddam-style moustache exiting the car. Finally it was Dusty's turn to pass the roadblock. Now all three vehicles were on the track.

The Commander stood in the middle of the road and watched as the three vehicles picked up speed and sped off in a cloud of dust. He lit a cigarette, and nodded to his Lieutenant.

It was the pressure wave that arrived first. It hit him in the chest like a sledgehammer, knocking him back into his seat and knocking the air out of his lungs. Then came a deafening *crack*. It jabbed inside his ear like a red hot needle as the mound of sand fifty metres down the track erupted. Mason searched for the white outline of the lead vehicle in the cloud of dust and debris that now engulfed the whole area. Nothing.

Mason had undergone extensive training on how to react to explosions. The 'flash bangs' or 'stun grenades' were tools used by the SAS during anti-terrorist operations. Years of training had taught him to ignore the immediate effect of the blast, and to concentrate on the outcome. As all of the men around him were dealing with the flash blindness and deafness caused by this concussion wave, this is where Mason's training kicked in.

'Drive. Drive!' he shouted at a dazed Thor as their vehicle entered the dust cloud, creeping forward until he had found what he was looking for. 'Stop here!' Thor drew alongside Billy's smouldering Land Cruiser that had been blown into the ditch at the side of the road.

Mason ran towards the stricken vehicle, desperate to check for casualties, as the ground around him began to erupt with splashes from the lead rain being poured in his direction.

Smudge, having recovered from the initial disorientation, could see what Mason was doing. He tried to cover him as well as possible by putting the rear Land Cruiser between him and the policemen who were now advancing up the track on foot. The sides of the steel-plated four-by-four sung as metal struck metal. Tommo had also regained his senses and, using the gunport cut out of the back door of the rear vehicle, began to put down suppressing fire with his Minimi in the direction of the police trucks.

The driver's door of the lead vehicle had taken the full blast. It was still intact, but the metal at its edges had fused, the intense heat of the explosion welding the battered door into its frame. He looked through the large hole that the projectile had punched through the B6 armour, and was met by a horrific sight: Paddy was sat slumped in the driver's seat. He had taken the full blast of the EFP, his body transformed into a bloody mess, his pale white skin showered by his own crimson liquid, he was an unrecognisable mass of ruptured flesh and bone.

Billy, sitting in the passenger seat, had fared better, but wasn't responding to Mason's frantic calls. Running around to Billy's door, Mason yanked on the handle. The door was intact, not damaged at all, but it wasn't opening. He planted his feet squarely on the ground, placed both hands on the handle and braced himself. On the third hard yank, he felt something give way. He pulled again with all his might. The handle of the door came off in his hand.

He noticed that the swing-out back door at the rear of the vehicle had popped open in the blast. Remembering the location of the tool kit, he ran to the back of the vehicle and started to rummage around in the metal box. This time he had more luck; the crowbar he was searching for was still there. As the crack and thump of the bullets began to intensify, he ran back to the passenger's door to try again. He pushed the flat end of the bar into the gap and began to work it back and forth, the size of the fissure increasing each time, as the metal gave. Encouraged, he threw his all into it, the hulk of the vehicle rocking back and forth with his efforts. After what seemed an age, it finally gave, Billy's body spilling onto the floor as its prop was removed.

Billy weighed ninety kilos wearing just his skimpy Calvin Kleins, the body armour and chest rig pushing him over one hundred and twenty. Mason picked him up like a rag doll, throwing him over his shoulder before sprinting back to his own vehicle. He opened the rear passenger door and threw Billy on the back seat, the impact suddenly bringing the ex-Marine back to the land of the living.

'Wake up, Billy! I need you to wake up,' Mason shouted at the moaning man, slamming the door shut and getting into his own seat. He grabbed the radio. 'Dusty! We've got to move NOW,' he said, through gasping breaths.

'I need you to drive west. Not too fast, mate. I don't want you to kill us,' Mason said as he looked over at Thor - who was shaking and was as white as a ghost. 'You've done great so far. I just need you to keep it together. Okay?' Thor just shook his head, the shock rendering him incapable of speech.

'Hello, Zero. This is Lima One Bravo,' Mason said into the radio handset. 'CONTACT, CONTACT, CONTACT!' This is the phrase most dreaded amongst soldiers and security contractors alike; it means that they had been attacked by the enemy. 'Five minutes ago, fifty metres west of red eleven. One vehicle disabled, one man dead, one injured. Call sign engaged by twenty-plus IPS with small arms and IEDs. Trying to break contact. IPS are in pursuit. Headed west towards the bridge at Yellow One.'

The five minutes of radio silence that had preceded the message had led Tonka to fear the worst. As soon as he had heard the word 'CONTACT,' he grabbed a pen and paper. His job now: to help his men by collating the necessary information. He sat and listened carefully, writing down the facts as Mason described them. Despite the life and death situation unfolding at the other end of the radio, he had to stay calm and business-like. He wanted to ask Mason so many questions. Who had been killed? Who was injured, and how badly? Was he sure it was IPS? The list was growing with every passing second, but he knew it would have to wait. 'Ronda, get me Brit Mil,' he shouted, rocking back on his chair. 'Mason's been hit.'

The Commander threw his cigarette on the ground, and stamped it out with his highly polished shoe. His plan had been to disable the lead vehicle, turning it into an obstacle on the narrow track, bottling up the other two Land Cruisers behind it. But the energy released from the hastily-installed IED had picked up the five ton armoured car as if it was a toy, and blown it to the side of the road. *A few minutes more and I would have had them*, he thought, as he looked at the cloud of dust disappearing down the track. *But all is not lost; they have nowhere to run to. It will just take a little longer than anticipated.*

'I want them finished,' he shouted at his Lieutenant. 'They will have alerted the British by now. It must be done quickly.' The officer saluted him and ran off to execute the order, while the Commander lit up another Marlboro and got back into his vehicle.

Mason had climbed over into the back seat. He was treating his blood-soaked casualty, who was lapsing in and out of consciousness. The most obvious injury was to his left arm. It had been blown off just below the elbow, leaving a mangled mess of bone and muscle tissue. *It's bad, but it's not life-threatening*, Mason thought, as he checked the rest of his body for wounds. *Luckily, nothing.* He took out a tourniquet, and strapped it above the left elbow. As he tightened it, Billy opened his eyes. 'What the fuck are you doing? Get off me, you stupid bastard!' he shouted, before looking at the mangled remains of his left arm.

'Billy. Look at me,' Mason said, taking hold of Billy by his shoulder straps. 'You've been hit. Your vehicle was destroyed by an IED. You're okay, but you've lost your left arm. DO YOU UNDERSTAND?' he shouted over the vehicle noise.

Billy calmed down as he processed the information. 'Paddy?' he croaked.

'He didn't make it,' replied Mason. 'I need you to hold this bandage TIGHT on your arm, and keep it elevated.' He took Billy's right hand and directed it to where the already blood-soaked bandage was.

Billy nodded again. 'My balls... are they okay?' he asked nervously, craning his neck to look at his crotch.

'They look fine to me, mate'.

'Thank fuck for that!'

Mason nodded and smiled. 'Tight, Billy.'

Mason jumped back in the front seat and grabbed the radio. 'Dusty, what's happening? Over.'

'There is a lot of dust. But it looks like there are at least two police vehicles following us. And they're getting closer. Over'

'Roger that. The plan is to keep heading west. We need to try to put as much distance as possible between us and the ambush site. Over.'

'Understood,' replied Dusty.

Mason was holding the radio in his hand when it came alive with the sound of Tonka's voice. 'Mason, Mason. This is Tonka. Are you receiving me? Over.'

'You're good to me. Send.' responded Mason.

'Brit Mil have a *helo* in the area. It will land in the open ground two-hundred metres west of the bridge at Yellow One. Can you get to it? Over.'

Mason quickly checked his map. 'Fifteen minutes to Yellow One. Over.'

'Good. I will let them know. Just keep moving. You're less of a target when moving. Over.'

'No shit, Sherlock,' Mason responded with sarcasm to his friend. 'Did you get that, Dusty?' Mason asked the rear vehicle.

'Yeah. Roger that. Helo extraction at Yellow One. Figures One Five,' Dusty repeated in his thick Australian accent.

The Commander had noticed how easily the B6 armour of the Land Cruisers had been able to resist the attack of his men's AK47s. Before the police had started to give chase, he had given new orders. As the Land Cruisers and the police vehicles bounced along the dusty track in a deadly game of cat and mouse - the lighter police pickups closing easily on their heavier prey - the commander's men prepared to carry them out.

Mason looked in his rear view mirror. Dusty's vehicle was slowing down again. 'Dusty! You need to go faster!' he ordered.

'We've been hit... they're shooting at our tyres... Smudge can't control the vehicle.'

As Mason turned to check on their progress, he saw the streak of an RPG warhead as it left the police truck. He watched as it hit Dusty's Land Cruiser squarely in the rear, the force of the explosion twisting the vehicle in a violent upward corkscrew. Mason watched in horror as the vehicle smashed into the ground, starting to roll over and over again. 'STOP. STOP. STOP,' he shouted at Thor.

Thor obeyed the order and slammed his foot on the brake, the vehicle skidding as it came to a halt in a huge cloud of dust. 'Now, REVERSE,' Mason shouted. Thor sat motionless, staring out of the windscreen. 'We need to go back and help them,' Mason said, looking over at his driver. There was no reaction. 'Look at me, Thor,' Mason continued, his voice now calmer. 'We have to go back.' Thor's head turned. Mason studied the young man's face. He could see the fear in his vacant eyes. The Americans in Vietnam had a name for this look: they had called it 'the thousand-yard stare'. Thor slowly nodded, and engaged the gear.

The area was covered in a huge cloud of dust, which hid the stricken Land Cruiser until they were right on top of it. It had rolled several times, finally coming to rest on its roof. As Mason got out, he could hear the engine spluttering, clearly entering its final death throes. As he got closer, he couldn't help but step in the liquid that was pouring out of the damaged fuel tank.

Dusty was lying in the track just in front of the vehicle. He had been thrown clear. He was bruised and battered but alive. Alongside him lay the trolley jack that they had used just minutes ago to fix the flat tyre. As Mason stooped to check him over for injuries, the engine gave a last cough and died. The shouts from the Iraqis were now clearly audible. *No more than fifty metres away*, he thought, *probably waiting for the dust to settle before making their next move.*

'Take this,' Mason said, giving Dusty his M203 rifle as he got to his feet. 'Don't fire until you can see them. I need to check on Smudge and Tommo.'

Mason climbed through the space where the front windscreen had been. Smudge was still in the driver's seat, his body held in position by the seat belt. Mason felt Smudge's neck, searching for a pulse from his carotid artery. There was none. Smudge was dead. Mason quickly surmised what must have happened. When the vehicle had rolled, the trolley jack, that hadn't been re-secured had kept on going. It had hit Smudge in the back of the head, breaking his neck, and killing him instantly. The jack had then continued with its forward momentum and smashed through the windscreen, making an escape route for the luckier Dusty.

There was a small explosion as the vehicle engine caught fire, thick black smoke pouring into the confined cabin, filling his lungs with acrid fumes. *Seconds* he thought as he rummaged round looking for his other teammate, *seconds before the whole lots goes up.*

He didn't have to look far. What was left of Tommo's massive body was in the back. When the RPG round had impacted on the rear door of the Land Cruiser, a shard of the B6 metal armour had sheared off and struck Tommo in the chest. His body armour would have saved him. But the shrapnel had punched a hole in one of the numerous magazines he was carrying. It had exploded, creating a chain reaction, the result of which was this sickening cobweb of flesh, muscle and blood.

Mason was momentarily transfixed by the gory scene, unable to pull away. But the noise of the police gunfire broke the fixation. *I can't do anything for these guys,* he said to himself, *but I can help the others.* He turned away from Tommo and climbed past Smudge. 'Mason, we need to go NOW,' Dusty screamed. 'They're coming!'

As Mason crawled out of the wreck, he could see that the dust cloud was settling. Dusty had dragged himself back to Thor's vehicle, and was engaging the silhouettes of the policemen as they presented themselves. Mason sprinted back to the last remaining Land Cruiser, and jumped into the front seat, just as Dusty squeezed off the last burst of covering fire and lunged for the rear door.

'Watch it, you fat bastard!' screamed Billy as the Australian opened the door and threw himself onto the back seat.

'Sorry, Billy,' Dusty blurted out, staring at the bloody dressing that was covering the stub of his arm.

Thor pointed at the radio. 'Tonka. Tonka,' he shouted,

still unable to string a sentence together as his foot slammed down hard on the accelerator.

Mason grabbed the radio. 'Tonka, this is Mason. Send your message.'

'The *helo* is inbound. It will be there in ten minutes. Over.'

'We've been hit again,' replied Mason. 'Another vehicle down. Two men KIA. Only one vehicle heading west to Yellow One.'

'Mason,' said Thor, shaking with fear, 'We're not going to get out of this, are we?'

'I will get you home. Don't worry. I give you my word,' Mason answered.

'You promise me?'

'I promise. Now shut up and drive,' yelled Mason as he searched the map, desperately looking for a way out of their deadly predicament.

'Listen in, guys,' he shouted above the noise of the racing engine. 'The *helo* is landing in a few minutes. You will drop me off here,' he said, showing them the map and pointing at a small bridge at Yellow One. 'This bridge is the only crossing point in the area. There is another bridge further to the south, but its five Ks away. It will take the police too long to get there. From the bridge, it's two-hundred metres to the landing site. I will hold them off at the bridge while you get out.'

'How will you get to the landing site?' asked Thor.

'I won't,' replied Mason. 'I will go to ground and lie up. You arrange for the *helo* to come back at dawn and pick me up.'

'That sounds a bit dodgy... leaving you behind,' said Thor.

'It's not the best, I agree. But... unless someone has a better plan?' Mason said, putting on a fresh magazine onto his weapon. 'Anyway, they won't be expecting a fight. And in all the confusion, getting away should be easy enough,' he lied.

126

They were on the bridge in three minutes. Fifty metres before the drop-off point, Mason threw a smoke grenade out of the door of the moving vehicle. 'No need to let them know what we're up to,' he said, with a wink to the nervous driver. When they were on the bridge, Thor slowed the vehicle, and Mason jumped out, his weapon at the ready.

The bridge was small, only five metres in length, its surface a mere metal sheet supported by a wooden structure. The body of water that it spanned just a metre below its deck. Mason noticed that a small boat had been tethered to one of the bridge's wooden beams. The bridge was just about wide enough for a motor vehicle to cross over. On either side, the river banks were covered in the tall marsh reeds so common in this area. *Excellent cover from view, but those reeds aren't going to stop any bullets*, Mason thought as he rapidly assessed the bridge and its immediate vicinity. *I need a good fighting position.* He spotted a shallow ditch on the far side of the bridge. *Perfect,* he thought, as he darted across the narrow span and took up a position. He laid his magazines out in front of him, flicked the safety catch to 'off' and listened to the engines of the IPS Ford Rangers as they approached down the dirt track.

Seconds later, the first vehicle came cautiously through the thinning smoke. The hunters were wary. Their prey was wounded but still dangerous - exactly how dangerous, they were about to find out.

Mason put two short bursts of automatic fire into the lead police pickup. One burst into the engine and the other into the windscreen. It had a devastating effect. The vehicle veered off to its left, the driver dead at the wheel. As the vehicle slowed, smoke pouring from its disabled engine, three panic-stricken passengers jumped out, rolling in the dirt as they hit the ground. They quickly recovered and jumped to their feet, only to be despatched by the ex-soldier's marksmanship. The second vehicle stopped just short of their comrade's pickup, which was now on fire, the three officers dismounting as quickly as they could to avoid the same fate.

Mason knew that he wasn't getting out of this one. *This is the end of the road*, he thought, as he checked his stock of ammunition. He wasn't frightened to die; he was calm. He would be with his girls soon, his suffering over. But, before that, there was work to do. He was going to do the job that he had learned and perfected during his life; he was going to hold this bridge and let his guys get away. He placed his sights on the next policeman that was going to get the good news, and squeezed the trigger.

Dusty had climbed into the front seat as soon as Mason had got out, and was trying frantically to contact the chopper. 'Heli call sign, this is Lima One. Can you read me? Over,' he said into the handset, again and again, but with no reply.

As they arrived at the open space, the three men heard a weak signal from the radio. 'Hello, Lima One. This is Whisky Two-Nine. Are you receiving me? Over,' said the crackly voice of the pilot, the noise of the rotor blades clearly audible in the background of the transmission.

'Thank fuck for that!' shouted Billy from the back seat.

'Yes, we are receiving you,' responded Dusty. 'What's your ETA to the HLS? Over.'

'We'll be with you in figures few,' answered the pilot. 'Do you have smoke?'

'We have red smoke,' said Dusty, holding the cylindrical smoke grenade ready in his left hand.

'Red smoke. That's a Roger. Pop it when you can hear us… Out.' The radio went silent once again.

Dusty sat back in his seat, and breathed a sigh of relief. 'If Mason can hold them for another few minutes, we'll be out of this death hole,' he shouted. 'Get your stuff together. The chopper is inbound. We've got minutes!'

The Commander had got to the bridge just in time to see

Mason destroy the first police truck. He was furious. This wasn't supposed to happen. Security teams were easy targets - especially to veteran soldiers like him and his men. But the body count was rising. At least five of his men had been killed so far, with a further eight wounded. Confronted with such losses, he briefly considered calling off the attack. But he quickly thought better of it. He was in too deep now. He couldn't allow any of the security guys to escape and report that the IPS had been behind the ambush. If the Iraqi government found out, he would certainly be out of a job. *And, in any case*, he thought, my men are not afraid to become martyrs for their country. He called his men around him, picked up a stick, and began drawing a quick sketch in the sand, explaining the plan of attack. 'This has to end NOW!' He shouted, as his men ran to their positions, and as a further four IPS vehicles arrived down the dirt track. He lit another Marlboro, and gave the signal.

Mason had been putting down a withering rate of fire. Everything that moved in front of him was getting hit. He'd had the advantage in the initial stages of the contact. But now he saw these four new vehicles turn up, he knew the tide was turning. He crawled back and moved a few metres down the ditch to the left, changing his firing position. *That should fool them for a bit*, he thought as he readied himself for the final round. *I will wait until I hear the chopper, and then I will give them everything I've got.*

He didn't have to wait long, the blade slap - the distinctive noise of the helicopter rotors cutting through the air - heralding the arrival of the ageing Royal Navy Sea King helicopter. He put on a fresh mag and checked that the grenade in his 203 was ready. As the thump of the rotor blade got louder, he started to count down, *ten, nine, eight, seven, safety off, five, finger on the trigger, three, second pressure, one.* He looked up - and just in time; ten metres in front of him were two policemen. They were dispatched with two short bursts.

I've had enough of hiding behind this bloody ditch, he said aloud as he leapt to his feet. He pulled the trigger of his 203 grenade launcher, the device emitting a 'pop' as the deadly projectile arced towards its target. It found one of the police vehicles, the high explosive detonation sending parts of the pickup in all directions. He pulled back the tube of the 203 and pushed another HE round into the barrel. 'Pop'. He watched as the grenade fell short of its target, exploding on the dirt track, sending a wave of grit and stones crashing harmlessly against the front of the vehicle. He reloaded and made the correction. 'Pop'. Seconds later, he could feel the heat as the second truck exploded.

In the confusion of battle, Mason hadn't seen the two policemen - one armed with an RPG - breaking away from the others and manoeuvring on his left flank, giving him a wide berth. And, while the ex-SAS Sergeant Major caused death and destruction amongst their colleges, they advanced unnoticed.

The rhythmic thud of the rotor blades grew louder as Mason readied himself for the next onslaught. He looked behind in the direction of the landing site, searching the blue sky for the dark outline of the chopper. *They're coming in low*, he said to himself, as he saw a plume of red smoke drift into the air. *Not long now*.

As he turned, his eye caught a slight movement off to his left. The policemen had got close, very close. As he brought his rifle into the shoulder and lined up his sights, he could see the streak of the warhead. It was headed directly for him, silhouetted against the reeds and closing at three metres per second.

'Lima One, we can see your smoke. Coming in for a hot landing. Stand by. Stand by,' said the pilot.

The two police trucks raced towards the landing site. They were fully laden with the reinforcements that the

Commander had requested from the station south of Majar Al Kabir. The trucks had crossed the small bridge five kilometres south of the landing site, and were now heading northwards, the men in the back of the open pickups hanging on grimly as the vehicles bounced along the uneven trail.

The Lieutenant in the front pickup was the first to see the red smoke. 'Yalla. Yalla,' he screamed at his driver, just as the silhouette of the helicopter broke the horizon.

The loadmaster, wearing a desert-coloured flight-suit, hung precariously out of the open door of the Sea King, as the aircraft levelling in flight as it began to descend onto the red smoke.

'I have eyes on Three,' the load master informed the pilot, as he continued to count down the height. '30 metres. Keep it level. No obstacles. 25... 20... 15.'

The three exhausted men crouched beside their vehicle as the downwash from the *chopper* enveloped them. They had to cover their eyes as the powerful rotor blades whipped up a storm, the hot air from the engine exhaust, mixed with the gravel, stinging their faces. But they didn't care. This magnificent machine was going to take them home.

The air gunner – the aircraft's only defence – stood in the doorway to the right of the loadmaster, traversing the area with his machine gun, his eyes on stalks, looking for danger, knowing all too well that this was the helicopter at its most vulnerable. He was the first to see the cloud of dust.

'I have two fast movers from the south,' he reported over the aircraft's intercom. 'Range: 100 metres.'

'Give them a warning shot,' ordered the pilot, concentrating on the loadmaster's instructions. '10 metres... 5... Keep the nose up... Nearly there.'

The air gunner let rip with a burst from his machinegun. The line of bullets landing neatly before the racing pickups, the cloud of dust from their impact instantly devoured by the maelstrom as the police vehicles charged onwards towards the landing site.

Bullets struck the fuselage of the helicopter, the

loadmaster alerted by the ping they made as they tore through the lightly armoured skin of the aircraft to the right of the open door. 'ABORT, ABORT, ABORT,' he shouted.

The pilot immediately pulled back on his controls, opened the throttle and pushed hard on the foot pedal. The three waiting men watched in horror as the aircraft climbed, banked to the left and sped off.

'Get them back, Dusty!' Thor shouted. 'Get them on the radio. They can't leave us.'

Dusty shook his head. 'Get in the vehicle,' he shouted. 'Our only chance is to keep moving.'

'Fuck it,' said Billy. 'I'm not running any more. This is as good a place as any to die.' He grabbed an M4 out of the back of the vehicle, and stood, resting the gun on the bonnet. He adjusted his blood-soaked field dressing, and aimed carefully at the enemy who had taken up defensive positions around their now-stationary pickup trucks.

His fire was accurate. The police quickly realised that the security men were a far harder adversary than the helicopter. This time, it was they who were pinned down and forced to run for cover as the bullets pinged around them.

'They're falling back,' shouted Billy, watching the policemen jumping into the drainage ditch at the side of the road. 'Let's make a run for it.'

'The track to the south links up with the main road,' yelled Dusty, as he pointed in the direction from which the police pickups had come.

'It's worth a go,' agreed Billy. 'Get in. I'll cover you.'

Thor and Dusty jumped into the front of the vehicle while Billy kept firing, doing his best to keep the cowering policemen on the back foot. It was his turn to get in. He let go of his gun, letting it hang by its sling from his shoulder, and tugged at the heavy door with his good arm.

As the door opened, there was a burst of gunfire from behind him. Billy's legs gave way, the bone and muscle in his limbs disintegrating as round after round tore through them. He fell against the door and slid down, coming to rest against the rear wheel.

There were shouts of celebration as the police advanced across the bridge that Mason had fought so hard to defend. The three men had been so engrossed in what was happening in front of them that they had failed to notice the movement to their rear.

Billy was grimacing in agony as his blood soaked the earth around him. But he would not give up the fight. The ammunition in his M4 expended, he unclipped the pistol from his leg holster, and fired desperately at the oncoming trucks.

'Get in, Billy!' shouted Dusty over the noise of the gunfire. 'We need to go,' he said, looking over at Thor.

The doorman from Watford looked back at him. 'We ain't going anywhere without Billy,' he said with clenched jaw.

The police on the southern side, seeing their comrades advancing, broke cover and ran towards the vehicle. Within seconds, the Land Cruiser was surrounded, the police shouting at Billy to put down his pistol. Billy screamed back at them, his words an incoherent torrent of rage. He raised the barrel of his pistol in a final act of defiance, and aimed at the man with the Saddam moustache.

The Land Cruiser rocked at the impact of the bullets. Billy's blood-soaked body streaked against the white paint as it slumped to the floor.

'Mason promised me that he would get me home,' Thor murmured to Dusty, tears streaming down his face. 'He promised me.'

PART TWO

CHAPTER FIVE

Masahuin Village, Iraq,
17.35hrs, 14 May 2007.

'It's my fault. I know it is.' Rachel confessed to the
gravestone as tears roll down her face. 'If I only hadn't
wished for more. If only I had just got on with my life, rather
than wished for another. I'm sorry, Mama... so sorry. You
believe me, don't you?'

It was getting late. The sun would be gone soon. She
knew that she'd lingered too long and that she would be in
trouble for neglecting her chores. Her aunt Miriam will scold
her. But still she didn't want to leave. She was frightened.

She stayed at the grave for as long as possible, making
sure that everything was perfect. But it was all done. No
need for more attention; even John's toy sword was as it
should be. No more excuses. 'Ah, well,' she said aloud. 'I
suppose I must go back and face Miriam.'

'Where have you been?' Miriam asked as she entered the
kitchen.

'I'm sorry, Aunty.'

'Have you been crying, child?'

She waited for the scolding, but it didn't come, somehow

replaced by a look of pity and a smile. 'Is it the man?' she asked.

'Yes, Aunty. He frightens me.'

'Don't be silly; he's only a man. Here, take this,' Miriam said, giving her a glass of water. 'Go and see if our visitor is awake.'

She stood outside the bedroom, listening; the heavy blanket hung from the simple frame, the only thing between her and the stranger. *Please let him live. If you do, Lord, I will never wish for the outside world again. I will stay here and look after my Papa, I promise. No more thoughts of aeroplanes and life in big cities. I promise. I promise. Please just let him live.*

Breathing.

It was faint but regular.

She pulled back the blanket and entered the room - her brother's bedroom. She knew it so well - every inch: the bed in the corner, the small bedside table where he would put his toys whilst he slept, and the little window above the bed where he would leave crumbs for the birds. All so familiar. Her realm - a place she would visit without thought. *But now he lies where my brother used to.* She noted the contours of his manly frame resting under the sheet, a stark contrast to the boy that would hide under the covers when they played hide and seek, thinking he couldn't be seen. Even the smell had changed. *It's not like Papa's*, she mused. *The strong musky scent takes my breath away. Everything is different now. He has changed it.*

The blanket moved behind her. She jumped. Her heart raced. Miriam entered, carrying a bowl of scented water. 'We need to bathe him' she whispered as she a put the bowl down on the three-legged stool - the place she would sit when reading John his bedtime stories.

There was a commotion outside. The noise of a crying child filled the air. 'You wait here,' Miriam said, as she pulled back the blanket. 'I will go and see what's the matter.'

When Papa had found the man, he was unconscious.

Miriam had helped Papa check for wounds, as they'd cut the ripped clothes from his bruised and grazed body. Rachel wanted to look, but couldn't. It didn't seem right, especially in front of Papa. But it wasn't new to her; from an early age, she'd been taught how to care. As the daughter of the Elder, her hands had healing powers, Papa had told her so. She'd hated the sight of ripped flesh and blood at first, but had soon become accustomed to it. To help her, she'd sung the old song that the healers had used for centuries.

In front of her lay the man, covered with one of the villagers' linen sheets. She pulled back the light cotton gently, averting her eyes as more of his body was revealed. At his midriff she stopped and looked away, her modesty winning out over her curiosity. She picked up the cloth from the basin and rinsed it out, the droplets echoing as they fall back. And then... she began her task.

She started on his face, dabbing at the cuts and grazes softly, wiping away the dirt and grime, singing softly as the scent from the healing water filled the room.

It was a dream; it had to be. How else could he explain the beautiful melody that wrapped itself around him like a blanket soothing his aching body.

Mason held his eyes closed, tight shut, not wanting to break the enchantment as he listened. But then the singing stopped. He pondered momentarily whether to look up, to search for the songstress. But, as quickly as it had stopped, it started again.

The unseen carer wiped his face and neck with the lightest of touches. His taught, stiff muscles were starting to relax, the pain subsiding as his nurse spread the wonderful-smelling liquid over his chest.

He began to check his body for damage, scanning from his head down, using slight movements of his muscles and joints to assess for serious breakages. Luckily, nothing obvious presented itself. Just bruised and battered, he thought as he lay back, not wanting this treatment to end. He was desperate to see his nurse, but he knew full well that revealing his consciousness would jeopardise his treatment. Finally, temptation proved too great. With the slightest of movements, he partially opened his left eye.

The room was getting dark. The last rays of sunlight dancing on the bedroom wall the only illumination. He could see the outline of her flowing robes, and as his eyes adjusted, a veil that was draped over her face. She stepped into the light. Her face set in by the iridescent rays; clear. Smooth, olive skin - translucent in the ebbing light - a perfect match for the green eyes. The small upturn on her nose effortlessly keeping the veil in its place. He was entranced; he had to see more.

As the girl turned to soak her cloth, he opened both eyes and raised his head a fraction off the pillow. She hadn't noticed. Unabashed, he continued to watch as her delicate, slight hands caressed his torso, the dark complexion of her fingers distinct against his own pale skin. Katie was the last one to touch him with such compassion. He hadn't known another woman since; he didn't have it in him.

But, as he watched the young girl, a wave of warmth crashed over him, its energy seeping into places that had been void for so long.

Engrossed with her task, she was unaware of her patient's attention. But when she rose to soak her cloth, she found him staring directly at her.

The shock made her jump from the bed. The sudden action allowing the veil to fall. Her face visible, caught in the waning sunlight.

As she faced him, the full story was revealed. Instead of the angelic sight that he had seen seconds before, he was now confronted with a twisted mass of scar tissue. Her face was split; on the left was that of a beautiful young woman, on the right a Halloween mask that spread from her right

137

cheek to her chin. She wrapped the scarf around her face and
ran.

John stood in the threshold of the Temple - the building that
had stood there in the centre of the village for centuries -
greeting the members of the village council as they arrived
with the customary kiss on both cheeks and the profuse
shaking of hands.

The men filed into the large hall at the end of their
long working day, and began to sit on the ornate cushions
strewn across the stone floor. Each family had its own place
in the hall, and these places had been handed down from
father to son over the ages. As the men settled, the boys of
the village brought around the traditional tea, *shay*, their job
being to ensure that weary men's glasses, or *istica,* never ran
empty.

Moving in front of the altar at the far end of the hall, John
readied himself for the meeting. He was seventy years old.
But despite his age he showed remarkable vitality, his
posture good, with no sign of senescence. His fair skin,
piercing blue eyes and light brown, wavy hair evidence of
his undeviating lineage.

'Brothers, we have a visitor amongst us,' he said, the
small crowd in the Temple coming to order as his words
settled. 'Yesterday, I moored my boat on the edge of the
marshes whilst I went hunting for rabbits. On returning, I
heard a great battle. It was the police. I watched as many
were killed.'

'The visitor: is he from the battle?' asked Michael, who
sat in the front row.

'Yes, my brother. The man I found had killed many
police before they struck him. I thought he had died, but
when the police had gone, I found him near my boat, still
alive. He is in my house; Miriam and Rachel are looking
after him.'

The hall came alive with the sound of excited voices, as

the villagers digested John's words and their implications.

'Look what happened when we helped the people from the city the last time. Saddam destroyed our village and all but wiped us out. Do you want this to happen again?' asked Peter, who was sitting further back.

'Peter is right, John. Didn't you think of the risk?' added Michael.

'Brothers,' answered John, as he tried to calm the council. 'No one needs to remind me what happened. We all suffered. I lost my wife and son, and my daughter still carries the scars,' he said as he moved behind the altar to take up the position normally reserved for the Holy days. 'I'm saddened every day when I look at her. But it is our duty,' he continued, placing his hand on the stone ossuary that stood in pride of place on the altar. 'Sir John taught us that we should protect the weak and defenceless. This is our creed: the Code of Chivalry that we live by.'

'The Code also says that we must always speak the truth,' answered Michael. 'Sir John knew nothing about aeroplanes and bombs when he gave the Code to our ancestor all those years ago. Times have changed, John. I say that this man must go before they come looking for him.'

'Brothers, I can see your concerns. But we cannot pick and choose what rules we follow; we must do our duty.'

'Our duty is to our families,' shouted Peter, 'not to this man who will bring only death and destruction.'

'Before you make your decision, brothers, I have something to add,' interrupted John as the men started to carry on muttered conversations between themselves. 'This man is not an Arab; he is from the West.'

The council was silent. His words had hit home. Now, certain of their full attention, he raised himself to his full height and threw back his shoulders. 'Brothers, you know the prophecy,' he continued. 'Sir John De Guise told our ancestors that when the Masahuin needed him the most, a knight would come from the West. His job would be to relieve us of our duty of guarding what we hold so dear, and which we hold for the good of mankind: the Treasure,' said John, placing both his hands on the ossuary. 'I believe that this is the knight. I saw him myself, fighting the corrupt police. He is a mighty warrior. I saw him kill many before he fell. He was spared, and I found him for a reason. I believe this is the man we have waited for.'

The silence was shattered, as Rachel burst through the door. 'Father! she gasped. 'He is awake. Come quick. Come quick!'

Yellow One,
The Day Before.

The police ordered the two prisoners to kneel next to the bullet riddled Land Cruiser. Dusty complied with their instructions, but Thor was having none of it. The body-builder from Watford had seen films of men being executed on their knees, and there was no way he was going that easily. The Commander had instructed his men to ensure that the two prisoners were taken alive. So, instead of bullets, the policemen just shouted and pointed their weapons menacingly at the man whose mass towered above theirs, staying well away from the large fists that hung freely at his sides.

The stalemate was solved by a blow to the side of the head with a rifle butt, delivered by a skinny policeman in an ill fitting uniform. Immensely proud of his handiwork, the man stood back like a lumberjack, admiring the enormity of his felled foe. His beaming grin, revealing the full dilapidation of his teeth, became bigger as each of his comrades patted him on the back with congratulations.

One of his captors stood on Thor's head. His open mouth was desperately grasping for air, but it was filling with dirt each time it was pushed further into the arid soil. Another two grabbed his arms and held them behind his back while a third fitted the handcuffs. Finally, all four seized a part of the limp body and hauled him to his knees.

Thor looked over to his right. Dusty was surrounded by men wearing blue shirts and black trousers. The Australian, secured by his captors, was punched and kicked. The movements made as if in slow motion. He tried to focus his blurred vision, but it was no good; his head was spinning, and the constant ringing in his ears from the explosions had made him deaf. Without his senses, he felt numb, detached, a voyeur to the acts around him. He didn't see the small hessian sack dropped over his head, robbing him of daylight and his modicum of vision. Now there was only darkness.

The stale dry air inside the hessian acted like smelling salts, reviving him. His hearing returned, compensating for the lack of vision as a fear grew in the pit of his stomach, fuelled by an acid of helplessness. He knew too well that, when they were bored with Dusty, their anger would turn to him. He tried to ready himself for the pain. He could hear the footfall as the group closed around him.

The blow, when it came, was devastating. The skinny policeman, encouraged by his previous success, drove his rifle squarely into Thor's face. The brass plate on the rifle butt struck him on the bridge of the nose, breaking it instantly, triggering Thor to gasp as his body was gripped by the intense wave of pain. He tried to breathe through his nose, but to no avail; it was blocked with blood. He tried his mouth, the foul air from the hessian sand bag burning his parched throat as his lungs gulped for life. He coughed violently, the irritation further robbing him of oxygen. The flow stopped. He passed out.

The police convoy sped along the pot-holed roads, carrying their two prisoners, their blue lights flashing and sirens wailing. The boom gate to the police compound was raised as the convoy approached. The pickups, soon inside, ready to unload their valuable cargo. The skinny officer jumped from the vehicle as it was still moving. Eager to continue his role as the main antagonist, he went straight to the back of the truck to greet the police station's new inmates. He took hold of Dusty's feet and pulled him straight off the back of the pickup like a carcass of meat that had just been collected from an abattoir. The compound filled with whoops of laughter as the Australian's limp body smashed into the hard surface. He then tried to perform the same stunt with Thor, but the unconscious man's weight was far harder to move. The applauders now became mockers, laughing at his futile attempts to move the dead weight. It finally took the effort of three to shift the comatose body.

Dusty was dragged through the station and dumped in the holding cell in the basement of the building. The eight concrete steps that made up the staircase impressed on his memory. As that was the number of times his head had hit the floor as he was pulled down the steep gradient.

Then it was Thor's turn. Dusty, still hooded, listened as the policemen struggled with the bodybuilder's weight. He couldn't understand Arabic, but it was clear that the policemen weren't merely exchanging pleasantries as they laboured with the body.

Finally, the cell door was slammed shut, the lock engaged, the footsteps gone.

As the silence settled, Dusty pulled himself over to Thor's side. 'Are you okay?' he whispered.

There was no reply.

Masahuin Village, Iraq,
08.40hrs, 17 May 2007.

From his sick room, Mason had got used to the sounds and smells of the village over the last two days. With Miriam, the middle-aged sister-in-law of the village Elder, tending to his bruised and battered body, while Rachel took on the less-intimate role of bringing him his meals.

For the first few days, Rachel had spoon-fed him a delicious chicken broth while sitting on the small three-legged wooden stool next to his bed. Mason, captivated by the girl, watched her every movement. Out of modesty, her veil was always fastened when she entered his room, the light fabric covering her face and hair revealing only her undamaged skin above the bridge of her nose. Her forehead, eyebrows and the skin around her eyes was unaffected by the disfigurement. The soft, delicate, olive skin on show, a complete contrast to the scar tissue that lurked under her flimsy scarf. But, once seen, its vulgar intrusion remained ever present, peeking out, allowing for an occasional glimpse as she went about her business.

He had bombarded her with questions with his rusty Arabic, unsure if she even understood him, her answers either a simple nod or shake of her head. But his persistence eventually paid off. By the second day, she had spoken her first words to him. To his amazement, they were spoken in English.

On the third day, he had risen early and put on the clothes that John had given him. His Nomex flight suit, reduced to tatters after the battle, had been burnt by his hosts, desperate to keep his presence in the village a secret. He hadn't minded, soon realising that this new local attire was far more comfortable.

As he sat waiting for his breakfast and the tour of the village that he had been promised, his mind wandered. *Paddy, Smudge and Tommo are dead, but at least the other three got out. By the time I get back to Basrah, they'll have been shipped out. But never mind. I can catch up with them back home.*

His thoughts were interrupted as the drape across the door was pulled back. Rachel entered, carrying his breakfast.

'Sabbah al khair, Rachel,' he greeted her in Arabic as she placed the tray down on the end of the bed.

'Sabbah al noor, Mr Mason,' she replied.

'Today we go out into the village?' he asked.

She paused as her brain translated his English into her Arabic and then her Arabic back into English. 'Yes,' she answered, 'but first - you must eat all of your, um, breakfast.'

He was ravenous. Since he had woken, his hunger pangs had been telling him that he needed food, and was relieved that he could finally pacify his stomach's loud cries for attention. The food was light and wholesome: boiled eggs, dates, goats cheese, flat bread and yogurt - a perfect mixture of protein and vitamins - ideal for an exhaustive day in the intense heat.

She watched him finish off the last boiled egg. 'I have this for... you,' she said, presenting him with a walking stick.

He took hold of the wooden staff, letting his fingers run along its uneven surface. It was old, its handle worn smooth from many years of wear. Down its shaft, sculpted in incredible detail, was a series of intricate carvings. 'This is beautiful.' he said, holding it up to the light for closer inspection. 'Thank you.'

'It is my father's. It has been in our family... long, long time. It tells of our history. He not need it now. He say you borrow it,' she replied, with smiling eyes.

'I would also like to thank him for all he's done for me,' he said as he stood up, transferring his weight to his walking aid.

'Yes...yes, you can talk to him later,' she said as she took his arm and led him out of the room.

Rachel led Mason up a dusty street that was lined on either side by buildings of mud-brick, their roofs thatched with reeds. From the outside, they appeared very primitive. But he was able to stand testament to the comfort. Their thick walls and tightly-thatched roofs provided protection from the heat by day and insulation from the chilly nights.

'What happened here?' Mason asked, pointing at some badly damaged houses in the eerily quiet street.

'They were... destroyed by Saddam,' she replied.

'Was there a big battle?'

'Yes. Very big. Many peoples die... very bad,' she continued. 'People who stay, rebuild house. People who go to city.... leave house like this,' she said, pointing at one of the damaged structures.

They continued walking as the street gradually inclined. Mason's progress was laboured. To help his legs stiff with pain, he dug the stick into the dust and pushed his weight forward. At the top of the slight hill he stopped. Catching his breath he took in the surroundings. The street had opened into a village square, at the centre of which was a building that rose above the houses and was constructed entirely from reeds.

From this vantage point, he was able to get his bearings. The village was built on a small island in the midst of a sea of reeds stretching as far as the eye could see. In front of him, at the end of one of the streets that led off from the square, was a wooden jetty, which pushed out into the still, brown water. Behind him was a track that ran for a few hundred metres and then disappeared into the reeds.

'Where does the track lead to?' he asked.

'It goes Al Amarah. Saddam's men build it... We no like.'

'What about this?' he asked, pointing at the reed building. 'Is it your mosque?'

Rachel laughed. 'Nooo. This no mosque. This Temple. We not Muslim like rest of Ma'dan; we Masahuin... We follow Jesus.'

'Can I go inside?'

'You? No - need permission. I ask father... maybe later. We go marsh now.'

'This way?' he asked, pointing at the jetty.

'Yes.'

Thanks for that. At least it's downhill!

❖ ❖ ❖

Along the length of the jetty were small boats moored to the tree trunks that had been driven into the mud to support the wooden structure. Mason sat on the edge and watched a herd of water buffalo wallowing in the shallows while their herder sat on the bank. He suddenly realised that, other than Rachel, this was the first person he had seen in the village that morning. *It's like a ghost town.*

'Where are all the people, Rachel?' he asked.

'Not many left now,' she said, as she took off her sandals and immersed her dusty feet into the cool water. 'After Saddam attacked, they leave... When I was a baby, many children play in the river. Now, no children. They go to Basrah... only a few people left.'

'You speak good English, Rachel. Did you learn it at school?'

'A little, but my mother teach me more.'

'Where is she?'

'Saddam men kill my mother... and my brother.'

'My wife and daughter were killed also,' Mason said after a long pause, as he took off his sandals and, copying Rachel, immersed them in the cool water.

'They bomb us with fire... many peoples die,' she said as she moved her feet back and forth. 'We run away into the marshes... lots of peoples too scared to return... Only a few left.' She started to count on her fingers. 'Only nine families left,' she continued. 'Used to be, ohhh, fifty or sixty. All gone now... or dead.' There was another long pause. 'How your family die?' she asked, looking over at him.

'Crash. They were hit by a truck'

'This is very sad. We both... lose. It is painful, no?'

'Very painful,' answered Mason. 'Death seems to follow me wherever I go. The other day, I lost three men that were close to me. It would have been more, but the others got away on a helicopter.'

Rachel looked at him, her mind analysing his words. 'No, Mr Mason. They not get away. Four man killed. Two man...

146

umm... prisoner.'

'What did you say?' he snapped.

Rachel was flustered by his sudden urgency, struggling to find the words. 'Helicopter no land. Mans get shot... Papa see police take two men away.'

'Are you sure, Rachel?' he demanded, grabbing her arms and pulling her out of the water.

'Yes. My Papa he say - not tell you until you are well,' she answered as she struggled to pull away from him. 'Please let go. You frighten me!'

He released her, and watched as her whole body began to shake with emotion. 'Please don't cry. I'm sorry... it's just that I thought they got away.'

'I only... wanted... to... help... you,' she panted between sobs.

He wrapped his arms around her and pulled her into his chest. *The last time I held Katie, she was crying. What's the matter with me?* 'Please don't cry. I am not angry,' he whispered. 'I need to speak to your father. Can you take me to him?'

'Yes,' she answered as she dried her eyes. 'I will take you.'

He tried to sit patiently on the bench outside the Temple where she'd left him while she'd gone in search of her father. But his brain was enjoying none of the calm of the surroundings. *Where are they? Are they being tortured? Are they still alive?* The questions raced through his mind, making his head spin.

He stood up and searched the street that she had run down, looking for a sign of her return. But there was nothing. The only movement was from a stray dog scavenging for food.

The wind had risen, picking up the heat from the midday sun and blowing it straight into his face, with the intensity of a hair drier. *Best get out of the sun,* he thought, taking refuge against the shaded wall of the Temple. It was then that he became aware of a mysterious sound.

The building was whistling, the hot wind passing through the reed walls creating an enchanting chord of notes; a captivating, almost bewitching, sound. It was as if the building were calling him. *I suppose I could go inside. It wouldn't do any harm. Nobody will know.* He made his way to the large wooden door and turned the handle; it wasn't locked. He pushed the door. It swung open.

He expected the interior to be dark, but had underestimated the porous quality of the reeds. They didn't just allow the winds to pass through; they also let the light stream in. Mason stood in awe, gazing at the beautiful patchwork of light and shade in the spacious hall interior. He was astounded at the way the ceiling rose high above him, the pillars made entirely from reeds supporting it arching above the floor, tapering from a cylindrical mass into the flat surface of the ceiling, the work clearly having been undertaken by an artisan in mastery of his craft. The hall's architecture bore an uncanny resemblance to a cathedral.

He stepped further into the Temple, his walking stick tapping on the stone floor, curiosity compelling him forward, his attention drawn to what seemed to be an altar at the far end of the hall. He saw that it had been draped with a dark red cloth, the corners touching the floor. On its surface were three objects. He directed his attention to the item in the centre: a stone box. He scrutinised the tablet placed on top of the lid. It was a portrait of a dark-skinned, clean-shaven man with a large nose, dark eyes and curly hair. The brilliant colours of this portrait stood vividly against the plain stone surface of the box.

On the right of the stone box was a kite-shaped shield nearly four feet in length, the front of its curved wooden structure plated with a layer of steel, painted white, displaying a large red cross. *This is old*, he thought, as his fingers touched the dents and gorges along its surface. *It looks like it could have belonged to a Crusader, but what the hell would he be doing here?*

The last object on the left side of the altar was covered by a leather sheet. His curiosity piqued, he moved towards it and gently pulled back the cover. 'It's a sword,' he said out loud. It was over three feet in length, its handle newly covered with leather and its highly-polished blade still looking razor sharp.

Mason couldn't resist the pull of the weapon; he had to touch it. He rested his walking stick against the altar and gently placed his hand around the grip. Carefully supporting the tip of the blade with his left hand, he lifted the ancient weapon clear from its protective cover. He was surprised at how light and manoeuvrable it was, the metal disc above the handle- the pommel - acting as a counter-weight to the steel of the blade, making the sword perfectly balanced. He remembered the walking stick. He had seen a shield and a sword engraved on the shaft when he had inspected it earlier. Holding the sword in one hand, he picked up the stick and studied it again. There they were: clear representations of the artefacts he was now examining. As he looked closer, Mason saw that they were being held by what appeared to be a knight in chain mail.

There were voices. They were outside and getting closer. He replaced the sword and made his way to the entrance as quickly as he could. As he closed the door to the Temple, John and Rachel rounded the corner.

'You must go,' John said, casting a grave look at Mason.

'Sorry, I didn't mean to look inside. But I couldn't help it,' replied Mason, believing that his curiosity had upset his hosts.

'The police are coming,' Rachel added, pointing at the cloud of dust that was closing on the village. 'They cannot find you here.'

'Quick, Rachel. Go and ready the boat,' John shouted, taking Mason by the arm. 'Come. You must move as fast as you can.'

As they reached the first planks of the jetty, the screaming engines of the police pickups could be heard racing through the village.

'Look!' shouted Rachel as Mason got into the boat. 'I can see them.'

Mason held out his hand to help John aboard. But, instead of his hand, John gave Mason a small sack. 'These are the rest of your belongings,' he said, before pushing hard against the boat. 'Go now. My daughter will take you to safety.'

'But you are in danger,' urged Mason, holding out his hand as the distance between them grew. 'You must come with us.'

'My place is with my people,' John replied.

Clear of the jetty, Rachel took hold of the long pole and drove it hard into the shallow water, the boat careering as she recovered, ready for the next stroke.

'Wait,' Mason shouted, as he remembered his earlier concern. 'My men: you saw them captured?'

'Yes. Two men,' shouted John. 'One was tall, with yellow hair; the other had a beard. The police have them.'

The boat sped forward again as the pole found solid ground, the reeds closing on the small craft like a curtain, just as the police trucks thundered down the street towards the jetty. By the time they'd stopped, they were completely hidden.

They peered through the tall reeds and watched as John, arms outstretched, welcomed his visitors. His cordial greetings were not returned. The police surrounded him. Mason and Rachel could hear the shouts. And they both saw the blow.

Mason grabbed her as she fainted, just stopping her from falling overboard. As he held her in his arms, he watched John's limp body being dragged into the truck.

Police HQ, Al Amarah, Iraq.

There were two cells in the basement. They lay beside each other, opposite the flight of eight concrete steps that led to the one door that constituted the only way in or out. A grid of iron bars separated the units, holding in place two doors with heavy locks, the whole frame being fixed into the floor, walls and low ceiling. The cell, closest to the steps was the larger of the two, and had the only window. The hole needed no protection, as it was too small for even the slightest of inmates to fit through its unglazed frame.

The concrete floor of each cell was smooth, its hard surface polished by the countless prisoners who doubtless had no alternative but to sit awaiting their fate. In the middle was the only sanitary provision: a small hole, the odour attracting a swarm of flies that merrily feasted on its contents. The mustard-coloured paint used to cover the lime plaster on the back wall was still visible in parts, but had mostly been worn away or covered with the brown streaks that spread sporadically across its surface.

'What do you think this is?' Thor had asked, as he began to trace his fingers over the thick brown streaks.

'That's blood. Don't touch it. You might catch something,' Dusty said, already having figured out the curious patterns for himself.

Thor pulled away, as if his hand had just touched hot metal. He stood back and looked at the smear, analysing it like an art critic trying to make sense of an impressionist painting. He could see it now: a significant gush of blood from a deep wound. He shuddered and looked away, feeling sick to his stomach.

Their hoods and handcuffs had been removed at the end of the first day. And, although their bruised and bloodied faces still bore the signs of that day's violence, there had been no more beatings.

The skinny policeman with the rotten teeth had been given the job of their gaoler. Each morning, he brought a pot of mixed rice, some hard unleavened bread and a canteen of water as their only meal of the day. They followed the same ritual: standing at the back of the cell, facing the wall, as he unlocked the door and slid the meal towards them with his foot. This was the highlight of their long, boring day which started at dawn when they were woken by the call to prayer from a distant mosque. For the rest of the time, they just talked about anything, trying to pass the time, each man trying to keep as busy as possible, trying to rid themselves of the constant fear that gnawed at them.

On the fourth day after their capture, the door at the top of the staircase burst open.

'What's going on?' whispered Thor as the skinny policeman descended into the basement, followed by two other guards.

'I think we're in for it,' Dusty answered as he moved into the corner of the cell, drawing his knees in close to his chest.

But they both breathed a sigh of relief as the guards ignored them and walked to the adjoining cell. The skinny policeman unlocked the door. The other two policemen passed their cell, dragging a body. Both prisoners watched as the new captive was thrown through the open cell door, disturbing the swarm of flies that were feeding on the filth of the open sewer.

The two guards turned on their heels and left immediately, not even bothering to look behind them, leaving the skinny policeman to secure the cell. On his way out, their gaoler stopped in front of their cell and looked at them, grinning. 'Fooking Christian,' he said, looking over at the new prisoner and making the throat-cutting sign. He spat on the floor before carrying on up the steps, laughing to himself as he went. 'Fooking, fooking, fooking...' he said, as he climbed out of the basement.

'They really went to town on him,' said Thor, picking up the plastic bottle containing what was left of their daily ration of water. 'Do you want a drink, mate?' he asked, walking over to the bars between the cells. The man looked up. His face was stained with blood, and both eyes were badly swollen. Thor went down on his haunches and offered the bottle through the bars. 'Drink?' he asked.

The man crawled to the bottle, taking it in both hands. He looked at his fellow captives as he took a small sip. 'Thank you,' he said in English, before handing the bottle back.

'My name is Thor, and this is Dusty.'

The man pulled himself up off the floor as best he could, and offered Thor his hand. 'My name... John'.

'Yes... yes. I understand,' said the Commander into his cell phone. 'They are safe. Don't worry... and the money?' He took a Marlboro from the pack on his desk, listening to the man on the other end as he lit up. 'Banks are no good; I want cash,' he interrupted. 'I understand that it will take longer. I am prepared to wait.' He hung up, placed the phone on his desk, and, as he took a long pull of the cigarette, glanced down into the courtyard. *I will be able to retire soon, very soon.*

'Sergeant!' he shouted, while stubbing the end into the already-full ashtray. 'Make sure that the prisoners are not harmed.'

'I have already given the orders, Sayeed.'

'And the food? Are they receiving any?'

'Yes, Sayeed. They're getting adequate rations.'

'Good, good. Oh, and Sergeant,' he said, stopping the man just as he was leaving. 'The ambush site: we need to make sure that it is cleared in case the British come looking.'

'Yes, Sayeed. I will go and check it myself to make sure it is done.'

'And what about the search for the infidel that got away?'

'We have arrested one of the Marsh Arabs, Sayeed.'

'Does he know anything?'

'We're not sure, Sayeed.'

'What do you mean?'

'He's old. And the boys were a bit rough with him…'

'We'll go on looking. He's out there somewhere. I need him found.'

Mason sat at the prow of the long Marsh Arab boat, as Rachel, who stood on the small platform at the stern, rhythmically worked the pole in and out of the shallow water, the boat's narrow beam allowing it to move easily through the dense mass of reeds. There was nothing in front for him to see, so he sat facing the stern and watched Rachel, the village Elder's daughter, deep in thought, totally oblivious to his stare.

Her veil had dropped, the hidden blemish once so fiercely guarded now exposed. Tear tracks, easy to follow against her skin, vanishing as they entered the mass of scar tissue. He watched as her small hands gripped the pole, working the long wooden stick in and out of the water like a piston. There was no let up in her rhythm; the physical effort, a practiced grace from years of refinement, allowing only the occasional grimace on what was an otherwise expressionless face.

'Do you want to rest for a little while?' he asked, after what seemed hours.

'No time,' she replied, without looking at him. 'Maybe later.'

He took hold of the bag that John had given him, and undid its fastening. At the top was a gourd that was full of water. 'Drink?' he asked, removing the stopper and offering her the vessel. She shook her head.

He was as thirsty as hell, but if she wasn't going to drink, neither was he. He put the stopper back in, and put the gourd back in the bag, his hand touching something hard and metallic. He pulled out the rectangular object. It was his satellite phone. *Just what the doctor ordered*, he thought, checking it out. The grey outer casing had been damaged, and the screen was cracked. But when he pressed the button, to his delight, it came on.

'Do you know what this is?' he said, showing the phone to Rachel.

'It's a... telephono.' she answered.

'Yes, you're right,' he answered. 'But this one is special; it will pick up a signal anywhere in the world.' He scrolled down through the saved numbers, found the one he wanted and was about to press 'call' when she interrupted him.

'There,' she said, looking at him for the first time since the journey had started, while pointing ahead to a distant feature. He stood carefully, trying not to disturb the boat's balance, and peered into the distance. He couldn't see anything. He shaded his eyes from the sun and looked again. This time, he could just make out the silhouette of distant objects as they moved rapidly along an elevated causeway. 'A road!' he exclaimed. With every stroke of Rachel's pole, they got closer, the colours and makes of the vehicles soon becoming distinguishable.

Rachel brought the boat to rest on a small beach at the base of the causeway, the hull of the boat scraping on the sand and pebbles as it ran aground. She leapt to the shore with the all the nimbleness of a gazelle, and tied the boat to a rock. Mason, tried to copy his companion, but fell like a sack of potatoes, his weak legs buckling as they hit the wet sand. *I'm getting too old for this shit*, he said to himself as he lay on the floor, his ego now as bruised as the rest of his body. 'What now?' he asked, as Rachel helped him to his feet.

'Now, we climb,' she said, pointing at the steep slope.

It took several minutes for them to reach the top of the embankment, their progress hindered by the uneven surface and loose sandals. Eventually, they both lay behind the silver crash barrier, their chests heaving from their exertion. 'Where does this road go to?' Mason asked, as he used his hand to brush the mud off the walking stick.

'To Basrah,' she replied as she began to scan the heat-hazed tarmac in both directions. 'Look,' she shouted, standing up. 'Military.'

She's right, he said to himself as he got up from behind the barrier for a better look. Closing on them fast was a column of Brit Mil Snatch Land Rovers.

'British... yes?' she shouted over the noise of a passing lorry. 'You British. This good?'

The Land Rovers were travelling down the white line in the centre of the road, the traffic around them struggling to get out of their way. When confronted with a military convoy, most Iraqis had learned to adopt the tactic of getting as far away from it as possible, some even choosing to drive off the tarmac and into the fields rather than risk an encounter with trigger-happy soldiers and security guards. Mason watched as the traffic parted before the convoy, the sight reminding him of a snow plough clearing a path. It wasn't long before he could make out the helmet and face of the soldier in the turret of the front vehicle. His LA85A2 assault rifle at the ready, pointing towards the traffic.

'Yes... British good,' he answered as he turned back towards her. But before he had a chance to stop her, Rachel had vaulted over the barrier and, with her arms waving, was running directly towards the convoy.

'Sarge, Twelve o'clock,' the soldier in the lead vehicle said into the radio, having seen the woman jump over the barrier and start running towards them.

'Roger. I've got her, eyes on,' replied the Sergeant. All vehicles STOP. STOP. STOP.'

The soldier looked through the magnified optical sight of his weapon, and studied his target. 'Sarge,' he continued, 'I reckon she's a suicide bomber.'

'Roger that,' acknowledged his superior.

Mason watched in slow motion as the situation developed in front of him. *This looks bad*, he said to himself as he watched the soldier in the lead vehicle train his weapon on the unsuspecting Rachel. Struggling to his feet he climbed over the barrier, waving his hands, frantic for their attention.

He tried to shout, but the words stuck in his parched mouth, his throat too dry to form the words.

'Sarge, that's another one over the barrier. He's waving like a crazy man,' reported the soldier through the radio.

'Fuck me. Looks like an ambush,' replied the Sergeant. 'Engage the first target. TAKE HER OUT!'

The soldier lined up his weapon. His target was thirty metres away as he zeroed the cross-hairs in the centre of her face. *No problem. Easy*, he thought, letting off the safety catch.

Mason was limping heavily, but was closing on Rachel, who, not realising that the convoy had stopped, was still running towards the lead vehicle.

The soldier squeezed the trigger, taking up the first pressure. Another slight movement of his finger would release the 5.56 millimetre bullet capable of eliminating his target. He squeezed again.

As Mason gathered speed, the pain in his legs disappeared as adrenalin surged through his body. As he closed on the hapless Rachel, he threw himself forward, just as the supersonic *crack* from of the bullet - leaving the muzzle at 940 metres per second - ripped through the air. Mason's body smothered her small figure, the pair landing on the baking tarmac in an awkward heap.

'Don't move!' he said, releasing his grip. 'They think you're a suicide bomber. Put your hands where they can see them and stay still.'

'Sorry,' came the murmur from beneath him. 'I only... wanted to try to stop them for you.'

The anxious soldier in the lead vehicle, eager for his first 'kill', readied himself for another shot. 'Permission to fire, Sarge?' he asked, before lining up Rachel in his sights for the second time.

'Wait,' replied the Sergeant, looking through his binoculars from the second vehicle in the convoy. 'Hold your fire.'

Mason knew that the next few seconds were crucial. He had to defuse the situation, or both of them were going to end up dead. 'I'm going to get up. You stay where you are,' he said, putting his arms in the air whilst slowly working his way up onto his knees. He looked directly at the soldier who had taken the shot. He couldn't see his eyes, as they were covered by sunglasses, but he knew that he was watching his every move. Deliberately, he opened his hands and turned the empty palms to his inquisitor. He then lowered them slowly, his fingertips searching for the hem of his shirt, pulling the loose fitting garment over his head and clear of his torso.

'Sarge, he's taking off his shirt,' the soldier relayed. 'Do you want me to take him out?'

'Negative. Just keep your sights on him,' said the Sergeant, now watching Mason throw the shirt to the floor and turn through 360 degrees, allowing them all to see that there were no explosives.

'Looks like he's unarmed,' confirmed the soldier.

'What's that on his right arm?' asked the Sergeant, as he tried to focus his binoculars on the dark patch on Mason's upper deltoid muscle.

'It looks like a *tat*, Sarge,' replied the soldier.

'Can you make it out?'

The soldier adjusted the telescopic lens on his weapon, the faint lines on Mason's skin gradually revealing the emblem of a parachute, set in the middle of a pair of wings.

'Fuck me, Sarge... the guy's a para.'

'We need to get going, sir,' the Sergeant explained, as Mason and Rachel sat in the back of the Brit Mil Land Rover. 'We've been here for too long. We risk becoming a target.'

Mason knew this moment was inevitable. But, even now that it had arrived, he still did not want to accept it. He was torn; part of him wanted to stay with her and help her find her father, but the other part of him knew that he had to get back to Basrah to get help. His men had to be rescued, and he couldn't do it on his own. 'Come with me?' he asked, looking directly at her, gazing into her beautiful eyes, which were so full of pain. He wanted to say more - to reassure her - to take away the hurt - to share the suffering that they had both endured. But he didn't know where to begin.

Rachel looked away. She had dreamt of this moment all her tragic young life - to be swept off her feet by a brave, handsome, hero. She wanted it more than anything. To be taken from the village and given the opportunity to explore the world - a world that, up until now, she had glimpsed only in the magazines and books her mother had smuggled into the village. But it came at a bittersweet price; she could have her dream, but it would be at the sacrifice of her father, her family and the rest of the Masahuin. 'No. I can't,' she protested, it taking all of her willpower to suppress her true desires. 'Must go back... must help Papa.'

She looked different to him somehow, her scars not even registering any more. It was as if the unblemished soul of the courageous young woman was now radiating outwards, her physical disfigurement paling into insignificance. 'You go now,' she said, unable to look at him.

He took the satellite phone out of the bag, and gave it to her. 'Keep this,' he said, pressing it into her hand. 'Turn it on at 12:00 midday every day. Only keep it on for five minutes. I will call. I will come back for you.'

She grasped the beat-up grey phone, and held it tightly - just as tightly as she wanted to hold the man standing opposite her. Looking at the floor, she nodded. 'When will you come back?'

'It will take a few days,' Mason said, putting his hands on her shoulders. 'But I will.' She looked up in response to his touch, and he stared deeply into her eyes. 'I promise,' he whispered.

She looked at him and smiled. 'I believe you, Mason,' she said, climbing out of the Land Rover.

'Wait,' he said, holding out the walking stick.

'You can give it me when you return,' she said, as she climbed over the barrier. She turned and looked at him, watching as the vehicle pulled off, continuing to follow it with her eyes long after he was no longer visible. Finally, when the Land Rover had all but vanished, she waved, turned and ran down the steep slope to her waiting boat.

She put the phone – her precious link to the man that had promised to help her - into the pocket of her long flowing dress, and picked up her pole. 'Papa', she said as she pushed off. 'Must find Papa...'

Military Field Hospital, BAS,
16.16hrs, 17 May 2007.

'Well, you're a sight for sore eyes,' said Tonka as he helped Mason out of the back of the Snatch. 'The military want to check you out. There is a cubicle ready for you. Do you want a wheelchair?' he asked, looking at the walking stick.

'I'm okay,' replied Mason. 'I don't need a check-up. Just give me some painkillers and I'll be fine. I can't be doing with all this. We have work to do. There are two guys out there still alive.'

Tonka looked at him in astonishment. 'Well, that's a turn up!' he exclaimed. 'Up until an hour ago, we thought that you were *all* dead. Who's alive?'

'Dusty and Thor. The IPS have taken them. Smudge, Tommo, Paddy and Billy are dead.'

'Are you sure it was the IPS?' questioned Tonka.

'Yes, mate. One hundred percent.'

'Whoa! That's going to cause a bit of a stink, since they're officially supposed to be on our side!'

'You're having a check-up,' said a plump woman in a camouflage uniform, the Staff Sergeant's badge and red cross patch on her right arm adding weight to her order.

'Start walking,' she said as she took hold of his arm.

'Okay, staff,' he replied, looking at the formidable nurse. 'Lead the way. I'm not going to argue. It's been a hard few days.'

'I'll start the ball rolling,' Tonka said as he held the door open for the nurse and her patient to enter the tented labyrinth. 'I'll get straight onto JJ. And I'll be back as quickly as I can,' he said, letting the plastic doors swing shut, sealing the hospital off from the dust-ridden air outside.

The hospital consisted of a long, tented corridor with doors leading off it at regular intervals. 'Our cubicle is at the far end,' the nurse told Mason. He gulped. The corridor looked like it went on forever. He knew that it was just an optical illusion, remembering what his instructor had said on his sniper course: 'things will look a lot further away when you look down a long narrow feature, like a street or a corridor; it's called 'telescoping',' the instructor had explained. *I know it's not that far,* he said to himself as he walked up the never-ending passageway. *But try telling my legs that.*

The ward housed twelve beds, six on each side, with all the usual medical paraphernalia in place between them. It looked no different from a normal hospital, except for the green tented walls and large, cream-coloured air-conditioning pipes that crisscrossed the blue plastic floor, allowing patients to recuperate at a comfortable and steady sixty-five degrees Fahrenheit.

The nurse showed Mason to a bed, telling him to strip and don the surgical gown that had been laid out ready. The doctor arrived soon afterwards, and after a cursory examination diagnosed him with dehydration, bruised ribs and muscle fatigue. The ringing in his ears, an occupational hazard for men on the base, would disappear in a week or so, as would the rest of his injuries.

No shit, Sherlock, thought Mason as he swallowed the Ibuprophen and antibiotics that had been given to him in a small paper cup while the doctor delivered his diagnosis. 'We are going to keep you in overnight,' said the doctor, in an authoritative tone, as he wrote on the clipboard. 'It's just a precaution. If the signs are good, you will be released in the morning.'

As Mason lay back and put his head on the crisp, white, laundered pillow, a pang of guilt ran right through him. Four of his men were dead, and another two were M.I.A John's efforts to help Mason had resulted in him being captured by the ruthless IPS, and Rachel was on her own. *Fuck*, he thought, *what a mess. I can't rest. I have to get it sorted.* He dropped his legs over the side of the bed, and was just about to get up when he saw three men enter the ward.

The first two were dressed in desert camouflage, their rank slides showing the single crown of a Major and the more junior insignia of a Second Lieutenant, or 'one pip wonder' - straight from the Military Academy at Sandhurst. Neither was wearing any unit insignia, but Mason knew instinctively who they were. The SAS had a nickname for them, derived from the unique colour of their berets. *Green slime*, he said to himself, *Intelligence Corps*.

The third man was trickier to place. His tan chinos, blue striped Ralph Lauren shirt and suede boots would not have looked out of place at any Mediterranean resort. In the current environment, the uninitiated would be forgiven for thinking him a member of the press or an NGO worker. But, in light of his present company, there was no mistaking his association: MI6, or simply *Six*, as the Hereford gang called them.

The Major made an innocuous introduction, referring to himself and his young assistant by name and rank only. Roger, the third man, was given only the slightest of mentions, and was quite happy to sit in the background as his uniformed colleagues took the lead.

After every operation, the men of 22 SAS were debriefed by Military Intelligence. Mason had gone through the questioning on countless occasions, the operatives always using the same methodology of questioning. So he knew all too well what was about to come. It was called 'the tree technique', the main thrust of the questioning being the 'trunk', with the sub-questions as the 'branches', and with answers potentially adding more lines of inquiry and subsequent branches.

Mason didn't need to see the sheet of paper to know what diagram the Major was drawing. He had a picture in his mind, and, unbeknown to the Major, it was he who was leading the interrogation. He began to shepherd the Major along the line of questioning that suited him, his answers revealing only the information he thought was required to aid the rescue of his men. The debrief lasted a couple of hours. Mason had known it to last days on some occasions. But, since he was acting so compliantly, giving the officers exactly what he thought they wanted, there was no need for them to string it out.

The Major closed his notepad, and looked over at the young officer smugly. The Lieutenant nodded his approval.

Roger waited while the two soldiers thanked Mason and exchanged a few pleasantries, hanging back as they made their way to the door. 'Good to meet you,' he said as he shook Mason's hand. He had realised about thirty minutes into the session that there was something not right. Alerted, he had sat back and watched Mason skilfully lead the Major from one question to another, and he was aware that there was a key question that the two interrogators had failed to ask.

'Do you have any military service?' he asked as he studied Mason's face. 'I know a lot of you security guys are ex-military, right?'

'My parent unit was 3 Para,' replied Mason. 'But I've been out for years.'

'I recall reading about the exploits of a Mason in Bosnia. I believe he was an ex-Para. He was serving with 22 SAS. Any relation?'

Mason smiled and nodded.

'Pleasure to meet you,' repeated Roger. 'I read your report. You did a hell of a job in Bosnia.'

Roger pushed open the plastic doors of the hospital and led his colleagues off to the side so as not to obscure the doorway, stopping opposite the memorial to the RAMC soldiers that had been killed in Iraq. It was a simple monument, a wooden cross supported by a base of large pebbles that were concreted together. As he lit a cigarette, he studied the long list of fallen soldiers, each name recorded on a brass plaque.

'This is going to cause a hell of a fuss,' he said, not even looking at his colleagues. 'Private security companies attacked, their men killed and abducted by the IPS? It's just not on.'

'How do you want to play it?' asked the Major.

Roger took a long pull on his cigarette and exhaled, the cigarette smoke quickly dispersing in the dusty air. 'If it was anyone else, we could make it go away,' he said, turning to face the two men. 'But this guy isn't *anyone*. He's a decorated senior rank from 22 SAS... Filthy habit!' he said, suddenly remembering he was trying to quit, and throwing the cigarette to the floor.

'22 SAS?' the Lieutenant mused checking his notes.

'Exactly,' continued Roger. 'I want you to check out his story. Send a patrol to the ambush location and interview the local Police Commander.'

'That's not a problem,' replied the Major. 'But what about the prisoners?'

'The only witness is an old Arab who has been taken by the same bunch. He may already be dead. Those two guys - Thor and the Australian - um...'

'Dusty, sir,' interrupted the Lieutenant. 'Yes, Dusty. If there are no witnesses to support the accusation, then Mason's account becomes purely 'third

164

party': anecdotal. It would never stand up in a court of law.'

'Understood,' said the Major.

'Oh, and by the way,' added Roger, 'make sure that Mason is on the first C130 out of here. If I remember correctly, this guy is a one-man army. I read his citation. It was pretty impressive.'

'Consider it done,' replied the Major.

'Good,' said Roger. I don't want him anywhere near this place. He might just do something crazy.'

M4, London,
18.05hrs, 17 May 2007.

It had been a glorious summer day, the type that was ideal for taking the kids to the beach, or relaxing in a quaint pub by the river and watching the sun go down, with a few pints of beer. James had done neither. His labour today was having to listen to John Joe O'Hare complain about Target's excessive wage bill. Today's penurious rant from the Glaswegian only stopped when JJ had been reminded that it was in his interest to pay the men as much as possible, since it meant greater profit. He couldn't wait to get away, and had made an excuse that he had to go to Vauxhall Cross for a meeting. Instead, he had jumped into his ageing Mondeo and headed for home. He was now sat in a queue of traffic on the M4 that had only moved a mile in half an hour. He could have had a company car, but, because he was based 'in town,' he had opted for the extra pay instead. So, amidst the breathless calm of the sweltering London evening, he sat wilting, his windows rolled down, cursing the fact that he'd forgotten to get his A/C unit fixed.

He slotted a CD into the stereo to revive his flagging morale. And above the triumphal tones of Handel's Scipio - the Grenadiers slow march, he only just about heard the incoming text. It read simply 'phone home.' He hit the speed dial button. The phone rang only once before it answered. 'I'd like to speak to mother,' he said as he watched the car in front of him creep forward.

'Who shall I say is calling?'

'Tango 1-9-0,'

'Are you calling from a secure line?'

'Yes.'

'Please wait,' came the reply.

'There's been a development in Basrah.' It was a different voice, the confident tone of his superior needing no introduction to James. 'The callsign that was ambushed has turned up a survivor. I've emailed you the report. It's got all the details.'

'The name of the survivor?' James quizzed.

The answer came as two syllables hitting his ears like an insult. 'Mason.'

He took the first congested exit in an effort to retrace his steps, and, as he waited at the off ramp for the traffic lights to change, he received the first of what he knew would be a string of calls from JJ O'Hare. He fumbled on the handset, reducing the volume to zero before putting it on the passenger seat, placing over it his copy of The Times. The CD was now playing the British Grenadier. He turned up the volume, his posture altering immediately as the stirring tones resonated through the family saloon. With his new-found energy, he decided to try the A/C once more. He turned the switch, and, to his delight, a gust of chilled air greeted him, his face feeling like it has just been wrapped in a barber's cold towel.

He enjoyed the drive back into town, tapping the steering wheel merrily, the scowl of earlier now replaced by a thoughtful smirk.

The Marshes, Iraq,
16.55hrs, 17 May 2007.

Checking the angle of the sun with the horizon, she could see
that it was way past its meridian; there was maybe just
another two hours before it got dark. But the darkness held
no fear for her; the marshes were her home. She could never
get lost here, even when robbed of the light. The stars were
her map. The birds, interrupted by her passing, produced
calls, acting as her signposts.

The marshes had been Rachel's ever since Papa had
shown her how to use the boat. The long pole, initially so
cumbersome in her small hands, had become so natural to
use twenty years later, its application an unthinking deed -
fluent, like that of a beating heart. She knew every inch of
the reed mass; she knew its size and uniformity. This
landscape may inspire fear in those who know not of its
wonders, but to the Masahuin, it is their home, their larder,
their protection, giving them everything, claiming only one
thing in return: isolation. But the Marshes had also been a
place of inspiration; this was where the seed of her yearning
had been sewn.

Her mother Fatima, with her enticing green eyes and
mane of dark curls flowing so easily down her back, was the
most beautiful girl in the village. She told Rachel that, from
a young age, she had been chosen to marry the Elder, a man
some years older than her. But it wasn't a forced match; she
already loved John deeply, the marriage only cementing the
inevitable, allowing them to produce a daughter who was the
image of her mother, and a son vital for the family line.

But her mother passed on more than just her features;
there were other qualities that she infused. Rachel
remembered the first magazine that she was shown. Her
mother had asked one of the men to get it from the city, its
pages a window into a world that lay beyond the marshes:
cars, airplanes and women in beautiful clothes. She'd hidden
the publications - sworn to secrecy. The only opportunity to

167

enjoy the pictures by candlelight when her father was at work.

Her mother loved the village. She loved the ancient simplistic ways, the loyalty, the love of her family. If, like her ancestors, she'd been unaware of the outside world, then she would have been happy with her lot. But her Mama knew that there was a life beyond the reeds. She knew of the universities where you could learn anything your heart desired.

It was Mama who started the school. The other men in the village didn't want it, but she persuaded her father. The schoolbooks were brought from Basrah, allowing her to nurture the craving that was growing within her daughter. Rachel would take the books onto the boat and glide into the cool, open space. And, whilst the water lapped against the hull, she would work through her lessons and dream.

She had a wonderful childhood. Daughter of John the Elder, head of the Masahuin, direct descendant of Sir John. But her happiness wasn't because of her status; it was because everyone liked her. But she was no angel. Oh no. Mischievous like the other children. She became a nurse - her mission to care for the orphaned and sick animals that the villagers found in the marshes. It was testing for her parents' patience. The *infirm ward* set up in the corral at the back of their house, robbing her father of sleep, as the sick animals called out incessantly. Her equally-mischievous best friend Tebo, *poor Tebo* - the donkey with the deformed leg that she'd rescued as a new-born foal, would raid the kitchen for cakes and follow her around like a puppy, waiting by the water's edge for her return. It was all gone now - all except her Papa. The nightmares of that day were all that remained - that horrible day when her life changed forever.

It was the only time that she'd heard her parents argue. The disagreement was about the city men that came in their dirty ripped clothes - in ones and twos at first, but then in tens and twenties. Fatima didn't want to help them. But her father insisted that it was his duty. And then came that afternoon. She'd spotted the airplanes while returning from the Temple with John and Papa, her father shouting for them to get inside as he ran back to protect the secret. The explosions. The panic as people ran from their houses, screaming. The horrific smell of burning flesh. She remembered running down the street to the jetty with her brother, their mother holding both their hands so desperately. And recalled the time waiting to escape as the men brought the boats... and then she remembered Tebo, *poor Tebo*. There was the run back to the corral to fetch the donkey. The explosion, and then the pain as the napalm hit her flesh, stabbing like a thousand red-hot needles, skin melting, coming off in her hands.

The rest of the day was a blur, as she drifted in and out of unconsciousness. The one vivid memory the sight that awaited her back at the jetty. The group huddled together there for protection, taking a direct hit. Burning bodies, their suffering etched on their knotted faces. In that instant, her life was changed. She'd lost her mother and brother. Her father was a broken man, all youth, innocence and beauty vanishing from both their faces.

The village was deserted - even the houses where the few remaining families lived. In darkness with heavy legs and great trepidation, hands bloody from burst blisters, she made her way along the empty street from the jetty. Muscles aware of the small gradient, mood black, the darkness enveloping her like a sodden blanket. She was desperate to know, but frightened of the truth. Finally, she could see the outline of the house. It too was in darkness; there was not even a trickle of smoke from a fire that - even during the most tragic of times – had always kept burning.

'Where's Papa, Miriam?' She asked the sobbing figure hunched over the kitchen table.

'The police took him' she says, shaking her head. 'They raided the temple too. They took the Treasure. It's gone - all gone. We're finished.'

Miriam's words confirm her darkest fears. She'd punted through the marshes, trying to hold on to hope, gripping the pole tighter, concentrating on the pain in her hands every time a negative thought had entered her head. But deep down she knew the truth.

Delirious from exhaustion and grief, Rachel walked back along the street, her steps dictated by some unconscious, inward drive. She wanted to lie down, to sleep, to never wake up, but her feet keep on moving. Arriving at the temple, the door left ajar, she calls. 'Are you there, Papa?' the emptiness answering with silence.

The waxing moon is rising, granting just enough light to see the altar. Miriam was right; both the Secret Treasure and Sir John's things are gone. This most familiar of places had always been filled with happiness, but now it was foreign, its sanctuary sullied. She closed the door, leaving it as it should always be left, and turned.

Every day since that terrible day when her mother and brother had been killed, she'd carried the burden of their deaths. But she'd not given in, doing enough each day to survive, spurred on by the knowledge that Papa needed her as much as she needed him. When he held her, he took away the pain. But now, he was gone. For the first time in her life, she was on her own, and sliding into a chasm of despair.

It was a perfect, cloudless night, the stars shining down with all their celestial brilliance on a marshland scene that has not changed for millennia. Fatima had told her it was believed that the Garden of Eden had been in the marshes. 'Which meant,' she had always said, smiling, 'that Adam and Eve would have looked at the same stars.'

Rachel looks up into the blackness. Above the iconic shape of Orion the Hunter, pinned to the evening sky. She searched for the three most prominent stars of the constellation, Orion's belt - the middle star of the trilogy with special significance. Fatima had schooled her on how to find it, explaining to her daughter that 'if she ever needed help, all she had to do was talk to it, and the ancestors would hear. As she watched the star sparkle against the pitch-black, its outline became blurry as her eyes filled. 'Mama, please help me,' she mumbled, as the tears began to flow.

Her body, heavy with tiredness collapsed. As she lay exhausted, she realised that her tired legs had brought her to the village graveyard. In front, is the simple headstone that marked the grave of her mother and brother. Pulling herself up, she kissed her index finger and traced the names so finely carved on the wooden cross – in the same way that she had done for the last fifteen years. 'Mama, I don't know what to do,' she sobbed. 'Papa is gone, and I am frightened.'

As she lay on the warm earth, the cool evening breeze began to grip her aching body. Against the cold, she thrust her hands deep into her pockets, her fingertips nuzzling against an unfamiliar object: the satellite phone. She took it out and held it with both hands close to her chest, at the same time pleading to the star.

'Sir John prophesied that a knight would come from the West to relieve the Masahuin of their duty,' she uttered with a whisper. 'Papa was right. Mason must be that knight. I will be strong,' she said aloud. 'I will find out where my Papa is, and where Mason's men are being held. And I will lead the village in my father's absence. It is my duty - just as it was for all my ancestors before me. I must not let them down. I will wait for his call every day at noon. And, when he comes back, I will be ready. He will come back. I know he will.'

CHAPTER SIX

BAS, Iraq,
03.15, 18 May 2007

Mason stood at the edge of the airstrip, flanked by two military policemen. Fifty metres in front of him stood a C130 Hercules aircraft, its squat outline distinctive against the night sky. Tailgate lowered - the red glow from the antiglare lights exposing its vast interior - it waited to receive its payload of passengers.

'I only found out an hour ago that you were on this flight,' Tonka shouted over the noise of the four idling Rolls Royce turbo propeller engines. 'I've packed your kit,' he said as he tried to give Mason his small North Face grip, its delivery intercepted by the MPs. 'You look a bit spaced out, mate,' he said, noticing how dilated Mason's pupils appeared in the red light. 'You feeling okay?'

Unbeknown to either of them, the medical staff had been ordered to administer Mason with a sedative, just in case he had showed a reluctance to cooperate with the travel plans arranged for him.

'I'm okay,' Mason replied with a yawn. 'Just feel sleepy, that's all. Aren't the stars bright tonight?' he said, looking up dreamily into the evening sky.

'Yeah... it's the lack of ambient light, mate,' replied Tonka, humouring his old friend. 'You have to be somewhere with no artificial lights to get a view like this.'

'Do you remember how to find South using the stars?'

'South?' said Tonka, looking puzzled.

'Yeah... North is easy but South is a bit... trickier.'

'Naaah, never been showed that one mate,' replied Tonka.

172

'Look at Orion's belt and take the middle star,' Mason said, pointing up at the constellation that was directly above them. 'Then draw a line through the sword, and follow it down to the horizon. That will give you South,' he said, punctuating his comment with a yawn.

'I didn't know that. That's very...' Tonka's reply was cut short as Mason grabbed him by the shirt, his mood changing in an instant.

'This is bollocks! Why am I being sent packing? I need to stay here. My men are out there. They're my responsibility. I have to find them.'

The two military police stepped forward, Tonka holding his hands up to defuse the tense situation. 'Steady, big fella,' he said, as he loosened Mason's grip. 'Just understand, this has nothing to do with me, okay? But don't worry about it... they just want you back to start organising the rescue.'

'That's nonsense, and you know it. The best place to organise it is right here,' Mason said as he dropped his hands to his sides. 'This whole thing stinks.'

'The good news is Brit Mil is sending out a patrol. If your guys are out there, we'll get them back... okay, mate?'

'I feel like shit,' Mason said, shifting his weight onto the walking stick. 'If I didn't know any better, I'd have said that fat Staff Sergeant has slipped me a Mickey Finn.'

The RAF loadmaster walked down the ramp of the Herc, and started to flash his torch. 'Okay, gentlemen,' said one of the MPs. 'Time to board.'

'Listen,' Tonka shouted as the MPs escorted Mason to the foot of the ramp. 'When you land at RAF Lyneham, there will be a car waiting to take you to London. JJ wants to see you, ASAP.'

Tonka watched as Mason was helped up the ramp by the two burly MPs, and put into the first vacant seat. As the tailgate went up, Tonka could see that his old friend was already asleep.

Battalion HQ, BAS,
earlier on the 17th.

The envelope that had landed on the Colonel's desk was marked 'URGENT'. He had opened it immediately, digested its contents and decided on a course of action in the cool, calm, and professional manner honed over his long career as a British Army officer. 'Sergeant Major,' he shouted to the SNCO sitting in the adjacent office. 'Get me the adjutant, immediately.'

'Ah, Tim,' the Colonel said, a few minutes later, as a tall, wiry man with a mass of blond, wavy hair entered the office. 'Thanks for coming so quickly. Please come in and sit down. We have a challenge,' the Colonel said, as his subordinate made himself comfy. 'It appears that a PSC got into trouble up in Al Amarah a few days ago.'

'Is this the incident where the helicopter was shot at?' asked the adjutant.

'Yes, that's the one. Division thought that the whole team had been killed, but a survivor's turned up with a different story. It's all in here,' the Colonel said, passing over the manila envelope. 'The survivor is saying they were attacked by the IPS. Four of the team were killed, while the other two survivors were taken prisoner.'

'That's going to cause a hell of a fuss,' the adjutant said as he opened up the envelope and pulled out the document containing Mason's statement. 'We've spent millions on training and arming the police. If it gets out that they're killing security guys and shooting up our helicopters, there will be hell to pay.'

'Absolutely,' the Colonel said. 'It would be very embarrassing. But the thing that's adding weight to the story is the survivor himself. He's ex-SAS, with a record that goes back as far as the Falklands. If this story had come from anyone else, we probably wouldn't be talking about it now.'

'So it's his word against the IPS?' the adjutant asked, studying the transcript.

'His word and that of the village Elder that rescued him.'

'Ah... I see,' said the adjutant, scanning the document for the relevant information on the Elder. 'But it says here that he was attacked by the IPS, and has been taken prisoner also...'

'Yes,' responded the Colonel. 'Look, Tim,' he said, leaning forward in his chair and lowering his voice. 'This is off the record... but it seems to me that this whole thing is a bit of a *can of worms*. With the oil companies pushing to open up the oil fields and all... well, if this is true, then the shit is really going to hit the fan...'

'I think that your assessment is spot on, sir,' replied the adjutant. 'The fallout from this could be huge. I think we can expect some heavy political involvement... never mind MI6 getting all over it.'

'Exactly,' answered the Colonel, sitting back in his seat. 'So, let's treat this as a priority, and do exactly what we've been ordered to do: get over there, and check out this guy's story.'

'Yes, of course, Colonel. What's the time line?'

'Now, Tim. Just make it happen.'

IPS Station, Al Amarah,
08.45hrs, 18 May 2007.

The Sergeant knocked the door and entered before hearing the customary reply. 'My apologies, Sayeed,' he blurted out, well aware of his action's departure from protocol. 'But we have an emergency.'

'What is it?' replied the Commander as he put down his pen, crossed his hands over his chest and sat back in his seat.

'The British, they are coming. They are on the road from Basrah.'

'How close are they?'

'Maybe twenty minutes or less.'

'Why was I not warned sooner?' the Commander said, slamming his hand down onto the desk. 'What imbecile is responsible for not calling? I will have them flogged.'

'All the checkpoints tried, Sayeed, but the British blocked the telephone signals. They have helicopters, too. I have only just got the news from one of our men - who was on a motorbike.'

The Commander nodded. *This is to be expected*, he said to himself.

'Shall I move the prisoners, Sayeed?' asked the Sergeant.

'No, that will not be necessary,' he said, sitting up and putting his elbows on his large desk, pressing his palms together. 'If they have helicopters, they are probably watching us right now on their long-range cameras. The prisoners will stay where they are. Get me my best uniform,' he ordered as he stood up. 'I want to greet the British properly.'

The two Snatch Land Rovers passed under the red and white hatched boom gate and entered into the dusty courtyard of the police station, the barrier snapping shut behind the ageing vehicles like the jaws of some monster devouring its prey.

The compound was in a square, with the main building situated on the left as you entered, running almost the entire length of the perimeter wall for forty metres. It comprised of two storeys, the white and blue police colour scheme - consistent throughout - giving an appearance of functionality and attention to detail. To the right of the main building – and in front as you entered - was a small barrack block built along the back wall. On the wall to the right was a number of outbuildings and room for the police vehicles. In the centre of the compound was a flagpole, surrounded by a frame of white painted stones, at the top of which flew the Iraq tricolour.

As the dust settled, the Commander watched the men

alight from their vehicles in formation, the British soldiers' well-rehearsed drills and actions providing them with all round protection - something that the men were not prepared to compromise, even in this supposedly friendly area.

The Commander counted ten men: two drivers that he knew would stay with the vehicles, and two turret gunners – one in each *Snatch*, their job to provide a fire base in case of trouble. That left a leader - his opponent in this game - as one of the six men that stood around the sand-painted armoured Land Rovers with their weapons at the ready. He watched closely, his trained eye following their movements, his perceptive stare eventually coming to rest on one man.

He looks young. Probably his first time in war, he thought as he studied his adversary like a veteran boxer, looking for the best place to land his opening blow. As the soldier approached, he smiled, catching a satisfying glimpse of what he was looking for. 'My dear Lieutenant,' he said, looking straight into the eyes of the fresh-faced officer while shaking his hand. *It was there. There was no mistaking it: fear. The soldier reeked of it.* 'To what do I owe this unexpected pleasure?'

Yes, the young officer had rehearsed his opening remarks, but his rehearsals were based on an assumption of a hostile reception; the Commander's cordiality had thrown him; he was already on the back foot.

'We've had reports that a PSC team was ambushed in this area a few days ago, and that some of their men have been taken prisoner,' he blurted out, skipping the normal pleasantries and withdrawing his hand from the Commander's lingering handshake.

'Ah, yes. I too have heard these rumours,' replied the Commander in his perfect English. 'But this is not the place to discuss such matters. Please come to my office,' he said, gesturing the Lieutenant towards the main entrance.

The two men climbed the small flight of steps that led to a veranda which ran the whole length of the police station, its shade provided by a lean-to roof of corrugated metal, giving the policemen welcome cover from the harsh Iraqi sun.

'Please,' said the Commander, holding open the double doors that led to the interior. 'After you.'

'I'll wait outside, sir,' suggested the radio operator, as both men entered the building.

'Okay, Corporal. That's a good idea,' replied the Lieutenant as he removed his helmet and sunglasses.

The first thing that hit the officer was the smell. A mixture of sweat and excrement percolating in the stagnant warm air. The stench, like the building's prisoners, trapped. The only effect of the ceiling fans whizzing above their heads to spread the pungent aroma further.

'That smell will be from the cells,' the Commander said, noticing the Lieutenant's pinched expression. 'We have six on this floor. You get used to it.'

'Don't you have any air conditioning?'

'They gave me a generator, but there is no budget for fuel,' the Commander answered with a tut.

The corridor that led off to the left had several metal doors, each leading to a cell. To the right was a staircase. 'Come... My officers are upstairs,' the Commander said, putting his hand on the blue painted metal balustrade and beginning to climb.

At the top was a landing and a window that looked onto the courtyard and an array of doors that copied the format of the ground floor. The rooms on this level, however, were securing paper rather than lost souls.

'Welcome to my humble office,' said the Commander, opening the door nearest the window.

The office was the complete opposite of the spartan, tired interior seen elsewhere in the station. The walls were decorated neatly with a cool red, the floor completely covered with decorative rugs overlapping each other, allowing none of the concrete construction to show through. To the right, in front of a large window that overlooked the courtyard, sat a dark wooden desk, to the left of which - in pride of place - stood the Iraq flag. The air was fresh with jasmine.

'Please take a seat,' the Commander said as he moved over to the window, watching as, below him, the Lieutenant's men searched his compound. 'Your soldiers are hot and thirsty, Lieutenant,' he said, turning to face his guest. 'Let me have some cold drinks sent out to them.'

'There is no need, Commander.'

'A good officer always puts his men first, Lieutenant. Surely they taught you that at Sandhurst?' he said as he turned and studied the young officer.

The Lieutenant looked at the impeccably dressed figure that stood framed by the window. The man had a natural air of authority - a tone that demanded respect. 'Yes, sir. That's correct,' he responded smartly, as if questioned by one of his old instructors.

'And anyway, Lieutenant. You are all my guests. And in my custom it is impolite for me not to offer you refreshments. Do you wish to offend me by refusing?'

'Of course not, Commander. Please excuse my ignorance of your customs. Of course you can give my men drinks.'

The Commander turned and walked away from the young officer towards the door, the Lieutenant unable to see the large smile on the old policeman's face. 'Sergeant, get the soldiers some cold drinks,' he barked out in English.

'Now, Lieutenant, how can I help you?' he said, sitting himself down behind his desk.

'As I said downstairs, sir, there was an attack on a PSC team in this area five days ago. According to the report, we have evidence suggesting that four were killed and two were taken prisoner.'

'I have already sent you a report on this incident, as was requested. Have you seen it?' asked the Commander.

'Yes, sir. I have read it. But it doesn't say a lot, sir.'

'I can only report what I know, Lieutenant. Would you prefer me to make things up?'

'No. Of course not, sir. It's just...'

179

'Just what, Lieutenant? What are you trying to say?'

'We have a report that the men who attacked the PSC were IPS.'

The Commander got up out of his chair and walked to the window. He watched in silence as his Sergeant gave out the ice-cold cans of drink to the soldiers, who, grateful for the opportunity to quench their thirsts, had stopped searching. He smiled again, and then composed himself for the next act.

'Are you saying that my men did this?' he shouted at the young officer. 'Well?' he demanded, as he walked back to the desk.

The young officer sat in silence, taken aback by the reaction, his mind racing as he searched for his next move.

'Look, Lieutenant. I understand that you are just carrying out your orders,' he said, his voice now calm, as he continued with his mind game. 'But you must see this accusation from my point of view. It is an affront to my men. We are in this together: the British, the Americans and the Iraqis. You have paid to train and equip my men. Do you think that I would repay you by killing security men?' He asked, his tone building in anger.

The officer listened. The young Englishman unable to control the sweat that ran from his face, down his neck, forming large damp patches on the chest of his mottled combat shirt. As he began to think through his next reply, he was interrupted once more.

'It is part of their plan,' the Commander said, sitting back in his chair, his role changing to that of the experienced older officer explaining to a young and naive subordinate how the world works. 'It's the insurgents. They dress up as policemen and commit these crimes. It's part of guerrilla warfare. Their objective is to destabilise - to create chaos. Surely you can see this, Lieutenant?' he asked, picking up a packet of Marlboros. 'They want you to think that it's the IPS. That way, they can drive a wedge between us. Smoke?'

'No thank you. Yes, I can see where you're coming from, Commander.

'Good. I'm glad that you can see the big picture. I can assure you that, if I found out that any of my men were involved...' he said as he lit up his cigarette, 'I would kill them myself.'

The conversation was interrupted by a knock at the door. 'Sir,' said the radio operator as he entered the office, 'I need a word.'

'Can you excuse me, Commander?' said the Lieutenant, getting up from his seat, thankful for the interruption. He made his way to the landing.

'The other call signs have searched the area where the attack supposedly took place. They've found nothing.'

'No burnt out vehicles?'

'Nothing, sir. Not even any empty cases from the bullets. They said it was as clean as a whistle.'

'Okay, Corporal. Tell the men to get ready. We're leaving.'

'I wish I could stay longer, Commander. But I have to leave,' the young officer said, as he walked back into the office and picked up his helmet.

'It has been a pleasure, Lieutenant. But it is unfortunate that we have to meet in such tragic circumstances,' said the Commander, as he escorted him out of the office and down the stairs.

'Have you searched the compound?' the young officer asked the Corporal as they reached the bottom step.

'We have checked everywhere, sir. Inside and out. We were just going to check the basement.

'The basement, Commander? How is that accessed?' asked the Lieutenant.

'Here is the basement,' the Commander said, walking over to a metal door. 'We have two cells down there, but they are both empty. Of course, you are welcome to take a look for yourself if you don't believe me?' he said, turning the handle and beginning to pull on the heavy door.

'No, no. That won't be necessary, Commander. But thank you, anyway,' said the young officer as he shook the

Commander's hand. 'Okay, Corporal, let's get this show on the road.'

The Commander accompanied the British soldiers out into the compound, maintaining his impressive act of bravado until the last vehicle had left and the gate had been secured. He turned his back on the dust-filled air, and walked back into the police station. As he walked past, he could see that the door to the basement was still ajar, just as he had left it.

'Sergeant,' he said, motioning his head towards the open door. The Sergeant followed his gaze, grabbed hold of the door and slammed it shut.

RAF Lyneham, UK,
09.32hrs, 18 May 2007.

The cold, damp Wiltshire air rushed into the hold of the C-130 Hercules as the tailgate of the RAF's trusty transport plane began to lower itself. The passengers, taking this as a signal that their journey had finished, rose en masse from their rudimentary aircraft seats, grateful for the opportunity to stretch their stiff, aching bodies. The flight had taken a total of eight hours, lengthened by a brief stop at RAF Akrotiri in Cyprus to refuel. But, from the smiles on the returning soldiers' faces, the long, uncomfortable flight home had clearly been worth every second.

Mason too tried to stretch off his sore limbs, but found the effort excruciatingly painful. Unlike his fellow travelling companions, he hadn't taken the opportunity to disembark in Cyprus. His body still held under the influence of the drugs; he'd happily dozed through the entire flight. But eight hours of continuous seating in cramped conditions had compounded the effect of his injuries, causing his body to seize. As he watched the crew secure the tailgate, the chilly air began to wrap around his battered body, making it convulse with uncontrollable shivers.

As he stooped to pick up his small bag, he focused his mind on trying to control his body's unwanted reaction to the cold. *Concentrate on the pain*, he said to himself as he stood up, knowing full well that the pain-sensing neurones in the human brain can identify only one type of discomfort at a time. As he shuffled down the aircraft ramp - his violent shivering decreasing with every step – he noticed a man in a grey suit standing at the end of the tailgate. His civilian attire making him the odd one out amongst the camouflaged members of the reception party.

This grey-suited man closed in on him as he reached the end of the tailgate. 'Mason?' he asked, his voice just audible over the noise of the four waning Allison turboprop engines. 'I've come to take you to London. Please follow me,' he said, taking off at a brisk pace. Mason followed him, his face expressionless, ignoring his body's tenderness, his bag in one hand and the walking stick in the other. As both men walked across the tarmac towards the waiting car parked on the edge of the airfield's apron, the grey suited man was unaware that his every move was been scrutinised by the ex-SAS Warrant Officer behind him - two paces back, one pace to the right.

As they neared the car, Mason spotted the action that he was looking for, the man's right arm momentarily hesitating on his right hip as they walked. He probably didn't realise that he was doing it, but it was something that Mason had been trained to look for. The man was carrying a pistol. There was no mistaking it, his right forearm unconsciously brushing against the pistol grip to ensure its presence.

There are very few organisations allowed to carry firearms in the UK, their carriage sanctioned only by the government, most commonly the police or the military. The man had a dark, suntanned face - evidence of long periods of time spent under sunshine stronger than that of the UK. And his smart, closely cropped black hair also suggested this guy was no copper; he was military. He was too neat and tidy to be Special Forces. By the process of elimination, there was only one option left: Military Intelligence.

The SAS used to be called upon to provide bodyguards for royalty and political dignitaries. But, as their worldwide counter-terrorism commitments grew, their close-protection responsibilities had been offloaded onto the Royal Military Police. The RMP had set up a close protection course at Longmore, which trained its bodyguards specifically for the job. The SAS were more than happy to step aside, as it allowed their men to avoid the tedious 'babysitting' responsibilities, and focus on the job they loved: soldiering. This grey suit was ex-RMP. He oozed it. Mason knew the type: the guy had done his full twenty two years of service, his background allowing him to take up a job with the security services or Military Intelligence to bolster his pension.

As the man opened the back door of the innocuous Ford saloon, Mason took the opportunity to pose the question that all ex-soldiers loved to ask each other. 'When did you get out, mate?'

'Last year,' Grey Suit answered.

'When did you do the Longmore course?' he continued, making himself comfortable in the back of the saloon car.

There was a long pause as the man looked at Mason in the rear view mirror. 'Ninety-Four,' he answered after a pause.

'Yeah. Thought I recognised you,' Mason lied, as he put his seat belt on. 'Oh, just one more thing. Be a love, and put the heater on. I'm fucking freezing.'

Battalion HQ, BAS, Iraq,
14.15hrs, 18 May 2007.

'Come straight in, Charles,' the Colonel said as the young officer approached the open door to his office. 'Thanks for coming at short notice.'

'Sorry about my appearance, sir,' the Lieutenant said as he tried to straighten his dusty uniform. 'But I was told it was urgent, so I came directly.'

'That's quite alright,' the Colonel said, offering his subordinate a chair. 'Look... I'm not one for breaking procedure, but I have been overruled on this one,' he continued, as he gestured towards the civilian sat in the corner of the room, his casual attire a stark contrast to the other uniformed visitors in the Battalion Commander's office. 'These gentlemen have insisted on a *hot debrief* on your patrol.'

'That's correct,' said the Intelligence Corps Major, as he and his assistant opened up their notebooks in anticipation for the questioning session. 'Can we first start with the location where the survivor alleged the attack took place?'

The Lieutenant looked at his questioners. It had been a long day - one that had started way before the sun up He'd taken his patrol deep into a hostile area. It was a mission that, even for the most battle-hardened of leaders, would have been difficult, and it had pushed his meagre experience to its very limit. That combined with the tension caused by being constantly alert, and the sapping summer heat, had taken its toll on him. He was exhausted, and was looking forward to a cold shower and an hour or two's sleep before putting pen to paper and write up his findings. No such luck. He now had to undergo interrogation, with his commanding officer listening to his every word, before he could relax. 'Do you think I could have a drink of water?' he said, as he gathered his thoughts.

'The callsign tasked with searching the contact area at grid... 8546 3452,' said the Lieutenant, looking into his note book, 'found nothing.'

'What do you mean by nothing?' asked the Major.

'Exactly that, sir... Nothing,' replied the Lieutenant.'

'What?... No empty cases?' asked the Major.

'Nothing, sir... There was no sign of hostile activity in

the area whatsoever... No sign of an attack taking place.'

'Did you search the police station?' continued the Major.

'Yes,' said the Lieutenant, trying to sound as alert as possible.

'Every room?'

The young officer paused. 'The entire compound: every room, every cell... from top to bottom. No hostages.'

'What about the police Commander. Was he there?'

'Yes, sir. I questioned him. I told him that we had had a report that the IPS had been involved in an attack.'

'And what did he say? How did he react?' probed the Major.

'He became very angry. He said that we were all in the fight together, and he told me that if he found out that any of his men had been involved that he would kill them himself.'

'And what was your opinion?' interrupted the man dressed in the tan chinos and the Ralph Lauren stripped shirt. 'Was he telling the truth?'

The Lieutenant drank the last of the water from the plastic bottle, as he reflected back on the immaculately dressed police Commander that he had met earlier that day.

'This is important,' prompted the man. 'I need your gut instinct. Do you believe him?'

'Yes, sir. I do.'

Target HQ, Belgrave Square, London,
11.24hrs, 18 May 2007.

There was no need to use the intercom outside Target Security HQ this time; his escort had phoned ahead. As he closed on the black door, it swung open. His entry encouraged by a gate to the left that exempted him of the rigmarole of the access control and security checks. Today, he was receiving the VIP treatment. Grey Suit led the way as they walked through the lobby area and up the stairs towards

JJ's office. Mason noticing the receptionist making a call as he swept past her, her eyes transfixed on the ex-SAS man's bruised face.

As they entered the office, Mason had a strong feeling of déjà vu. It was as if nothing had changed. The two men were in the same places as they were when he left, JJ in his power position behind the ornate desk, James at the window, looking out over the scene of Belgrave Square. As Mason entered, JJ rose from his staged position, while James, following the script, turned nonchalantly and peered down his nose at the visitor. 'Come on in, mate,' said JJ, rushing forward to greet him, grabbing Mason's hand. 'Come and sit down. You must be exhausted?' he said, ushering Mason towards a dark red Chesterfield. The sofa sat behind a coffee table adorned with an array of biscuits, ornate cups and a cafetiere full of coffee. Mason sat in the middle of the three seat sofa, the soft, deep buttoned upholstery forming around him, while JJ and James took up their positions on the two chairs opposite. With all three settled, JJ began pouring coffee, the delicate china cups seeming out of place in his large, rough hands.

As he had dozed in and out of sleep on the long flight, his every waking thought had been about what would happen during this meeting. He had already written the report that he would give to the Hostage Extraction team leader in his head; he just needed to get hold of some maps to confirm a few of the details. Keeping calm and professional, he mused, was the key to the whole thing. Clear concise answers were needed. Such answers would allow a plan to be developed to get the guys out. But he was also adding questions of his own to a growing list: why had he been pulled out so quickly, and why had he been met at the airport by an armed intelligence operative?

He wasn't in the mood for pleasantries. But he was thankful for the hot coffee that he swished around in his stale mouth.

'A wee toddy for your coffee?' suggested JJ as he picked

up a strategically placed bottle of whisky from the floor.

'Haven't touched a drop since London,' Mason replied, topping up his cup with more of the black steaming liquid, watching as the other two men exchanged a furtive glance.

Rebuffed, JJ quickly started the meeting. It was cordial enough, with Mason doing much of the talking. He ran through the whole sequence of events - up until his involvement with his rescuers, the Masahuin. He referred to them fleetingly, not disclosing surplus details, much as he had done with the military back in Basrah.

'So, let me get this right,' James asked, when Mason had finished. 'The only witness to Dusty and Thor being taken prisoner is the village Elder. Is that correct?'

'Yeah. That's correct,' Mason nodded. 'But why are you so concerned about that? We have a witness to say that these men are alive and have been taken by the IPS. That's all we need,' he answered, trying hard not to lose his temper.

'My dear boy,' replied James, his patronising tone in danger of pushing Mason over the edge. 'It's not that we are doubting you or the credibility of the witness. But we have to get the facts straight. After all, this is a hell of an accusation that you're making - the consequences of which could have far reaching ramifications. So the only witness has now disappeared?'

'Correct again,' answered Mason. 'I saw him taken by the IPS. Look, you guys do what you need to do,' he continued, his frustration building. 'I need to get back to Basrah. My guys want rescuing.'

'That's all in hand,' said JJ. 'Brit Mil sent a patrol out this morning. We should have the report later today'. During the whole time that Mason spoke, JJ didn't take his eyes off him. He studied his facial expressions, the movement of his hands, his body language. During their days in the SAS, they had spent a great deal of time together, each man relying on the other's judgment and professionalism, their lives dependant on the trust they placed in each other. There was no doubt in JJ's mind: he knew that Mason was telling the truth, however inconvenient that truth sounded to him. Dusty and Thor had indeed been taken prisoner.

'So, now what?' asked Mason.

'We wait,' JJ replied. 'The fact is that nothing is going to happen until tomorrow. So, go and get some rest. We have arranged for you to stay at the Victory Services Club.' He could see that Mason was unhappy with this answer. 'We have people working on this,' he continued, trying to calm the situation. 'As soon as we have got something, we will call you.'

This is not good, he thought to himself. Every soldier knows that the best time to escape his captivity is early on. The longer you leave it, the more chance the enemy has to organise; the harder it gets. He wanted to hear that all the stops were being pulled out to rescue his men; he wanted reassurance. But what he was hearing was making him angry - very angry.

'Take this,' JJ said, handing him a small cardboard box containing a mobile phone. 'It's charged. And all the numbers you need are in there.'

Mason stood up and took the box, looking first at JJ and then at the ex-Guards officer, who, still seated, had showed no emotion throughout the whole of Mason's rendition. He wanted to lash out. He wanted to hurt them – to let them feel pain like he had endured. But, as he breathed out, the anger subsided. *What about the other questions?* he said to himself, squeezing the box tighter and tighter, channelling his anger onto the flimsy cardboard. *Not now, they can wait. If I start, I might not be able to stop,* he said to himself as he left the office, the box becoming more and more distorted in his hands. By the time he got to the car, the box was virtually destroyed. He climbed into the back of the Ford.

'Where to?' asked Grey Suit.

'Victory Services Club,' replied Mason through clenched teeth.

'So, what do you think?' said James, re-filling his cup. 'I think he's messed up, and he's grabbing at straws to save his sorry neck,' he said, taking a sip. 'I mean - a village elder that was also taken by the same bunch that killed his men? You'd think he would have come up with a better story than that. But why involve the IPS? That's what I don't understand. It would have been a lot easier to say it was just a bunch of insurgents.'

JJ stood and walked towards his desk. He picked up the photo which stood in pride of place on his desk: a black and white picture of the bunch of bedraggled but victorious paratroopers on the slopes of Mount Longdon. He sat back in his chair.

'As I said to you yesterday, this is a very tricky time for Target. We need things to go as smoothly as possible. Two hostages being paraded around on TV in orange jumpsuits is going to go down like a lead balloon. The deal will be off in seconds,' continued James, picking up a bourbon biscuit. 'Mason is a drunk that can't take responsibility for his actions. Let's face it. He's been running away for the last six years. I reckon he just wants to cause as big a stink as possible by biting the hand that's fed him. That's gratitude for you.'

JJ could remember the bitter cold, the biting wind, the exhaustion, the hunger and thirst, and the pair of piercing steel blue eyes behind the gun pointed directly at his face.

'I mean, it's up to you. It's your call, at the end of the day,' added James. 'You know him better than I do. But, if you want my opinion, I think he's lying.'

JJ carefully put the picture back. 'You're right,' he said, as he eased his head back onto the rest. 'He's lying - lying through his teeth.'

CHAPTER SEVEN

IPS Station, Al Amarah, Iraq.

It was dark, but he knew where the noise was coming from. The mournful sob had been getting worse and worse over the last few days. Now it was stopping him from sleeping.

'You okay, mate?' said Thor, crawling towards the figure sat in the corner, legs tucked up to the chest. The man's head resting on arms that were themselves crossed tightly above a pair of knees that rocked back and forth slowly.

'We won't be here much longer. Another couple of days and they'll find us,' said Thor, placing himself alongside his comrade, putting his big arm across the other man's shoulders. 'Trust my bloody luck. I should have listened to my mother; she didn't want me to come out here. I only did it for the girlfriend. She's pregnant. Wanted to get a deposit together for a mortgage. Trust me... First bloody mission and all...'

Dusty stopped rocking and looked across at Thor. The small amount of moonlight able to penetrate the cell's meagre window reflecting in the tears welling in the man's eyes. 'I'm scared,' he whispered.

'It will be okay,' said Thor, pulling him in close. 'This lot can't go shooting up helicopters and get away with it. They're bound to find us before long. The whole of the British army must be looking for us.'

'Do you think so?'

'Absolutely, mate. They could turn up at any time,' Thor said, bringing his own knees up to his chest, copying his cellmate. 'It could be worse, though; you could be like that poor sod next door. John... John... You awake?'

Both men listened for the reply. There was none, just

erratic breathing. 'I reckon he's on his way out; he's hardly moved all day,' Thor said, as he stretched his legs out slowly.

'They beat him up pretty bad.'

'Hey, but tell me something,' Thor said, as he huddled in close to his comrade for warmth. 'I thought you SAS guys are used to all this stuff: interrogation, escape, evasion and all that. I watch all the programmes on the History Channel; love all that Special Forces stuff.'

'I lied. I never got in. Did a few years in the RAR, went on selection and failed,' Dusty said, looking at the floor.

'Yeah? Well... it doesn't make any difference now,' Thor said as he pulled on the man's shoulders.

'If I hadn't stopped to fix the puncture, do you think we might have made it?'

'Dunno, mate. Mason is the only one that could answer that, I suppose.'

'Do you think they will kill us?'

'Nah. We're going to get saved, mate. If Brit Mil don't come for us, Mason will. He's a mean old bastard. Scares the shit out of me.'

Victory Services Club, London,
14.37hrs, 18 May 2007.

The Victory Services Club was down a side street at the expensive end of the Edgware Road. It was a hotel designed to provide cheap board and lodging for serving and former members of the armed forces who were passing through the capital. It had been a few years since Mason had last visited, during which time the building had undergone a major refit. As Grey Suit filled out the paperwork, Mason familiarised himself with the new decor.

The most striking addition, in pride of place over the fireplace in the bar, was a magnificent painting of an officer on horseback. 'Bloody marvellous, isn't it?' came a gruff voice from behind him, as Mason stood admiring the portrait.

'It is at that,' replied Mason, turning to see a short, plump man with a bright red nose and a beaming smile cradling a half empty pint of beer.

'Field Marshall Allenby at Jerusalem on the eve of the battle,' continued the tipsy guest. 'It was only the second time in history that a Christian army had taken the city, the other time being during the First Crusade. You know, he got off his horse as a mark of respect and walked through the gates of the city on foot? What a gentleman.'

'Thanks for the history lesson,' Mason said, and headed back to the reception desk to see if his room was ready.

'You're in room 603. Here's the key,' said Grey Suit, dropping a plastic card in his hand. 'We'll be back tomorrow to pick you up.' Mason put the key on the reception desk and watched as the man left through the main entrance and got straight into the parked Ford.

'Is there something I can help you with?' asked the receptionist.

'Yes, please. Can I use the Internet?'

Mason entered 'M A S A H U I N' into the search engine and waited for the results to load. 'Holidays in Florida'. *How the hell did it come up with that?* he thought as he clicked on the link to the second page. 'Car insurance, pet insurance, waste of bloody time,' he said aloud, irritably clicking on the third page. Something caught his attention: 'Masahuin. Cornelius Gregory, All Saints College, Oxford'. *That looks interesting*, he thought as he clicked on the link.

His kit bag, which he had placed at his feet, began to make an unusual sound. He opened the zip and discovered that the crumpled box was ringing. He tried to prise the phone out of its damaged packaging. But he had made such a good job of crushing it that it did not give up its contents easily. By the time the device was free, it had stopped ringing. He put it on the desk and went back to reading the web page.

The phone vibrated into life once more. He picked it up and opened the message: 'Meeting tomorrow, pick up at 1400hrs'. Mason pressed 'Reply' and typed in 'Roger' before hitting 'Send'. As he went to put the phone down, he hesitated. He typed in 118118 and pressed the *green telephone*. 'What number would you like?' replied the voice at the other end.

'All Saints College, Oxford, please.'

His exhaustion had initially dragged him into a deep sleep. But he had awoken at 3am, his mind overactive and unsettled. He had simply watched the clock after that. Just before 6am, he had got out of bed and pre-emptively turned off the alarm clock, grateful for the end of another long, searching, mournful night without rest, glad to see the early morning rays creeping through the curtains, lighting up the room.

He drew back the drapes and looked out from his sixth floor room over the rooftops, their surfaces glistening with the rain that had fallen overnight. As he stood admiring this view of West London, he let his mind wander to the previous times he had visited the city. He had brought his girls down for weekend trips whenever he could. The last time, it had been to see 'The Lion King' musical in the West End. Isabella had been so excited that she'd not slept the night before and had dressed up as Simba for weeks afterwards, running around the house pretending to be a lion cub. He rubbed his face to erase the memory, and limped to the bathroom.

He looked at his face in the mirror for the first time since the attack. The scabs on the cuts and grazes were beginning to fall off, and the swelling around his eyes was subsiding, the dark bruising turning to a more subtle yellow as his body healed itself. *You look like shit,* he thought to himself, turning on the hot tap and starting to lather up the soap.

The small bathroom quickly filled with steam, the mirror above the sink clouding over with a film of condensation. As he watched his features gradually blurring, his mental process too seemed to lose its clarity, a wave of sadness suddenly flooding through him. It left him feeling empty. He had felt like this a thousand times since the accident. The feelings had temporarily subsided during his time in Iraq, when he was intently focussed on the job at hand. But it was these dark lonely times - when there were no distractions – that he found the hardest. His tried-and-tested solution for the last six years had been to reach for a bottle and drink until the pain faded into the background.

The voice inside his head began to talk to him. *It's easy,* it whispered. *All you have to do is go and find an off-licence. You could be back in this room in twenty minutes. And in thirty, your mind and body could be numb. You can drink to your heart's content. Take away the pain.*

'But who would help Thor, Dusty and Rachel?' he asked himself as he took his towel and wiped the moisture from the mirror, his battered and bruised face coming into focus once more. 'Do you want to help them?' he asked himself. He knew what the answer was. He knew that he could not trust anyone else to find them - not JJ, not Tonka, not Brit Mil. He was the only person who could save them now, and he couldn't do it from the inside of a bottle. *Better get cleaned up,* he thought, as he spread the lather on his beard and picked up his razor. *Can't go around looking like a tramp, can I?*

The cleaners were busy in the lobby as Mason exited the lift, skirting around the freshly cleaned floors as he made his way to the reception desk. 'Morning,' said the young receptionist in a thick Eastern European accent as he approached. 'Can I help you?'

'Do you have a piece of paper?' asked Mason.

195

'Yes. Of course,' replied the receptionist. 'Would you like a pen also?'

'No, thanks,' answered Mason, as he took hold of the sheet of paper. 'This will do just fine.' He stepped out into the street, stopping directly in front of the hotel entrance while he examined the blank sheet of paper, before folding it neatly and putting it into his pocket. He then turned right and set off at a very slow pace towards the Edgware Road, his walking stick tapping on the damp pavement.

At the pedestrian crossing, he stopped. Traffic was light and he could have easily made a dash for it. But that wasn't in his plan. Instead, he pressed the 'pedestrian' button, and waited for the signal to change. As he waited, he took the blank piece of paper out of his pocket, glanced at it once more, crumpled it up into a ball and, just as the light changed to green, threw it on the ground.

The coffee shop on the corner had only just opened, and was beginning to fill with people needing their first caffeine fix of the day. Mason didn't join the queue, but instead went straight to the large shop window that looked out onto the Edgware Road. He sat on one of the stools and looked closely at the progress of his piece of paper - which was still lying on the pavement opposite. He watched as a man dressed in blue jeans and a brown leather jacket approached the pedestrian crossing. As the man waited for the signal to change, he stooped down, picked up the paper and put it into his pocket. The signal changed. But, instead of crossing, he turned around and went back down the street towards the hotel. *What a fucking amateur*, Mason thought as the man disappeared out of sight. *JJ wants to get some better surveillance operators; that guy fell for the oldest trick in the book.*

He had the coffee to go, and crossed back over the road, retracing his steps to the hotel. 'Can I help you, sir?' asked the receptionist once again as Mason put his coffee down on the counter.

'Hopefully,' replied Mason. 'Look, I'm staying in 603. I

am completely jet lagged... Been travelling for days. I'm going to go back to bed, and don't want to be disturbed if at all possible. Is there any chance you can keep the housekeeping staff away? I could really do with a few more hours' sleep.'

'Of course, sir. I will let them know.'

'Thanks. You're a star,' Mason said with a smile, as he headed for the lift. Once inside, he pressed the button for the first and sixth floors. When it stopped at the first floor, he got out and headed straight for the staircase, following it down to the basement, checking for CCTV cameras as he went. He was lucky; there were none. In the basement, he found what he was looking for. 'For Emergency Use Only' read the sign above the exit. The door opened out into the street at the back of the hotel.

The back of the hotel was deserted. The naked streets a difficult area for surveillance operators. He picked up his pace, and headed west through the side streets, performing a series of anti-surveillance drills as he went. Satisfied that there was no one on his tail, he headed for his destination.

Paddington Station was busy, the platforms full of commuters disgorged from their transports. Mason watched their faces as he weaved his way through the densely packed throng, some still half asleep as they were carried along. He had no need to look at the information signs. He knew exactly where he was going. The plan of the station - from many counter-terror exercises - was imprinted on his brain. His target was the ticket office against the left wall of the iconic building, the electronic door closing behind him as he entered, the noise of the maelstrom of the station momentarily extinguished.

'Can I help you?' the man with a light blue turban said from behind the thick glass.

'Return ticket to Oxford, please.'

All Saints College, Oxford,
09.55hrs, 18 May 2007.

'Hello, Professor. It's Bill from the porter's lodge. I have a man here that says he has an appointment with you. His name is Mason.'

'Yes. That's right, Bill,' replied the Professor. 'I'll be right there.'

The Professor lived on the top floor of the main building of Chapel Quad, the grander of the three quadrangles around which the college buildings were laid out. It was so named because of the small eighteenth century chapel that sat in the north-west corner. His accommodation consisted of a bedroom, study and a bathroom - all very small but very homely. Most of the other college fellows took lodgings outside the college. But Cornelius chose to live in, convenient for the committed bachelor. His washing and ironing were done for him by his *scout*, and his meals - which he ate in the dining hall on the Master's Table, dressed, as custom dictated, in his black flowing gown - were all prepared for him by the college kitchen staff.

As he entered Chapel Quad, he was always amazed at how tranquil the college was, today being no different. The noise of the busy city outside never seemed to permeate through the institute's seventeenth century limestone walls, leaving the college like an oasis, an academic Xanadu, hidden away from the modern world. It was a perfect environment in which to pursue serious academic work. It was term time. The college was full of eager undergraduates, and yet the quad was practically deserted at this moment - except for a handful of students who sat on the lawns, in the shadow cast by the tall, grand buildings, fully absorbed by the weighty tomes they were reading, or looking earnestly through reams of handwritten notes. The rest of the students, Cornelius assumed, would either be in the college library or in their rooms, working on their numerous assignments.

One of the devices used to keep the outside world at bay

198

was an ancient iron-bound gate at the main entrance of the college, which would have looked at home at the end of any castle drawbridge. Behind the gate was an archway that housed the porter's lodge. Mason had signed the visitor's book and passed through the lodge into the college's oldest quad, where he now stood in the centre of the lawn, looking up at the buildings that surrounded him.

He heard footfall on the cobblestones and turned around to see a scholarly-looking man in his mid-thirties, with pale skin and a mass of unkempt hair, running towards him. The man looked horrified, and was shouting something at Mason, which he could not quite make out. 'Get off the grass! Get off the grass!' he now heard, as the animated Professor approached him. Mason was caught off-guard. He limped off the lawn as quickly as he could and stood on the paved path that circled the lawn, and watched as the man closed in on him.

'Mr. Mason?' the man said, panting as he offered his hand.

'It's just Mason,' he replied, warily, as they greeted each other.

'Ah, very good. I'm Professor Cornelius Gregory. Sorry if I scared you just now, old boy. It's just that no one is allowed to walk on the lawn of the Old Quad. There are fifteenth century monks buried underneath it, you see. The entire lawn is basically a grave. Respect for the dead and all that,' the Professor said with a smile.

Listen, I don't have a lot of time,' continued the Professor, looking suspiciously at Mason's bruised face. 'I have a plane to catch and a meeting with the Dean in, uh...'. He checked his watch 'thirty minutes.'

'Thanks for seeing me at such short notice,' replied Mason. 'Thirty minutes is fine. I won't take up too much of your time. I have to be back in London for 2pm myself.'

'Please follow me,' said the Professor, ushering Mason down the cobbled archway. 'We can talk in my office.' He stopped momentarily and looked down at the walking stick that Mason was leaning on. 'Are you alright to walk?' he asked.

'I'm fine, Professor,' Mason answered.

The archway opened up into a quadrangle, with light-brown limestone buildings on all four sides, looking down onto another perfectly manicured lawn. 'This is the Middle Quad,' remarked the Professor as they walked in the shade of the buildings. 'All of the old colleges in Oxford are built around quadrangles - we call them *quads*' he continued. A worried-looking student, wearing a black suit with a white bow-tie, ran past them, his gown trailing behind him, blowing in the wind. 'Morning, Professor,' he shouted, without checking his pace. Mason noticed that the young student had a red flower pinned to the lapel of his suit jacket.

'He's on his way to an exam,' the Professor explained to Mason. 'His final exam, by the look of things. The students have a tradition of wearing a red carnation for their last exam, you see'.

'I thought the students only dressed like that for their graduation ceremony after they'd completed their degree?' said Mason.

'No, no. This is Oxford, old boy. We have traditions. When taking their exams, the students have to wear their suits and gowns - or *subfusc*, as we call it. If they don't, they are barred entry to the examination halls and are fined. When in the examination halls, if they are postgraduate students who already have their degree, they have to wear their mortar-board caps as well. But if they are caught wearing their cap *before* they've graduated, they also get fined.'

'Sounds a bit like the army.'

'What kind of work are you in?' asked the Professor as they passed through the archway that led to Chapel Quad. Mason hesitated, momentarily breathless at the beauty of the scene as the quad opened up before them. At the far end of the lawn, behind a neat row of shrubs and bushes, the magnificent nineteenth century hall was illuminated by the early morning sunshine, the colours on its large stained-glass windows vibrant with the sun's rays.

'Security,' Mason answered, once he had caught his breath. 'Professor, this is incredible!' he exclaimed, as he continued to gaze.

Cornelius puffed out his chest at Mason's reaction. 'Isn't it?' he agreed. 'This is widely considered to be the most beautiful quad in all of Oxford.' He looked over at Mason once more. 'Security in Iraq?' he asked.

'Yes. Iraq,' replied Mason, as he rubbed his jaw. 'I was involved in a car wreck there a few days ago.'

'Ah, I see,' said the Professor, satisfied at the explanation for Mason's appearance. Relieved this man was not simply a ruffian, as he had initially feared.

The Professor stopped outside an old, weathered, wooden door with ornate metal hinges. 'This is my office,' he said, as he opened the antique portal. 'Mind your head.' Mason stepped through, ducking as he did so, avoiding the low-hanging antique beam of the doorframe, which had no doubt claimed many academic foreheads over the past centuries.

The Professor's office was small, with just one door and one window. However, the size of the latter easily made up for the lack of numbers; the large bay window with its checkerboard of small lead frames, stretched almost from floor to ceiling, providing inspiring views of the Chapel Quad from the Professor's desk, which had been placed right in front of it. Even though every inch of wall-space was covered with shelves jam-packed with books of every size and colour, there was still insufficient room, the surfeit of papers spilling into piles on the floor, leaving just enough space for the two men to walk. The wall visible to the right as they entered had a magnificent old fireplace that had been blackened by an incalculable number of heart-warming fires during cold winter evenings. On either side of the hearth, facing each other, was a pair of battered old armchairs.

'Professor, since neither of us has a great deal of time, I would like to get straight to the point,' said Mason, as both men sat. 'I have just come back from Iraq, where I met some very interesting people. They call themselves the Masahuin. I put that into a search engine yesterday. And your name came up.'

'I see,' said the Professor. 'Was this after your car crash?'

'Yes,' answered Mason. 'They helped me.'

The professor sat back in his chair and crossed his legs. 'I see. So you've actually met the Masahuin, Mr Mason - ah, sorry, Mason? They are a tribe that live in the marshes north of Basrah. But that much you know,' he said, adjusting himself to a more comfortable position.

'Yes. And they are Christian, right?' added Mason.

'I'm not sure about that, but my studies would indicate that they're certainly not Muslims. I've been researching them for a numbers of years you see. One of the questions I'm trying to answer is why this group of Marsh Arabs is different to the other Ma'dan, when they live in a part of the world that is otherwise almost exclusively Muslim. We have only been aware of their existence since the First World War. Gertrude Bell - one of the architects of modern Iraq - mentions them in her diaries, as does T E Lawrence - Lawrence of Arabia, that is - but there has been remarkably little contact with them, on the whole. They appear to be an incredibly insular tribe, shunning all outside contact, even with other tribes in the marshes. And, of course, when you take into account the remote and impenetrable nature of the marshes, and the great deal of political instability within Iraq in recent years, it's no wonder there's been so little contact with them. The last reported contact was in 1942.'

'You can add 2007 to your list,' said Mason. 'I met them last week, and I can confirm they are very much alive.' Mason sat forward in his chair. 'Professor, I understand that you are the leading expert on the Marsh Arab tribes. Why do you think that the Masahuin don't follow Islam?'

Cornelius looked deep in thought as he considered Mason's question. 'What's your theory, Professor?' Mason prompted.

'My theory? My theory... is controversial,' said the

Professor as he sat back in his chair, churching his fingers, pausing as he marshalled his thoughts. 'It starts with a parchment that was found in the sarcophagus of Saladin in Damascus in 1894. As you may be aware, Saladin was the man who led the Muslim opposition to the European Crusaders. The parchment was found as a result of a visit to the region by the Archduke Franz Ferdinand of Austria, who, in the process of having Saladin's remains placed into a newer casket, found a parchment in Saladin's shroud. Now, this is where it gets interesting,' he said, sitting forward. 'You see, according to Islam, when a Muslim dies, he must go to meet Allah bereft of any belongings. So this parchment must have been immensely important to Saladin for him to have been prepared to break this rule.'

'Where is this parchment now?' asked Mason.

'Alas, it disappeared shortly after it was found,' continued the Professor. 'The courier taking it to the Arch Duke was robbed in the street and killed.'

'A cover up?' asked Mason.

'Possibly... No one will ever know,' said the Professor. 'But, luckily, they made a transcript from the original before it went missing.'

'What did it say?'

The Professor picked up a well-used book from his desk and, using a colourful marker as reference, opened it at the desired page. 'Here you are,' he said, offering the book to Mason.

Mason began to read. After a few minutes he looked up. 'Sounds like a confession.'

Cornelius smiled. 'It certainly does!' he agreed. 'Let's remember that Saladin was an excellent yet ruthless general, who mercilessly killed thousands of the invading Crusaders. He does not seem like a man who would confess wrongdoing easily. So this confession must refer to an act he committed that he must have regretted immensely. What do you know of the Crusades, Mason?' he asked, probing his new student.

'I know that there were many of them, and that they were

203

launched from Western Europe, intended to restore Christian access to the holy places in and around Jerusalem. Jerusalem itself, however, has been taken only twice in its history: once during the First Crusade and once more by General... Allenby, I think, during the First World War,' he answered, thankful for the brief history lesson he had received the day before at the Victory Services Club.

'That's correct,' the Professor said. 'The Crusades were a series of Papacy-sanctioned military campaigns undertaken for a mixture of religious, economic and political reasons. We count nine, but there are a few more, the after-effects of which we are still feeling today. They lasted for over two hundred years, with most scholars agreeing that they ended in 1291. Your history seems to be in good shape,' he continued, changing his posture. 'How is your geography?'

'It's a few years since it's been put to the test,' quipped Mason.

'Do you know where Acre is?'

When he was 'in the job', he would have been able to run off the longitude and latitude, population demographics, routes in and out, cargos and even the maximum draft of ships able to enter the strategically important Mediterranean port. Now he was just happy to settle for the basics. 'Israel.'

'Correct again,' said the Professor, pleased at Mason's response. 'There is an interesting story of a knight who was at the fall of Acre during the Third Crusade. The Third, apart from the First of course, is probably the most famous of the numerous Crusades - because of the involvement of Richard I, Coeur de Lion. But he wasn't the only king involved,' he said, adjusting his glasses. 'Leopold V of Austria and Phillip II of France also participated. Our knight was working at the behest of the French King. On the morning of the fall of the city, he was ordered to take a small group of trusted men and rush to the city's treasury, in order to secure it from looters. The story goes that, when the knight got to the treasury, he found that all the gold and silver had already been taken. However, in a chest that contained fragments of the True

Cross - the holy relic taken by Saladin when he defeated the Crusader army at the battle of Hattin - the knight found evidence of a treasure that was far more valuable to the Crusaders than gold or silver. The treasure in question had been hidden in the ancient city of Palmyra, which is in the desert, north-east of Damascus, in modern day Syria.'

Mason sat forward in his chair, enthralled by the story. 'Please, Professor, go on,' he said.

'Well, Coeur de Lion was more interested in Jerusalem and was not as prepared to divide his forces, as was Leopold. But Philip sent a small force north-east under command of this trusted knight, to look for the secret treasure. When Saladin's spies informed him of the quest, he too sent a party of Saracens to stop the knights from taking the treasure - or to destroy it rather than let it fall into their hands. The knights never returned, and we don't know what happened to the Saracens.'

'So that's where the Saladin parchment comes into it?' Mason interrupted, his excitement getting the better of him. 'He thought that the treasure had been destroyed.'

'Yes. That is my theory,' replied the Professor, his eyes burning with passion. 'Whatever it was that Saladin ordered destroyed clearly had a great significance to both the Crusaders and to him. His decision to destroy it rather than let the Crusaders capture it clearly haunted him to his grave. But the story doesn't end there,' he said, tantalisingly, as he sat forward in his chair once more. 'According to a chronicle written by Ernoul, a historian active at the time of the Third Crusade, one of the knights escaped the battle with Saladin's men and fled to the east with a great prize, but was never heard of again.'

'So he would have fled into what is now Iraq?' asked Mason.

'Precisely. The knight went into Iraq and down the Euphrates. My theory is that it was he who was responsible for creating the enclave that exists in the marshes to this day.'

'Did the chronicle mention the name of the knight?'

'Unfortunately not. But, through my research, I have narrowed it down to three possibles.'

'Does Sir John de Guise sound familiar?' asked Mason.

The Professor sat motionless as he absorbed the sound of this name. 'What did you just say?'

'Sir John de Guise? Is he on your list?'

'He's not only on it,' replied the Professor, his actions becoming more animated as Mason's comment continued to sink in. 'He's at the top of it. But how do you know his name? My list has never been published.'

'The Masahuin saved my life,' answered Mason. 'They rescued me and took me back to their village. In the village was a church made of reeds. I managed to sneak inside, and I saw for myself a medieval knight's shield and sword. It was kept on the altar.'

The professor jumped out of his seat as though someone had just poured boiling water on him.

'You saw his shield? You saw his sword... Sir John's?'

'It didn't have his name on it. But I'm assuming it was his. After all, there couldn't have been that many medieval knights knocking around in the backwaters of Iraq,' said Mason with a grin.

The Professor sat speechless, absorbing the significance of what Mason had just told him. His eyes had a faraway stare as he stood up and walked over to his desk, grabbing its corner to steady himself.

'Oh. There was one more the thing you should know,' Mason said, still smiling. 'The village Elder's name was also John. He was six foot tall, fair skinned, with blue eyes. Might he be a direct descendant of your knight?'

The Professor's legs gave way and he collapsed into his desk chair. 'You don't understand what this means to me,' he said, his voice shaking with emotion. 'I have been ridiculed by my peers about my theory. I have been made a laughing stock amongst Arabist scholars; I've been a man with a theory but no evidence to back it up, and now... and now, you walk into my office and tell me that I have been right all along.'

'It appears so,' Mason said, as he stood up and walked over to the Professor, handing him the walking stick that he had been carrying all morning. 'They gave me this when I was injured. It has some very interesting carvings on it.'

The Professor took hold of the stick, his gentle touch like that of a mother picking up a newborn baby, and stared in wonder at the intricate carvings along its length. 'The sword,' he said, pointing in amazement, 'and the shield.'

The Professor's perfect moment was interrupted by a loud knock on the door. And, before the stunned academic could react, it burst open. 'I say, Professor' said the small man who stood in the doorframe. 'The Dean is waiting. This isn't on, old man.' The Professor looked at his watch. He'd been so carried away that he had forgotten about his appointment. 'Look, Mason. I have to go,' he said, getting up from his chair. 'I have to see the Dean. But I have to talk to you more about this,' he said, looking at the ancient wooden staff. 'There's one more part of my theory that I haven't told you - and it's the most important.'

'Does it have anything to do with a stone box?' asked Mason.

'You've seen it. You've seen it! I was right!' shouted the Professor as he started to dance around the room.

'Professor!' exclaimed the man in the doorway. 'This behaviour is most unacceptable. The Dean is waiting. He will see you NOW!' he shouted, before turning and storming off.

Mason and the Professor stepped outside the office onto the college quad. 'Please wait. I need to talk to you. So much depends on this,' the Professor pleaded.

'Look I have to catch a train,' Mason said, looking at his watch. 'I'd love to stay and talk more, but I can't miss this meeting. My train is in an hour. Do you know the cafe opposite the train station?'

'Yes. I know it,' answered the excited academic.

'I'll be there.'

'Splendid. I will be as quick as I can. Please forgive me for not showing you out,' said the Professor as he marched off across the quad in the direction of the Dean's office.

'Oh, and Professor,' Mason called after him, holding out his hand. 'The walking stick?'

'Ah, yes. How silly of me,' the Professor replied, returning the stick to Mason. 'As quick as I can...'

CHAPTER EIGHT

The Siege of Acre, The Holy Land,
July, 1191.

It was night, but the heat still remained, the parched soil and rocks continuing to radiate what they had stored from the fierce July sun. The soldiers' only respite from the heat, the cooling breeze that blew in from the Mediterranean. They were exhausted, their bodies drained by the relenting sun that beat down through cloudless skies and endless days of toil that had brought them to this point. But spirits were high. Tomorrow would mark the culmination of their two years of hard work and meticulous planning; tomorrow would be the day of the battle to bring about the fall of Acre. Their King, Philip II, provided for them well that evening; each man received a hearty supper of chicken, lentils and olives, washed down with the last of their supply of wine. All knew that, for some, this would be their last meal. But there was probably not a single man in the whole camp who believed this would apply to him. For those men who survived tomorrow's battle, however, the plundering of the rich Ayyubid port would bring great wealth.

The six men sat around one of the camp's innumerable fires, digesting their meal and finishing off the last mouthfuls of wine from their heavy earthen flasks. When they had left their homes in Northern France two years earlier, the crowd around their camp fire had been much bigger - so much bigger that the men had had to jostle to get near the flames. But the long, treacherous journey and fierce battles of the intervening years had taken their toll; now there were just six remaining from a company of fifty.

'I am going to buy myself an inn,' boasted Christopher,

who was laid out on his blanket, pouring the last of the wine into his open mouth. 'And I will have a different wench for each day of the week.'

'Will they be big?' jibed Peter, as he sucked the last piece of meat off a chicken bone, before tossing it casually into the fire.

'Aye. The bigger the better. You need something to hold onto,' replied Christopher, to the delight of the gang, who erupted with hearty laughter.

Their merriment was cut short as three men approached the fire, their heavy swords clanking against the chain mail as they strode towards the open hearth. They searched the flame-lit faces, looking for the man they had come to find. On recognising him, they closed in.

'Sir John,' said the leader of the trio. 'The King requires you at his tent.'

'Tell him I will come soon,' replied the knight. 'But, pray, let me digest my food first.'

'No, sir. He has requested you come immediately. You are to follow us.'

The knight rose wearily to his feet and picked up his sword, fastening the belt around his waist. 'You must tell me of the rest when I return, Christopher,' he said with a smile, before turning his back on the amber flames and following his escort into the darkness.

'Yes, John. Hurry back, and I shall tell you of my fat wenches,' he heard Christopher call after him as he left the light of the fire behind. There was another wave of deep laughter from the men.

As they made their way through the camp, towards the King's tent, Sir John looked in wonder at the countless camp fires that were spread out on the plateau in front of them for as far as the eye could see.

'It is a magnificent sight, Sir John, is it not?' asked the Captain as they walked.

'Aye, Captain, it is that,' replied the knight. 'I think there are as many camp fires as there are stars in the sky.'

'Nothing can stop us now. We will sweep them away tomorrow,' said the Captain.

'I am certain we will...'

As they walked, they saw on either side of them scenes similar to that which Sir John had just left behind: bands of men relaxing around fires, talking excitedly about what the morrow would bring, and what they would do with their newly won wealth. The friendships around each campfire had been formed long before the Crusade had begun. In most cases, men from the same village had joined the enterprise together, at the behest of their local lord. These friendships had been strengthened, and many more forged, by the hardships the men had endured together.

'They say you have been with the Crusade since the beginning. Is that right, Sir John?' asked the Captain.

'Aye, that is so,' replied the knight. 'For two years now, I have fought for the King, and I have served him in fiefdom for over ten. But tomorrow, when the city finally falls, I will be free of my vow.'

'Will you take land here, Sir John?'

'No. I will return to France. I have had enough of this country. My wish is to return home and, God willing, it will happen soon.'

As they approached the large tent, the Captain announced their names and their business to the two sentries blocking the entrance. Satisfied, the two guards stood aside, and the Captain pulled open the flap on the tent's entrance, allowing the light from within to spill out into the darkness. 'Good luck on the morrow, Sir John,' said the Captain, holding back the flap for the blond-haired knight to enter alone.

'And you, Captain,' replied the knight.

'I hope you get your wish.'

Sir John hesitated and grasped the man's hand. 'I hope so, Captain. I hope that tomorrow we all get our wishes,' he said as the flap fell closed.

'Ah, Sir John de Guise,' said the man that was sitting at the head of the long wooden table, facing the entrance to the tent. 'Please join us.'

'Thank you, Sire,' replied the knight as he entered further into the canvas enclave.

The tent was lit by several candelabras, the flames of which flickered and swayed as they were buffeted by the hot wind of the Holy Land, causing shadows to dance on the fabric walls of the tent. Around the table, scattered like the remnants of their feast, sat the commanders of tomorrow's battle. As he approached, the men stood in turn to greet him - Guy de Lusignan, Gerald de Ridefort and Robert de Sable - men who had trod a bloody path through countless skirmishes since departing France two years earlier. On the opposite side of the long table sat two men who, because of their recent arrival at the Crusade, he had not met properly. The rank and status of the nobleman evident from the men at arms that flanked each one, their escutcheons proudly displayed, resplendent even in the subdued light. They were Leopold of Austria and Richard of England. 'My lord,' John said to each monarch in turn as he passed. At the end of the table stood the man that had summoned him: Philip Augustus, the King of France.

Philip was slightly shorter than John although both men shared a similar physique, honed by the constant *tourney du combat,* the chivalrous mock-fights that were commonplace at the King's court. The men were of similar age, with the main difference between them being the King's brown hair which, cut short for the campaign, contrasted with John's thick yellow mane.

'My lords,' said Philip, grasping the knight's forearm, 'you all know Sir John. He has served me for more than ten years now, standing by my side in battle, ever faithful and never once to be found wanting. He is an ancestor of Charlemagne. Isn't that right, Sir John?' he asked.

'Yes, Sire. On my father's side,' replied the knight.

To all the men present, Sir John's illustrious lineage was evident in the man's appearance and demeanour. The knight was tall, towering above most of his comrades by easily a head or more. His skin was fair, but had browned from the years under the eastern sun, causing his piercing, blue eyes to stand out even more vividly. At twenty-seven, he had about him an air of authority which normally came with age, but which to him was innate. 'Who better than this to lead the attack on Acre,' continued the King, holding up Sir John's hand like an arbiter announcing a fighter's victory. The group cheered and clapped in excited agreement.

'Now you know the reason why I sent for you,' the King said, as he placed his hand on the knight's shoulder. 'In my eyes, there is no man that has earned this honour more than you,' he whispered into his ear.

Sir John watched as the men around the table picked up their goblets and toasted him cheerfully. 'My lords,' he responded when they had settled, 'I would like to thank my Liege Lord for bestowing this great honour upon me. I will try my utmost to live up to his expectations, and not let him down.'

'Nonsense,' said Philip. 'The city is ours for the taking. You have never let me down, and nor will you start on the morrow.' The King fell back into his chair, the half empty goblet of wine he was holding in his left hand tipping over his surcoat, the leather jacket reaching to his knees, emblazoned with his coat of arms of a Target of azure blue strewn with golden lilies, unbuttoned against the warm night.

Richard, displaying his normal terseness, had been silent up to this point. Content to observe the Commander of the army's vanguard for the impending attack from a distance. He was the only one of the assembled noblemen who was dressed in armour. His hauberk - the shirt of chain-mail that reached down to his knees - was, like his sword, always on his person. Finishing his wine, he stood and advanced towards the knight. His armour, beneath the crimson tabard decorated with the three Plantagenet lions, hissing, as his athletic frame quickly closed the short distance.

'I think you have chosen well, my brother,' Richard said to Philip as he stood, hands on hips, appreciating the appearance of the warrior, before slapping John heartily on the back, much to the enjoyment of the well-oiled guests.

'What is the plan, Sire?' asked Sir John.

'Ahh, the plan... Yes. We must talk of the plan,' replied Philip. He looked to his right, extended his hand and beckoned for someone to come forth from the shadows. 'You must meet Ashott. He is the plan.'

Oxford, UK,
11.27hrs, 18 May 2007.

The coffee shop was empty. Mason ordered a double macchiato and took a newspaper from the rack and sat down on a table that allowed him to watch the café entrance. He propped the walking stick up against the wall, took a sip of his coffee and unfolded the paper.

'Ex-SAS Man Responsible for Death of Security Team in Iraq' was the headline on the opening page. He read the heading slowly, underlining each word with his index finger before moving onto the main text. 'An ex-SAS soldier, who had been thrown out of the elite regiment because of alcoholism, took his security team into a very dangerous area in Southern Iraq, showing no regard for their safety. A Target Security spokesperson said that the team was ambushed by local insurgents, resulting in the death of six members of the team. The ex-Sergeant Major himself had returned to the British Base in Basrah unharmed...'

The sensation was as if he'd been kicked in the chest. The pain instantly spread through his body. As he read the article again his breath quickened. The full burden of this small block of neatly-cast words had landed on him like a lead weight, almost paralysing him.

'JJ... You bastard!' he shouted, pounding his clenched fist on the wooden table. He shot up, knocking his chair over, and ran out of the coffee shop towards the taxi rank outside the station. 'How much to London?' he asked the driver of the first cab in the line.

'It's going to be a ton, easy, mate. Maybe more,' the driver replied with a smile.

'Have you seen a man with some bruises on his face?' the Professor asked the girl behind the counter as he scanned the empty cafe. 'I was supposed to meet him here.'

'There was a man here a few minutes ago. He had... like...black eyes.'

'Yes that's him. Where is he?'

'He ordered a coffee and sat over there,' said the waitress, pointing at an empty table.

The professor walked over to the table and looked at the steaming coffee and the walking stick against the wall. *He can't have gone far*, he said to himself as he sat down and took a well-worn file out of his briefcase. *He's probably just popped out for something*, he said, opening the file and running his fingers over the picture of a medieval knight dressed in armour. *I'll just hang on; he'll be back soon.*

The Siege of Acre, The Holy Land, July 1191.

The man stepped forward out of the shadows. He was dressed in a white turban and baggy robes that were drawn in at the waist by a belt that held his curved scimitar. His black beard was speckled with grey, and his eyes - which were so dark it was difficult to see their pupils - were set deeply into their sockets, revealing no emotion whatsoever. He had a large scar on his face that started above his right eye, reached across his nose and ended in a deep gouge on his left cheek. The man looked as hard as flint. His body lean and muscular, perfectly adapted to the harsh climate in which he lived.

'Sir John, may I introduce Ashott?' Philip said, getting up out of his chair.

The two warriors looked at each other across the tent, their keen eyes, honed by a lifetime of combat, studying each other, instinctively looking for any sign of weakness. The Armenian mercenary bowed his head in acknowledgement of the chain-mail-clad knight who, as politeness dictated, inclined his head in response.

'Come closer, gentlemen, and I will explain the stratagem,' said Philip, as several squires hurried to clear the feasting table, replacing the eating vessels with a map of the besieged city.

'Tomorrow, as the first rays of the sun break the horizon, our friend Ashott will open the East Gate of the city,' Philip said as he picked up a bejewelled dagger, plunging it into the parchment at the location where the breach would occur, '...and our men will pour in. To facilitate this, there will be a diversionary attack against the West Gate,' he said, looking up at John. 'My cousin Richard will lead this attack in order to draw the enemy forces as far from the East Gate as possible. Guy will lead the eastern attack, with help from Robert.' He paused and looked up at the two knights he had named, both of whom nodded solemnly.

'John, you will be at the front of the column, with your six trusty men.' He looked up at the knight. 'You, sir, will be the first man into Acre,' he said, slapping the knight on the back. 'Once you have entered, I need you to make your way directly to the Treasury. It is located within the citadel, not far from the eastern gate. Ashott knows the city well, and will show you the way. You need to secure it, and make sure that it is not looted. When the people know that we have entered the walls, they will panic; they will likely take everything that is not nailed down. We have all seen it before, have we not?' said the King, scrutinising the knights around the table.

'Aye, my lord,' they answered.

'When they know we are amongst them, the terror will

216

spread like wildfire,' added King Richard.

'You are to take and hold the Treasury at all costs. I will send men to help you, but, until they arrive, you must hold. Do you understand?' continued Philip.

'Yes, Sire. It will be done,' answered Sir John.

'Good man,' said Philip, taking hold of John's hand. 'Are there any questions, my Lords?' he asked the gathered nobles.

'Nay, my lord. The plan is simple,' answered John.

'We will have our victory. It has been long in coming, but we will have it on the morrow,' smiled Philip. 'Now, my Lords, if there is nothing further, I will bid you goodnight.'

As the noblemen drifted away, Philip placed a hand on John's shoulder. 'Wait,' he whispered as he looked over to the corner where Ashott's brooding frame lingered. 'Ashott, go and make ready for the morning,' he commanded. 'You must be alert and strong.' The Armenian bowed and backed into the shadows, without taking his eyes off Sir John, and was gone - just as silently as he had appeared.

'Sire, what do you know of this man? Do you trust him?' asked Sir John, in a concerned tone, when they were alone.

Philip sat back into his chair. 'Please join me,' he said, gesturing in the direction of the chair to his right hand side. 'Truth be told, I know very little of Ashott. He rode into my camp two days ago. The sentries saw him leave the city with two other men. But, when he arrived at my camp to demand an audience, he was alone. The sentries later found his two companions with their throats cut. My guess is that he had been sent to deliver to me a message from the Caliph of the city, but instead had decided to present me with a proposition of his own,' he said as he picked up his goblet of wine.

'I have sat with him over the last day or so, trying to gauge him. I thought him an assassin at first, but this is not so. He has had many an opportunity to take my life, but has made no attempt.

'He has told me that he is Armenian - a Christian by

faith, and a mercenary, like his father before him. He is currently in the pay of Saladin. But, prior to that, he took the gold of the Fatimids of Egypt.

'I am not naive, John,' he continued, as he drained the ornate cup. 'I have met men like Ashott before. My reading of him is that he places money above all else. He is not like you or I, who live by a code of honour; he is a rat, living in the filth, getting fat from the remains of men who have fallen.

'Do I trust him? No I do not, and neither should you. But can I use him? Yes. I have offered him a share in the treasury if he betrays the Caliph on the morrow, and successfully opens the gate.' Philip took Sir John by the shoulders. 'He will be well paid for his work,' he said, looking directly into his eyes. 'But be aware that we are taking a gamble: if things do not progress in the manner of his liking, he may turn on you. If he does, you must be ready for him. I am sure that he would not think twice about cutting your throat and leaving you by the roadside, as he did to his two companions.'

'I will watch him like an eagle watches his prey,' answered Sir John. 'And if he makes his move, I will swoop on him. It will be his last.'

'Now, you must go and get some rest,' Philip said with a smile. 'You will surely need it. The day will be long, but the rewards will be great. Tomorrow, Sir John de Guise, we make history!'

M40, UK,
13.15hrs, May 2007.

Six men dead, Mason raged to himself, as he sat in the back of the black cab as it made its way towards London along the M40 motorway. *What was JJ playing at? There were still TWO alive.* As he tried to find a comfortable position for his aching body, he watched as the traffic slowed, the queue began to build as they reached the city's outskirts. *I bet the patrol found nothing. The bloody IPS covered it up,* he said to himself, taking control of his anger. *He's just prepared to let it go. But why?* His mind raced through the possibilities. But there was only one that would stack up: the sale of Target to Navaro Oil. It had to be that. Two hostages being paraded around on TV would be the last thing JJ needed. After all, who would be crazy enough to buy a security company and inherit a hostage problem that could last for months, if not years? *They were loose ends,* he said to himself, *and I am the string being used to tie them up.*

It all made sense now: the rushed exit, the armed guard at the airport, the surveillance. They had kept a keen eye on him while JJ had arranged the coup de gras. There was no coming back from this. No one was going to listen to him now; his credibility had been destroyed. *He's done a good job on me,* he said to himself as the taxi pulled up at the rear of the Victory Services Club. *But it's not over yet.* 'I need you to wait here,' he said to the taxi driver. 'I have to get my stuff. I'll be back in ten minutes.'

'I will have to see the colour of your money first, guv'na,' said the driver. Mason glanced up at the meter. It read £127. He took out a handful of twenty pound notes he had taken from a cash-point earlier that day, and handed them over. 'Ten minutes,' he said as he got out of the cab, walking towards the rear entrance of the hotel. The driver nodded his agreement while holding the notes up to the light to check their watermark.

Mason had anticipated a quick move before he had left for Oxford, and had packed up all his stuff in readiness. He entered the hotel room, grabbed his small bag and left, making sure the 'do not disturb' sign was still hanging on the outside doorknob. There was one more job to complete before he left the hotel. And for that, he needed the help of the receptionist. He exited the stair well on the ground floor and went straight to the Internet room. The room was around the corner from the reception, with no line of sight. He put his bag in one of the cubicles, and made his way to the reception.

'Can I help you, Mister... uh... Mason, isn't it?' asked the receptionist, remembering him from that morning.

'Yes. That's right. Room 603,' Mason confirmed. 'Could I have an Internet card please?' he whispered.

'Yes. Of course, Mr Mason. Shall I charge it to your room?'

'Yes, please,' Mason replied, adding a fake yawn and stretch.

'Caught up on your sleep then?' asked the receptionist.

Mason smiled as he took the ticket. As he turned, he noticed a man wearing blue jeans and a brown leather jacket sitting on the sofa next to the door. 'Oh, there was just one more thing,' he added to the receptionist, this time loud enough for all to hear. 'Could you have room service send a burger and fries to my room please?'

Mason didn't wait for the receptionist's reply; he was already heading back to the computer, conscious there was no time to waste. He unzipped the small bag that Tonka had packed for him. *All the things a man on the run needs*, he thought to himself, with satisfaction, as he rummaged through its contents: passport, credit cards, $5,000 in $100s, pants, socks, a clean shirt and a basic unlocked Nokia phone. *It's not so much a weekend bag as a 'bug out bag,'* he thought to himself.

The webmail site loaded, and he quickly composed the email, scanning it when he had finished, to make sure his big fingers hadn't caused any spelling mistakes. Satisfied, he pressed 'Send'. And, within a few minutes, he was in the street at the back of the hotel.

The taxi was where he had left it. As he walked down the backstreet, he took the phone JJ had given him out of his pocket and opened its plastic casing. He threw the SIM card down between the bars of a storm drain cover, tossing what was left of the phone into a refuse bin.

'Where to now, gu'vna?' asked the driver as he got in.

'Heathrow.'

The Siege of Acre, The Holy Land,
July, 1191.

The four hundred men had assembled while it was still dark, with Guy and Robert at the front, leading the long column as it snaked its way along a dried up river bed running parallel to the city's wall. The men moved as stealthily as they could, their weapons wrapped in cloth so as not to clang and give away their position to the sentries on the wall.

Guy gave the order for them to stop when they were about fifty metres from the East Gate. For now, they had the cloak of darkness to hide them. But it would soon be dawn. And with daybreak they would lose the advantage, becoming easy targets for the skilled bowmen on the battlements above them. There was no sign of the sun yet, but the darkness was fading, the sky turning from black to an inky blue, colours returning to the landscape with every passing minute. It would rise behind them, and it would not be long. They lay in wait, listening to the faint sound of trumpets as, on the opposite side of the city, the diversionary attack advanced towards the West Gate. The inactivity was excruciating for the men lying still in their meagre cover, waiting for their turn to join the battle. John could feel their anxiety, but he knew that to charge the gate, unless unlocked, would be suicide; its sturdy wooden planks fortified by an array of iron nails.

The three Kings, their banners unfurled and blowing freely in the predawn wind, advanced to the shrill call of trumpets. They were the red flag to the bull. And, for the plan to succeed, they had to draw as many men away from the East Gate as they could. Philip was in the centre, his white Crusader's cross tunic plain for all to see. Leopold on the left had also chosen to wear the Cross. But Richard, on the right flank, mace in one hand, shield in the other, walked amongst his men, resplendent in his crimson tabard.

'Where is he?' whispered Guy to Sir John.

'Patience, my lord. He will come... His task is not

221

an easy one.'

'We will be stuck like pigs with arrows if he doesn't complete his task soon,' joined in Robert.

The wave of men that was the diversionary attack crashed onto the rock that was the city's great walls, their shouts, and the clash of metal, clearly audible to the men who crouched in the dry riverbed on the eastern side of the city. Some began to curl themselves into small shapes, attempting to hide from the growing light. Others held their weapons tightly, desperate to move, or at least do something.

'This is treachery,' hissed Guy, clenching his teeth in anger. 'He has delivered us into the hands of the bowmen, the Armenian swine! We are done for.'

All the previous night, Sir John had been plagued by suspicions that the mercenary had manipulated the Crusaders, and was leading them to destruction. He was not prepared to voice his doubts; he trusted the judgement of his King. But, moreover, he knew that to question the plan so soon before the battle would create panic and confusion amongst the already nervous men. Even now, Sir John would not admit that the Armenian had betrayed them, and instead urged the knights to place their faith in a higher power. 'My lords, we must trust in our Lord God,' said Sir John to Guy and Robert. 'If he wants us to take the city, then the gates will open. We must stay here. If we run now, all will be lost.'

Sir John left the two leaders, and crawled the short distance to the head of the column, where his six men were in a close huddle.

'What is the word, John? Are we trapped?' asked Christopher, nervously.

Sir John smiled at him, reassuringly. 'Nay, my friend. The gate will open. Trust me. And when it does, you will all need to stay close to me. We must move as one. Do you understand?'

'Yes, John. As one,' replied Christopher. The others nodded.

'Don't worry, my old friend. You will have your inn and your fat wenches,' said John, with a smile.

A cry came from the battlement. The men hiding below could not understand the foreign words. But there was no mistaking their meaning; it was an alarm. They had been seen.

Target HQ, Belgrave Square, London, 19.05hrs, 18 May 2007.

'I've got some bad news,' James announced as JJ walked into the office. 'They lost him.'

'What the fuck do you mean: you lost him?' JJ screamed, turning his attention to the two men that had followed James into his office. 'One simple job: if he leaves the hotel, you follow him. And you lost him? You're a pair of fucking idiots!'

'We think he got out the back way,' answered the man in the brown leather jacket.

'The back way? Of course he got out the back way, you fucking retard. But you were meant to be covering the back, weren't you?'

'Yes, boss,' the two men answered in unison.

'He made a phone call to an Oxford number... uh... All Saints College,' said Grey Suit, hoping to save the situation.

'A phone call, a fucking phone call. Is that all you can give me?' JJ screamed, his temper clearly besting him again. 'So what do you think he was trying to do? Enrol in the Open Fucking University?' he screamed.

James's suit pocket came alive with a bleepy rendition of a *A British Grenadier.* Saving the fortunate man from having to give an answer which would no doubt have angered JJ even more.

The conversation was brief and one sided, the only words offered by James being an initial 'Hello,' and a 'Thanks very much.'

'We need to talk,' he said to JJ as he put his phone back into his pocket.

'You pair, get out of my sight,' shouted the angry Glaswegian at the two men. 'Go to Oxford and find out what he did there,' he barked as they left, both glad to be out of the firing line.

'I'm having his credit card and passport tracked,' said James as the door closed. 'He left on a British Airways flight to Beirut at 18:30. One way ticket. What the hell is going on, John?'

'What do you mean?'

'This guy is supposed to be nothing more than the hopeless alcoholic that got his team killed. We expected him just to climb back in his bottle, not run away to Beirut. Christ, this is getting ugly. He's going back isn't he? He believes his men are still alive. And he's going back to try and rescue them...'

'Nah. If he was going back, he would have taken the shortest route. Kuwait is only a few hours' drive from Basrah; he would have gone there. I know I would have.'

'But that's just it, JJ. Mason *isn't* you.'

The two men sat in silence, both running through the options. Only the noise of the early evening traffic, seeping through the double-glazing, offered any distraction. 'There are two scenarios,' James said as he sat down on the Chesterfield. 'Either he's running away, or he's going back to attempt a rescue. Correct?

'Aye. I would say that about sums it up.'

'The Lebanon is a pretty queer place to travel to if you're running away. So I think we can rule that one out. That leaves us with scenario two,' he said, searching JJ's face. 'If, by some freak set of circumstances, there *are* two hostages still alive - and he ends up rescuing them - you're done for, old chap.'

'Nah, nah,' interrupted JJ. 'We might have to put the deal with Navaro on hold for a while. But done for? I think that's a wee bit much.'

'John, you're only here because MI6 chose you. We can't afford to be associated with a company that might have abandoned its men. What do you think the fallout would be if those two hostages turn up?'

There was a long pause as JJ chewed on the information. 'So, let's get rid of him, then.'

'What are you saying, John? Order a hit on Mason?'

'Aye. It wouldn't be the first time that Six has taken someone out.'

'My dear boy, I belong to the British Secret Intelligence Service. We don't just go around killing people at the request of members of the general public.'

'Now, you just wait a damn minute!' JJ said, his temper again beginning to surface.

'No, John. You hang on,' James said, springing up from the Chesterfield, his patience exhausted. 'If Mason manages to pull it off, the press, the government, the whole lot will be screaming for blood. No one could survive the storm - not even you. Six will be looking for a scapegoat. And you're going to be it.'

'So what are you suggesting?'

'I can make this go away,' James said, as he walked up to the desk, his hands grabbing the ornate top, his scowl an indication of the weight of his statement.

'How?'

'Two million and your problems disappear.'

'What the fuck? Are you serious?'

'Two million,' James repeated, sitting on the end of the desk. 'And in answer to your question: yes, I've never been more serious in all my life.'

PART THREE

CHAPTER NINE

Beirut International Airport, Lebanon,
01.35hrs, 19 May 2007.

The British Airways Airbus 320, having performed a
large circle around the peninsula holding the sprawling
city of Beirut, landed at the International Airport. As it had
banked over the historic metropolis - which
historians have estimated was inhabited one and a half
thousand years before Christ - Mason had stared through
the porthole into the darkness, trying to identify any
familiar landmarks. The best he could do was to make out
where the land ended and the Mediterranean Sea began.
Frustrated at his inability to conduct an aerial
reconnaissance, he had instead sat back and concentrated on
his plan to recover his men.

The jet rocked gently to a halt, the seatbelt sign on the
panels overhead pinging into life. Mason quickly grabbed his
bag and attempted to make a quick exit from the plane, but
was soon hampered by the slow, tired shuffle of passengers
in front of him. Although he had not checked in any luggage,
it still took him an hour to clear immigration and customs.
As he emerged, groggy and irritable, into the arrivals area,
he looked at his watch: 01:35. *I need some rest*, he said to

himself as the automatic doors parted. *A cheap airport hotel will be fine.*

He headed straight for the line of taxis directly opposite the entrance. To his astonishment, the first vehicle in the line was a Ferrari, its red splendour glistening in the bright artificial light. The taxi drivers had all abandoned their humdrum, yellow sedans, and were huddled around the sports car, admiring its Latin lines with loving adoration. Skirting around the edge of the crowd, he made for the next vehicle in the line: a beat-up old Mercedes. As he opened the taxi door, he heard his name. 'Hey, Mason,' shouted a voice from within the swarm. 'Do you want to ride with me?'

A man broke from the dense ranks and stepped forward. He was dressed in a Hawaiian shirt, long shorts and flip-flops. His deep suntanned face was covered with a dark manicured stubble, the dark shadow an impeccable match for his thick, dark curls, the deep cleft on his chin projecting through the shallow growth.

As he walked clear of the crowd, Mason observed that the man, despite his obvious wealth, had not yet sacrificed his body to over-indulgence. The muscles in his legs were lean and defined, his frame athletic. Aside from these impressive physical attributes, his most striking feature - the one that caught everyone's attention - was the black eye patch that he wore over his left eye.

He was a handful of years younger - and a few inches shorter - than Mason. This height difference apparent as he threw his arms around Mason - in a massive bear hug.

'It's great to see you, man,' he said, squeezing his friend tight.

'I didn't expect you until tomorrow,' replied Mason.

'Yeah... yeah... I know. But when I got your email, I got so excited that I had to come and meet you off the plane.'

'How did you know what flight I was on?'

'I didn't. I've been waiting for hours. And this is the last flight from London; if you weren't on this one, I would have had to go home disappointed,' he said, looking down at

Mason's bag. 'Is that it on the luggage?'

'Yep... Travelling light.'

Mitch was an American who had joined the French Foreign Legion and gone on to the French Special Forces. He had bumped into Mason on an operation *that never existed* in Beirut fifteen years prior. The comradeship they had forged during that long, hot, crazy summer, was unquestioning. They had kept in touch. But after the accident - like everything else in Mason's life - it had fallen apart. This was the first time they'd met since Katie's and Isabella's funeral. But the bond was still there, as tight as ever. Mason never falling off the pedestal on which Mitch had placed him. After all, the Englishman had saved his life.

Mitch led Mason through the crowd of excited taxi drivers. 'Ferraris look great, but the storage is useless,' he said as he popped the hood. 'Should just be enough to accommodate your bag, though,' he laughed.

'I suppose I'd better put this on?' Mason said as took hold of the seatbelt, the soft calf-leather seats of the Italian sports car wrapping themselves around him.

'Roger that, mate,' answered Mitch, with a fake English accent, as he got behind the wheel. 'Buckle up. It's going to get gnarly.' He revved the engine and took his foot off the clutch, the car lurching forward with a screech of tyres, leaving behind a cloud of smoke, the smell of burnt rubber and a mass of ecstatic taxi drivers.

Mason was tired, bruised and battered. He'd lost his reputation, his team and his life. And he was going on a rescue mission that would probably end up with him getting killed. He felt as low as a snake's belly. But, as the sports car raced along the deserted city streets, the warm Mediterranean air blowing through the open top, the tyres screeching around corners, the guttural growl of the exhaust ripping through the still night air, he somehow found himself smiling.

'I am trying to be covert,' shouted Mason over the roar of the engine, 'and here I am, riding round Beirut at a hundred a fifty miles an hour in a Ferrari, with a crazed ex-Legionnaire who's wearing an eye patch.'

Mitch looked over at him and laughed, his toothy, North American smile illuminated by the light from the dashboard. 'You know me, brother: too fast to live...' he said as he depressed the accelerator once more, the car thrusting forward, pushing them back into their seats. Mitch slowed the beast as they approached a large tower block that was set back from the road. There was not a single light, the building's form silhouetted black against the backdrop of the city's evening glow. As they drew up alongside, Mitch stopped. The marks and holes on the concrete skin of the building made during the country's bloody civil war still evident, even in the darkness. 'Is that 'sniper central'?' Mason asked, looking at the infamous building that had once been home to countless sharp shooters.

'You bet. The old Holiday Inn - all twenty-five floors of her,' Mitch said, tapping the steering wheel.

'It seems like only yesterday. The explosion... and you, screaming like a baby,' Mason laughed.

'Yeah, I remember that day. Fourth floor, remember? They set up a booby trap. But I was lucky. The guy in front of me took the blast. He died. I lost an eye. And Sergeant-Major Mason of 22 SAS pulled me out.' He looked over at his old friend. 'I owe you, man.'

'I thought they'd have knocked that down a long time ago. Why is it still standing?'

'Ah, that's a good question,' Mitch said, slipping the gear stick in to neutral. 'I've heard that the owner doesn't want to develop it. Apparently, he bought it on the cheap and likes it the way it is.'

Mason smiled. 'Oh yeah? Who owns it now then?'

Mitch rubbed his chin, as if searching for the answer, delighting in the game that he'd started. 'Uh, that will be me.'

'No way?' Mason laughed. 'How much did it cost you?'

'It was a cool million, US.'

'So what you going to do with it? You can't just leave it like that?'

'This is Beirut; I can do anything I like. This is my town,' he said, cockily. 'I'm going to keep it as a monument to my eye,' he laughed. 'It was a good eye; I was very fond of it. I'd had it since I was a kid,' he said as he engaged the gear stick and depressed the accelerator pedal, the car thrusting forward with a deafening roar.

During the Lebanese civil war, the British and French governments had received an urgent call for help. The Lebanese government had - for safekeeping - placed a large number of extremely sensitive documents in the strong room of one of the city's largest banks. The bank had been in a Christian enclave. But, due to advances by Hezbollah (the Iranian-backed Shia militia), the bank found itself right on the frontline. A plan was hatched for a joint Special Forces operation, the objective to attack the bank and rescue the documents before they fell into the wrong hands. As Britain and France were not involved militarily in the conflict, the mission was designated a 'black operation'. In other words, it *never existed.*

Sergeant Francois Mitchell or Mitch of the Foreign Legion's 2e Regiment Etranger de Parachutistes was on secondment to the French Special Operations Command when he had received the call. His team had been picked to lead the assault. In support were elements of B squadron, 22 SAS.

Mitch was from Louisiana. He had joined the American 82nd Airborne straight from school, his interest aroused one summer's afternoon with the arrival of a recruiting Sergeant who talked of God, country, honour and excitement. He didn't care too much for the first three of these concepts. But the last one – excitement – hit home. His parents had scraped a living in Louisiana, his father's spine curved from a lifetime of heavy work in the docks, his mother having to make ends meet by cleaning for rich folks - both of them growing old, living from one pay check to the next. That wasn't for him; he wanted a uniform and the chest full of medals. He signed the contract and enlisted just in time for his first taste of combat: the invasion of Grenada. After the adrenalin had settled, and the weapons cleaned and restored to the armoury for safekeeping, his unit returned to peacetime duties. After a year of tedium, he'd had enough. He packed his bag and deserted. His search for excitement took him to the other side of the Atlantic, fighting for a unit where his Créole language skills would serve him well.

The French had been in Beirut for a while; to the SAS it was a new area of operations, so it was agreed that the French would take the lead, with the SAS providing the outer layer and security cordon. Planning and rehearsals went well, the covert attack to be launched in the deserted Beirut street just as the bank opened on a Monday morning. At first it all went to plan. The documents had been identified and were being loaded into the unmarked vans outside. Then all hell broke loose. Hezbollah had been tipped off that something was happening, and soon surrounded the area with its fighters. The ensuing battle was intense, incoming fire arriving on the battle-scarred street from all directions, the derelict buildings making ideal locations for the Shia militant snipers. To make their exit, the assault team 'popped smoke', covering the whole area with a thick layer of yellow haze as they made their getaway.

The mission had been successful. The vault had been cleaned of all its delicate stationery, but there was also an unexpected twist: in the process, all the bank's gold bullion had also disappeared.

Mason, along with the whole team, was questioned extensively. But, being part of the outer cordon, it was accepted that he had played no active role within the bank. None of the other witnesses summoned were able to help with these enquiries, as the blanket of smoke the forces had used to make their getaway continued to obscure the whole affair. The fact that the mission was a 'black op' was the deciding influence. Because the mission never officially existed, the missing bullion was never adequately chased, the whole matter eventually being dropped by the presiding regime. Privately, the blame was commonly pinned on Hezbollah.

The two Special Forces teams hung around Beirut for a while, conducting mop up operations – in one of which Mitch lost his eye. But eventually the foreign forces were sent home. All the authorities were able to do was to monitor the men's bank accounts and look for deposits unbecoming of soldiers. Mason knew that none of the Brits were involved in the larceny, but he had never found the right opportunity to ask Mitch. In an atmosphere where it was frowned upon to ask your colleagues where they'd been - never mind what they'd been doing there - secrecy soon veiled the whole incident. The Beirut bank job passing into legend. The closest Mason ever got to the truth was a cheeky wink one evening when both men were drunk.

Mayfair, London,
02.40hrs, 19 May 2007.

JJ had worked late, talking to his legal representative in The Virgin Islands. His attorney - currently sitting in his air-conditioned offices on the Caribbean island - assured his client that the new account for Mr Smith would be up and running in a few days. The contractor would be able to receive the first of the two scheduled payments - each of a million pounds sterling - from one of Target's offshore accounts by the end of the week.

Despondent at the prospect of having such a large amount of cash leave his account, he'd grabbed a bottle of Teacher's, and had spent the last couple of hours in his penthouse decanting it into his favourite Edinburgh crystal tumbler. This also gave him time to search for answers, whilst looking out at the incredible view of West London from his high-rise apartment. Bereft of ideas, and annoyed at his lack of ingenuity, he finally succumbed to his alcohol-induced tiredness, climbing into bed.

By 3am, his unconscious had worked it out: 'James,' he mouthed into the phone at his bedside table, 'Beirut... I know why Beirut. He's gone to meet Mitchell.'

'Who the hell is Mitchell?' said the quiet, predawn voice on the other end.

'Don't worry. I'll explain it in the morning. We've got him.'

The Siege of Acre, The Holy Land, July, 1191.

The arrows started to fall like raindrops in a summer shower, lightly at first but with ever increasing intensity, as the defenders obeyed their captains' calls to arms. Their accuracy was improving with every passing minute. 'Get your shields up,' Sir John shouted, as he strode along the column of dismayed Crusaders in the dry riverbed. 'Make yourselves ready.'

Sir John looked at the men that were pitifully huddling together for protection. In the darkness of night, they had been faceless shapes. But now, in the early morning light, he was able to see them clearly, their wretchedness unsheathed like the weapons they held in their unwashed hands. His men had taken the vow and followed their lord on the Holy Crusade. Some of them had died quick, clean deaths in battle. But most had died of starvation and disease, their bodies wracked in pain as they lay on piles of straw and waited for their life energy to dissipate. To fill the ranks of their fallen comrades, the Pope had ordered the jails of Europe to turn out their inmates. The result; a motley bunch of thieves and murderers, pressganged into doing God's will in whatever way they saw fit.

The screams of wounded men began to fill the already-crowded air as the wooden shafts, with their deadly iron tips, found exposed flesh. Sir John de Guise looked on in disgust at the men cowering around him. *I will not flinch as these peasants do*, he thought, thrusting out his chest and drawing himself to his full height.

'Sir John,' shouted Guy, as he ran towards the knight, his body arched in an attempt to protect himself from the deadly arrows. 'We are done for. The rat has sold us out.'

'I know but one thing, my Lord,' replied Sir John. 'If we stay here, we will all surely perish.'

'It is decided then. We shall fall back,' shouted Guy.

'Nay, my lord, not back – forward,' John said, pointing at the gate. 'If we can draw the attention of the defenders, then the diversionary attack on the western gate might succeed.'

'But that will be suicide, John,' protested Guy.

'That might be, my Lord,' answered Sir John. 'But it has taken us two years to get here, and we have lost many good men on the way. We owe it to them to at least try. Are you with me? For if you are not, then I will rush the gate with just my six men.'

Guy looked at the man standing proudly erect before him, his shield and sword at his sides, impervious to the danger around him. He had seen this man do unbelievable things over the past two years - feats of bravery that were already the stuff of folklore.

Sir John stared at Guy with his steely blue eyes. 'Are you with me?' he repeated.

'Aye, I am with you,' Guy answered.

'Good. I will lead. Ready your men. We must move quickly.'

'Guy!' shouted Sir John, as his fellow knight turned. 'I cannot think of a better place to die. Can you?'

Sir John was the first to leap out of the dry riverbed as the trumpet sounded, urging the rest of the attackers forward as he ran towards the city's walls. The other men were more hesitant about exposing themselves fully to the bowmen, the captains having to get in amongst the reluctant mass urging and coercing them forward with threats and strikes, using the flats of their swords. Like a great boulder caught in a landslide, the four hundred moved, slowly at first, but gaining momentum as the men, hysterical with fear and rage, were driven on a collision course towards the East Gate.

As the Crusaders attacked, the defenders fired volleys of arrows into the raging mass, causing many casualties, but not nearly enough to stop the Crusaders' advance. Sir John was the first to reach the gate, his men surrounding him, their shields held high, protecting their lord as he beat on the great door with the pommel of his sword. 'Ashott!' he cried. 'Open the gate!' But there was no answer, the huge mass of solid wood remaining shut, intransigent.

'If this gate does not open soon, we are done for,' shouted Robert, as he too reached the huge door.

'Bring the scaling ladders to the front. If we can't go through, we can go over,' Sir John shouted in answer.

As the minutes passed, the defenders on the walls took the opportunity to reorganise themselves, taking advantage of the proximity of the attackers to deploy the other weapons in their arsenal - weapons that required far less finesse and skill than that of an archer, but which had a far greater effect at close range. As the first ladders went up against the smooth walls, the heavy rocks came crashing down into the dense mass of men, cracking skulls and crushing bones with ease.

The Crusaders had not equipped themselves with the heavy engines needed to breach the city's defences; after all, they were supposed to go through the gate. The few ladders that they had brought were soon destroyed by the determined men on the wall who were fighting for their lives. As the battle raged, the Crusaders in their exposed position began to suffer increasing casualties. Sir John turned and scanned his men to evaluate the losses. Of the four hundred men that had started the day, he estimated that half already lay dead, dying or injured.

'We cannot stay here!' shouted Guy. 'We shall all be dead in minutes.'

Sir John knew that he was right. Without the gate open, they would all perish. 'Our cause is useless,' he shouted in answer. 'We must fall back and re-group. Guy, sound the retreat.'

A loud trumpet call pierced the air, the men gladly obeying the order, walking backwards in a tight group, their large shields held high above their heads to protect them from the arrows. When they had walked only twenty metres or so from the wall, a shout went up. 'The gate is opening! The gate is opening!' Sir John turned and shouted to Guy. 'The gate. The gate, Guy. We must attack!'

Sir John's men were the first to respond, rushing at the gate and pushing at the huge wooden structure, eager to widen the small gap that had appeared. As the opening grew, Sir John stepped through the opening: the first to enter Acre.

Beirut, Lebanon
02.02hrs, 19 May 2007.

The Ferrari turned onto a wide boulevard lined with palm trees. On their right was an ornate white painted balustrade that marked the edge of the esplanade and the beginning of a beach that led down to the Mediterranean. On their left was a row of tower blocks that rose twenty four floors above the gentle lapping waves. The lights in the trendy apartments flashed out to sea, serving as fashionable lighthouses.

'I know this place,' said Mason. 'Isn't this St George Bay?

'Yep... Looks a lot different from the last time you were here,' replied Mitch as he slowed the car to negotiate a small access road leading to the front of a high rise building. 'This is where the 'well-heeled' Beiruties live,' he continued, parking the car outside a luxurious looking bar on the ground floor of the tower block.

'So, I take it that this is where you live, then?'

Mitch nodded, before springing out of the car. 'Fancy a drink?'

'Do I have a choice?' asked Mason.

'No... not really. Catching up is best done over a few drinks, wouldn't you agree?'

The bar had been decorated in the style of a London gentleman's club. The walls were lined with oak panels, adorned with prints of soldiers in nineteenth century uniforms, Napoleonic battles and an array of swords, helmets and assorted militaria. The lighting created even more ambiance. Concealed spotlights illuminated the antiques on the walls. Red table lamps in the secluded booths seemed capable of delivering intimacy and facilitating decadence. It was both the place to be seen and a place not to be seen at all - a venue for doing deals.

Mason followed Mitch to a raised booth that overlooked the entrance and the long, teak-finished bar. At one end of the booth - in the prime spot - was a large armchair of magnificent cherry-red leather. Either side of the antique table that squatted in the middle of the ensemble were two three-seater leather sofas. As both men relaxed, a waitress came to take their order. 'Usual, Mitch?' asked the pretty young hostess, who Mason noticed was wearing little more than a smile. Mitch nodded. 'What's your poison, Mason?'

'I would love a cup of tea.'

Mitch gave a disapproving look. 'Give him that with a bourbon chaser,' he said, as the waitress disappeared.

'Business is slow tonight; I think we're the only ones in here,' Mason said, looking around as he made himself comfortable on the sofa.

237

'Yeah. Pretty much,' agreed Mitch. 'The place should have been closed tonight - but they've opened for a special occasion.'

'Oh yeah? What's that?'

'For you,' Mitch said as he sat back in his chair and took two Cohiba cigars from the leather case in his breast pocket. 'Smoke?' he asked as he sparked up his Zippo lighter.

'Yeah, why not?' answered Mason.'

The two were still lighting their Cubans as the waitress bent over and put their drinks down on the table, Mitch giving her a smack on the butt as a reward for her timely service.

'Nice of them to stay open,' said Mason as he sipped his tea.

'They didn't have much choice,' replied Mitch with a grin.

'Oh, I get it - you own the bar, right?'

Mitch clapped his hands and smiled broadly. 'Yep. And I kept it open for you, me old muckka,' he said, using his fake English accent again. 'Actually, I own the whole building. I built it. This is Mitch Towers.'

'You've done well for yourself. How did you achieve all this, then?' he said, taking a sip of his tea.

'Well, you know… I had a good pay out for my eye from the Frenchies. And I invested it well,' he said, with a cheeky wink.

Mason returned the grin. *I'm not even going there* he thought.

'But enough of me,' Mitch said, changing the subject and picking up his drink. 'I heard you retired. What you been up to?'

Mason sighed. 'To be honest, I climbed into a bottle of whisky for a while, and tried to drown myself in self-pity.' He took another sip of tea, and looked up at Mitch. 'I think I'm over it now. But I don't want to test it. You know what I mean?'

'Man, don't I feel like a fucking ass hole?' replied Mitch

as he slid the glass of bourbon away from Mason. 'So you said in the email that you need a favour?' he said, after an uneasy pause.

Mason squirmed in his chair. He loathed asking favours of anyone. 'Look, I hate doing this, but my back is against the wall and you are the only person I could think of.'

Mitch could see how uncomfortable his old friend looked, and decided to help him out. 'Look man, you saved my life. If it weren't for you, I would be six feet under now. Name it, brother, and it's yours.'

'Do you remember JJ O'Hare?' Mason asked.

'Yeah. How could anyone forget that prick?' snorted Mitch.

'Well, he's done really well for himself. He now owns a security company that has got a really big contract in Iraq. I went out there to work for him. But it all went horribly wrong.'

'How wrong?'

'Four dead and two hostages wrong.'

Mitch whistled, 'That's wrong, all right. So what's the prick doing about the hostages?'

'There's something you should know before we go any further,' Mason said, looking straight at his old friend. 'There's been some bad stuff said about me in the UK press.'

'How bad?' asked Mitch.

'Pretty bad. JJ has got to the papers, and they've done a hatchet job on me; they are saying that it was all my fault.'

'Why would he want to do a crazy thing like that?' replied Mitch, as he started on Mason's unwanted bourbon.

'He's selling the company, and wants a nice smooth ride. Two hostages would make it very bumpy for him. So he's decided to make them go away. As far as he and everyone else are concerned, they're all dead.

'So, he blames it on you. What a complete bastard.'

'That's the way he operates; he's totally ruthless. It's been made easy for him though. There is little proof of the guys been taken captive. The only witness is an old Marsh

239

Arab who saved me near Al Amarah. And he's now gone missing - taken by the same people. But I know they're alive, Mitch,' he said, looking straight at his friend, with all innocence. 'I can feel it in my gut.'

'Who are the bad guys in all this?' asked Mitch.

'The Iraqi police.'

'Ouch,' said Mitch, swilling the ice cubes round at the bottom of his glass. 'That's not good for the peace process. So, let me get this right,' he said as he finished off the last drops. 'JJ has abandoned these guys, and now they stand a good chance of getting their heads chopped off?'

'Yep, pretty much. But I'm not going to let that happen; I'm going back to get them out!'

'Man! I knew when I saw the email this wasn't going to be a social call.'

Mason turned to Mitch. 'I need help with the logistics. I need to get into Syria and then across the border into Iraq.'

Mitch whistled through his teeth as he sat back. 'So... let me get this right,' he said, sitting forward and arching his fingers. 'You want to cross over into Syria, travel across the Syrian Steppes, into Iraq, and then down to Al...'

'Al Amarah,' finished off Mason.

'And somewhere along the way, you need to pick up some guns, and put together a course of action to spring your guys?'

Mason's initial plan to free the hostages had involved a full-scale military operation. But his plan had since been downsized to that of a one-man band. He'd had time on the flight to go over some scenarios. But at this stage, all he had was a general outline. He was only too aware of the need to add the technicalities – the nuts and bolts. But as Mitch hooked details onto Mason's empty hangers, he realised how difficult the whole thing was going to be.

'You do realise that the border between Syria and Lebanon is as tight as a duck's ass right now?' continued Mitch. 'Tensions are running pretty high. Lebanon is expecting an attack from Syria or even Israel at any time.

240

But that's not the biggest problem. It's *game on* at the Syria and Iraq border. The Green Berets are all over it like stink on shit. The border is one of the main routes for Al Qaida into Iraq, and they are engaging anything that moves,' he said, before trying to get the waitress's attention. 'And if the American SF don't get you, the Hellfire missiles will. It's going to be difficult. Very difficult.'

Mason shook off his negativity. 'Look. I know it's not going to be easy. But I am not prepared to stand by whilst my guys are held hostage. I don't leave people behind.'

Mitch sat forward. 'I can testify to that. After all, you came back and got me out of that burning building. Man! I thought I was a goner for sure,' said Mitch, taking a big puff on his cigar. 'Okay. I agree it's not going to be easy. But it can be done,' he said as he exhaled a large cloud of expensive smoke.

'You picked the right guy to ask for help,' Mitch smiled. 'If anyone can set this up, it's me. You're looking at the King of Beirut.' He began gesturing with a dramatic sweep of his arm. 'This is the realm of King Mitch. This is where I hold my court. And this,' he said, banging the thick leather arms of his chesterfield chair 'is my throne.' Mitch paused as he looked Mason straight in the face with his good eye. 'It's not going to be cheap, though, my brother.'

'I have some money put away,' interrupted Mason, knowing that the conversation had at some point to turn to money - a subject he hated. 'The rest I will have to pay off in instalments. How much do you think it will cost?'

'You know... I'm a very rich guy,' said Mitch, thumbing his lighter, his tone sombre. 'My time is very expensive. You can appreciate that?

Mason went to answer, but Mitch held up his hands, indicating that he hadn't finished. 'My involvement in your enterprise will come at a price which will be non-negotiable. It's important that you understand that from the outset,' he said, placing his lighter on the table with a tap, the punctuation allowing Mason to re-enter the conversation.

Mason had only known Mitch as a soldier - a non-pretentious guy that just wanted to get the job done. No agendas. He wasn't sure if he liked this new Mitch. 'So what's it going to be, then?'

'The payment is simple. For me to do this, I just need one thing from you, one thing only,' he said, looking directly at his old friend. 'I want to go on the mission.'

Mason sat back. His mind had been racing with monetary considerations. Mitch's answer had taken him completely by surprise. 'You want to come along?' he asked, wondering if he'd heard it right.

'Damn right.'

'No way,' said Mason, recovering from the surprise. 'This is my problem. I don't want anyone else getting hurt.'

'Look, you don't have a choice. I'm the only guy who can help you. And, if you want this to happen, you have to agree to my terms. I'm pretty good at negotiating, Mason. Look around you - this is mine, all mine. I've built it all from scratch. One way or another, I always get what I want.'

'Look... you said yourself that it was going to be difficult. And that was being optimistic. To be honest with you, I think it's got all the hallmarks of a suicide mission.'

'You know what? I have to agree with you,' he said, laughing.

'Why would you want to risk it then, when you have all this?'

'I have my reasons... Okay, okay. Let's not fuck about. I told you in the beginning, this is non-negotiable. Remember? Take it or leave it.'

I shouldn't have involved him, Mason thought as he looked at his friend across the table. This was still the old Mitch. *I can't let anyone else get hurt*. At the same time, he knew that on his own there was little hope of success, but with an operator like Mitch helping him, the odds of pulling it off had more than doubled.

'Well?'

'Is there any way I can talk you out of this?'

'None whatsoever.'

'Then I reluctantly agree.'

'I knew that you would see reason,' said Mitch, rubbing his hands. 'Right. So I'm assuming that you want all this to happen, like... yesterday?'

'You know the score,' said Mason. 'All offensive operations are fighting against time. We need to get these guys out ASAP before they appear in a video, wearing orange jump suits and a guy with a big sword standing behind them.'

'Gotcha. We'd best get some sleep, then,' he said as he stood up. 'We've got a hard few days ahead of us. Let's go. I'll show you where you're sleeping.'

'What about my bag?'

'It's already there, my good fellow,' Mitch said with his fake English accent, giving his bruised and battered comrade a pull out of his chair.

Mitch walked to the back of the bar and stopped in front of one of the oak panels – decorated with a print of a young Napoleon Bonaparte. He pulled at the frame, the picture moving easily, revealing a small keypad. He punched in a handful of digits and - to Mason's amazement - the whole panel to the right moved, revealing a lift door.

'Whoa, James Bond or what!' Mason laughed, as the lift door opened with a ping.

'You better believe it, brother. I love all this shit. When I was a kid back in New Orleans, I always wanted my own private lift. This one goes straight to my penthouse. What use is money in the bank? You can't take it with you,'

Mitch grabbed Mason around the shoulder and pulled him in to the lift. 'Man, you don't know how good it is to see you. It's never been like you to disappoint, and you sure ain't starting now.'

There were only two floor buttons in the lift: one reading 'Down' and the other 'King Mitch.' Mitch pushed the latter and looked at Mason, grinning. 'The old team, back together. Those guys have no idea what's about to hit them!'

Pretoria, South Africa

We are pleased to confirm your recruitment for the consultancy position described in the previous correspondence. The immediate task requiring your services is to be accomplished in Beirut, Lebanon. You will be retained under the existing contract obligations, the fee of $100,000 being paid into your nominated account on completion of your duties to our satisfaction. All assets required for the task will be made available to you in-country. This job is URGENT; please acknowledge acceptance and details of travel so we can arrange transfers.

'Gert?' the voice was thick with an Afrikaans accent, the guttural character of the language compounded by a growl at the back of the throat.

'Yes, Colonel.'

'I have just received an email. We have a job. Is Ernst with you?'

'Yes, sir. We're having a braai.'

'Good. We need to leave immediately.'

'When can I expect you, sir?'

'I will be there in an hour.'

Siege of Acre, The Holy Land, July 1191.

John stared at Ashott as he pushed his way through the gap in the heavy door. The mercenary was stood in the middle of the covered archway that held the gatehouse, his eyes bulging, teeth white against his dark skin, the morning light exposing a macabre grin, as his mouth gulped to feed his heaving chest. In his right hand lay a curved scimitar; in his left: a long dagger, both dripping with the blood of the men that lay dead or dying at his feet.

'You took your time, Ashott. But I can see that you have been busy,' Sir John said as he was pushed forward by the men starting to pour through the ever-widening gap behind him.

'Follow me. We have little time,' said the Armenian mercenary as he turned and sped off.

Sir John called his men forward, and together they ran after Ashott, who had set off down the cobbled street at a fierce pace. Ashott knew the route extremely well, not hesitating or slowing once as he led the Crusaders through a maze of small back streets. The route avoiding the main avenues that criss-crossed the ancient city. It made use of alleys so narrow that only one man could pass through at a time, a tactic to nullify any numerical advantage that the defenders might be able to impose on them if caught. The Crusaders struggled to keep up with the Armenian, their chain mail armour, swords and shields weighing heavily on their already-tired legs, as he led them upwards towards the Treasury.

Ashott pulled them up short of a small cobbled square - that was lined with houses on the right and left and a high wall with a gatehouse on the far side. 'That is the Treasury gate,' he said, pointing at the entrance that was thirty metres away on the other side of the square. 'Wait here. I will get them to open it.' He sheathed his sword and rearranged his clothing and headdress before stepping out into the small square.

The sounds of battle could be heard clearly in the distance, but the square was eerily quiet, allowing Ashott's knock on the gate to be easily heard.

'Open the gate!' shouted the Armenian.

A small hatch at head height opened, the obscured face peering into the empty square before speaking. 'Who bids entrance?'

'It is I, Ashott, Captain of the garrison and servant to the Caliph. Open this door immediately.' There was the sound of metal bolts sliding out of their locks. And then the heavy gate opened with a creak. Just before Ashott entered, he looked back at the waiting Crusaders, beckoning them forward with his left hand, while his right unsheathed his deadly scimitar.

The Crusaders rushed across the square and into the open gatehouse just as Ashott's razor sharp blade fell on the neck of the hapless gatekeeper kneeling before him. Sir John looked at the body lying in a pool of blood and then at Ashott. 'Where is his weapon?' he asked. 'Was he unarmed?'

'He had none,' replied Ashott, wiping his blade the dead man's blood-soaked clothing.

'Why did you kill him, then?' demanded the knight.

'It makes no difference - armed or unarmed. Ashott decides.' He nodded towards the weapon Sir John was holding. 'You have no blood on your sword, Crusader. You have not worked today,' he sneered.

'I don't care if my sword never sees a drop of blood again,' said the knight, striding towards Ashott, outraged at the Armenian's lack of chivalry.

'My lord, we have more important work to do,' said Christopher, grabbing Sir John's shoulder and holding him back. 'Let us settle this later.'

'Come. We waste time. Bolt the gate,' shouted Ashott, as he sprang off again further into the complex.

The gatehouse led onto a large courtyard that was framed on three sides by austere looking buildings that rose several stories above the cobbled surface. They featured few windows, and those that existed were randomly set into the smooth walls. They were too small, barred and high to facilitate forced access, the only entrance to each building a small door, set into a limestone portico, big enough for only one man to enter at a time.

Ashott tucked his body closely against the smooth wall, and began to skirt around the square towards the door on the building to the left. The Crusaders, following his example, quickly fell in behind him. On reaching the door, he took hold of the large iron ring and turned it to the left, the locking mechanism disengaging with a hefty click. He braced himself and heaved against the heavy door. It gave. His momentum carried him forward. The Treasury was theirs.

Target Compound, BAS,
09.40hrs, 19 May 2007.

Tonka must have read the email twenty times in the last hour, his brain still finding it difficult to appreciate the full implications of the dispassionate missive.

Tonka,
Coalition forces have searched the area where the alleged attack took place on Target callsign Tango One, and have found no evidence substantiating the claim that the callsign was attacked by the Iraqi Police Service. Based on the findings of the military search, it has been decided that there is no call for further action. The members of the callsign are listed as MIA - presumed dead - unless evidence to the contrary is found.

Please ensure that all personal belongings of the MIA are shipped to the home address listed on each man's file. Replacement team members will be issued in due course.

The six men had ceased to exist. They were gone; these two paragraphs of electronic text had verified it. Now it was down to him to put what remained of the men's belongings into boxes and transfer the weight of their passing to their grieving families. 'I hate this fucking job,' he shouted, slamming his fists down onto the desk. 'JJ, you bastard!'

When things went wrong in Hereford – and they often

did – there was always someone Tonka could turn to and seek advice from. With his friends, he could work it out. Here, he was on his own. His mind raced with things he could do. *I can go and demand that Brit Mil conduct another search mission. I can get a team together and go and search myself. I can phone JJ and make him listen. I can phone the press and tell them that JJ is a ruthless bastard, or...* He reached for the bottom drawer and took out the bottle of Johnnie Walker. *Or...*

Outside Police Station, Al Amarah,
11.55hrs, 19 May 2007.

At 11:55, the ritual began.. Rachel took the satellite phone out of the bag, unwrapped and extended the small aerial. She pressed the green button displaying a small picture of a telephone handset. As it beeped into life, she checked the display. Acquiring the signal from the invisible orbiting satellite miles above, it read, 'Thuraya, Iraq'. She held it up to the sky with both of her hands, like an offering to an ancient god.

It had been nearly a week since her father was taken and since Mason left. Almost overwhelmed with anxiety, she had left her aunt Miriam to tend over what was left of the house, and set out in search of Papa and the hostages.

Her first port of call had been the big station on the road to Al Amarah, where she'd asked the Sergeant behind the desk if he had any knowledge of her father. The man, in his light blue shirt and dark trousers, treated her with contempt. He had told her that if she asked any more questions, or even spoke of the incident again, she would be arrested. As she stood in front of him, she bit her lip to control the anger, turning as he shouted. As she walked away, her fists clenched, she couldn't erase the image of the Sergeant's sneering face from her mind. It had then dawned on her that

248

she'd seen the man before. It was on the day that father had been taken. He was one of them.

Since then, she has regularly sat under the large tree opposite the entrance of the police station, watching the courtyard, through the entrance guarded by the red and white boom gate, a scarf covering her face, hand extended, mouth muttering the occasional word to passers-by – just as beggars do.

The display read '12:05'. *Mason said to keep it on for only five minutes.* She closed her eyes and wished for it to ring, but the only noise was her heart as it marked each second. Nothing. The display read '12:06'. She wanted more than anything to keep the phone on, but knew what needed to be done. Her thumb hovered over the 'off' key. 'Tomorrow,' she said. Yes. Tomorrow it will ring for sure. She depressed the red key with her thumb. The screen went blank.

The door at the top of the steps opened, and four guards quickly descended into the wretched basement. 'On your knees... Face the wall,' shouted the Sergeant, as he unlocked the cell door.

'What's happening?' Thor asked Dusty, as the two men assume the requested position.

'Stop talking, and put your hands behind your backs,' barked the Sergeant, as two of his guards enter the cell. Their hands were quickly bound with zip ties, masking tape wound around their heads and over their eyes, acting as a rudimentary blindfold. Thor listened as Dusty was pulled to his feet and led off, the Australian's questions unanswered by the guards. He was manhandled out of the cell and up the stone steps.

Thor strained his ears, moving his head slowly, first to the right and then to the left, listening for any noise that might give him an advanced warning. 'SLAM'! Thor's body jumped with fear as the cell door was flung shut, the noise crashing into his body, making his hair stand on end.

He listened as the key was put into the hole and the lock slowly engaged. He could sense that he was being watched, his every move scrutinised, his tormentor relishing his discomfort. His body started to tremble, his body shaking uncontrollably. But it wasn't the temperature that was making his body shake; it was fear. He tried to replace his quick, shallow breaths with longer, deeper ones. But it was hard; his ribs were still bruised and painful from the previous beatings. He fought the pain as the air rushed into his lungs. His efforts were rewarded as the involuntary action stopped and his composure returned. He took another deep breath and pulled back his shoulders - a display of defiance against the invisible antagonist. He was regaining control.

The piercing noise of the gunfire outside smashed into him like a train, his body's resilience disappearing in an instant. As he fell to the floor, a wave of despair washed over him, engulfing every inch of his body in a tight knot of helplessness. The shaking returned, this time accompanied with a wail - a crazed cry that evoked despair - emanating from the pit of his stomach and echoing around the cell.

Rachel has just put the phone away when the commotion began. She witnessed several policemen burst into the courtyard from the main building carrying a blindfolded man, his feet trailing behind him. His boots kicked up a cloud of dust as he was dragged through the open space. She didn't recognise him – why would she? But his clothes looked familiar; they were the same clothes that Mason had worn the first time she'd seen him - an all-in-one tan suit with a long zip down the front. She got up and walked slowly to the other side of the road, trying her best not to draw attention as she settled into a position for a better look. *He must be one of Mason's men.*

She watched as he is dragged around the back of the police building and out of sight. Seconds later, a volley of gunfire ripped through the air. As the sharp cracks faded, the only noise is a flock of birds in a nearby tree, startled, taking to the sky in a flurry of wings.

She walked back to her spot under the tree, fighting the urge to run away as a swell of fear gripped her shaking body. She sat and once more resumed the guise of the beggar, wanting nothing more than to flee, to get away from this horrible place. But she couldn't; she stared at the compound. *My duty is here.* She forced her eyes to look up, to gaze at this evil place. But, to her dismay, the policemen have dragged another man from the building. He too was dressed like the first. *No, please no…*

CHAPTER TEN

Mitch Towers, Beirut,
09.02hrs, 19 May 2007.

Mason woke with a start. He looked up at the
unfamiliar ceiling. *Where the hell am I?* he wondered as he
studied the room. *Beirut, Mitch's place.* The details
began to trickle back in to his groggy mind. He threw back
the covers and sat up on the edge of the bed. The stiffness
in his body made every movement painful. *I'm not
getting any younger,* he thought as he slowly stood up,
taking hold of the cream leather headboard to steady
himself as he went in search of somewhere to relieve his
bladder.

His bedroom looked like something that would be found
on the pages of a glossy magazine - the type engineered
by an interior designer. But the bathroom was even better!
He walked into the shower cubicle - which he realised
was as big as his whole bathroom back in the UK - and
turned on the taps. The hot water gushed from every
direction, with nozzles to the sides and above delivering a
torrent of warmth that truly soothed his aching frame. It was
the type of shower that he could have stayed in until the
water turned cold. But there was a job to do. So, after a time
that was nowhere near long enough, he determinedly turned
off the taps. He dried off in one of the abundant thick
Egyptian cotton towels, dressed, and went in search for
Mitch.

His bedroom entered onto a corridor. To the left – which
he took as the back of the apartment - was a floor–to-ceiling
window that allowed light to flood into the hallway.
Opposite him were two doors, which he assumed were more
bedrooms. To his right: sheer opulence.

The living space was tastefully decorated with several

modern leather sofas, their slim proportions, elegant lines and pastel colours matching the silk Persian carpets that broke up the marble floor. To the left, there was a kitchen, with a long bar fronted by chrome-legged stools, the dull stainless steel of the kitchen utensils looking like they'd never been used. But the pièce de resistance was the view; the external walls were made entirely of glass, allowing an incredible panorama of the city and the Mediterranean - which stretched in front of the penthouse like a thick, blue, azure carpet.

Mason opened the French doors that led onto the sun terrace where Mitch was busy on the phone. 'There's coffee in the pot, and some breakfast in the fridge,' said Mitch, interrupting the call by putting his hand over the telephone receiver.

Mason walked back into the kitchen, his nose tracking the smell of ground beans until he came across a jug of freshly brewed coffee. He poured himself a cup, and, as he sat on one of the bar stools, taking in the apartment's splendour, he noticed that to the right of the hallway leading to the bedrooms was a mosaic of photographs. He picked up his coffee and went to investigate.

It was Mitch's trophy wall: an array of neatly hung pictures, all presented in matching frames, featuring men in uniforms with guns of every description. Mason found one of himself and Mitch standing in front of an armoured vehicle, surrounded by a desert landscape. But most of the faces in the other pictures he did not recognise. They were friends of Mitch's from a different time, men with whom he'd shared experiences in perilous locations, undertaking questionable tasks, their camaraderie their only real motivation. The stories behind these photographs and the events they depicted would never be made known, the real truth stored solely in the memories of these ageing ex-soldiers, who, despite the hardships they had endured, still had the energy to smile for the camera.

Pride of place on the wall was given to the picture of a

group of smiling kids in front of a colourfully-painted concrete building. It appeared to be a school. The inscription at the bottom of the photograph read, 'To Papa Mitch. With thanks from Free Kids Orphanage.

Mason could hear Mitch's footsteps behind him. 'What's with the orphanage picture?' asked Mason, without turning around.

'Ah, it's nothing,' answered Mitch. 'I just donated some stuff for the Beirut orphans. Thought I needed to cancel out some of the bad shit I've done and get into God's good books. Know what I mean?'

'They look pretty happy. What did you donate?'

'Ah, I built them the orphanage. There are three hundred kids there now. That should get me into heaven, don't you think?' said Mitch, smiling.

'Yeah. It's a good start,' laughed Mason, as the two men stepped back out onto the terrace and into the sunshine.

'This place is incredible,' Mason said, sipping his coffee and walking over to the edge of the infinity pool, the water stretched out before him, appearing to fall over the edge and into the Mediterranean.

'That's what most people say,' Mitch said as he sat down in one of the thick-cushioned patio chairs. 'But, to be honest, its novelty has worn off on me. I take it for granted now. But yes… I suppose it is pretty impressive.'

One of the three phones that Mitch had laid out on the glass table in front of him began to ring. He answered it with the phrase 'Salaam alaikum,' and then proceeded with the conversation in fluent Arabic. The conversation was brief, with Mitch scribbling down a few words on the note pad in front of him. He thanked the caller, ending the conversation with 'Shukran habibi.'

'I have been busy this morning whilst you were sleeping. That was the last piece of the jigsaw,' said Mitch as he put down the phone. 'We're all set. Sit down and I'll run you through it,' said Mitch, as Mason sank into a chair, impressed by his friend's efficiency.

'Okay... so we leave early tomorrow for the Syrian border. When we get there, we will be met by our contact - who will have already paid off the necessary people. Visas are not going to be a problem. We go through passport control and will be met on the Syrian side by another contact, who will take us on to Damascus. You ever been there?' asked Mitch.

'Never,' replied Mason as he finished off the last of his coffee.

'Great. You'll love it. We stay there overnight, so I will show you the sights. I have arranged the weapons. It was short notice, and I could only get AK47s,' he continued. 'Is that okay?'

'Happy with an AK; they're a good bit of kit,' confirmed Mason.

'Yeah, that 7.62 can do a lot of damage,' agreed Mitch. 'We will pick them up the day after tomorrow, at the Baghdad Cafe, in Palmyra, on the way to the Iraqi border. My Syrian contact has suggested that the best way for us to get to Basrah is by boat - all the way down the Euphrates. He will arrange everything. He knows some pretty effective smugglers who operate between Iraq and Syria. They have been doing it forever, so we're in good hands.'

'Have they had much experience smuggling people?' asked Mason.

'Funny, I asked him that,' replied Mitch. 'Apparently, they do. He said that the only thing coming out of Iraq these days was refugees. Most end up in Syria or Jordan. But the ones with money go on to Europe. The only people who want to go into Iraq these days are terrorists.'

'So your smugglers help them?'

'Yep. They help Al Qaida get in, and anyone with money get out.'

'Sounds pretty lucrative,' replied Mason, holding his face up to the early morning sun. 'So, after we pick up the weapons, we go on a mini cruise down the big river,' Mason said, turning to his old friend. 'It sounds like you have it all sorted.'

'Yup. I think I've got it all covered. The only thing left to do is to get some kit in the local shops. You know... some camping gear and that. Oh... and we need to arrange the party.'

Mason looked confused. 'What party?'

'The going away party for tonight.'

'I should have guessed,' said Mason as he stood up and went in search of more coffee.

Beirut International Airport, Lebanon,
12.47hrs, 19 May 2007.

The greeter outside the airport held up a sheet of A4 paper in a transparent plastic cover. It carried the single emblem ø, in bold, with 72 font.

'I think you are here for me,' said a man in a deep, rasping Afrikaans accent.

'Your name, sir?' asked the greeter, with laboured English.

'Abraham,' replied the South African, with a guarded tone, revealing his codename.

'You are three?'

The man nodded and waved at the two men some distance behind, gesturing for them to close in.

Colonel Hans Marius - codename Abraham - was in his mid-fifties. He was tall, but carried no weight. His gaunt frame, impaired by his preference for alcohol over food, contributed to his haggard expression and hanging skin, his appearance made worse by his reliance on cigarettes, the smoke staining his hands, grey beard, moustache and producing a guttural growl in his speech.

His travel companions - brothers Gert and Ernst - filed in behind the Colonel as the group followed their greeter to the transport. Gert was the eldest by a year. He was tall, with a powerful set of legs and a thick chest from endless hours of sport played under the warm South African sun. But he now preferred to watch rather than take part, the bulk on his midriff an indication of his supporter's status. His head was covered with a down of recently close-cropped hair, its grey colour matching his scruffy beard.

Ernst hardly ever spoke. As the youngest sibling of six, he found there was no need; his brothers and sisters had done it all for him. The silent habit had stuck into adulthood and, by the time he had joined the military for his national service, the trait of not talking had become ingrained. When he wanted to communicate, he used as few words as possible, relying on primeval grunts and facial expressions to get his point across. It had led to many fights in the army, but his superiors had turned a blind eye. The plus side of his personality being an ability to carry out the hardest and most thankless tasks efficiently and without complaint. His appearance was as nasty as his attitude, his thick lips and bent nose protruding from a massive head that was thickly attached to a squat torso.

The minibus pulled into a tree-lined avenue on the outskirts of the city. The large cedar trees - *cedrus libani* – the cedars of Lebanon, the national emblem, provided a comfortable dappled shade along the quiet suburban boulevard. The safe house was set back from the road, and was surrounded by a two-metre high wall that ran the length of the perimeter, completely enclosing the building and its substantial garden. The only way in or out was through the gate that was set at the top of a short drive that led onto the silent street, where everyone kept to their own business.

'You go there,' said the greeter, pointing at the gate.

Hans exited the minibus, leaving the others to settle up with the driver. He walked up the driveway. The entrance consisted of two gates - one for vehicles and the other for

257

pedestrians. Both were painted a lime green and crowned with razor wire. To the right of the pedestrian gate was an intercom and CCTV system. He pressed the button and waited.

'Yes?' asked the electronic voice.

'I have an appointment,' answered Hans, looking directly into the camera.

'Your name, please?'

'Abraham.'

There was a pause and a buzz as the lock disengaged. 'Please come in.'

The three men were met at the front door by a short fat man in a dark three-piece suit and a comb-over, the dark strands of which matched his bushy moustache. 'Gentlemen, our meeting will be brief,' he said with perfect English that was laced with a hint of an Arabic. 'Please, follow me.'

He ushered them through a double set of doors that led off from the central foyer and into a large room. It looked like it had once served as a reception area for the large two-storey house. But it now lay bare and unfurnished, save for a large table and several chairs that sat in the centre of the poorly-lit, empty space, its curtains drawn against prying eyes.

The short fat man flipped the light switch and walked to the table. 'This is for you,' he said, pointing at a large manila envelope that was resting on the otherwise empty table.

The *target pack* had few details. It contained several pictures of Mason and a physical description, an address and a picture of Mitch Towers from several angles. The information was scant. But Hans wasn't here to write the man's biography; he was here to kill him.

'Who is the other man?' Hans asked, pointing at a picture of a man with an eye patch.

'He is a Beirut businessman. American by birth. He is very well known. We would prefer it if he was not harmed,' said the short fat man as with his index finger he separated the picture of Mitch from the others. 'This envelope does not leave this building. Please ensure that everything is committed to memory?'

The three men gathered around the table and studied the information. 'Do you have anything else for me?' asked Hans, after several minutes of cramming.'

'Of course,' said the fat man, with a hint of annoyance. 'We have a car in the garage. It has a hidden compartment in the boot. In it you will find what you need to complete your task. When you have finished, you will put the weapons back in the compartment, and drive to the Jordanian border. Leave the car in a car park and dispose of the keys. The vehicle has a tracker device so we will know where to recover it. Get a taxi to Amman and wait for the email confirming your flights. When do you anticipate the 'event' taking place?' said the fat man, taking out a packet of cigarettes and offering one to Hans.

'Either tonight or first thing in the morning,' Hans answered as he lit up.

'Good. The less time you spend in Lebanon, the better... Oh, and one more thing. Under no circumstances are you to come back to this house. Are there any more questions?'

Hans shook his head, taking a long pull on the cigarette. 'No questions.'

'Good. Then follow me. I will show you the car.' The basement had been turned into a garage, the underground space allowing several vehicles that were covered with dust sheeting to be stored adequately. The short fat man took hold of the sheet of the nearest obscured vehicle and yanked. The covering fell away to reveal a black, four-door Mercedes saloon, the sides of which bore the marks and dents of several years of use on the Lebanese roads. He rolled up the dust sheet and placed it on a workbench at the rear of the Mercedes. He then opened a box that was fastened to the wall, and unhooked an electronic key from its interior and pointed it at the car.

'Gather around, gentlemen,' he said, as the boot popped opened.

He reached inside and removed a patch of the fabric lining. Underneath was a metal strip that was two foot long, six inches wide, and fastened at either end by a large screw. He opened the screwdriver blade on a small penknife that was attached to the key fob, and undid the fixings. He then placed the cover to one side and put his hand into the opening, fetching a long object wrapped in a cloth and put it to one side of the spacious luggage hold. Repeating the process, he retrieved another three bundles.

He uncovered the first three parcels, each revealing a Krinvok assault rifle - the weapon that was a miniature version of the AK47. It had been designed for use by the Russian special forces - the Spetsnaz - and was also the rifle of choice of Osama Bin Laden. It was small – less than two feet in length - its butt able to fold away, making it very concealable. It was also extremely powerful, and was particularly effective at short range. As the weapons were uncovered, each man picked one of them up, and tested its operation.

'Ernst, I think that is the first time I have seen you smile in a long time,' said Hans, sarcastically looking at his colleague.

Ernst's reply was a hollow grin that was made slightly wider as the fourth bundle was uncovered, revealing six magazines filled with 5.45 ammunition and three silencers.

The Colonel had known his two companions for many years. They had worked for him in the same police unit, the Civil Cooperation Bureau (CCB), under the Apartheid regime. Their job had been to assassinate enemies of the state. In real terms, that was anyone that had stood up to, or publicly criticised, white rule in South Africa. If they had put a notch in the butt of their weapons for every man and woman they had killed, those butts would be withered stumps. But, even after apartheid had collapsed, the Colonel was not short of work. His well-honed skills were in great demand from a number of other African countries. And it was on such a mission that he had come to the notice of the British SIS. He had done them a favour by eliminating a troublesome politician in a West African state and in doing so, had ascended to the top of their *preferred contractors* list. Hans never worked without his two companions. What they lacked in people skills and good looks they made up for in loyalty to their Colonel. Hans knew that his men would do anything that he ordered them to do, without question.

The three former CCB operatives had used their Krinvoks to great success throughout their career. But, unlike professional snipers - who would wait patiently, taking out their target with stealth and precision - the CCB relied on brute force, their modus operandi consisting of kicking down doors and shooting anything that moved. This tactic had served them well in Africa, where police intelligence was scant. And, even if they were compromised, a few hundred-dollar bills placed in the right hands would always ensure a favourable outcome. SIS had refrained from using the three operatives outside the African continent for this very reason. But, unbeknown to them, it wasn't SIS that was paying this time. This was a private job. And the reason they had been picked was because they were cheap.

The three men loaded into the car and set off towards the city. 'We need to recce this location first,' Hans said, pointing to Mitch Towers on the street map that he found in the glove box, Gert straining to look at the map as he drove through the Beirut side streets. 'We need to decide how we're going to take them out.'

'Them?' asked Gert. 'I thought it was just the one?'

'Naaah...' replied Hans. 'I don't want any witnesses. It looks like our friend with the eye patch just became collateral damage.'

The man stood in the hallway of the treasury, his arms filled with parchments, his body paralysed with fear, as he stared at the blood-stained Armenian and his armoured companions. 'Who are you?' demanded Ashott as he closed on the stunned man.

'I am Yusef Al Bakhir, keeper of the Caliph's Treasury,' he answered, with a trembling voice. 'And who might you be, sir?'

Ashott's answer was a mighty blow with the back of his right hand across Yusef's face, sending him reeling backwards. 'I ask the questions, you eunuch dog,' shouted Ashott as he stood over the shaking administrator. 'If you are the keeper, then you are well placed to show us the Treasury store,' he snapped, kicking the man, who had assumed the foetal position, in an attempt to protect himself. 'On your feet, you snivelling coward. Lead the way.'

They followed close behind Yusef, the man guiding the group through an arch and down a winding staircase at the bottom of which was a metal door. Ashott pushed the man aside, and tried the handle. It didn't move; the door was locked. 'Open it, dog,' he snarled at the petrified Yusef. The treasurer fumbled with a cluster of keys that was attached to his thick leather belt with a big iron ring, his nervous fingers hurriedly inspecting each in turn before slipping one off the loop. He tried to insert the key into the thick iron lock, but his hands trembled so much that he dropped the heavily cast metal object before it could reach the aperture, the noise of iron on stone echoing throughout the staircase.

'Imbecile,' shouted Ashott as he pushed Yusef out of the way once more. He picked up the heavy key and pushed it into the lock, smiling as he turned it, bathing in anticipation of the wealth that would soon be his. The lock clicked and the door gave way, the Armenian pushing it open excitedly before stepping into the treasury, closely followed by the Crusaders.

There were no windows in the subterranean strong room, the only light emanating from candelabras that stood in each of its four corners, the mass of candles flickering as the air was disturbed. All present could see that the room was empty, save for a line of four chests against the back wall. 'Where is the gold,' shouted Ashott. 'Is there another room?' He went back outside and grabbed Yusef, who was crouched against the wall, pulling him up and throwing him into the treasury.

'I had instructions to move it all, sir. It... it... is... gone,' whispered Yusef, fearful that his answer would bring him more pain.

Ashott grabbed Yusef's tunic with his left hand, and raised his scimitar to the man's throat, the curved blade piecing into the man's skin, the blood from the wound mixing with his sweat, before running down his neck and onto the collar of his white tunic. 'Where has it gone?' Ashott whispered.

'I do not know.' Yusef broke into tears. 'Soldiers came and put it on the ships. I don't know where it is now.'

Ashott paused. It would take only the slightest movement of his right hand, and the razor sharp blade would cut so deep as to sever the man's artery. Ashott looked into the man's eyes. Yusef stared back, unable to look away. Yusef was looking at the face of death.

A chain-mail-clad arm reached across and grabbed Ashott's hand. 'He is worth more to us alive than dead, Ashott. Let him live,' said Sir John in a hushed tone in his ear. Ashott looked towards the knight. 'Let him live, Ashott. We need him,' the knight repeated, slowly letting go of the mercenary's hand. Ashott pulled back his sword, and threw the terrified prisoner aside like a rag doll.

'What are they?' asked Ashott, pointing with his sword at the four thick, wooden chests that lay against the far wall. The sturdy containers were all the same size: three foot wide, two foot deep and two foot tall, their sides reinforced with iron; each box sealed with a heavy lock. Sir John looked back at Yusef, and pointed to the locks. The keeper of the Caliph's treasury took the cue and scurried forward fumbling with his keys, eager to show his worth to his captors. Starting from the left he opened each lock in turn. The first three boxes were full of silver coins. In the fourth box were a number of rolled parchments, a crucifix of wood in a gilded frame and a small casket, the exterior of which was inlaid with precious stones.

'Ask him how many boxes have been taken,' said Sir John to Ashott. A brief conversation took place between the two men in their native tongue.

'Eighty four - all of the same size - filled with gold and precious stones. These were the last, and it was planned that they would be taken this evening,' replied Ashott, the anger and disappointment clear in his voice. Ashott broke away from the Crusaders, who were still examining the silver coins, and started to pace the room, shouting angrily to himself. They didn't know what he was saying, but they could tell he was furious. As Ashott raged, Yusef hid in amongst the Crusaders, peering out from behind the armoured men, hoping that the enraged Armenian would not vent his anger on him.

Sir John walked over to the last box and looked inside. 'What is here?' he said looking at Yusef, and pointing at its contents.

Yusef began a stream in his local dialect only stopping when John raised his hand. 'What's he saying Ashott?' the knight mused.

'He says that it's the True Cross, taken by Saladin at the battle of Hattin,' Ashott said as he continued his pacing.

Yusef smiled and gestured towards the relic. The ancient wooden fragment enlarged by its ornate frame - once paraded so proudly at the head the Crusaders army –

incongruous in its latent setting.

Sir John knelt and crossed himself, his men gathering around him, following his example. After they had prayed John rose and pointed at the small box 'And that?'

Yusef reached into the chest, picked up the bejewelled box opened it, and with the biggest smile that he could muster offered it to Sir John. Inside was a rolled parchment that was held in place by a gold clasp. Sir John slid the parchment out of its holder and unrolled it. It was old - very old - and on its surface were inscribed characters that looked familiar. As his eyes became accustomed to the letterings he realised that he could read it; it was written in Latin.

'What is it, John?' said Christopher. 'What does it say?'

'It speaks of a great treasure that was taken for safe keeping from Jerusalem to the ancient city of Tadmor - after Jesus' crucifixion,' answered Sir John. He read on. 'Only a select few knew of its existence. And, to ensure its safety, it was buried in a vault in the sand.'

'What type of treasure?' asked Christopher.

'It doesn't say. But it gives directions and a map of how to find it.'

Ashott had stopped pacing when he heard the words 'great treasure,' and was listening intently to Sir John. 'Maybe not all is lost then,' he said, rubbing his hands.

'Where is Tadmor?' asked Sir John.

'Tadmor, 'the bride of the desert',' announced the Armenian with a smirk. It is north-east of Damascus on the caravan route. The Arabs call it Tadmor; the Romans called it Palmyra.'

Saracen Encampment, The Holy Land,
July 1191.

The first Sultan of Egypt and Syria, the Great Ayyubid general, Saladin, sat on the cushioned floor of his campaign tent, surrounded by his officers, waiting for the sun to set before they started their evening meal. 'Sire,' interrupted the Captain of the Guard, 'there is an urgent dispatch from Acre.'

'Show him in, Captain,' answered the general with a wave of his arm.

The messenger entered the tent, his clothing covered in dust from his long, arduous journey. He approached his general. Kneeling before him, and reached into the leather pouch slung across his shoulder and with his long sinuous fingers offered the dispatch.

'You have come far. We thank you for your endeavours,' said the general as he accepted the scroll of parchment from the exhausted rider. 'Captain, make sure this man receives nourishment,' the general said, turning his back to the rider as he opened the dispatch.

There was a long pause while Saladin read and digested the information. 'Gentlemen, I'm afraid these are bad tidings,' he said to the assembled officers as he put the parchment into his pocket. 'As I feared, Acre has fallen.' There was a murmur as the news settled.

'We saved the treasure, at least,' the general said, more for his own benefit than his listeners', trying to focus on something positive. 'The Caliph got it out over the last three weeks. Thankfully, we have the money to re-arm our troops,' he continued, as he sat back down. 'But the Caliph was unable to get all the treasure chests to safety. His spies have reported that the chest containing the True Cross and more importantly the map of the Great Treasure buried at Tadmor have fallen into the hands of the Crusaders,' he said, deep in thought. 'It appears that the Caliph has put more weight on securing the coinage than on the Holy relics. Foolish... foolish... We all know what will happen if the Crusaders get wind of the Great Treasure,' he said, addressing the assembly. 'They will stop at nothing to possess it. They will be driven on again, destroying our lands and killing even more of our people. Captain,' he said, his course of action decided, 'I need to write a despatch.'

The scribe entered the tent and knelt close enough to the general so that he could hear his hushed tone. 'Take a handful of your best men and leave for Tadmor immediately,' dictated the general. 'To the north of the city walls is a small craggy outcrop, at the base of which is an underground tomb. In the tomb is hidden the Great Treasure. You must be swift as the Crusaders are searching for it. It must not fall into their hands. You are to destroy the Great Treasure.'

The scribe blew on the ink, and sprinkled drying powder, before melting a blob of wax ready for his master's seal. 'Give this to the Commander of my Guard,' said the general, as he pressed his ring into the hot wax.

'Yes, my Lord Saladin,' answered the scribe. 'Consider it done.'

Police Station, Al Amarah, 12.30hrs, 19 May 2007

John looked up when he heard the door go. *That was the second time*, he thought, straining to see what was happening. Every movement was difficult, his whole body racked in agony from the beating he had received. *A week ago?* he asked himself, *or was it longer?* He tried to count the days. How long had it been? There was too much pain; he couldn't concentrate. He looked up and saw the guards throwing one of his fellow prisoners into the cell. Minutes later, they did the same with the second man.

He'd heard shooting outside and had feared the worst. But they were both back now, and he was glad. He had grown fond of them. They had given him water and food - even though their ration was meagre - and had engaged him in conversation, allowing his mind to focus on happier times. As he lay in the corner and wrapped his blanket around himself, he listened to the two men. *I'm cold. Ever so cold,* he thought, as the fever gripped his body.

'You okay?' asked Thor as he peeled the masking tape from around his own head.

'Yeah, I think so,' answered Dusty. 'I think one of the bullets must have ricocheted, 'cos something hit me in the side of the head. Take a look, will you?' he asked as he began to unwind the tape that been used as a makeshift blindfold.

'It must have been a bit of plaster,' said Thor, tearing off a part of his sleeve and pressing it up against the bleeding gash. 'It's a flesh wound. You'll live,' he continued, sticking a bit of masking tape over the dressing to keep it in place.

'Why did they do that, Thor?'

'Fake execution, I guess. I saw it on the TV. It's a power thing. They do it to fuck with your head.'

'Well, consider me fucked up, 'cos I can't take any more of that shit. I would rather them shoot me and get it over with.'

'Yeah, you're right. Sick bastards,' Thor said, glancing at his cell mate.

'I hate them. I hate them all,' said Dusty, his voice breaking with emotion. 'Why are we still here? They should have come for us by now. Where are they?'

'Mason told you that he wouldn't leave us,' Thor said as he put his hand on the Australian's shoulders. 'Hang in there. He'll come back. It could be worse, I suppose,' he continued, motioning towards John, the Elder, 'We could be like that poor sod over there.'

'He doesn't look good, does he?' said Dusty, moving over to the barred wall that joined the two cells. 'Are you okay, John?' he whispered. 'JOHN, can you hear me?' he asked, raising his voice. There was no reply.

'Do you think he's dead?' asked Thor.

'No. I am not dead, my friends. I am just tired and cold - very cold,' John answered. Dusty picked up the metal water cup, pushing it through the bars. 'Here. There's a mouthful of water. Take it. It will make you feel better.'

'You are too kind,' replied John, 'but you must keep the water. You need it more than I do.'

'No. Come on. Take a sip,' insisted Thor. 'Then you can tell us some more stories about the village and your daughter. Tell me the one about the donkey that would follow her everywhere like a dog. What was the donkey's name again?'

'Tebo. The donkey's name was Tebo... Yes, you are right. He would follow her everywhere,' said John, sitting up and taking the smallest of sips. 'Yes. Those were good times... good times,' he continued, passing the mug back through the bars. 'Thank you once more for your kindness. I am ever indebted to you.'

'No problem, mate,' replied Dusty. 'I'm glad of the stories too; they take my mind off this place.'

'I will repay you. And if I can't, then my daughter Rachel will repay you in my stead.'

'There is no debt. It's just some water,' Dusty said taking a sip from the nearly-empty mug.

'You mentioned a man just now by the name of Mason,' John said, as he pulled the blanket over himself. 'I helped an injured man called Mason.'

'What? Did you just say that you helped Mason?' asked Thor, sliding over to the bars.

'Yes. I helped him to escape. He is the reason I am here.'

'Why didn't you tell us earlier?' asked Thor.

'I did not know that there was a connection. It is only when I heard you whisper his name that it came back to me. But, come to think of it, he was dressed like you when I found him. I should have realised. I'm sorry... My mind... My mind is not...'

'Don't worry,' replied Thor. Can you tell us what happened?'

'Yes, there is more to tell. But first, I must rest. I am so tired.'

'Okay. Get some sleep. And then you can tell us everything,' said Thor, as they watched John trying to make himself comfortable. 'He doesn't look good at all,' whispered Thor to his cellmate. 'He's as white as a ghost.'

'Yeah. You're right. If he doesn't get released soon, I reckon he'll be dead in a few days.'

'Mason alive!' said Thor as he sat back against the wall. 'That's the best news I have heard for ages. 'I bet he is out there, planning our rescue right now,' he said, a smile breaking out on his face.

'I hope so, mate. I really bloody hope so.'

Mitch Towers, Beirut,
01.23hrs, 20 May 2007.

Mitch had gone through his address book, and had invited everyone he knew. The venue was his bar on the ground floor and, as the sun tucked itself behind the Mediterranean, it came alive with Beirut's trendiest set. The revellers, taking full advantage of the *open bar,* soon got into the swing of things. The music became louder as the partygoers became more and more drunk.

Mason had considered the party a bad idea and had a feeling that it would end badly. So he never ventured far from his flamboyant host's side all night. He'd tried counting the drinks that the intoxicated guests had brought their host, but his reckoning had gone by the first hour. Eventually, with his bladder bursting from soda water and blackcurrant, he had to put his body guarding duties aside, and take a piss.

When he returned, the bar was empty. *What the hell is going on now*? he thought, running to the entrance. When he got closer, he could see through the glass that all the inebriated guests had gathered outside. He arrived just in time to witness the taillights of Mitch's Ferrari disappear into the large swimming pool that fronted the building. 'What the fuck?' he shouted, as he ran towards the pool, pushing his way to the front of the crowd.

Luckily, the top was down, and Mitch floated harmlessly to the surface. The car, however, didn't fare so well; it now lay at the bottom of the pool, its headlights still on, its windscreen wipers trying in vain to clear the six-foot of water that was above it. Mitch was swimming on his back, spitting water into the air like a whale. The crowd was hysterical, the chants of 'Mitch! Mitch! Mitch!' reverberating through the sultry night air.

'What's going on, mate? You're acting like a mad man,' said Mason as he pulled Mitch out of the swimming pool.

'I love you, man,' was Mitch's answer. 'It's so good to see you again. I love you, man.'

'Yeah, yeah. Let's get you inside and out of these wet clothes,' said Mason putting his arm around Mitch's waist to support him. Mason somehow steered him back into the building. When they got inside, Mason bundled him into the lift. 'That's enough for you,' he said, pressing the button and trying to keep him from sliding down the elevator wall at the same time.

'What's the matter with you tonight? I've never seen you like this. Anyone would swear this was the last party you'll ever have,' Mason said as he took hold of Mitch's arm and threw it over his shoulder. He carried his friend into the apartment.

'It is, man. It *is* the last party ever... That's why it needs to be so radical,' Mitch cried out as he was thrown onto his bed.

'Look, I know it's not going to be a walk in the park but there's a good chance that we can survive it,' said Mason as he pushed Mitch back down on the bed.

'Not for me, man. I'm not coming back. It's a one-way ticket, daddy-oh.'

'You're pissed. What are you on about? A one-way ticket?'

'I've got cancer, man.'

Mason stared at him, not sure whether he was telling the truth or whether this was some kind of sick joke.

'I was diagnosed six months ago,' Mitch slurred. I've tried everything. Seen all the best doctors. But it's no good. I'm a dead man walking... or lying... swimming or... whatever.'

Mason sat on the edge of the bed and stared at the sopping wet Mitch. 'Cancer?' The word formed like acid in his mouth, stinging his lips as it fell out. 'Cancer?' He repeated, only this time as if it were an obscenity.

'Got it big time... Yep. They wanted to give me chemo. But not for old Mitch! I ain't loosing my hair and dying in a hospital bed. I am going to die like a Viking, with a sword in my hand. Straight to Valhalla. That's why I was so glad you came, man, it was meant to be,' he said as he fought with his jeans.

Mason took hold of the legs of the jeans, and pulled them off, the heavy denim landing in a heap on the marbled floor. He was devastated, his stomach cramped as though he had received a heavy blow to the guts. He watched as Mitch struggled with his t-shirt. Stepping back from the bed Mason collapsed into a chair, like a boxer returning to his corner after a hard round. He needed time to think.

'You see? That's why this *is* the last party ever. This is my 'death party'. Man. Who the fuck has one of those? Mitch Mitchell. That's who!' he said, as he managed to free the shirt from his head, throwing it at Mason.

❖ ❖ ❖

Twenty-four floors below, the party was still in full swing as the black Mercedes with its three occupants drove slowly past the bar.

'That looks like a crazy party, Hans,' said Ernst from the back seat.

'Yah, yah, too many people. We can't do it tonight. This will work for us though. We'll come back in the morning, when they are all suffering from their hangovers. This should make our job easier - much easier.'

The Treasury, Acre,
July 1191.

'You will be glad to know that the city is ours,' said King Philip to the assembled men in the Treasury Square as he dismounted from his horse. 'And what of your task, Sir John? What of the treasury?'

'I'm afraid my news is not as fair as yours, Sire. We took the Treasury as planned. But we found it empty. There are only three chests of silver left.'

'Is the treasure still within the city?'

'Nay, my lord. I think not. We captured the Treasury keeper,' he said, nodding towards Yusef. 'He's told us that most of it was taken away by ship when they learned that we'd received reinforcements.'

'It seems that my lord Saladin is a canny opponent,' Philip said as he looked at Yusef. 'Could he be lying?'

'He's lost everything, and has nothing to gain by lying. I believe him.'

'This is not what I wanted to hear,' said Philip as he paced before the men. 'We were counting on the booty to help pay off some debts and enable us to re-arm.'

'There is consolation, however, Sire,' Sir John interrupted. 'In one of the chests, we found the True Cross - the relic that was lost at the Battle of Hattin,' he said, pointing at the chest resting on the cobbles.

'This is excellent news,' Philip said as he approached the strongbox.

One of John's men opened the lid as the King approached, all of the other men kneeling as the artefact was laid bare. 'There is also this, my lord,' Sir John said, handing Philip the small bejewelled box. 'There is a parchment inside, written in Latin.'

Philip opened the box and read the parchment, his harsh expression mellowing the more he read. 'What do you make of this, Sir John?' he said, putting the parchment back in the box and looking up at the knight.

'It is something that they obviously placed at a high value, Sire. Yusef has informed me that the box has been there ever since he can remember. I think that the parchment and the treasure of which it speaks are genuine.'

'As do I, John. And a truly great treasure it seems. But how shall we go about recovering it?'

Ashott stepped forward. 'Let me go, my lord,' he said enthusiastically. 'If the treasure is there, I will find it.'

'Thank you for the offer, Ashott. But to send you alone would be... far too dangerous.'

'It would be better for me alone, my lord,' argued the Armenian. 'I can move swiftly and unseen. I would soon bring it back to you.'

'Yes. I am sure you would, Ashott,' replied Philip. 'Sir John, what do you think?'

'Ashott will need help, Sire. Someone should accompany him. How else could he carry the treasure back? In his pockets?'

Philip smiled. 'I agree. But who should it be?' he said, as he again began to pace the cobbled floor.

'I will go, Sire,' said Sir John.

'Nay, John. You have done enough. I would not ask this of you.'

'Sire,' John said, his tone hushed, out of Ashott's earshot. 'I have the measure of him. If anyone should go, it should be me. But I speak only for myself. My men have their own voice,' he said, louder - for all to hear.

'But who will stop you from getting into trouble?' butted in Christopher. 'If you go, then so shall I.'

'And I!' 'And I,' sounded off Sir John's men, '..We shall all go!'

'It is decided, then,' Philip said with a smile. 'What shall be our next move, Ashott?'

'We shall set off at nightfall, and will travel only in the dark. Saladin has many spies. But hopefully, the blanket of darkness will assist us in staying alive and unnoticed,' Ashott answered, with a scornful face.

Sir John's band of men gathered their belongings and readied themselves for the walk back to their encampment. Yusef looked on with horror as his protectors started out on their march. He recognised that his usefulness had already been expended, his fate likely to match that of the city's other inhabitants: certain death. Sir John caught a glimpse of the keeper of the Treasury in the corner of his eye, and stopped. 'Yusef,' he called. 'It is not fitting for a knight to carry his own baggage. I am in need of assistance,' he said, beckoning the frightened man. Yusef ran as fast as he could across the courtyard, unsure what the knight had just said, but heartened by his tone of voice. He took the knight's shield that John held out towards him, and fell in behind the Crusaders as they marched through the streets of the fallen city.

With the battle won, there was no need for the men to use the small back streets as they had done that morning. Instead, Ashott took them down the main avenue that dissected the city east-west, heading towards the East Gate. When they had first entered the city, there had been no sign of its inhabitants; the frightened people had hidden from the Crusaders' onslaught, leaving the streets deserted. But, on the way back, things appeared markedly different.

The Crusaders who had stormed the walls and defeated their enemy, were not content with the blood they had let during the battle. After their victory, they had lined up their prisoners and executed them whilst singing hymns. Their blades had scythed at the defenders' necks; their severed heads collected like some gruesome crop in pyramid-shaped piles on the city's streets. And yet the Crusaders' blood-lust was still not satisfied, and with the two thousand men of the Acre garrison soon annihilated, they turned their attention to the city's citizens.

As the small group walked down the newly liberated streets of the city, they were met with a horrific sight; packs of Crusaders were running from house to house, turning their occupants out into the streets and killing them where they stood. None were spared - men, women nor children. The victims stood in small groups, waiting hopelessly to be butchered, their faces etched with utter horror as their friends and loved ones were murdered all around them.

Sir John understood the argument underpinning this practice. He was well aware of the requirement to eliminate combatants. He himself had previously made the error of releasing prisoners under their promise that they would take no further part in hostilities, only to find the same individuals fighting again, days, weeks or months later. But he believed in the code of chivalry. He had never taken a man's life in cold blood. If his opponent surrendered, he would be spared and taken prisoner. According to his code, prisoners may be ransomed, but never executed. What he and his men now saw on the streets of Acre sickened them all. It was wholesale slaughter. He felt the anger well up inside him. He thought of stopping one group of Crusaders. But if he did that, what of the next group? And the next? There were so many employed in this hideous work. He could not stop them all. He averted his eyes, choosing to look down at the ground rather than at the faces of the condemned. But even that was no good; the sticky red liquid from their opened flesh ran in rivulets between the cobble stones, accumulating in the gutters at the road side, where it became a torrent, coating everything in its path. Acre was being washed in blood.

The horrid walk seemed to go on forever. But eventually, their blood soaked feet led the party to the place where the fate of the city had been sealed: the East Gate. As they entered the gatehouse, a young child blocked their path, screaming uncontrollably. The first two men steered around the toddler, ignoring him. But Sir John stopped beside the crying child. He followed the infant's petrified stare, and was horrified by what he saw. The child's mother was being raped in the corner of the gatehouse by a Crusader, whose bloody tunic had been thrown to one side for the act. Sir

John, enraged, grabbed the man by the scruff of the neck. He pulled him off the weeping woman and onto his feet. The man gasped for breath, his chest still heaving from his exertions, unable to speak. As he recovered, he tried to justify his actions to the incensed knight. Sir John de Guise had reached the end of his tether, channelling all his anger and frustration into a single blow to the man's face. It broke the rapist's jaw instantly, sending him reeling backwards, his unconscious body landing in a heap on the blood-soaked cobblestones.

Sir John took his shield from Yusef, and pointed to the child and his mother. 'Help them,' he said, 'and follow us.' Yusef nodded, and pulled the woman to her feet, the young child running instinctively to its mother for protection. She scooped up the infant and, helped by Yusef, walked behind the group as they departed Acre.

Sir John's party, with their three refugees, were soon back at their encampment on the plateau outside of the city walls. During the journey, Ashott had wanted to go to his quarters to gather what belongings he had left. But Sir John would not allow it, asserting that it was too dangerous for him to be seen in the city, even with an escort. The real reason, though, was that he didn't want Ashott out of his sight for a single moment.

Sir John's men had gone straight in to their well-rehearsed routine, half tending to their weapons and armour whilst the others lit the fire, and began to prepare the food for the evening's meal. The mood should have been a joyous one. After all, they had achieved what they had set out to do; Acre had been freed from the barbarians. But instead, the men were sombre, each reflecting on the haunting and horrific scenes they had witnessed.

Sir John went to where Yusuf, the mother and her child sat on the ground, huddled for protection. The woman held her child closer to her chest as the iron-clad knight approached. Sensing their fear, he turned and looked for Ashott, finding him in the shade of their tents, sharpening his scimitar. 'Ashott,' he called, seeing the man's head rise at the call of his name. 'I need you to talk for me.' Ashott rose, sheathing his sword as he walked towards the knight.

'Ask her: what of her husband?' Sir John instructed, as Ashott closed on the knight.

'Dead,' was the mercenary's brief, uncaring reply after a quick exchange of words.

Sir John untied a small leather pouch which hung from his belt and took out three silver coins. 'This is for them,' he said to Ashott, putting the coins in Yusef's hand. 'Tell him that they are free to go, and that he is to look after this woman and her child as if they were his own.' Ashott translated. Yusef nodded. 'He must swear this, on all that is Holy to him.' Yusuf fell on his knees and kissed the knight's hand, his eyes filling with tears. The woman too kneeled before Sir John in gratitude.

Yusef looked up at the knight and spoke. 'He said that you are most merciful. And he will do as you request. He swears it to Allah,' said Ashott.

'Go now. Go far from this place and try to forget what has happened here,' John told them, with the help of Ashott's translation.

Yusef and the woman rose to their feet and started off down a path, quickly disappearing as the footway wove its way through the rocky hillside. Sir John stood and watched until he could see them no more. He then turned and walked with Ashott back to where his men were sat eating.

'You are a good man, John,' said Ashott as they walked. 'It's a pity they will be all dead before nightfall.'

'That I have no control over,' replied the knight. 'But at least they now have hope, where before they had only despair.'

As his men ate, John sat alone on a rock overlooking Acre, the city for which they had marched for two years to reach. In the process, he had lost many of his men. He had openly wept tears of joy when he had first entered the Holy Land,

278

believing that - for his penance - God would absolve him of all his sins. But, as he watched the smoke rise from the burning buildings, the fires set by the marauding bands of Crusaders, he wept again. This time, his tears were of anger and disbelief.

He reached for the Crucifix that had been hung around his neck by the Bishop of Metz over two years previously – a blessing before his departure. Finding the leather cord, he took hold of it in his powerful hand, and tore it from himself. He looked at the simple wooden cross that he had worn with pride, and had held every time he prayed to his beloved God. *I knew that there would be bloodshed*, he thought as the tears streamed down his face, *I am not naive. But the brigands and thieves that make up this army of Crusaders have ruined the sanctity of the Holy Land. This place - where Jesus had died a thousand years before to absolve mankind for their sins and to make the earth a better place - was now awash with blood. And Jesus had done nothing to stop it.*

He, like all of the Crusaders, had believed that their quest was just. The *Muslims had no right to seize the Holy Land.* They had all been agreed on this, as they sat around their campfires during their long campaign. John had participated and acquiesced in the questionable things he had witnessed, believing them to serve a greater good, even though they weighed heavily on him. He had been sure that, when he had fulfilled his vow - when the Holy Land had been freed from the heathens' hands - his sins would be absolved, washed away like dirt from a pane of glass in a summer shower. They were to be cleansed by the thankful God. But now, it seemed, it wasn't so.

He looked up at the city, its mass engulfed by a bright yellow and orange blaze. As the fire took hold, his grip on the wooden cross that he held between his hands tightened as his anger grew. There was a snap as the Crucifix broke. And, at that moment, he knew it: his faith was dead, like that of so many of the innocents whose bodies now lay in heaps outside Acre's walls.

'Sir John, Sir John,' said Christopher, shaking his arm. 'It is time for us to leave.' The knight opened his eyes. He'd fallen asleep sitting upright, leaning against a rock in the same spot from which he had watched the city burn. He rose slowly, his body stiff from the day's exertions and from his awkward sleeping position. 'Why did you not wake me earlier?' he said, as he stretched.

'You were peaceful. We thought it better to leave you. It is no matter. Your kit is packed. We are all ready. But you need to put these on.'

'Arab clothes?' said the knight, as he took the garments.

'Aye... it is Ashott's bidding.'

Ashott had already mounted his brown mare. As Sir John approached, the mercenary explained his intentions. 'We will travel at night, and lay up far from the road in the daytime. If we see any troops, we will run rather than fight, for we are to bring as little attention to our party as possible. I have arranged our clothes and animals so as to look like we are Arab merchants. So please do not talk to anyone, as your voices will surely give you away. Remember, the further we get from this place, the more dangerous it will be. But, when we reach Damascus, the danger will pass. The city is full of merchants who do their business along the silk route to the East. And no one there will give you a second glance.'

As the sun set in the west – seeming to hover over their distant homelands - the group of seven headed north-east towards Damascus.

Police Station, Al Amarah,
07.05hrs, 20 May 2007.

He'd seen the Commander lose his temper on many occasions before. Once, during the Iran-Iraq war, two of their men had been found sleeping at their posts. He had had them arrested. And, at dawn the next day, in front of the whole unit, they had been paraded before him. His tone to begin with had been like that of a headmaster: scholarly. While pacing through the ranks, he had lectured the assembled on the rights and wrongs of being a good soldier. However, as his address had progressed, his voice had grown louder, his annoyance at the two miscreants - who stood in the middle of the parade ground with heads bowed – soon turning to hatred. With white spittle clinging to his lips, he had shouted at the officers to make the men kneel. And, as the two men were pushed down, he drew his pistol from the polished leather holster attached to his belt. Walking behind them, he shot one, then the other, the two corpses falling together in a macabre embrace, as their bodies' vital liquids exited from the wounds in their skulls.

As the Sergeant watched his Commander, all he could see was the same spittle on his lips and the memory of those two bodies slumped together on the parade ground. *Why did I let the men conduct their fake executions? I am such a fool,* he thought to himself.

'You are an imbecile. These men are worth money - a great deal of money - and you would squander this for fun? You are an idiot. What if one of the men missed and killed one of the prisoners? What would we do then, imbecile? How much would we get for dead men? Not fucking much, I can tell you,' the Commander ranted.

Like a dog showing its submission to the leader of the pack, the Sergeant avoided eye contact at all cost. He knew that if their eyes met, it could send his boss into a killing rage. He kept his head bowed, his eyes fixed on a flower pattern woven into the ornate carpet in front of the Commander's desk. The Commander approached his victim, drew his hand back and slapped him hard against his cheek. The abuse stopped, as if the blow had acted as a pressure valve. The Commander picked up a packet of Marlboro cigarettes from his desk and sat back down in his chair.

'Muhammad, look at me,' he said to the Sergeant.

The man raised his head slowly, his eyes still fixed on the spot on the carpet.

'LOOK AT ME,' he shouted, as he banged his fist on the desk. 'Never disobey my orders again. Do you hear?'

The Sergeant rotated his eyes upwards, until they came to rest on his Commander's face.

'Do you understand?'

'Yes, Sahib. It will never happen again,' he croaked in answer.

'Good, good. Our Iranian friends are coming soon. I want the prisoners in good condition. I'm holding you personally responsible. We will soon be rid of them, and our bank accounts will be much fatter,' said the Commander, with a hint of a smile. 'Are there any questions?'

'No, Sahib. No questions.'

The Commander pulled deeply on the cigarette, and sat back in his chair. The Sergeant didn't take his cue to leave, and hesitated at his mark.

'What is it?' the Commander said as he blew out the lungful of smoke.

'The old man, Sahib. He does not look well. It looks like the life is draining out of him.'

'Yes, I had forgotten about him.' He took another pull on the cigarette. 'It is God's will... if he dies.'

'Inshallah,' repeated the Sergeant. 'What of his property, Sahib? The shield, sword and stone box?'

'Where are they?'

'We have stored them downstairs, Sahib. They are old - very old. Such things are worth money.

'Yes. Thank you, Sergeant. You're right. Such things are valuable. We will take them to Kuwait. We will find a fool there who will buy them.'

Mitch Towers, Beirut,
07.15hrs, 20 May 2007.

The black Mercedes drove down the cornice, past the driveway that led to the apartment block, and turned down the first available road that led off St George Bay. Touched by the cool morning sea breeze, the street was quiet, save for two joggers and an old woman walking her dog - neither of whom paid any attention to the three men dressed in dark grey boiler suits as they alighted from the vehicle. As Ernst retrieved the small bag from the boot, Gert made sure that the car was ready for the rapid exit to follow, while Hans leaned against the family saloon, nonchalantly reading a paper whilst checking the street for activity. Each satisfied, they walked briskly towards the tower block entrance.

They stopped just out of sight of the smoked glass door, the bag and its heavy contents clunking as Ernst grounded it. 'Ski masks,' Hans grunted, as he unzipped the holdall and pulled out the black hoods. With their faces hidden, each man grabbed one of the three lethal assault rifles. The men were professionals; their rifles had been made ready before they were placed in the holdall, the lethal, shiny, metal projectiles lying in wait in the chambers, ready for immediate use. The men knew that in a *hot* situation, a fraction of a second could mean the difference between going home Club Class, or in a body bag.

The concierge with his back to the entrance was arranging his morning paperwork when he heard the door open. He turned around, his cheerful greeting sliding off his face as he looked down the barrel of three guns.

'PENTHOUSE!' one of the masked men screamed at him, shoving the muzzle of the rifle into the man's face, knocking him backwards into his seat. Another of the masked men grabbed his shirt, pulled him off his chair and threw him against the wall. The concierge fell to the floor and began fumbling for the keys that were attached to his belt, releasing the bunch and holding them up like a talisman, hoping that they would protect him. 'Yes, Yes. Key for lift. Penthouse,' he stammered.

Hans took hold of his shirt and pulled him to his feet, pushing him towards the lift door. 'Penthouse. Mitchell. Do you understand?' he said, pointing upwards. The concierge nodded, put the key into the lock that was labelled 'Penthouse,' turned it and pressed the button. Within seconds, the lift began to move.

All four men watched as the green lights on the panel illuminated with each passing floor. As the elevator slowed, the three men readied for action. This was when they were at their most vulnerable. If their prey had been alerted to their presence, this was where it was going to get *loud*.

As the door slid open, Gert and Ernst burst out, one to the left, the other to the right. Hans pushed the concierge forward, clear of the lift. And, as the shrill *ping* - the announcement of their arrival – dissipated, they stood motionless and listened. Silence. The only noise was the lift door as it closed – that and the heavy breathing of the petrified concierge.

The foyer was a box. No windows, some plants and a few pictures on the walls. Ahead of them was a set of double-doors. 'Key?' Hans said, pointing at the entrance to the penthouse. Hoping that his part in this ordeal would soon be over, the man fumbled through his collection of passkeys, holding up the result of his search with a faint smile. Hans took the key from the man's shaking hand. With a flick of his head, he motioned the petrified man towards the lift. As he turned and presented his back, Hans fired. The first two rounds hit the concierge in the neck. The third went straight into his skull, killing him instantly. The only noise was four thuds – three as the bullets hit home from the silenced weapons, the fourth as the lifeless body landed in an ungainly heap.

The three hooded men - so ungraceful and cumbersome in normal circumstances - were now in their element. They worked as a well-oiled machine, moving around the apartment, each man covering his teammate, knowing from experience what the next move would be.

It was soon evident that their quarry was still in bed, the only rooms they had not checked being the bedrooms at the rear of the building. Hans pointed for the two men to move to the rear of the apartment. Ahead of them was a corridor that had three doors: two on the right, one on the left. At the end was a large picture window, stretching from floor to ceiling. Hans signalled Gert to advance. In the lead, Gert worked to facilitate entry for Ernst, who, following close behind, was the 'entry man'. His job was to take down any targets that presented themselves. Hans's job was as 'rear protection'. They had practiced this same room clearing technique - to devastating effect - for decades.

From experience, Hans knew that bedrooms could be tricky, as people sometimes lock them. They had a choice: they could either try the handle, and risk alerting the occupants if the door was locked. Or they could kick it in. But that would alert the occupants in the other rooms. He signalled for them to try the handle. Gert turned the handle of the first room on the left. The door gave, Ernst rushing past his brother, his weapon on his shoulder, eyes fixed on the rifle's sights, trying to identify a target. There was none; the room was empty.

By the process of elimination, they knew that any occupants had to be in the other two rooms. There was no need for silence any more; they would kick both doors in simultaneously - Gert on the right, Ernst on the left.

Hans held up his fingers and counted down from three. On his mark, they kicked the doors, the two men rushing into the bedrooms, looking for their victims. Gert unleashed a hail of bullets at the figure that was sound asleep under the duvet, the body jerking as the lead projectiles impacted at supersonic speed, ripping through soft flesh, severing arteries and smashing into bones. Within seconds, crimson patches began to stain the white bedclothes, growing bigger as the blood gushed from the many wounds.

Hans looked into the other room. Ernst had done the same, the bleeding form under the duvet going into a into a death twitch. The feathers from the pillow - ripped apart by the bullets - settled like snowflakes of the convulsing body. Hans put a round straight into its head. The body went limp. Mission accomplished.

CHAPTER ELEVEN

En route to Damascus,
1191.

The first night's travel had gone well, the only fight the Crusaders having to wage being that against tiredness. Sir John had ridden back and forth along the line of exhausted riders to make sure that none had fallen off or gone off in the wrong direction in the inky blackness. When the sun had come up, they had stopped and hid amongst the desert rocks. They had remained there, like lizards, resting, eating and trying to avoid the powerful rays of the summer sun. The second night had been harder, as they had steadily climbed hour after hour. But Ashott seemed to know the route well. And true to his word, he had kept them away from unwanted attention. At daybreak on the second day, they reached a plateau, which Ashott had called the Heights of Golan. It was here that they had rested. However, when they began to prepare food, they discovered that the bag containing their rations had been lost during the arduous journey the night before.

Ashott had eagerly volunteered to go and forage for fresh rations. Sir John, reluctant to let the Armenian go on his own, decided that sending him in this way was preferable to splitting his force; he couldn't afford to send two of his men as Ashott's escort. He had told him to be quick and to bring enough rations to last the rest of the journey. The Armenian had quickly completed his mission, and had returned within a few hours with a sack full of food to replace the one lost from the night before, the multitude of fresh fruit and dried foods putting smiles on the faces of the famished Crusaders.

As the men had sat on the grass under the shade of a

copse of trees, surrounded by beautiful green hills and enjoying the food, they had no idea how close they had come to death that day.

Although Ashott's homelands were to the north of Damascus, his people had been spread all over the Holy Land, some settling in the Golan Heights. He had travelled this route many times, and this was the reason why he knew the path so well. Unbeknown to the Crusaders, it was he who had cut the bag of food that was tethered to one of the sleeping men as they rode. His plan: to be allowed to go to his people's village, for the clandestine intention of enlisting their help in overpowering his travel companions. With these foreigners out of the picture, he would be able to pursue the treasure for himself. But Ashott was furious to arrive at the village to find that all the men of fighting age had gone, their help needed by the Armenian settlement under attack, two days' ride to the north. There were only old men and young boys left in the village; no match for the seasoned Crusaders.

Disappointed, but not deterred, Ashott had given instructions to the Elder that, when the village fighters returned, they should to travel straight to Damascus - where they would find him at the caravanserai of his old friend Arslan, deep inside the walls of the great city. The village Elder, enticed by the prospect of sharing in Ashott's great treasure, eagerly agreed to do all he could to help.

After Ashott had eaten his fill and loaded his saddlebags with rations, he'd handed a note to the wrinkled old village Elder. It contained one word; valerian. On reading this scrap of parchment, the old man had laughed and patted Ashott on the back. 'You must ensure that Arslan has this waiting for me,' he'd said, climbing on his horse. The Elder, his face cracked with a knowing grin, had touched his nose with his index finger several times. He was still laughing as Ashott had ridden off.

It had taken the Crusaders five nights to cover the one hundred and forty miles to Damascus. They had finally reached it on the morning of the sixth day. The terrain had been much easier after descending from the Heights of Golan; crossing the flat, barren desert, heading north-east towards the city, had allowed them to regain some energy and morale.

Now, as the yellow sphere rose before them, they were greeted with a magnificent sight. The illustrious city lay silhouetted by the sun's rays, its towers, minarets and crenulations of its great walls, standing out against the ochre backdrop. As the band approached, they could hear the ancient metropolis come to life, the sound of the call to prayer emerging from one minaret at first, before being taken up by another, and another, the haunting call rippling through the still morning air.

'I'm not happy with entering the city, Ashott,' said Sir John as the two rode side by side.

'But we have to stop,' replied Ashott. 'Palmyra is still a long journey away, and we need fresh horses and provisions. Do not worry,' he sneered. 'You and your men are well disguised; to them you are but merchants.'

They entered through the great city's western gate as it opened at dawn, the huge slabs of wood remaining open throughout the day, closing only again at sun down. As they joined the throngs of people in the already busy streets, they dismounted, and led their tired steeds.

'How far is it to our lodgings?' asked Sir John to Ashott – is a whisper, so as to avoid prying ears.

'It is not far. You can rest then. But for now, enjoy the city,' Ashott said with almost a smile. As they walked through, they were pestered by merchants trying their hardest to get a sale from the tired travellers. And, although Sir John was exhausted, he found himself beginning to relax and enjoy the experience. The city was vibrant and alive with incredible colour and delightful smells that wafted over them from the food being cooked by the roadside vendors.

They turned a corner and Ashott suddenly stopped. 'This is the Street they call 'Straight',' he said, looking at Sir John. 'Or as the Romans called it, 'Via Recta.''

'What? The Straight Street? The street mentioned in the Acts of the Apostles?' asked Sir John.

Ashott nodded, '...and God said unto Ananias, visit Saul at the house of Judas, on the Street called Straight, and there lay hands on him to restore his sight...' recited Ashott. He pointed at an old two-story building that looked like it was on the verge of collapsing, 'That is the house of Judas.'

Sir John approached the old wooden door, and, with the fingers of his right hand, touched the crude crucifix that had been painted upon it. The other Crusaders bowed their heads and made the sign of the cross as discreetly as they could before setting off once again down the straight street.

As they got closer to the centre of the walled city, the already-hectic roads became busier. Luckily, apart from the street beggars, no one else gave them a second look. Damascus had been a melting point for a millennium; its inhabitants were used to seeing pale-skinned foreigners walking amongst them. As far as they were concerned, this was just another group of merchants - here to buy and sell goods, or else to rest and resupply before continuing their journey along the ancient trade routes.

The Crusaders looked around them as they walked, taking in the amazing sights, sounds and smells of the metropolis. It was alive - a living organism. As they weaved their way through the narrow streets, John began to notice that the merchants' stalls seemed to be grouped according to the wares they were touting. One moment, they were surrounded by stalls selling every type of nut you could think of. Meanwhile, twenty paces further down the street, the stalls were all selling spices, vegetables or leather goods. It seemed like every stall or shop owner was trying to outdo its neighbour with lavish displays of exotic goods. As the Crusaders walked, they marvelled at the sheer opulence of the displays, and were mesmerised by the differently coloured silks and cloths draped from the merchants' windows, the rich fabrics falling to earth like brightly coloured waterfalls. The tired men were almost sorry when

Ashott told them they had reached their destination, the Armenian taking them down a side street and stopping in front of a large archway blocked by a hefty wooden door. The bland and unassuming appearance of the outside gave no clue as to the splendour of the interior - which was revealed to them as the door was thrown back and as they entered under its portico.

'What is this place?' asked Sir John, gazing at the hive of activity in the large courtyard before them. Various stable boys were busy helping merchants to load their pack horses and camels, the unruly animals spitting and nipping at the stable boys when they got within reach, punishment for loading them with their heavy burdens.

'It is called a caravanserai or - as some people call it - a khan,' replied Ashott. 'There are such places all along the silk routes. It is where tired merchants can rest while keeping their animals and goods safe from bandits.'

'We have them in our land also,' replied Sir John as they entered into the square courtyard. 'We call them inns. But they are in no way as grand as this.'

Ashott led the small group into a quiet corner, where he was met by a short man with a huge stomach and a beaming smile. The short man and Ashott embraced, exchanging pleasantries in their own tongue. 'This is Arslan. It is his caravanserai,' said Ashott, turning to Sir John. Arslan put his hand on his chest as he smiled at the knight, his grin revealing the only two teeth that remained in his mouth.

'Follow me. Let us get out of this mayhem,' said Ashott, over the din of the animals, as he entered an archway housing a staircase that led to the first floor. 'The animals sleep downstairs, but we sleep here,' he continued, ushering the men through an open door at the top of the staircase that entered into a large room. The area contained a number of beds that were topped with straw mattresses and lined up against the walls. In the middle of the floor was a large table, low to the ground, surrounded by colourful cushions. The room was well lit by a row of windows in the ornate, domed ceiling above them. The slats had been left open, allowing the space to be ventilated, the breeze from the windows and the thick stone walls and floor making the room a welcoming sanctuary from the intense heat outside. 'Make yourself comfortable. Arslan will make sure the food arrives shortly,' continued Ashott.

As promised, the food arrived in good time, and was swiftly devoured by the ravenous men. They sat around the table together, their morale lifted by this hot meal and by the imminent prospect of resting their aching bodies on a proper mattress. 'We must sleep in watches,' said Sir John as he mopped up the last of the sauce with his flat bread. 'I will take the first watch with Christopher. Sleep with your swords within reach,' he said, as he rose from the table.

Sir John stood on the balcony outside the room, watching as the caravan departed from the courtyard below, the noise decreasing with every beast that passed through the ornate entrance. When the gate finally closed behind them, the tired knight was able to appreciate the splendour of his surroundings. He looked around the empty building in amazement. In the centre of the square courtyard was a stone fountain, which had previously been obscured by the caravan, but which could now be seen in its entirety. Sir John listened as the water trickled from its spout into the ornate reservoir. This fountain was not only decorative but also highly practical; it made it easy for the stable boys to dispense water to the thirsty animals. The courtyard was divided into four areas, each quadrant covered by a raised dome that stood atop five intricately carved pillars, leaving only the central area around the fountain uncovered and open to the elements. Just before the apex of each dome, there was a row of windows, allowing sunlight to gush into the enclosed space. Each quadrant had an archway with a staircase - just like the one they had used earlier - leading to accommodation on the first floor.

The knight gripped the balustrade, tilting his head back to take in the full view of the arches and the dome above him.

Their limestone surface was covered in intricate symmetrical shapes, rendered in dark basalt, ensuring that every detail in the complex patterns could be easily recognized. 'Magnificent,' he said to Christopher, who stood beside him, cleaning his nails with the tip of his dagger. 'Truly magnificent!' His companion looked up at him and grunted.

When Sir John woke, it was dark. He reached instinctively for the sword that lay next to him on the bed, his fingers wrapping around the familiar leather bound handle, the sword instantly becoming an extension of his arm. *Something is wrong*, he thought, rising to his feet. He could hear the snores from his sleeping men as he moved quietly towards the shaft of light leaking into the room from the gap under the door. He slowly opened it. The light from the lanterns in the corridor rushed into the room. He stopped when the door began to creak on its dry hinges. Sir John counted the shapes on the ground - still snoring. There were six. *Who is on guard*? he thought to himself, his anger growing. The reason underlying his men's inattention became obvious when he saw the earthenware casks on the table. Wine! He could smell it, the stale aroma souring the stuffy air.

Idiots, he thought, as he went to Christopher's bed, shaking the sleeping man frantically. 'Wake up, Christopher. All is not well,' he whispered.

'What is it, my lord?' said Christopher shaking off the heaviness of sleep.

'The men are drunk. And I expect an attack. We must to arms,' answered the knight.

The two men tried desperately to rouse their sleeping comrades, slapping their faces, pushing and shoving them. But to no effect. 'This is no ordinary sleep, John,' said Christopher as he threw a jug of water over one of his sleeping companions. 'They have been drugged.'

'Grab your sword, Christopher. They are too far gone,'

said Sir John, registering the sound of fast moving footsteps on the cobblestones below. John looked urgently for the bolt to lock the heavy door, but it had been removed. The footsteps were coming up the staircase. He had only seconds to prepare, but he knew exactly what he must do. He stepped back from the door and readied himself, his sword poised in his powerful arms.

The first man was pushed through the door by the weight of the throng behind him. He received the first blow, his head cleaved cleanly from its shoulders following a lopping blow from John's sword. The head was sent soaring over the other attackers and back into the corridor. The second blow followed swiftly from the first, as John swung his sword from his left side, severing the next attacker's right arm, just below the shoulder.

The assassins were not expecting a fight. They had been told to slit the throats of several drugged men as they slept. These two battle-hardened swordsmen standing in front of them were not part of that proposal. But, rather than retreat, the assailants pushed forwards, enraged by the sight of brothers and cousins killed. Plans of murder and robbery now gave way to sentiments of blood feud and revenge. The sheer weight of numbers pushed the two Crusaders back from the doorway, allowing more of the bandits to enter the room. Those thugs that were not engaged in fighting swept around them and launched a frenzied attack on the helpless drugged men, stabbing and cutting relentlessly. Sir John and Christopher fought desperately to intervene, to save their comrades from being butchered. But, at every attempt, they were pushed further and further back.

Eventually, the two Crusaders, overwhelmed by the sheer weight of numbers, found themselves pinned into the corner of the dimly lit room. Suddenly, the fighting had stopped, the impromptu pause welcomed by all, as men on both sides tried desperately to fill their heaving lungs with the oxygen their burning muscles required before the final onslaught.

'I think this is it, my friend,' panted Sir John.

'Aye, my lord. I think you are right,' replied his loyal servant.

Sir John wiped the sweat from his eyes, and gripped his sword. 'I think it best to attack, don't you?' said the knight.

'Yes, my lord. It is not good to die in a corner,' replied Christopher.

'On the count of three, then, old friend,' said Sir John. '...One... Two...' He looked up to see Ashott standing in the doorway. He gritted his teeth. '...Three!'

Damascus, Syria,
14.30, 20 May 2007.

The hands of the Rolex Submariner glowed against the black face, allowing even the most hungover eyes to read their message. 'Two thirty...? Where the fuck are we?' came the subdued voice from the back seat.

'We're just on the outskirts of Damascus,' Mason answered, turning to face the shape that lay sprawled out on the back seat.

'I can't remember crossing the border...'

'I'm not surprised. I virtually carried you. Lucky you paid off the guy in advance, 'cos there was no way we were getting in otherwise. I told them that you were ill... Here, take these,' said Mason, handing Mitch two aspirins and a can of Coke. 'Best thing for a hangover.'

'Where are we staying?' Mason asked.

'Four Seasons. You can't miss it. It's on the left as we run in towards the centre,' mumbled Mitch, clutching his aching head.

Mason looked over at the driver. 'Four Seasons?' he asked.

'Mafii mushkeela, no problem', said the driver with a smile.

The people carrier sped down the Mezzeh highway, a six-lane road that led to the city centre. On either side, the vast city of nearly two million inhabitants sprawled out onto the Syrian plain. The massif to the left was the mighty Jabal Qasion - the Biblical mountain where Cain had murdered his brother Abel - looming over them majestically, standing guard over the oldest continually-inhabited city in the world.

'What is that building?' Mason said, as he pointed to a large concrete structure on the high ground to his left.

Mitch lifted his head up just long enough to acknowledge the austere building that commanded the heights. 'That's the Presidential Palace,' he replied.

'It's shaped like the Sphinx,' observed Mason.

'Yeah, you're right. It's like a cat waiting to pounce. They say that there is a huge window that El Presidente sits behind - to watch his minions as they scurry about in the city below. I can just imagine him with a Cuban and a good Cognac, mulling over who to fuck up next.'

The twenty-five-floor high-rise was by far the biggest building in downtown Damascus. Its architect had been told that the hotel had to blend into its ancient surroundings. And so, he had decided on a step pyramid approach, with a concrete facade that wouldn't have looked out of place in Las Vegas. 'It's quirky, right?' said Mitch, as they pulled up outside the impressive hotel entrance. 'I don't know whether to love it or hate it.'

The smartly dressed doorman, wearing a scarlet tunic, piped with gold braid, slid the door open as the car stopped. 'Mr. Mitch, delightful to see you again,' he exclaimed as he recognised the passenger. Mitch took his bill-fold from his jeans pocket, unrolled a hundred dollar bill and put it in the man's palm as they shook hands.

'And delightful to see you, Mustafa,' he responded.

'No wonder they remember you,' said Mason as they walked towards the reception.

Word of Mitch's arrival spread. It was like someone had kicked an ant's nest. Within seconds there were bellboys everywhere, frantically looking for Mitch's luggage, in the hope of benefiting from his well-known philanthropy.

'Ah, Mr. Mitch. How delightful to see you,' said the receptionist, with a polished English accent. 'Your suite is ready.'

'Thank you, Abdul,' said Mitch, handing over his black American Express card.

'I didn't know that Amex did a black card...' Mason said, as they walked towards the lift.

'Yeah. They don't advertise them. They save them for their best customers. They're going to be so pissed with me when I don't pay next month's bill. I must've run up about fifty grand so far,' said Mitch. He called over a disappointed bell-boy who had missed out on the opportunity to carry his luggage, handing the boy the half-empty Coke can he had been carrying around with him. 'Take this to my room, boy,' he said to the smiling youth.

'Come and look at this,' Mitch said, as they entered the suite on the twenty-third floor, taking Mason straight to the window. 'Man, I love this place,' he said, both men looking out at the incredible view of the ancient walls circling the old city. 'Come on. We've got some time on our hands. Let's go for a walk. I need to show you this place. It's alive with history. It's been here forever, and it will be here long after we're gone.'

'I also know the best place in the world to cure a hangover. You're going to love it,' said Mitch. Soon, they were walking along the tree-lined Damascene boulevard towards the Souq Medhat Pash and the entrance to the Old City. Just before the Souq's entrance, Mason stopped to look at a striking statue of a man on horseback. 'Who's that?' he asked.

'Saladin. He's buried in the Umayyad Mosque, at the end of the Souq. I can show you if you like.'

'If we've got time. We're meant to be picking up the

weapons tomorrow, right?'

'Yep. In Palmyra. But relax… We're in Damascus. We'll sort out tomorrow when it comes. Now, we live for today.'

They entered the Souq, the covered street running for two hundred metres before them, its sides lined with shops selling everything from motor oil to gold. As they walked through, the shopkeepers - immediately aware of their identity as Westerners - tried to cajole them into a sale. 'Hey, Mister. You come see my shop,' a man shouted. The two men were quickly surrounded by salesmen eager to help part them from their cash. Mitch stood up, saying nothing while he waited until a crowd of about ten had gathered around him. Then he held up his hands like a conductor in front of an orchestra. Their attention secured, he started speaking in fluent Arabic. This was totally unexpected. Mason tried to follow what he was saying, but couldn't keep up with the flow of the throaty words that Mitch poured out on his audience. He looked at the crowd. They were enthralled, each face holding a beaming smile. After a couple of minutes, the crowd were howling with laughter, patting Mitch on the back and shaking his hand as the two men continued their journey.

'What was all that about?' asked Mason.

'I told them a joke about the Iranian man and his donkey,' answered Mitch. 'They think the Iranians are really stupid; they lapped it up.'

'I could see that,' Mason said, laughing, as they stepped out of the covered walkway through the ancient remains of Roman columns and into a square overlooked on its far side by the wall of the huge Umayyad Mosque.

'This is the start of 'the street they call Straight' - you know, the one from the Bible.' said Mitch.

Mason nodded. 'Yeah. I've heard of that. Something to do with Paul, right?'

'That's right. I see you were paying attention in Sunday school. It runs all the way through the city from east to west. Saladin is buried there,' said Mitch, pointing at the mosque.

'But we are going in this direction.' Mitch led Mason down a street that was filled with spices and all manner of exotic herbs, lining the thoroughfare and infusing the air with such intensity that it stung their noses.

Mitch stopped outside an arched opening that was set between two shops, both outlets selling nuts, each vendor trying desperately to outdo his neighbour with intricate displays of kernels. 'This is it,' he said, pointing at the carved sign above the doorway, which was set with an array of Islamic geometric patterns. 'Can you read the sign?' teased Mitch. 'Just in case you can't, it says that it was built in 1154 at the time of the Crusades. Man, can you imagine what this place has seen?' he said, ducking his head beneath the low beams. The two men descended the well-worn steps to reach the entrance. 'This is the Nureddin Hammam. It's like a Turkish bath. The steam room and massage will either kill ya, or cure ya,' he continued, as he greeted the receptionist with his big smile.

By the time the masseur had worked his incredibly strong fingers into every muscle group of each man's physique, they both felt totally invigorated. Mitch's hangover was a thing of the past, and even Mason's bruised, battered and stiff body felt like it had received a new lease of life. 'Oh, I forgot to tell you, but after you passed out last night, two drunken girls turned up looking for you,' said Mason as both men lay on the high benches, letting their muscles relax, covered from head to toe in towels.

'Leggy blondes?' asked Mitch.

'Yeah. That's right. Can't remember their names.'

'Gretchin and Heidi,' Mitch answered. 'We hang out.'

'I tried to get rid of them, but they were pretty drunk. I let them crash in the bedrooms. I checked, and they were still there this morning when we left. Hope it was okay.'

Target HQ, Belgrave Square, London,
15.07hrs, 20 May 2007.

'What do you mean they killed the wrong people? How can
you kill the wrong people? Are you fucking crazy?' JJ
screamed, as he bounced around his office.

'They thought that they *were* the targets. They were
covered in bedclothes, apparently. They thought it might
have been a trap,' replied James, himself furious at the
team's ineptitude but not willing to show that the situation
was getting away from him.

'A trap? Covered in bed clothes? Sleeping? Who was
going to trap them? The fucking Sandman?'

'Okay, John. This isn't helping,' James said, just before
the torrent of abuse started up again.

'Oh, please excuse me,' JJ's tone was laced with
sarcasm, 'but it's not you that is spending two million for a
bunch of idiots to go around killing the wrong people. That's
a lot of fucking money. I can be as angry as I like!'

There was a pause while JJ reloaded for the next
broadside. 'They found a note pad with locations and dates. I
know where they're going,' James jumped in before JJ
launched another onslaught.

JJ hesitated. 'Where?' he asked as he rested back on the
desk.

'Palmyra,' James offered as he walked to the world map
that hung on the wall, his finger searching for Syria,
Damascus, and then north-east to Palmyra. 'It's the perfect
place to stage an entry into Iraq,' he mused aloud. 'It looks
like he's definitely heading back to Basrah.'

'When?'

'The 21$^{st.}$'

The cessation in anger came to an end abruptly. 'That's
tomorrow, for fuck's sake,' he shouted.

'It's okay... I've sorted it. They've been dispatched.
They will be there to meet them.'

'I hope for your sake that you have,' JJ sneered.

Damascus,
1191.

Ashott had played chess all his life. His father had insisted his son learn the game, the tactics of which could be used on the battlefield as well as in life. He learned that the winner was the one that was able to anticipate his opponent's next move, and, in doing so, outmanoeuvre him. He had also learned never to commit himself unless he was certain of victory, making all his decisions from the head, and never from the heart - to be cold and calculating.

As he stood in the doorway, he looked at the carnage before him, the room cluttered with the dead and dying of both sides. His gamble hadn't paid off. The band of killers had only done half the job; two of the fearsome Crusaders still survived. Yes, they were pushed into a corner with their backs against the wall. But they were very much alive. With his warrior's skilful eye, he observed that, although they were hurt and their position weak, they were still dangerous, very dangerous. He noticed the steely resolve in their eyes, comparing it to the hesitancy he saw in his own men. This wasn't checkmate; it was only check.

He drew his own sword, just as Sir John shouted '...Three...,' the two remaining Crusaders charging into the mass of men in front of them. Ashott too stepped into the fray, the assassin nearest him smiling when he saw him, glad for another pair of hands to help them complete their bloody work. But the man's smile soon turned into a look of horror as Ashott drew back his blade and delivered the man a deadly blow. The rest of the assassins, on seeing their relative kill one of his own, buckled and ran, howling in dismay and confusion, their already weakened morale now in tatters as they scurried down the stone stairs and out into the night.

'Where have you been, Ashott?' Sir John screamed, between gasps for air, as he looked at the Armenian.

'I had business. I do not answer to you for my comings

301

and goings,' he replied, picking up one of the empty vats of wine and sniffing at it. 'It appears that your men were drugged.'

'How do you know that?'

'The wine smells sweet. The women in this area mix the root of the valerian plant with wine. They use it to calm people. But in large doses, it sends them into a deep sleep. It appears you have been ambushed.'

'Ambushed by your friend!' shouted John, angrily.

'Arslan is not my friend; he is merely someone I do business with. Anyway, did you not tell your men *not* to drink wine on this journey?'

Sir John didn't answer. He chose instead to pick his way through the bloody scene, checking his fallen men for signs of life. *Ashott was right; he had told them to refrain from drinking. Foolish men,* he thought as he closed the eyelids of yet another one of his dead countrymen. *They have paid for their lack of discipline with their lives.*

Palmyra, Syria,
16.05hrs, 21 May 2007.

The road shot out in front of the speeding people carrier as straight as an arrow for as far as the eye could see. On either side of the strip of dark tarmac, Mason witnessed a barren landscape of sand and rocks, interspersed with the occasional clump of desert grass desperately trying to survive in the parched soil. He had studied the map of Palmyra before leaving Mitch's flat, wondering why the ancients had built the city in such an isolated position in the middle of the desert. As they crested the brow of a small hill, his question was answered. Ahead of them lay a green blanket of palm trees that stretched out to the horizon: a luscious oasis. 'Palmyra?' he said to the driver, pointing at the forest. 'Naam, Palmyra,' said the driver with a big grin.

'Jameel! Beautiful, yes?'

Mitch, waking from another travel-induced nap in the back seat, rubbed his eyes and gazed ahead. 'Some people reckon that Palmyra took its name from the palm trees,' he said, yawning. 'Funduq Al Shams,' he said to the driver, leaning forward and patting the man on the back. 'I've stayed at this hotel before. You're gonna love it. Agatha Christie stayed one time when she was writing one of her books. It's on the other side of town. We should get a nice view of the ruins as we drive by.'

Mitch was right; as they drove to the hotel, they enjoyed a magnificent view of the ruined city of Palmyra. Mason looked on, captivated by the sheer size of the archaeological site that stretched off into the skyline, the streets of the once great city still legible, their edges marked with intricately carved, honey coloured columns that had stood for millennia, marking the ancient thoroughfares where its citizens had gone about their business. The buildings that once housed Queen Zenobia and Emperor Vespasian were ruined, but the columns still stood proud against the backdrop of the green vegetation.

Mitch sent the driver back to Damascus with a hundred-dollar tip and an even bigger grin on his face. He then checked into the hotel with his black Amex card, both men agreeing to meet after they had freshened up. *Mitch was right again*, Mason thought, as he made his way to his room; this is gorgeous.

The reception desk of dark mahogany was set in the middle of a large foyer. Behind it was a staircase of the same black wood, its treads covered with a rich red carpet, held in place by shiny brass rods that led to the first floor. The same colour theme was carried throughout, the claret-coloured floor running the whole length of the downstairs corridor, the dark door-frames separated by woven damask fabrics, their intricacy emphasised against the whitewashed walls. The high ceilings were appointed with fans, their slow moving blades cutting through the warm desert air with

303

an effortless swish.

It was the deepest bath that Mason had ever been in. The tub sat on its four ornate feet in the middle of the sumptuous bathroom, holding on to him, encouraging him to top up the cooling water twice before he was interrupted by the knock on the door. 'Just had a phone call,' shouted Mitch through the slats of the louvre door. 'My guy is downstairs. He's in the bar.'

Mitch led Mason out of the main entrance, following a stone path that led to the right of the hotel and a cloistered walkway. The arches, their ceilings etched with Islamic patterns, were supported by columns and stone utilised from the ancient city, built in a time before conservation was fashionable. Halfway down the colonnade that ran along the hotel, its length furnished with wicker chairs and tables, was a stone doorway marked on either side by gaslights that flickered in their red, glazed holders.

Ahead of them was a flight of well-worn steps that plunged into the darkness. 'It used to be a wine cellar,' Mitch said as he ducked his head to avoid the low beam at the bottom of the flight of steps. 'It's the hotel bar now. But everyone in the trade calls it the Baghdad Cafe. You remember the pack of playing cards with the pictures of Saddam's most wanted guys?' asked Mitch. 'Well, most of them have been through here at one time or another. A lot of money has changed hands over these tables. Everything's for sale here: weapons, explosives, freedom, you name it. If you've got the money, someone here will sell it to you.'

Before them was a small bar area that was framed by thick stonewalls and low ceilings. The lighting was dim and unobtrusive; the strategically placed, red-covered lampshades throwing out the bare minimum of light, the luminescence blending perfectly with the antique rugs that were scattered on the stone-paved floor. Either side of the small wooden bar were small corridors that had once contained wine racks but which now had tables tucked away into their recesses, the light in the corners even dimmer than those at the bar. The visibility was made even worse by the cigar smoke that, because of the low ceilings and poor ventilation, hung thickly in the air. Mitch led Mason to a table that was occupied by an Arab man in his late twenties, who was wearing an LA Lakers T shirt and, despite the poor lighting, was still wearing a pair of mirrored sunglasses on his unshaven face.

'Habibi, it is good to see you again. It has been a long time,' said the man rising and grabbing hold of the American with a bear hug.

'Mason, let me introduce you to Hollywood,' he said, after being released.

'Good to meet you,' said Hollywood as he shook Mason's hand. 'Please sit with me and have a drink,' he said as he poured three shots from the open bottle.

'Did Mitch give you the nickname 'Hollywood'? asked Mason.

'Yes... yes. How did you know?' laughed the Syrian, exposing his white teeth behind an easy smile. 'I have been trying to get to the US since I was a kid. But the fuckers won't let me in,' he said shaking his head. 'Said I am an undesirable. That's bullshit, though, right Mitch? Just 'cos I got caught gun running. I mean, a man has to make a living.'

'Amen to that, brother,' Mitch answered with a smile. 'Did you get what I asked for?' he asked, as he picked up his shot of Jack Daniels.

'You bet,' answered Hollywood. 'Russian AKs - none of the Chinese shit - for my friend.'

'What about the magazines?'

'Russian also. I checked the springs and loaded them with the best ammo I could find. It's all good, my friend. They work; I tested them myself. Do you want to check them out?'

'We'll have time in the morning,' answered Mitch. 'You're still coming to the border with us, right?'

'Yes. Of course, my friend. I have arranged the boat. Everything is taken care of.'

'Excellent. Then tonight we can pull up some sandbags and tell some war stories,' said Mitch as he slapped Hollywood on the back.

'Mason... ah, Mr. Mason. Is that you?' came a voice from the darkness.

Mason looked up to see a man with pale skin and dark, floppy hair, standing in front of the table, dressed in a crumpled shirt and trousers and a dusty pair of boots.

'I thought it was you. How astounding to see you here. Unbelievable, absolutely unbelievable! I missed you in Oxford. I went to the coffee shop, but you must have just gone. I waited for as long as I could, but you never came back,' the Professor blurted out as he approached their table.

'Yes, I'm sorry about that,' replied Mason. 'Something came up. I had to rush off.'

'Well I would be lying if I said I wasn't disappointed. But the gods have seen fit for us to meet again,' continued the Professor, excitedly. 'What a coincidence! I can't believe it. May I join you?'

'Sorry, Professor. We're discussing some business. Bit busy at the moment. Perhaps later.'

'Nonsense,' interrupted Mitch. 'We're finished with the boring stuff. It would be a pleasure for you to join us. Please sit down.'

'Then let me introduce Professor Cornelius Gregory of All Saints College, Oxford,' announced Mason, as the Professor sat in the fourth seat.

'Pleasure to meet you, Professor. Any friend of my old buddy here is a friend of mine,' said Mitch as grabbed the academic by the shoulder. 'I'm Mitch, and this is my associate, Hollywood,' he continued, pointing at the smiling Arab. 'Wow, Mason, I am impressed with your choice of new playmate. You're not turning in to a closet intellectual, by any chance, are you?'

'No, no,' answered the Professor on Mason's behalf.

'We only met a few days ago. Mr. Mason showed an interest in my work. But we never had chance to finish the conversation.'

'He's been a very busy boy,' answered Mitch in his friend's defence.

'Are you on your way to Iraq?' asked the Professor.

'Woah, steady tiger! Where did that come from?' butted in Mitch.

'I'm not an idiot. Why else would you be here? You're certainly not tourists,' the professor continued, his voice amplified by several beers. The three men looked at each other and over their shoulders. Mason squirmed. Hollywood's smile had vanished.

Oblivious to his indiscretion, the Professor continued. 'This is the Baghdad Cafe, after all. There are all sorts of dodgy deals that go on in this place, or so I've heard. And they all seem to involve Iraq. For all we know, the man sitting on the table opposite could be CIA, and the man he is talking to could be Al Qaida. They could be doing an arms deal for all we know.'

'So, Prof. What exact line of work are you in, these days?' Mitch asked, changing the subject.

'I teach history at Oxford. My speciality is the Crusades, and I've come to Palmyra as part of my research. I'm on a dig,' he said, ending the sentence with a hiccup. 'Mr. Mason came into contact with an elusive group of Marsh Arabs that I've been studying. Oh, by the way, I have the stick... You left it in the café.'

Mason nodded, 'Yeah... thanks.'

The Professor couldn't hold himself any longer. A few days ago in Oxford he'd come so close to hearing answers to the questions that had perplexed him for years, only to have had them ripped away. He was frightened that he would lose them again. He sat forward, gaining the three men's attention before whispering his next question. 'Can I come with you? I've spent so long writing about the people you are going to meet - my whole life's work is based on it.'

307

Mason was losing patience. 'Look, Professor. We ain't going to Iraq. And even if we were, there is no way we would take you along. Okay?' he answered, pausing for effect. 'Now, if you will excuse me,' he said, getting up 'I'm going to my room. 'You coming?' he asked, turning to Mitch.

'Nah, I'm going to finish off the bottle and have a chat with the Prof about history stuff,' he said, pouring three more shots - one of which he slid across the table to Cornelius. 'Catch you in the morning, nice and early.'

As he walked through the lobby, Mason looked at the three men who were in the process of checking in. They're not tourists either, he thought to himself as he made his way past them, his ear catching the harsh sound of the Afrikaans accent from the tall man with a scruffy grey beard.

Damascus,
1191.

John wanted revenge for the cowardly attack, but Arslan had disappeared, leaving the caravanserai deserted. He knew that to stay there longer would only bring more trouble. So, after arrangements had been made for his men's funerals, John, Christopher and the Armenian mercenary carried on with their journey.

On the trek between Damascus and Palmyra, the three men hardly spoke. The mood was sombre as both Crusaders mourned the loss of men with whom they had shared so much. Ashott had suggested that they stay in the caravanserai so abundant on the Silk Route as they headed for Palmyra through the Syrian Steppes. But Sir John was having none of it. Instead, as before, they travelled at night, skirting around sun-baked villages, keeping a careful distance from other travellers, taking refuge by day amongst the rocky crags.

As the days passed, John's melancholy became worse. Christopher, in all the time that they had been together, had never seen his lord so despondent. But the cause of his anguish was not the loss of his comrades. True, he felt anger and sadness that they were gone. But, over the last two years, he'd become almost used to his men's passing. His feelings numbing as their number dwindled. Nor was it fear; he'd stared at death many times in his life; death was an old adversary he had the measure of. The emotion he was experiencing was new. There was a feeling of emptiness gnawing at his soul. The faith that had kept him warm at night and allowed him to make sense of the horrific events he had been through had been ripped from him, torn like a beating heart from his chest. He realised that it had been thrown on to the blood-soaked streets of Acre, where he had watched it die. He had lost the thing that he held most dear. For the first time in his life, he felt all alone.

It was just after dawn on the fifth day that the trio caught their first sight of Palmyra. Its temples and other high buildings, thrust up from the desert floor, were supported by ornate columns outlined clearly against the backdrop of green foliage. But Sir John had no time for the frivolity of sightseeing. He stopped and studied once again the information that was written on the historic parchment. There was no doubting it: the map was taking them north, on a course skirting the outer wall of the ancient city, which stood before them in the distance, rising above a sea of palm trees. 'The map is taking us away from the city,' he said as he showed it to Christopher.

'Aye, you're right,' replied Christopher. 'I would have thought they would have hidden such a great treasure in a fine palace within the city's walls.'

'It looks like it is taking us to base of that small hill,' said Ashott, shading his eyes from the rising sun and pointing at the craggy outcrop that lay a mile in front of them.

'Yes. You are right. As good a place as any,' said Sir John as he took in the reins of his horse and spurred the beast's sides. 'Let's finish this,' he said as his mount leapt forward, spraying his companions with gravel.

The small hill rose from the desert plain, the large rocks that made up its interior bared on the easterly-facing slope towards the rising sun and the city. As they approached, they could see a thin wisp of smoke coming from a small hut nestled at its base. This, according to the map, was where the great treasure was buried. 'There are horses outside,' said Ashott, peering into the distance. 'Let me go ahead and I will find out who they belong to.'

'No,' answered John, desperate to see the task finished, but not foolish enough to let Ashott out of his sight. 'We stay together.'

They were about a furlong from the hut when Ashott stopped in his tracks, his horse's hooves skidding on the dusty surface of the road. 'What is it, Ashott?' demanded Sir John, as he pulled in his reins.

'Go no further. They're Saladin's men.'

'They've beaten us to it, there must be eight, maybe ten horses,' Christopher said, as he doubled back to Ashott.

'Yes... and each mount ridden by a Saracen warrior,' Ashott said as he rubbed his chin for inspiration.

'The odds are against us, but I have faced worse,' said John, as his right hand dropped the reign and reached for his sword.

'No... We cannot attack them now. That would be foolish. We must wait. This calls for more than just brute force,' Ashott scoffed at the two Crusaders.

'Where are the riders, anyway?' asked Christopher. 'Are they in the hut?'

'It looks too small to accommodate a group that big,' said John, dismounting, his impetuosity now under control. 'Ashott's right. To do this properly, we need to plan. Let's get off the road before they see us, and find a place where we can watch our new friends.'

To the left of the road, running towards the hill, was a dried riverbed. 'Let's see where this leads,' said John, taking his horse by the bridle and leading it off the track. The wadi climbed steeply on the southern side of the hill. At the end of ten minutes' scrambling amongst the marooned rocks, they reached a large boulder. Clambering on top, it gave them an excellent vantage point over the hut below - and its guests. As their chests heaved, they watched men dressed in white turbans and scarlet topcoats emerging from what seemed to be a tunnel, the mouth of which was directly in front of the hut.

'This is too much of a coincidence,' said John as he surveyed their new foes. 'These men must be seeking the treasure also. And they look to me as if they have just arrived - probably despatched by the great general to safeguard his possessions.'

'You are correct. These are not ordinary soldiers; they're from the personal guard of Saladin himself... look... they carry his mark on their coats,' Ashott pointed out. They watched the Saracens mount their horses and ride off towards the walled city, leaving two sentries behind.

'This is the first good luck that we have had since Acre,' said John. 'We must attack now.'

Ashott spat in contempt. 'They think that they have secured the treasure... that they have done their job... and now they can go and indulge themselves. Hah!' he sneered. 'They are weak. Let us go and make widows of their wives.'

The two guards stood at the entrance of the tunnel, warming themselves in the morning sunshine, unaware of the three men that stalked them. When the attack came, it was deadly, the guard to the right of the tunnel dying instantly from the Armenian's deadly scimitar. The second, having received a heavy blow from Christopher's broadsword, fell backwards into the hole.

The three stood at the edge of the opening and peered down into the darkness. They could see that it wasn't a natural cave; the opening was manmade. A flight of twenty or so steps - hewn into the living rock - ended at a large iron door. It had broken the fall of the injured Saracen, who now lay in a heap before it.

The three men descended cautiously, swords drawn, the groans from the injured man getting louder as they neared the bottom. On the last step, Ashott readied his sword. *A quick thrust to dispatch the dog,* he thought, looking for a naked blood vessel to pierce. But as he pulled back his arm in readiness, he felt the knight's hand on his arm.

'Spare him,' ordered John. 'He might give us valuable information.' The Armenian hesitated. *Possibly,* he thought to himself, as he lowered his sword and kicked the groaning man in the ribs to gauge his level of incapacity. The groaning intensified as Ashott grabbed hold of him and dragged him roughly to one side, clearing the door.

John took hold of the thick metal handle and turned. The lock disengaged, and, with Christopher's help, the heavy door was pushed wide enough for a man to pass. John went first, his sword poised. What he had expected was a dark, dank cave. What he found was the complete opposite.

The large central room was lit by oil lamps, their modest light reflected and intensified by the smooth surfaces of the limestone walls, so that it clearly illuminated the colourfully painted reliefs which decorated the chamber. Left and right from the central room branched two corridors filled with two rows of rectangular niches carved into the rock, like a shelving system. Crouching at the end of the corridor to his left, Sir John spotted the figure of a man who had fear written all over his startled face.

'Ashott, ask him what this place is?' Sir John ordered. The Armenian growled a few words at the cowering man as he and Christopher dragged the injured Saracen through the opening.

'He says it is a tomb,' Ashott translated. 'He is a eunuch, as was his friend whom the Saracens killed earlier. Both of them are the guardians. They live in the hut outside.'

'When did these Saracens arrive?' asked John.

'He said they came just after dawn. They have gone to get food from the city, and will return shortly.'

The conversation was interrupted with a large groan from the injured Saracen, who, in trying to get up, had been flattened once more by the Armenian.

'Ask the Saracen who sent him,' Sir John said, switching his line of questioning.

With the tip of Ashott's scimitar at his throat, the Saracen needed no more encouragement. 'He said they received an order from Saladin. They were told to ride as quickly as they could to Palmyra.'

'Why?'

'He says he doesn't know.'

Sir John strode towards the injured man, his face and tone needing no translation. 'I do not have time to waste. Tell him that he will tell me the truth or I will run him through.'

There was a pause while Ashott translated. 'He says that they were sent here to destroy something.'

'What?' shouted Sir John, as he brought his sword to bear on the battered Saracen.

'He does not know what... now he asking Allah to save him... he says his Captain was the only one who knew... now he is pleading that he has a wife and seven children... now he is saying that the Captain has gone to Palmyra... the Captain mentioned a treasure...' Ashott looked weary. 'Can I kill him now?' he asked.

'Wait! He mentioned a treasure. Ask him if it was that that they came to destroy?'

'He says Yes. Saladin gave orders for the Great Treasure at Palmyra to be destroyed.'

'Why would he want to destroy the Great Treasure?' wondered Sir John. 'Ask the eunuch what he knows of this.'

Ashott turned his head towards the man, who was still cowering in the corner. Their exchange of words bringing a broad smile to Ashott's face.

'What did he say?' shouted Sir John, his patience wearing thin.

'He said that the treasure is here... In the tomb... He will show us.' The eunuch rose to his feet and nervously made his way over to were the knight stood, pointing at the wall as he did so, uttering more foreign words that the Crusaders could not understand.

'He said that the treasure is here in the wall.'

All three men looked at where the eunuch was pointing. There were markings on the wall that they could not quite make out. Sir John moved closer, and Christopher grabbed a torch from its bracket on the wall, to make their search easier. It was then that they heard the noise - from outside - of galloping horses.

Palmyra, Syria,
07.45hrs, 22 May 2007.

Mitch was sat alone at breakfast in the hotel restaurant, his remaining eye red from another night of overindulgence. 'What time did you finish last night?' said Mason as he sat down opposite him.

'About one a.m. I just couldn't get away from the Prof. He was telling me all about the Ma....Masa...?'

'Masahuin,' Mason finished off.

'Yeah, Masahuin. So those were the guys you met in the Marshes?'

'Yep, that's right. The man that saved me, John, was the village Elder.'

'And he is related to the knight, Sir John De Guise, who founded the settlement when he fled to the east with the treasure, right?'

'If Cornelius's theory is correct, yes,' answered Mason.

'And you saw the knight's shield and sword in the church at the village? Wow, that's incredible.'

Mitch's breast pocket started to vibrate. He opened the phone and checked the text message. 'The package has arrived, amigo. It's right outside.'

Hollywood had parked the battered, black Land Cruiser

in the hotel car park as far from the main building as he could. As the two men approached, he met them at the tailgate. 'Here you are,' he said, unveiling the fruit of his labour. 'All oiled and ready to go.'

On the blanket in the boot space were two Russian AK47s and a number of magazines. After checking that no one was looking, both ex-soldiers took hold of a weapon each, and began to dismantle them, checking the working parts and the firing mechanisms. When they were both satisfied, they reassembled them and put them back under the cover of the blanket. 'Nice doing business with you, amigo,' said Mitch as he unrolled several one hundred dollar bills from the wad in his pocket. 'You get the rest when we get to the boat.'

'Look out. There's someone coming,' said Mason, as he spotted a man in a bush hat approaching the Land Cruiser from the hotel.

'It's okay,' answered Mitch. 'It's just the Prof. I've invited him. He's going to show us his dig.'

'We need to get off,' said Mason. 'We've not got time for this. We have a hell of a long journey ahead of us.'

'Yeah, man. I know. But how often do you get the chance to have an Oxford Professor show you around a dig? Come on, we can spend an hour, surely?'

Mason looked at Mitch, and then at Cornelius, who, by this time had joined them at the back of the four-by-four. 'An hour, maximum,' he said, looking at his watch. 'And then we're off.'

'I come here every opportunity that I can,' explained the Professor as the three men drove towards the Old City. 'It won't be for much longer though - not if All Saints has its way. The Dean is going to sack me; he says that my infatuation with my theory has gone too far.' He pointed to the left as they drove down a dusty track. 'That's where the Italian mission have discovered another church. That's the fourth within the city walls now. But this one is the biggest by far. It's a real whopper – about half the size of a

315

football pitch.'

'So what?' sighed Mason, moodily, still annoyed at the interruption to his mission.

'One must remember that Christianity was in its infancy when these churches were built,' continued the Professor, oblivious to Mason's sarcasm. 'It is unheard of for such a new religion to have so many places of worship in such a small area. One would expect possibly two at the most. But to have four - and of such great sizes - is extremely unusual. From this and other discoveries, we are finding that Palmyra was a very important site to the early Christians.'

'Is that why the Italians are here?' asked Mitch. 'Because of the early Christianity thing?'

'Yes. I suppose you could say that, Mitch,' replied the Professor. 'A colleague of mine thinks that they're spies sent by the Vatican,' he laughed.

'Espionage in the archaeology business? Whatever next?' said Mason dryly.

'Actually, you would be surprised,' answered the Professor. 'Remember my story about the bearer of the Saladin parchment to the Arch Duke. The rumours at the time were that Vatican spies had killed him.'

'Well, it's just a story, after all,' jibed Mason. 'If it wasn't them, perhaps it was the Mafia?'

'The Catholic Church is very sensitive about the early days of Christianity,' continued the Professor, ignoring Mason's comments. 'We must remember that Christianity was not always the well-structured religion that we have today. It took a millennium to create the doctrines and constitutions. It was a very different religion in the first few centuries after the death of Jesus. And we've seen what happens when new documents are discovered - documents that even the cleverest of theologians can't fit into the established doctrines. There is outrage. Look at what happened when they found the Dead Sea Scrolls...'

'He's right, Mason,' said Mitch, who was hanging on to the Professor's every word.

'It wouldn't surprise me in the least if the Italian mission here was supported by the Vatican. That way, they'd be perfectly placed to deal with any contentious finds that might prove embarrassing to the Catholic Church. Such intervention would be perfect for making problems go away quickly and discreetly. Turn right here,' said Cornelius to Hollywood, pointing at a small track that led off towards a small craggy outcrop. 'My site is just at the foot of that small hill ahead of us.'

The Land Cruiser stopped at a small mound, the entry to which was secured by a metalled barred gate. 'It's Friday. My locals have got the day off,' said Cornelius, as he took out the padlock key from his trouser pocket and unlocked the gate. 'This is a necropolis. Palmyra has a number of them - all outside of the city walls, as it was not the done thing to bury one's dead inside the city. Some of the necropolises are towers where the bodies were interred, while others - like this one, date from the first century AD - are hypogeum, underground chambers. This one belonged to a wealthy merchant...' the Professor paused. 'Does anyone know of a man called Balthazar? Are there any biblical scholars amongst you? Mitch?'

'Sorry, Prof. Doesn't mean anything to me,' replied Mitch.

'Wait, Balthazar... Wasn't he one of the three wise men?' answered Mason.

'Excellent!' exclaimed the Professor. 'Yes. You are correct. One of the three Magi who visited Jesus at his birth was called Balthazar.'

The Professor pushed open the gate and picked up a Maglite torch that had been left at the entrance. 'Welcome to his tomb,' he continued as he descended the flight of stone steps. 'Balthazar amassed great wealth during his lifetime, but this tomb is not his alone. As was the custom in Palmyra, it not only housed him and his family but also any other wealthy citizens who could afford to pay the price of an eternal 'des res'. He pushed open the heavy metal door at the

317

bottom of the flight of stone steps and walked through. 'Behold Balthazar's Tomb!' he said with great pride.

Before them was a large stone chamber, with two corridors leading off to either side.

'Let me show you where our friend Balthazar resides,' said Cornelius, taking them down the corridor on the left. 'As was the custom at the time, the bodies were first left out in the dry air until most of the flesh had gone and the bones could be collected. Then they were put into small stone coffins, or ossuaries, which were then placed in these niches. It's a bit like a shelving system, really,' explained Cornelius, as they walked down the passageway. 'I am not sure whether the builders of the necropolis were driven by how many eternal spaces they could sell, but they sure tried to pack a lot in.'

Cornelius stopped opposite one of the recesses and shone his torch. 'This is Balthazar. See how there are two tiers of shelving: one at ground level, and the other at chest height. They slid each coffin into its own separate niche headfirst. Balthazar's coffin is on the bottom tier. It is highly unusual for the owner of the tomb to be located on the bottom bunk, as it were. They are always on top. Now look at the stone plaque,' he said, shining his torch on the painted relief that showed the portrait of a grey haired man with a beard, dressed in a crimson tunic. 'This was used to seal the niche, to enclose the tomb. It carries the likeness of the person buried within, and also states their name.'

He pointed at the faded letters on the base of the stone tablet. This is written in Aramaic, the language of Christ. It says 'Balathazar'. Cornelius turned to Mason. 'Have you seen anything like this before, Mason?' he asked.

Mason looked up. 'Yes, in the Marsh Arab Church, there was a tablet just like this,' he said, much to the delight of the Professor, whose face lit up with a huge smile.

'When I discovered this tomb five years ago, it was completely buried. Artefacts in the rubble that had been used to cover the entrance and seal the tomb were carbon dated to the 12th Century. That means I was the first to enter for over eight hundred years. In the niche above Balthazar,' he said, shining his torch into the empty space, 'I found something very unusual. It was the remains of a man whose body - not in a coffin - had been placed there in a hurry and without ceremony. The remains were dated to the same period, but it is his clothes and ancestry that are the most intriguing. He was dressed in a mixture of clothing: long-flowing local robes on top and European garments underneath. The clothing on its own is not conclusive evidence of anything - after all, the city is on the silk route and Europeans, although not common, were known to have visited. But the manner of death is very intriguing. When we investigated further, it was found that the man had been stabbed, the point of the blade broken off and left in his body. It was a Saracen's blade. Something of great importance was buried here, gentlemen,' he said, looking gravely at the two men.

'The treasure?' asked Mitch.

'Yes. I think so,' replied the Professor. 'And I think it was kept here,' he said, placing his hand in the empty niche above the tomb of Balthazar. 'It was important - so important that the man I found, and possibly many other men, gave their lives for it. And, when he died, his comrades put his body in the place where it had once been.'

'You think that the coffin I saw in the village of the Marsh Arabs used to sit there, don't you?' Mason asked.

'Yes,' the Professor nodded. 'And I also think the man I found was a Crusader - probably one of Sir John de Guise's party - sent to rescue it from the hands of the Saracens.'

'Phew,' Mitch whistled. 'So, what do you think the 'treasure' actually was?'

'I have a theory: one I would have gladly shared with you that day in Oxford. But you ran off,' he said, looking at Mason. 'Do I have your attention now?' asked the Professor.

'You certainly have mine,' said Mitch. 'Like you just grabbed my balls.' Mason nodded.

'Good! Let's go up in to the sunshine. I will show you

some of my work, and explain what I think the treasure is, or was.

'Hey, Mitch,' shouted Hollywood from outside, his voice echoing around the dark tomb. 'There's a car coming. Get up here quick; I think they've got guns.

Palmyra,
1191.

The three men stood in the doorway at the entrance of the tomb. The dust from the ceiling, dislodged by the horse's hooves, settling on their shoulders. 'What now, Sir John?' asked Christopher.

'I don't want to die underground like a rat. Let's meet them head on. Die with the sun on our faces?' said John. 'What say you, Ashott?' The Armenian nodded in agreement.

As the three warriors readied themselves for the imminent clash, swords drawn, ready to climb the steps, the eunuch ran over to John and grabbed hold of his tunic. 'What's he saying?' asked the knight as the eunuch continued speaking in his native tongue whilst pointing at the end of the corridor.

Ashott's stern face broke into a grin. 'He says that there is a tunnel at the back that leads to the surface.'

Sir John looked at Christopher. 'The door,' the two men shouted simultaneously, both leaping into action, putting the full weight of their bodies behind the half-open, heavy, metal door, a thick cloud of dry earth engulfing them as it slammed shut into its solid frame.

In the commotion, no one saw the injured Saracen pull the knife from his boot. With his comrades outside, it was time for him to act. He jumped up, and with his razor sharp dagger, lashed out at the two men that were blocking his escape route. Christopher caught the blow and fell back against the door, clutching his chest. The dagger had gone straight through his lung - the curvature of the thin blade increasing the internal damage - and had snapped as the Saracen had tried to withdraw it. Retribution was swift and lethal, the Saracen clutching the handle of his broken dagger - his only defence – no match for the long curved blade of Ashott's scimitar, the razor sharp edge of the Armenian's blade delivering several cuts in quick succession, dispatching the assailant with ease.

As Christopher dragged himself to one side to attend to his wound, Ashott took his place at the door. 'Is there a bolt?' shouted Sir John.

'I cannot see one,' Ashott shouted back, turning to the eunuch and asking the frightened man the same question in his own tongue. The man shrugged and muttered a few words.

'What did he say?' asked the knight.

'He said that the dead cannot lock doors, so why put a bolt on the inside?'

'Then we need to secure it as best we can,' said Sir John. 'Help me move the stones behind the door,' he said, pointing at the neat pile of carved blocks in the corner. 'They will buy us some time.'

'It doesn't look like I will get my tavern,' Christopher said in a weak voice, as crimson bubbles began to dance on his lips.

John turned to where his friend was slumped against the wall and knelt down beside him. 'Nonsense. You will survive. We will all live to fight another day,' he assured the injured man.

'I fear not, my lord. This is not piss I sit in; it is my blood. I never knew I had so much in me,' he said looking at the growing red stain that had already engulfed them both. 'The Saracen has finished me.'

Sir John looked at Christopher. His youthful face, bronzed by the sun of the Holy Land, had always held a smile, even through the hardest times. But now it was pale and fearful. He'd always been John's favourite. Just eighteen when he had set out on the Crusade. John had watched as his mother had kissed him goodbye. That day - the day they had left the village - her own pain and worry were clear on her face as she had pleaded with Sir John to take care of her Christopher, and bring him back safely. 'I will take care of him, madam. Do not fret,' had been his bold reply.

John took hold of the hand of the man who had bravely fought side by side with him since their departure from France. He had watched the boy grow into a man - a man who flourished in the kind of harsh conditions that had seen lesser men wither and die. But now it was his turn. The lifeblood that had coursed through his youthful body, allowing him to live with such vigour, now lay around him in a dark slippery pool. John was watching him die. He felt like screaming. He couldn't bear it.

'I am cold, John... and tired... so very tired.'

'Sleep then, my friend. For, when you wake, you will be in a better place,' answered the knight, trying to mask the emotion that was taking hold of him. Christopher clenched Sir John's hand in a strong grip and squeezed tightly - like a candle burning brightest just before it expires. His grip weakened. He was gone.

Palmyra, Syria,
09.17hrs, 22 May 2007.

The Land Rover was heading straight for them, the cloud of dust thrown up by its tyres marking the vehicle's route from the main road. There were two men in the front cab and another one standing in the back, holding on to the vehicle's roll bar, the dark silhouette of a small rifle clearly visible against the blue sky.

'Are they the police?' shouted Mason.

'The police don't use Land Rovers,' answered the Professor.

'Well, whoever they are, they're sure in a hurry to meet us,' added Mitch.

Mason and Mitch looked at each other. The glance only lasted for a split second, but it was enough for each man's finely tuned military mind to analyse the situation and decide upon the appropriate course of action. Not a word was said as both men turned simultaneously and ran to the Land Cruiser, their legs pumping like pistons as the ground around them erupted, bullets beginning to tear at the surface.

'Hollywood! Get the Prof back into the tomb and lock yourselves in,' shouted Mitch, as both men snatched their AK47s from the back of the vehicle, the drills that they'd practiced over decades readying the weapons in seconds.

'What d'ya reckon?' asked Mitch, as both men crouched at the rear of the vehicle, fingers on the triggers of their AK47s.

'We draw them in,' answered Mason. 'They don't know that we have weapons yet. Remember: 'SAS: Speed, Aggression and Surprise'.

The firing stopped as the Land Rover screeched to a halt forty yards from their position, the three assailants jumping from their vehicle and taking up firing positions behind it. Within seconds, they were unleashing a withering hail of bullets, all directed at the black Land Cruiser. There was a loud crash as the tinted windscreen exploded, the ping of metal against metal as the projectiles ricocheted off the vehicle's solid engine block, causing the four-by-four to judder. Both men were now on the floor, trying to make their bodies as small a target as possible, knowing that the vehicle's thin metal shell only gave them cover from view, not protection. It was only a matter of time before the Land Cruiser would become more of a hindrance than a help.

'They probably think they have got us,' said Mitch, when there was a lull, taking advantage of the hiatus to crawl

323

under the vehicle and into a position where he could take a shot.

'Not yet,' said Mason. 'We need to take some more punishment. Just hang tight. We need them to get closer.'

Mitch nodded and grinned. 'Roger that. On your word,' he answered.

The firing started again. But this time it was lighter, the aimed shots more selective, their purpose being to keep heads down. 'One has broken off,' shouted Mitch from his vantage point. 'They're trying to outflank us.'

'Seen,' shouted back Mason in acknowledgment, watching the man dash between the rocks to their left.

'If he gets round any further, we're going to be fucked. They'll have us both ways,' Mitch shouted.

'I thought we'd be able to tempt them out into the open. But these guys are professional. It's time we gave them the good news,' shouted Mason, kneeling up and flicking his safety catch off. 'Fuck it... let's win the fire fight.' Mason put the weapon on automatic, and squeezed the trigger just enough to unleash two or three rounds of 7.62. The AK came to life, its loud aggressive bark taking their assailants totally by surprise. Now it was *their* turn to take cover.

'Fuck me, Hans, where did they get weapons from? You never said they would be armed,' shouted Gert.

'Shut up and put some fire down. We've got a fight on our hands,' said Hans as he clipped another full magazine on his Krinchov.

'We need to get away from the vehicle,' shouted Mason as he continued with small bursts of accurate fire into the side of the Land Rover. 'It's acting like a bullet magnet, and if that other guy gets round the back of us, we're finished.'

'Where to?' shouted Mitch over the sound of the gunfire.

'Look half right: Group of rocks. Twenty yards. Seen?'

'Yeah... I can see it. Ladies first,' shouted Mitch.

'Okay... on Three,' Mason shouted back.

Mitch increased his rate of fire on the utterance of the word 'Three', giving cover as Mason ran to the rocks, and emptied a full magazine of thirty rounds into the Land Rover, silencing the two men that hid behind it. He quickly pressed the catch in front of the trigger guard, allowing the empty banana-shaped magazine to fall away, before replacing it with a fresh one. And, as he brought his weapon back into the shoulder, he glanced to his right to check his friend's progress.

Ernst had bobbed and weaved amongst the large boulders, trying to make his cumbersome torso as elusive a target as possible. By the time he had reached a place where he was able to see the back of the Land Cruiser, he was exhausted. His eyes had been fixed on the man hiding behind the vehicle firing short bursts of accurate fire at his comrades. As he'd looked down the short, stumpy barrel of the Krinchov, he'd tried to line up the front and rear sights on the man. But it was no good. Every time he'd breathed, the target had moved out of the circle of his sights. He took a few more breaths, wiped the sweat from his brow and tried again.

The deep breaths worked. The requisite oxygen finally flowed through his arteries, delivering energy to his screaming muscles, allowing him to control his movements. He squeezed the trigger just as his stationary target began to run, the bullets hitting the back of the vehicle in a small cluster - exactly where the man had crouched just a fraction of a second earlier. He adjusted his aim and unleashed a long burst at the back of the sprinting man, keeping his finger on the trigger until all the ammunition in his magazine was expended. The South African didn't see the impact, but, as he looked on, he could see his bullets had had the desired effect; the man fell to the floor. The target had been hit.

Mitch glanced over to check Mason's progress. Mason's body lay in a crumpled heap just before the rocks, his limbs distorted from his fall. He stared for what seemed an age at the motionless body before a great well of rage surged from within him. 'Fuck. Fuck. Fuck. You fucking fuck!' he shouted aloud as he gritted his teeth and crawled backwards from under the vehicle. As he emerged at the back of the Land Cruiser, bullets began to whiz around his head, the supersonic projectiles punching holes into the flimsy metal skin of the vehicle. *It's the third man*, he thought instantly, *the bastard has got round behind us*. He crawled back under the vehicle. *Deep breaths. Consider your options. They've got me both ways. There's no way out. It's only a matter of time before they finish me.*

'Fuck it!' he shouted, as he rolled out to the right from under the pulverised Land Cruiser. 'Fuck it!' he shouted as he stood up and walked towards the Land Rover, his weapon in the shoulder, his index finger on the trigger, his eye staring down the sights, searching for a target. He didn't have to wait long; as he walked forward, a head presented itself from behind the Land Rover's shattered windscreen. The snap shot was instantaneous, the three rounds that had left the muzzle within thousands of a second of each other quickly finding their mark, jerking the head backwards as the skull exploded.

The sand around him was alive, bubbling from the bullets that were ripping into the ground around his feet, but he didn't care. He was too far gone; the red mist of revenge had taken control. All thoughts of personal safety had gone out the window. After all, this is what he wanted: to die like a warrior, with a weapon in his hand and adrenalin pumping through his veins. As he advanced, he kept a constant rate of fire on the Land Rover, making sure that the other would-be killer hiding behind it couldn't get a shot back.

The man behind the Land Rover didn't show himself until Mitch was right up on him. But when he did, he had Mitch's full attention, the ex Legionnaire letting rip with a long burst. It emptied his magazine and ripped the fat man's chest apart. Mitch wasted no time; he threw down his empty weapon and picked up the smoking Krinchov of his dead adversary. *One more to go*, he said to himself as he replenished his ammunition by picking up a spare mag and putting it in to the back pocket of his Levi's.

His blind rage faded. His blood lust had been fed. He was calmer now, and the odds were far better. He couldn't see the third man, but he knew exactly where he was. The hunter had become the hunted. He began to move silently in a big loop, like a lion stalking his prey, stopping every few seconds, checking: left, right and behind, listening for movement, his weapon ready. Time stopped. Everything stood still. The only sound the distant cry of an eagle carried on the hot wind. The only people on the whole planet were Mitch and his adversary, playing their deadly game. Eventually he had it - the ample torso of his opponent - in his sights. 'Drop your weapon!' he shouted.

The man spun round, letting rip with a harmless burst of gunfire into the desert sky. Mitch retaliated with a burst of his own, his accurate bullets smashing into the legs of the man that stood ten yards in front of him. The man dropped his weapon as he fell to the floor, his hands instinctively grabbing his shattered legs as the pain exploded in his brain.

'Who sent you?' yelled Mitch, as he kicked the wounded man's weapon from his reach.

'I don't know. I'm not the boss,' screamed Ernst.

'Wrong answer,' said Mitch as he kicked his legs. Ernst screamed even louder. 'Who sent you?' The man looked pitifully at Mitch.

'Please don't kill me,' Ernst babbled.

'If you tell me, I will let you live. Now. Who sent you?'

'O'Hare. The job is for Target Security. That's all I know. Please don't kill me,' he pleaded.

'Where you're going, you'll wish I had,' answered Mitch. 'Have you ever been inside a Syrian jail? They're going to luuuuv you.'

The voices were angry. They had found their slain comrade.
There was footfall on the stone steps, and then a loud bang
as the door's strength was tested. 'Quick! The treasure!'
shouted Ashott. 'We must act now.' He began to dig
frantically with his dagger, in an effort to prise the limestone
portrait of a dark skinned, clean-shaven man, with a large
nose, dark eyes and curly hair, from the tomb opening. The
Armenian, working in a frenzy, paid no heed as the tablet
with the painted relief dropped to the floor. The eunuch let
out a scream of horror as he saw it fall, and held out his
arms, his fingertips grasping the object just before it crashed
into the hard stone surface. Ashott, unperturbed by the antics
of the eunuch, reached inside of the niche, took hold of the
stone coffin and yanked it out. The eunuch, who was back on
his feet, this time managed to catch hold of the other end of
the ancient casket, just as Ashott pulled it clear of the lip of
the shelf.

Sir John, oblivious to the noise of the attackers, and to the
feverish work of his travel companion, placed Christopher's
hand on his chest, gently, as if not to wake him, and softly
closed each eye. He stood dazed, watching, as the Armenian,
teeth bared like a scavenging hyena, worked fanatically. His
blade darting over the stone surface of the ossuary,
desperately trying to find an opening to prise off the stone
lid. As the bangs on the door grew louder and louder,
Ashott's knife found a chink. He worked it, adding his
fingers to the effort of the sturdy blade, making the opening
grow. Finally, there was enough room for leverage. Using
his hand, he pulled desperately at the stone lid. With a loud
rasp, the top was free.

The eunuch was overcome with emotion. He was looking
at the treasure that he had guarded for as long as he could
remember, never thinking in his wildest dreams that he
would ever get to see it. He fell to his knees. *I should not*

gaze upon it, he thought as he covered his eyes, overcome with reverence and trepidation.

Sir John looked on towards the ossuary. The stone box was carved from a single piece of limestone, and was filled with human remains. The bones, still with traces of skin attached, were stacked neatly inside the chiselled interior. He took a step closer - so as to ensure his eyes were telling the truth – and he began to laugh. 'For this... for this?... all my men died for this?' he exclaimed, with mock humour.

Ashott wasn't laughing; he was deranged with anger. He grabbed the eunuch and started to shake him, like a starved dog with a piece of meat. 'Where is the treasure? Where is it? The gold... the jewels... where are they?' he screamed at the eunuch.

'There are no jewels, no gold,' replied the frightened man.

'Do not take me as a fool, or I will skin you alive. Where is the treasure?'

'It is here, master. This is the treasure; there is no gold, nor jewels. This is the thing that has been buried here - a secret - for over a thousand years.'

'These are bones. How can they be called great treasure? Who was this man?'

The eunuch looked at him, his eyes wide. 'You mean you don't know?'

'If I knew, I wouldn't ask you, you dog.'

'Sorry, master. I thought you knew. This is the body of the prophet, Jesus!'

Sir John had no understanding of the conversation that was going on between the two men, but the name Jesus was common to both their tongues. 'Did he just say Jesus?' he asked Ashott.

Ashott let go of the eunuch. 'Yes, the fool said that this is the prophet Jesus.'

Sir John's mind was reeling. The banging on the door, which was now constant, prevented him from thinking clearly. 'It sounds like they have a battering ram,' he shouted

329

over the noise.

'We must go now, or else we will be captured,' replied Ashott.

Sir John went to pick up the coffin, but stopped. 'Ashott, before we go, help me with Christopher.'

Target HQ, Belgrave Square, London, 10.14hrs, 23 May 2007.

James climbed the plush staircase one step at a time, resting at the top of the stairway opposite the print of the Duke of Wellington. He carried a sealed manila envelope, tucked under his left arm. He was dreading what was to come next. After spending several minutes looking into the eyes of the Iron Duke for inspiration, he opened the door, resigned to what was to come.

'You need to read this,' he said as he placed the envelope on JJ's desk before retiring to his favourite location in front of the French windows. The fuse had been lit; James readied himself for the explosion.

'What the fuck is going on?' JJ slammed his fist down on the desk, the proud picture of Tony Blair toppling over with the quake. 'How the fuck could this happen? They are fucking useless,' he shouted, out of his chair, thrusting around the room, the message crumpled in his hand. 'So, let me get this right - there are two dead, one of which is the boss? What's his name again?'

'Hans,' replied James, happy to be able to answer an easy question, but well aware that the exchange was going to be all downhill from here.

'And what's the score with the third man?'

'The Syrians have him. He's been shot in the legs - nothing life-threatening.'

'More's the pity,' JJ snapped. 'Better if they were all dead.'

'Yes, it would have been cleaner that way,' agreed James. 'But he's no longer our responsibility. He's a disposable asset. It comes with the job.'

'Fucking right he's not my responsibility; he's yours. And you've fucked up AGAIN. It's a good job that I only paid you a deposit. A million quid for what? A useless bunch of amateurs who go and get themselves shot up.'

'They'd never let us down before,' James said, regretting the remark as soon as it had left his pursed lips.

JJ stormed over to where James was standing. 'Don't test my patience,' he said, waving the message in his face.

'And Mason?'

'The only bodies recovered were the two South Africans'. There was a blood trail from a fourth victim, but the Syrians are being tight-lipped. That's all I could get from HQ at Vauxhall Cross.'

'So, best-case scenario is that Mason is dead. But we just don't know.'

'Correct,' answered James, acclimatising to the barrage.

There was another tense silence as JJ sat down at his chair. 'He's not dead. Not him. He's got a charmed life. Not Lucky... lucky Mason. Nooo. He's out there. The next we will hear from him is when he pops up on the radar with the two bloody hostages.'

'Not unless you stop him.'

JJ shot James an assertive glance. 'I could do a lot better than your lot. That's for sure.'

There was a pause as JJ sat back in his big leather chair, locked his fingers and placed his hands on his barrelled chest. 'I know how these guys operate. I can put in an ambush that will kill them all.'

'You can't do it on your own.'

'Don't have to. I have some good Iraqis that I used on some dodgy stuff in the early days. For the right amount of money, they will do anything.'

James nodded, glad to be out of the firing line.

JJ pressed the intercom button on his desk. 'I should have

done this in the first place,' he said aloud as the secretary answered. 'Yes, Mr O'Hare.'

'Get me a flight to Basrah.' As the secretary rung off, he turned to James. 'I'll sort YOU out when I get back,' he growled.

❖ ❖ ❖

'Hold still. How can I stitch this up properly if you're moving around?' said Mitch, as he pinched the two folds of skin together with his thumb and forefinger, piercing the puckered flesh with the suture. 'You're acting like you've never been shot before.'

'That's because I *have* never been shot before,' Mason said, through gritted teeth, as the needle went deep into his flesh.

'You've never been shot? What kind of soldier are you?'

'A lucky one.'

Mitch pulled the curved needle through the wound, like a tailor putting on a new button. 'I've checked the hole… can't see any bone fragments. And the exit wound is nice and clean. An inch higher and it would have gone through your scapula. Then you would have been in a whole world of shit. You *are* lucky, my friend.'

'Lucky? How the fuck did you work that out?' replied Mason. 'I've just been shot and knocked unconscious. What's fucking lucky about that?'

'Those Krinkovs fire a 5.45 mm round. If you'd been hit with a 7.62 from an AK, it would have taken your arm off.'

'What's the time?' asked Mason.

'It's time you shut up and let me get on with this,' replied Mitch, as he inserted the suture for another stitch, his tongue sticking out of the side of his mouth as he concentrated on his handiwork.

'I have to phone Rachel. I told her to put the phone on at 1200 hours each day.'

'Shit, man. I was just beginning to enjoy myself; it's been ages since I played doctor,' said Mitch, turning his wrist and reading the time off the black face of his Submariner. It's 1150.'

Outside the Police Station, Al Amarah,
11.55hrs, 23 May 2007.

Rachel studies the small wristwatch - the one she'd received from her mother as a birthday gift many years ago. At first, she'd only worn it on special occasions, frightened that it would be damaged, or worse: lost. For safekeeping it had been displayed in pride of place on her bedroom table. But now, it is part of her daily routine - a vital accessory. Its slow moving hands are closely monitored from the moment she wakes up each day, willing forward the small black markers across the white face, their progress always too slow for her impatient eyes.

But now they have finally reached their mark; it is time for the ritual to begin.

It is 11:55. The phone is made ready, the signal obtained, the device carefully placed in a convenient nook - the best place she has found for reception - just above her head, in the trunk of the palm tree that stands opposite the entrance. This tree is her new home - her begging pitch - the place where she stands vigil. Racing anticipation surges through her veins as she again glances at the silent watch. The second hand continues its slow sweep, pulling the minute hand laboriously towards the top of the face. And then: a noise! A chime! The face of the satellite phone shines yellow - alive with an incoming call.

She reaches up to grab the phone. But her impatient fingers are too quick, pushing instead of holding. The phone jumps from its resting place, bounces on the floor and tumbles down the bank that lines the road.

She follows, hands outstretched, reaching for the small grey plastic block as it careers, still chiming, down the steep slope, heading towards a puddle of stagnant water. A fraction before the puddle, the stumpy antenna catches a loose mound of dirt. Acting like an anchor, it stops the phone abruptly. But she's still chasing, headlong and out of control. Her hands make contact, but her speed is too great, her fingers not quick enough, their tips pushing the phone into the stagnant pool.

It's immersed, but only for seconds. Quick hands scan the oily surface, completing the rescue. It has stopped ringing. But the screen is still animated with symbols and digits. As she wipes the greasy mud from the surface, a long bead of water runs from the hard casing. The screen flickers. It dies.

CHAPTER TWELVE

Palmyra,
1191

Ashott led, torch in hand. Sir John and the eunuch followed down the narrow tunnel, the entrance of which had been hidden behind an empty tomb. It was small, even for the slight frames of Ashott and the eunuch. But, for the muscular frame of the Crusader dragging the ossuary, the experience was positively gruelling. After what seemed an age, all three men finally emerged into the sunlight. John collapsed into an exhausted heap, as Ashott and the eunuch rolled a number of large boulders across the exit of the tunnel, blocking the advance of any unwanted followers.

'I will fetch the horses. We must make our escape,' Ashott said, between snatched breaths.

John nodded. 'Go... I will wait here,' he answered, getting to his feet.

As Ashott moved stealthily off in the direction of the horses, John shaded his eyes and searched around him in all directions, looking for any signs of danger. He held his ear to the ground and listened for the sound of galloping hooves. *Nothing.* The only noise was the screech of an eagle carried on the hot wind. He walked over to the ossuary and began to study it. In the bright sunlight, every detail of the stone casket was clear. Along the lid were a number of carved words, most of which made no sense to him. But then he found a phrase in Latin. He ran his fingers over the chiselled characters, mouthing their sounds as he did so. 'Jesus of Nazareth, son of Joseph, The Messiah.' He thought that his eyes were playing tricks. He rubbed them and read them again, spelling out the letters louder this time, loud enough for the eunuch to hear

335

'Jesus of Nazareth, son of Joseph, The Messiah.'

The eunuch spoke. 'Yes... Jesus... Messiah,' he smiled. Sir John motioned for the eunuch to help him remove the lid once again. But the guardian, after his initial bout of curiosity, had reverted to his pious role. He shook his head and fell to his knees in prayer. John didn't press him. Instead, he carefully lifted the lid, letting it slide gently backwards, cushioning it with his foot, before resting it on the sand.

The lack of moisture in the dry desert air had mummified the remains, leaving skin, teeth and tufts of dark hair on the dead man's face. But the face was distinguishable, matching the likeness of the fresco that lay off to the side, carried so gently by the eunuch on their escape. He moved the shroud that wrapped the rest of the skeleton to one side, exposing the bones of the lower arm: the ulna and the radius.

His eyes followed the bones down to where they met at the wrist. The joint was covered with a decaying dressing. He carefully pulled back the bandage on the right, and then the left wrist. There was no mistaking it; both wrists had clearly been punctured by a small implement, revealing a hole that went all the way through the skin and bones. He checked the feet. They were also covered with bandages, the puncture wounds imitating those of the wrists.

It was if he'd been struck by a lightning bolt. His whole body was locked, his legs giving way. He fell to the ground. And, as he stared at the open coffin, he began to cry. A wave of sadness engulfed him, his sorrow unleashing a torrent of tears that burst from his tired eyes.

He cried for Christopher.

He cried for his men murdered in Damascus. He cried for the rest of his companions lost on the way to the Holy Land. He cried for the men that he had killed. He cried for the innocents, the children, the mothers, the elderly – all of whom had been caught up in the savagery of the Crusade.

He didn't know how long he had wept; it could have been

mere minutes, hours, or perhaps days. Time was lost to him, his senses returning only when he felt the rhythmic beating of the horses' hooves on the ground. He looked up. Ashott was back.

'There is no sign of the Saracens, but we must go now - back to Damascus,' he said as he dismounted his horse and let go of the reins of the other two mounts he had been leading. Sir John stood, his legs unsteady, the strange enervation still gripping his muscles. He looked directly into Ashott's dark, unforgiving eyes. 'Damascus?' he queried.

'Yes. Damascus. And then back to Acre. King Philip will pay a handsome sum for the body of Jesus.'

Sir John looked at him, as his weary mind made sense of the words. 'You mean to take this back to Philip?' he said, pointing at the open coffin.

Ashott shot him a glance, his anger and hatred simmering under the surface. 'Crusader, you are a fool! You are weak. You are all weak. You come to this land and you think that you can beat us. You will never! This country will soak up all your blood and devour you. I am Ashott. This is my land. I will do as I please,' he said before spitting on the floor.

'This is the body of Jesus, our Saviour, who died for us on the cross. But he did not rise to heaven; he is here in front of us. 'Do you know what this means?' he said, staring at the Armenian. 'This means that he was not the Son of God. He was just a man - like you and I. If you reveal this to the Crusaders, they will unleash a whirlwind of destruction that will make the carnage at Acre seem tame. All that they hold dear will be taken from them. The reason for their Crusade, the way they live their lives, all gone... They will lash out against the people of this land with an anger that knows no bounds. Do you want that?'

The Armenian sneered. 'It is not for me to decide.'
'But it is! We can bury the coffin and keep our tongues still.'

Ashott laughed. 'Bury the coffin? After all that I have gone through? Never! Ashott will take the coffin back to your King and will be well rewarded. Damn everyone else.'

Sir John knew that there was no reasoning with the mercenary. As Ashott turned away from him, he grabbed the handle of his sword and drew it from its leather scabbard. But he was weak, so weak. His muscles reacted in a way that he had never experienced. His sword - usually the extension of his arm - felt heavy and cumbersome as it cleared the end of the scabbard.

Ashott, hearing the familiar noise of a blade being drawn, turned instinctively, drawing his scimitar in readiness. The Crusader was coming towards him, but Ashott could see something was wrong. The knight, a worthy opponent, whom he had seen defeat so many, was behaving strangely, his body moving in slow motion. The Crusader made a cut which Ashott stepped away from, and then a slash, which a child could have delivered with greater effect. Again and again the blows came. All to nothing.

Ashott, tired of the futile display, advanced towards the Crusader, readied his sword and thrust deep into John's abdomen, the point of the blade glinting in the sun as it emerged through his back. Completing the move, he withdrew the sword and watched as the knight fell to his knees.

'It appears that your journey is over,' he said, kicking John squarely in the chest, sending the knight sprawling backwards. 'It is your time, Crusader. Prepare to meet thy maker,' he said as he placed the point of his scimitar on the throat of his hapless opponent.

John, his eyes swollen and blurred from his tears, watched as the dark figure of the mercenary stood above him, clear against the backdrop of the bright blue desert sky. He felt at peace. There was no fight left in him; his anger and despair had vanished.

He stretched his head back and extended his throat, presenting his executioner with an easy target. Ashott responded by placing the bloodied tip of his scimitar on John's throat just above the jugular. As John waited for the thrust, he listened to the distant screech of the solitary eagle.

The thud came from nowhere. The dark figure above him swayed, the cold steel removed from his neck. Another thud and Ashott was on his knees. The silhouette of the mercenary replaced by that of the eunuch, the screech of the eagle gone. The only noise: a sickening thump as rock met flesh and bone, as the eunuch finished his gruesome work.

IPS Station, Al Amarah,
14.04hrs, 23 May 2007.

His complexion was far paler than that of the Arabs that surrounded him - an indication of his diverse Persian ancestry. He could even have passed for a European, his well-fitting suit making him stand out amongst the loose-robed Iraqis. But the thing that clinched it was the collarless shirt that he wore under his suit; there was no mistaking he was Iranian.

'Would you care for a cigarette?' asked the Commander, as the man who sat opposite him was presented with a cigarette box by one of the Commander's men. He reached into the ornately decorated container, picked out a Marlboro and held it to his lips. The attendant then undermined the finesse of the gesture by lighting the cigarette with a disposable lighter.

'Leave, and make sure we don't get disturbed,' said the Commander as the attendant put the lighter back in his pocket.

The Iranian took a long pull on the filter, and sat back in his chair. 'It is good to see you again, Commander,' he said as he exhaled. 'It must be, what? Twenty years now?'

'Nineteen,' replied the Commander.

'Yes, yes, of course. Nineteen, you are correct. How silly of me. How could I forget that date. August 20th 1988: a historic day. You were a Major then, were you not?'

'As were you. You have a good memory,' answered the Commander.

'It is one of my better attributes,' he said, tapping the Marlboro with his index finger. 'Yes. That monumental day when the war ended. I shall never forget the meeting in the tent between our two generals.'

The Commander nodded. 'Would you care for a drink? I have a good single malt, given to me by the British.'

'That would be very kind.'

The Commander got up from his chair and poured two drinks. 'To our fallen comrades,' he said, passing one glass to his guest and raising his own tumbler in readiness for the toast.

'To our fallen comrades,' repeated the Iranian. 'Who would have thought then, nineteen years ago, that we would be sitting opposite each other, enjoying a wonderful Scotch, and doing business?'

'Not I. That's for sure. There was so much death and destruction... so much...'

'Anger?' The Iranian butted in to finish the sentence. 'And yet here we are,' he continued, sensing pain in his host's answer, not wanting to dwell on the past. 'We must look to the future now, Commander. And business is good, is it not?'

'Yes. Business is good,' the Commander replied as he stroked his empty glass.

'Are you aware that the Americans and the British have plans to open up a huge oil field right under your very nose?'

The Commander paused. 'I'd heard rumours,' he lied, as he pushed the tumbler away from him with his index fingers.

'Let me be the first to tell you that the rumours are correct; they plan to drain the marshes and make an oilfield that will become one of the biggest in the world.'

'Would you care for another?' the Commander asked, as he stood and moved to the drinks cabinet. He had been put on the spot, and needed time to think. The Iranians had always had a good intelligence agency, but he was furious that he knew nothing of this oil field. *Was he bluffing?* the Commander thought, as he refilled the glasses.

'They are trying to take our land. And we have to stop them,' the Iranian added, nonchalantly, as he sipped his whisky.

'Our land?' asked the Commander with a surprised voice. 'The last time I looked, the Marshes were in Iraq.'

'Metaphorically speaking, of course,' said the Iranian, with a smile. 'After all, we are virtually brothers. The only thing separating us is the border.'

The Commander drank what was left of his second glass of Scotch and put the empty glass neatly onto a coaster. Without taking his eyes off the Iranian, he opened the top drawer of his desk, placing his hand slowly into the wooden recess, his fingers quickly finding what they were searching for: the cold steel of his Beretta pistol. 'That border you spoke of cost the lives of many of my men. Would you have me forget their sacrifice so easily?'

'Of course not, Commander,' answered the Iranian, annoyed at himself for his poor choice of words. 'We both lost men - good men - but it is all in the past. Now, we have to move on. There is a great deal of money to be made. The infidels think that they can come here and rape our land. But we can stop them. You are with us, are you not, Commander?'

The Commander opened the drawer fully and looked inside. The pistol was sat on top of a photograph, the handgun obscuring the picture. He pushed the weapon to one side and looked down on the photograph. This was his prized possession - something that he could no longer openly display. It was a picture of him standing next to another man in military uniform. He too had a large moustache, but there was no mistaking his features. It was Saddam Hussain. As he stared at the picture, his mind went back to that glorious day when he had been rewarded by his president. It was the proudest day of his life, his broad smile captured for posterity. In fact, he mused when seeing it, the picture only showed a glimmer of how proud he really was. He gently touched the glass. 'I am sure we can do business,' he said, as he closed the drawer. 'After all, the enemy of my enemy is my friend,' he said offering his hand.

'Excellent, I knew that you would see it favourably,' said the Iranian as he grasped the man's hand. 'And so to business. I would like to see your prisoners.'

Mayadin, River Euphrates, Syria,
22.47hrs, 23 May 2007.

They had moved into the small port under cover of darkness to avoid unwanted attention, but it turned out that they needn't have bothered. Mayadin was a smuggling town, and had been a centre of illegal activity between Iraq and Syria since the British and French had re-drawn the borders of the two countries just after the First World War. The locals never asked questions; it was not in their nature to do so, and if they looked, they did so only fleetingly. Everyone kept themselves to themselves.

They'd only just been able to start the assassins' Land Rover after the fire-fight, the Land Cruiser, riddled with bullets, had given up the ghost. But the old British four-by-four - hanging on for dear life – had somehow lasted until they reached the quay, the long jet of steam from the radiator signalling its demise.

'My cousin,' Hollywood pointed, as a man approached the Land Rover. The man was stocky, his shaved head sitting on a thick set of shoulders, the well-developed deltoid muscles giving the impression that he had no neck. 'His name is Captain Mahmood. He is the best smuggler on the river Euphrates. He will take you wherever you want to go.'

'Okay. Let's get this show on the road then,' said Mitch, grabbing a kit bag out of the back of the dead vehicle.

'No, no, Mister. Let me,' insisted Mahmood as he took

the bag from Mitch. The weight of the small canvas sack was deceptive; it took the Captain by surprise. But just as it was about to hit the floor, the Captain regained his balance, moving his feet quickly, like a fighter, to adjust for the load. The bag pulled up short, its metal contents shifting and clinking together. The Captain looked at Mitch and smiled. He had moved too many weapons in his life not to recognise the noise.

The river dhow, or badan, was not a new boat. Even if it had been, there was no easy way of identifying it as such; the shape hadn't changed much over the centuries. It was less than forty feet in length, eight foot wide at the beam - its thickest point - and was steered from a small wheelhouse at the stern that was only big enough for two. The wheelhouse overlooked the open hold area, which was covered over with an old sail, so as to shade the cargo and passengers from the sun. Beneath the wheel house was a small galley. And beneath that, the engine room, containing Mahmood's pride and joy: two Volvo Penta V8 marine turbines with a combined power output of several hundred horses. The rusting bolts covering the hull were there to give an impression of dilapidation. The real story, however, was that these two pulsating engines turned into beasts when the throttles were pushed forward. At least, this is what they had been told a hundred times by Hollywood on their journey from Palmyra.

Mahmood sailed just before midnight, the diesel engine of the boat humming them to sleep as they lay on sacks of maize, their slumber difficult, broken by hordes of hungry mosquitoes. They had crossed over the border in the middle of the night, with little ceremony, the customs officials on either side always glad to see the generous tipping skipper. In the morning, they were woken by the crew with hot shay. Taking their fill of the sweet tea, they watched as herds of buffalo, sheep and cows gathered on the riverbank to drink their fill in the still morning air, the spectacle idyllic.

'Did you know that the first recorded Englishman to sail

down the Euphrates was Ralph Fitch in 1583?' said the Professor, breaking the silence. 'He was carrying letters from Queen Elizabeth I to the Grand Mongol Emperor of China,' he elaborated, standing and stretching the sleep out of his body. 'He reported seeing lions prowling along the riverbanks in the mornings, looking for a kill,' he continued, maintaining his firm hold of the boat's handrail.

Mitch stood, stretched and yawned, copying the Professor's example, adding a loud fart to his routine - a defiant act of individualism - as he stuck his hand down the front of his jeans to rearrange himself.'

'Hey, you never got to finish your story yesterday, Prof. Come on. Spill the beans. We've got plenty of time on our hands.'

'You're right. A lot of high octane stuff yesterday. This trip has been full of firsts. A gunfight and now a boat trip on the great Euphrates. It just gets better and better.'

Mason looked over with a frown of indignation as he finished his tea.

Mitch waved at Hollywood up in the wheelhouse. They had agreed for him to remain with the party for a few days, while the heat died down. 'Can we get some more tea, please?' Mitch shouted.

'No problem, boss,' answered the man - with a smile that could blind.

The Professor went and sat on the sack of wheat next to Mason, both men waiting for Mitch, who had decided to empty his bladder over the side of the dhow. Mitch stood on the end gunnel, held a rope to support himself and thrust his hips forward. The urine had left his body in a perfect arc, clearing the side of the boat, its journey ending in the calm water of the Euphrates.

Cornelius looked at Mason in amazement. 'You'll get used to him,' Mason said, with a shrug of his shoulders, 'It takes time and patience. But you'll get used to him.'

'OK, Prof. You may begin,' Mitch said, plonking himself down on a sack of grain.

'Well... my theory starts with the death of Christ. We all know the account of the crucifixion - with Jesus being speared by the Roman Centurion, and how he is taken down from the Cross. It's what happened next is subject to debate. The Bible tells us that Jesus' body was interred in the tomb of Joseph of Arimathea for safekeeping and a rock rolled in front of the entrance. When his followers returned, they discovered that the corpse had gone. Jesus then appeared alive in person to his followers, and - depending on which account in the Bible you follow - ascended to heaven between three and forty days later. Correct?'

Both men nodded in agreement.

'The resurrection is a key tenet in Christianity. Jesus's death and resurrection was the proof needed to sell the concept of 'eternal life' to the masses. Followers believing that, if they took up the new religion, they too would rise after their deaths, and ascend to heaven.

'So there we have it. That's the story from the Bible that we've all grown up with. But there is another school of thought – one that believes that Jesus didn't die on the cross. He was wounded, yes, but was taken down from the Cross still alive. There are tales, folklore, saying that Jesus travelled east. Some say that he reached as far as Srinagar in modern-day India - Kashmir, to be exact - where he lived out his days. There still exists a shrine to *Yus Asaph* - Jesus the Gatherer in the local language - purportedly built in the immediate aftermath of his death. But I don't agree with that theory,' Cornelius said, as he pushed his thick dark glasses back onto his face. 'There's no hard evidence to back it up'. He paused. 'I *do*, however, believe that he travelled east.'

'Look, Prof... I'm not religious. I mean, I go to church, like, once a year: at Christmas. But that doesn't sound right to me. Everyone knows that Jesus died on the cross. Isn't that right, Mason?'

'Sounds like blasphemy to me,' said Mason, his voice laced with pain as he stretched his aching body. 'But let's hear what he has to say.'

Cornelius smiled. 'To continue, let's look at the events thirty-three years before the Crucifixion - at the time of Jesus' birth, to be exact. We all know the story of the three wise men, or Magi: Melchior, Gaspar and, of course, our friend Balthasar. Now, Balthasar was present at the birth of Jesus. And we now have evidence suggesting that Jesus was buried in his tomb. So he was there at the beginning and the end. Yes?'

Both men nodded.

So... we're in agreement. Balthasar, the rich merchant is one of the main protagonists. He would have been well into his seventies - maybe older - at the time of the crucifixion. Certainly he would have been too old to be making such arduous journeys – journeys that were tough even for the young. So how would he know of Jesus's death? After all, the events leading up to the crucifixion happened very quickly. It would have taken weeks for the message to get to Palmyra.'

'There was someone there, watching on his behalf?' suggested Mason.

It was Cornelius's time to nod. 'Yes. That's what I think. Balthasar might have thought of himself as a godfather figure - after all, his name translated means *protector of the King*. He might have spent his whole life watching over the Messiah. And, when he was too old, he may have sent someone younger in his stead.'

'So the injured Jesus is brought to Palmyra by one of Balthasar's men?' Mitch interrupted, his face etched with concentration.

'Correct. Brought here, away from his enemies. How else would Jesus' body come to rest in a tomb in the middle of the desert?'

'So, did Jesus die in Palmyra, then?' asked Mitch.

'I can't say for sure. But I think so. From inscriptions in the tomb, we know that Balthasar died a year after the Crucifixion. And the reference to 'following the Messiah into heaven' that was carved into the lid of his ossuary, suggests that Jesus had died some time before.'

'So he didn't last long, then?' asked Mitch.

'No. Remember that he was badly wounded. I think he was alive when he reached the city, but died shortly after.'

'So why did the Muslims wait all that time before they tried to destroy Jesus's remains? Why straight after the fall of Acre, over a thousand years later?' asked Mitch.

'They wanted to deny it to the enemy,' said Mason. 'Exactly,' answered Cornelius. 'King Philip only knew of it as a 'Great Treasure'. He must have thought that it was gold or silver; he had no idea what it really was. The Crusaders had just murdered and pillaged their way across the Holy Land. Can you imagine what they would have done if they knew that Jesus's body was actually at Palmyra. They would have carried on their bloody mission, stopping at nothing, cutting a bloody swathe through what is now Lebanon and Syria. It was only when the knight - Sir John De Guise – actually found the treasure that he discovered what it really was.'

'And we know he got to Palmyra because of Ernoul's chronicle, right?' asked Mitch, recalling the Professor's words from the night at the Baghdad Café.

'Yes. Sir John De Guise went on a mission to the east - a mission from which his company never returned. I think he made it to the tomb of Balthasar, and he took the ossuary east.'

'Why east, Prof? You'd have thought he'd have taken it back to the Holy Land,' quizzed Mitch.

'If he'd done that, there would have been chaos,' answered Cornelius. 'There is a passage in the Bible. It's by Paul; the first chapter of Corinthians'. The professor paused to gather his words. 'How do some among you say that there is no resurrection of the dead? But if there is no resurrection of the dead, then not even Christ has been raised; and if Christ has not been raised, then our preaching is vain, and your faith is also vain…'

'I think that our knight realised something,' Cornelius

347

continued, breaking the silence. 'To go west with Jesus's body would have caused a rift in Christianity such as had never been seen, pitching dissenters against believers.'

'A civil war' proclaimed Mason. 'It sounds to me like he'd had enough. Enough of the killing and the stench of death.'

'I would agree. He went east away from the Crusader Army, and south to the Mesopotamian Marshes, taking the treasure with him. He knew that to take it back to Philip would cause pain and suffering on an unbelievable scale.'

'And you saw his shield and sword?' asked Mitch.

'I saw a shield and a sword. I don't know who they belonged to.'

'They must have belonged to him. How many other knights are going to be running around the Iraqi Marshlands? So if we find this ossuary and the knight's stuff, your theory gets proven right?' asked Mitch. 'What's the knight's name again?'

'Sir John de Guise,' answered the Professor.

'Yeah, that's right. Sir John de Guise. He sounds like a hell of a guy, taking one for the team like that. A real hero. Hell, Mason, he reminds me of you!'

The Euphrates,
1191.

Sir John watched the deck hands as they undid the ropes holding the river dhow tight to the wooden jetty. The sailors pushed with their oars until the boat was clear of the landing stage, the lateen sail unfurled, the loose canvas flapping in the summer breeze until captured by the wind. Only then was it blown into its distinctive triangular shape. Their journey down the great Euphrates River had begun.

Sir John and the eunuch had arrived at the small port two days before, after a dusty journey through the Syrian

Steppes. The knight had thought that he was done for, the hole from Ashott's blade gaping at the moment he lay injured - surely a signal of his imminent passing. But the eunuch had rubbed dust from inside the coffin onto the wound and bound it. And, as they had ridden through the Steppes, his strength had gradually returned.

At first, there was no common language between them, so they communicated by sign, each man sharing words daily to build a hybrid vocabulary. Gradually, John was able to unfold his companion's story. His name was Naseem. He'd spent his whole life in bondage, and, together with the slave killed by the Saracens, had tended the Great Treasure for as long as he could remember. The owner had offered very little material comfort to his two guards, the dishevelled appearance of Naseem testament to his former master's thriftiness. His dark hair was matted and un-groomed, his face dirty, the grime highlighting scars of an old disease that had healed but nonetheless left its mark, with deep holes in his young skin. If he'd stayed at Palmyra, he would have been killed. And why stay anyway? His lifelong friend was dead. And the meaning of his existence - the object he had spent every day protecting - was now in the possession of the knight. He knew nothing else. His job – even now - was to stay with the treasure.

When they had reached the great river, the two travellers had set up camp outside a small port, both men bathing in the cool water, washing the dust and dirt from their tired bodies. Sir John had sent Naseem into the port to sell the horses, find a large chest, gain provisions and buy passage on a boat going south. He had also told him to buy new clothes for them both. When he returned, John had made a fire with Naseem's old garments, much to the delight of the now-smartly-dressed servant, whose smile glowed bright as he danced around the campfire. In the chest, Sir John placed the stone casket, shield and sword. Securing the artifacts away from prying eyes, its contents guarded with a large padlock.

Naseem had kept Ashott's scimitar after he had buried the Saracen at Palmyra. With Sir John dressed in his new attire, Naseem had given him Ashott's deadly blade. The knight copied the Armenian, the scimitar hanging from the thick belt that drew in his loose, flowing robes.

As the sail filled with the hot wind, John stood at the bow of the boat. He looked back at Naseem and smiled, watching as the young man - who was still enthralled with his new clothes - patted the material with relish. *Things have changed*, he thought as he turned, taking hold of a rope to steady himself, watching as the bow cut its path through the brown expanse of water. *Changed forever*.

The progress down the Great River was slow, their journey lengthened as their dhow stopped regularly at the busy ports that lined its length to load and unload cargo. The two travellers quickly became liked by the crew, Sir John helping them with the heavy sacks at each port, and Naseem singing and dancing, providing welcome entertainment for the men as they ate their meals at the end of their exhausting days. The further south they travelled, the hotter it got, and the wider the river became. The fast-moving, brown water alive with the assorted colours of a myriad of sailing boats. When the vessel was at sail, Sir John would sit at the bow and keep watch for rocks or obstacles in their path, waving at the children as they swam in the river, some using inflated animal skins to keep themselves afloat. At every bend, it seemed that the Euphrates gave up a new story to its observers. He watched one day as a lion stalked a water buffalo on the river bank. Around the next bend stood a mass of Bedouin tents stretching out for miles, the nomadic tribe's horses and camels crowding on the bank, quenching their thirst.

For once in his life, the knight had the time to reflect, to ask himself questions. The answers to these questions needed time to formulate, their resolution only made possible through the absence of external pressure. The savagery of the Crusade weighed on him heavily. Like many

Crusaders, he'd hoped that his sins would all be absolved when they had conquered the Holy Land - washed away by a thankful God. It had not been so; instead, his faith had deserted him. But why had he, of all people, been given the body of Jesus to safeguard? He was not a saint; he was just a man. Moreover, he was a man who had lost his faith. Why him? Was it not better for the task to be carried out by a more pious man - a man that still believed - a man like he used to be?

As the journey progressed, so did his resolve. During the Crusade, he'd not been able to control the actions of the massed horde that the campaign had attracted. But this was something he *could* now control. He realised that to take the treasure back to his King was to call into question the very basis of Christianity: the understanding that Jesus had died on the cross, was resurrected, and ascended to Heaven.

The evidence of Jesus's earthbound remains polluted this understanding. He knew that the faithful would never believe it. But there would be many others; men and women who'd lost their faith: apostates, followers of different callings, all of whom would be able to capitalise on the new circumstances to serve their own agendas. Civil war, death and hardship, chaos and bloodshed, would surround the announcement that Jesus was but a man.

It was decided. He was now the guardian of the treasure, and he would not allow that to happen. He was going to take it as far away as he could. Make sure it remained unrevealed. He would guard it for as long as he was able to - as his penance for having partaken in the savagery of the Crusades. His determination became stronger with every day that he spent on the great river of Mesopotamia.

Sir John was at his post at the bow when realised that the riverbanks on either side had fallen away. The men had entered into a vast lake, the far shore of which was nowhere to be seen. It took them the rest of the day to reach land, the crew finally securing the vessel to a jetty, the wooden landing filled with boats at the mouth of a wide river that poured from the lake.

Sir John stepped onto the wooden landing stage and stretched his legs. As his muscles loosened, he turned and watched the remnants of the sun sink into the great lake, the sphere cut perfectly in two by the horizon. 'A perfect sunset,' he said, standing mesmerised, unable to break his gaze until its whole had vanished. When it had, he knew that his journey down the great river was at an end.

He walked back to the boat and shouted for Naseem to gather their belongings. The crew, unhappy at their departure, pleaded with him to eat one more meal with them. That night, they feasted with the crew for the last time, with Naseem dancing and singing until his voice could no longer hold a tune. In the morning, the two men departed as the sun rose. The crew lined the boat as Sir John and Naseem walked down the quay, the crew's tears betraying the fondness they had developed for these two mysterious travellers.

So, this is where the Tigris and Euphrates meet, Sir John said to himself as he drank his shay and looked at the map that the merchant had unrolled for him - the old man's hut on the jetty providing welcome shade from the burning sun. The old merchant gave a toothless smile and nodded. 'Al Qurna, Al Qurna,' he said, placing his finger over the spot where they were located. 'Al Basrah,' he continued, pointing to the next town on the great water course.

Sir John nodded. 'Al Basrah,' he repeated after the merchant. The knight pointed to the area east of Al Qurna, where there were no towns. 'Ma huna?' he tried to ask the man in his native tongue. 'What's here?' He had learned some basic Arabic on the boat, the crew laughing at him as his uninitiated European tongue tried to pronounce the difficult rasping sounds. He could ask basic questions, but his meagre lessons had not equipped him to understand the answers. 'Torathe alanguar,' said the merchant. 'Hadda, Torathe alanguar,' he repeated. Sir John shook his head to the unfamiliar words, the merchant in answer pointing to a nearby clump of reeds. 'Torathe alanguar,' he repeated, pointing at the vegetation.

'Ahhhh,' answered Sir John, finally getting the explanation, 'Marshlands, Torathe alanguar,' he said, pointing at the map, much to the delight of the merchant.

From what money was left, Sir John bought a boat big enough for the heavy chest. And the next time the sun rose, it found the two travellers setting sail on another journey - this time not down a great river, but instead into the still waters of the fabled marshes - the place that, unbeknown to Sir John, had been the site of the Garden of Eden. The two travellers were going back to where humanity had started, and to where God had completed his greatest creation, Adam.

They travelled for three days, sleeping in the boat at night, for want of dry land, Sir John insisting that they push further and further east into the dense marshland, driven by impulse, as if his actions were being guided by an unseen hand. Naseem became frightened and, after the third day, began to weep. The claustrophobia caused by the tightly packed reeds, as well as sheer exhaustion had taken a grip of his very being. Sir John managed to calm his companion. And luckily, on the morning of the fourth day, their spirits were lifted, when they spied a column of smoke rising into the sky from a distance.

It was a village that had been built on the first hard ground that they had seen for days. The many huts - made from mud brick, with thatched reed roofs - rose above the water on a small hill, the high ground overlooking a wooden landing stage where many small boats were moored. As they tied their boat alongside the jetty, they watched as the men tended their water buffalos and the children played in the open water.

'I knew not of this place's existence. But now that I have found it, I know that this is what I have searched for,' Sir John said, looking at his tired companion with a smile. 'This is our new home, Naseem. Our journey is at an end.'

The door at the top of the concrete steps opened, the Iranian following the Commander and his entourage down into the dark, foul-smelling room.

'Make them stand,' ordered the Iranian, stopping half way down the small flight of steps, and taking a handkerchief out of his trouser pocket. 'I want to see that they are not damaged,' he continued, holding the material close to his nose.

'I think we're on display,' said Thor, as the Commander barked an order at his men. 'Who do you think he is?'

The cell door was unlocked, one of the policemen entering the small, barred room, indicating - with the tip of his truncheon - for the prisoners to stand. 'SILENCE,' shouted the Commander, in English, as the policeman raised his truncheon in readiness to punish the infidels for any insolence.

'They seem to be in good order,' remarked the Iranian. 'I have seen enough.' He turned to leave, but hesitated when his eye caught sight of the crumpled body on the floor of the adjacent cell. 'Who is that?' he asked, pointing at John.

'He is of no consequence,' replied the Commander.

'May I suggest you move him. You cannot afford your other guests to get sick. It would also make the smell in here a little more... tolerable,' he said, as he continued to climb.

'I will be back in three days' time with the money. The exchange can take place then,' said the Iranian as his men opened the door of the waiting car. 'See that nothing happens to them in the meantime.'

'Where will you take them?' asked the Commander.

'There is no need for you to know that, my friend,' he said as he turned to get into his car. 'Ah, I suppose there is no harm in telling you,' he paused. 'You will see them soon enough on TV, so there is no real point in secrecy. They will be given to one of the Shia groups in Baghdad. They, in turn, will ask for some outlandish conditions from the British and Australian governments for their release - which will of course not be met. Their appearance on TV will highlight the cause of our people; it serves as a form of communication. And then their execution will be filmed and seen all around the world. Barbaric, I know. But it is symbolic. After all, they were not invited here; they're invaders. A warning to future meddlers to stay away.' He shook the Commander's hand. 'Thank you for your hospitality, Commander. It is good to see you again.'

The Commander watched as the car left the compound, the dust from its tyres rising into the air. He turned to his Sergeant. 'Release the old man, and give the two prisoners a good meal,' he said, lighting up another Marlboro. *They will need it, where they are going*, he said under his breath.

River Euphrates, Iraq,
11.55hrs, 24 May 2007.

'It looks good. There's no infection. And the swelling is coming down nicely. I'll give you another shot of my wonder drug,' Mitch said, as he dipped the needle of the syringe into the small bottles in front of him, each labelled with their contents: antibiotics, anti-inflammatories, pain-killers.

'What time is it? Mason said, with a slight wince, as the needle pierced his skin.

'Rachel?'

'Yeah... she's not answered in the last two days. I'm getting concerned.'

'Okay, just hang on a minute while I sterilise the wound.' There was the noise of a cork popping from a bottle. 'Brace yourself. Here it comes.'

'Ouch! What's that smell?'

'Jack Daniels. It's the only alcohol I've got. You should

be honoured; it's my last bottle.'

The display read 12:00. He pressed the call button, held it to his ear and waited. The unseen signal shot into space, bounced off the satellite orbiting hundreds of miles above him and fell back to earth, ready to connect to Rachel's sat phone. Nothing. He tried again. Still nothing. He turned the phone off and on. But still there was no connection. He looked at the phone display. 12:03. I *will try once more. If there's no answer, I'll leave it 'til tomorrow*, he said to himself. He hit the button again. There was a delay, but this time it rang. Once, twice and then there was a voice. 'Mason! Mason? Is that you?'

'Yes. It's me.'

'I broke the phone. It was my fault. I couldn't get it to work. But I took it to a man, and he fixed it. Mason. Is it really you?'

'Yes, Rachel. It's really me. I told you I would come back.'

'I know you promised. But people break their promises.'

'Are you okay?'

'Yes... yes. I am fine. I know where your men are. I found them.'

'What. You found them? Where are they? Are they in danger?'

'The police have them, and I think that my father is with them. You have to hurry. It is very bad here - very bad. Where are you?'

'Rachel, listen to me carefully. You must not put yourself in danger. I'm one day away. You must stay safe until I get there. Do you understand?'

'Hurry. Please hurry. I am frightened.'

'Rachel, I need you to do something.'

'Yes, yes. What is it?'

'Press the menu button on your phone. It will show you a number of options; pick the one that says 'navigation'. Do it now.'

'Okay. I have it. What next?'

'Choose the option that says 'current position', and press it.'

'Yes, yes. I have done that. It says 'acquiring satellites'... Now it says 'longitude and latitude.''

'Great. Now choose the option 'send as SMS', and send it to this number.'

'Yes... yes. Wait. I will do it.'

There was a pause, and then Mason's phone buzzed into life registering a text message. He opened it up and smiled. 'Good girl. I've got it. I know exactly where you are. Now, keep out of sight. And I will call you tomorrow. I will leave my phone on. If there are any problems, just call me. Okay?'

'Yes, Mason. I understand. I will put the phone on again at the same time tomorrow.'

'Good girl. You are fantastic.'

'I was lonely and frightened. But now I know you come. I am strong again. Please be quick.'

The line went dead. Mason put the phone down on the sack next to him and breathed out deeply.

'Good news?' asked Mitch as he took a swig from the bottle of whisky.

'We're in business, mate,' replied Mason as he lay back, folding his arms behind his head.

GCHQ, Cornwall, UK.

The locals that lived on the North Cornish coast thought that they looked like golf balls. But the strange looking spheres were protection for the highly sensitive satellite dishes contained within them. This was GCHQ, the British monitoring station, located in an old World War II RAF station near Coombe in Cornwall. Its job: to relentlessly monitor satellite and radio communication from Africa, the Indian Ocean, all of mainland Europe and the Middle East. The secret systems within the intelligence base were installed for the purpose of capturing communications from terrorists, criminals and any other troublemakers wishing harm against Her Majesty's Government.

There was no criminal intent from the incoming message that the highly sensitive computer received from Coombe. But the operator in London handling the alerts didn't know that. The fact was that the phone number was on a 'watch list', the event causing an automatic email to be sent to SIS at Vauxhall Cross, London. The email had flashed up on the desk officer's screen as he enjoyed a cup of coffee.

The officer put *The Guardian* newspaper aside, opened the email and scratched the detail down on his notepad. He then picked up his phone and dialled '9' for an outside line.

'Hello. Is that James? This is Oliver.'

'Oh, hello, Oliver. Yes, this is James. How's things?'

'Wonderful, thanks. Look, I've got some information for you on that phone that was lost in Iraq. Our boys at GCHQ have intercepted a text message that gives its exact location. Have you got a pen?'

'Fire away... longitude... yes. Latitude... yes. That's fantastic, Oliver. Give my regards to Melissa. Thanks awfully.'

PART FOUR

CHAPTER THIRTEEN

Basrah International Airport, Iraq,
13.20hrs, 24 May 2007.

The plane couldn't make a normal approach. Instead, it had
to descend directly over the runway, the pilot of the small jet
liner constantly adjusting the controls, as the aircraft
descended in the pattern of a giant corkscrew. This unusual
approach was normally used by military pilots at 'hot'
locations. The technique adopted by all the planes landing
here, after a Russian cargo plane had been shot at with a
missile from the nearby city the year before. No one was
taking any chances, for this was no ordinary airport: this was
Basrah International.

JJ looked out of the small window from his seat in
the first class section at the front of the plane. He watched as
an aircraft beneath him turned and turned in its downward
spiral, the eventual contact with terra firma marked with
a puff of smoke as the tyres struck the baking tarmac. As
his own aircraft lost height, he was able to identify line
upon line of vehicles, the desert camouflage doing its
job and obscuring the angular outlines. But, with the ever-
decreasing altitude, his trained eye was soon able to

pick out the silhouettes. They were the machines of war. As he recognised them, he said their names quietly to himself, *Challenger Main Battle Tank, 432 Armoured Personnel Carrier, Scimitar Reconnaissance Light Tank.* Bump! He had been so engrossed that he hadn't realised how close they'd got to the ground. He sat back in his large first class seat and listened to the engines as they roared with reverse thrust, the fuselage rattling from their effort. *Shit,* he thought. *I hate this place.*

Tonka was there to meet him. The greeting emotionless, the pleasantries exchanged out of common courtesy. JJ didn't care what Tonka thought of him. But for his plan to succeed, he needed him. He had to win him round.

'I suppose I'm the bad guy,' JJ said as he climbed into the white four-by-four. 'The shit on everyone's shoes. But I'm here now. And I'm going to sort this mess out.'

'Okay,' Tonka nodded in reply, raising the clutch and pulling off.

'What sort of answer is that? Okay? What the fuck does that mean?' snapped JJ.

'It means 'good'?' replied Tonka, without taking his eyes off the road.

'Then why didn't you say 'good', then?' continued JJ on the offensive. 'Listen. I don't give a flying fuck what you think. At the end of the day, I'm the boss, and the buck stops with me. Do you understand?' he said as he fastened his seatbelt into the lug. 'I'm here to sort this fucking mess that Mason has left behind him. Has he been in touch?'

Tonka shook his head as he gripped the steering wheel.

'I asked you a fucking question. Has he been in touch?'

'No, he hasn't,' said Tonka through gritted teeth.

'Exactly! The fucking drunk hasn't been in touch. And you know why. Don't you?'

Tonka looked over at JJ. 'No, I don't know why. Enlighten me.'

'Still mates, then?' said JJ with a short sarcastic laugh. 'Still mates with the guy that used to get so drunk he would pass out and piss himself. He was thrown out of the Regiment because he was a drunk - a fucking drunk that couldn't hack it. He couldn't hack it then and he can't hack it now. Where is he?' JJ paused, as Tonka recalled the sad sight of Mason passed out in the mess. 'I'll tell you where he is; he's climbed back into the bottle again. He's trying to drown himself with self-pity. Look at me, and tell me I'm wrong?'

Tonka looked straight ahead, gripping the wheel harder, his knuckles bleached from the effort.

'Look at me, damn it,' JJ shouted. 'Tell me I'm wrong.'

Tonka slammed on the brakes, the wheels locking momentarily on the dusty surface as the vehicle came to an abrupt stop, kicking up a huge dust cloud. 'So, if the guy's a hopeless drunk, why did you hire him?' Tonka said as he hit the steering wheel with the palms of his hands.

'Yeah. You're right; I hired him. It's my fault. I suppose I shouldn't have given him the second chance. Must be getting soft in my old age, eh?'

'It was a dodgy fucking mission,' shouted Tonka. 'It should never have gone ahead.'

'Look, mate,' replied JJ, his voice calmer. 'All these security guys are here of their own choice. We all know that. We're not like those poor sods in camouflage uniforms that are out here for Queen and Country. We're all here for the money. And if a security guy doesn't like it, he has the privilege of just holding up his hand and saying 'I want out'. Am I right?'

Tonka stared at JJ, the anger still knotted in his face.

'You know I am,' JJ answered on his behalf. 'These guys get paid pop star wages for going to the gym and watching DVDs. Fuck me. Half of them are off their heads on steroids and the other half are gun-toting homicidal maniacs; they couldn't make it back in the normal world. I asked them to do a job. Yes, I agree, it was dangerous. But they all accepted - even that fucking drunk friend of yours.'

Tonka turned away. He was controlling his urge to punch

him straight in the face. But, deep down, he knew JJ was right. The only thing that was keeping the Target operators in-country was the money - they could leave at any time they wanted. There was a long pause as Tonka stared out of the windscreen and tried to calm himself. 'So what now, then?' he asked.

'If the guys are out there and still alive, I want to get them back,' answered JJ. 'But I can't do it alone; I need your help. Are you in?'

'I'm in.'

'Good. Let's get back to base. We have a lot to do.'

Tonka moved his foot off the brake and onto the accelerator. As the vehicle pulled off, JJ turned and looked out of the side window, his face hidden by his hand. The fake concern that had been written large across it was now gone - replaced by a suppressed smirk.

The two men stood in silence in the middle of the empty operations room staring at the large map that covered the wall, their eyes transfixed on the spot that was marked by a red pin. There was string wrapped around the marker, leading to a yellow stick note, which read simply '6 KIA'.

'I don't need to be reminded of this,' JJ said as he walked up to the map and pulled off the luminous paper note. He threw it in the bin. 'Brit Mil don't believe Mason's story about the two hostages,' said JJ, taking a black moleskin notebook out of his jacket pocket. 'You know that, don't you?'

'Yeah. I know that. They didn't find anything.'

'There were scorch marks where the vehicles were burnt out, but that was about it. Whoever cleaned up the area did a thorough job. I can't ask Brit Mil for any more help.' He pulled at the elastic fastener and opened up at a marked page.'

'So what's the plan, then?' Tonka asked, looking directly into JJ's face, searching for an indication of sincerity.

'Whatever we do must be under the radar... Brit Mil mustn't know. If they found out that we were continuing the search, they'd be all over us like a rash.' His finger scrolled down the page until it rested on a sequence of numbers written neatly along the thin blue line. 'We've got to do it alone,' he said as he looked at the map, his other finger searching for the coordinates. 'Here,' he said taking up a yellow pin and placing it at the tip of his finger. 'This is where we need to look.'

'Are you saying you know where they are?' Tonka said, as he grabbed JJ's arm and spun him around.

'This conversation doesn't leave this room. Do you understand?' JJ said in a low tone, looking down at Tonka's hand.

'Yeah... yeah. Of course,' answered Tonka, taking the hint and releasing his grip.

'I was given some information - apparently one of the satellite phones that was carried by the team went active recently. It sent a message with the phone's location.'

'Who the hell gave you that?'

'It doesn't matter who gave me the information. That's not important; what is important is that we have a new lead.'

'So you think there's a chance they're still alive?' asked Tonka, as he put his finger on the yellow pin.

'We don't know who sent it. But it's quite possible that Thor and Dusty still have the phone, and they've managed to get the message off. What's for sure is that the sat phone is still in the area. It looks like the old Arab might have been telling the truth after all. 'You might not like me, and neither might the guys who work for me,' JJ said as he put the book back into his coat pocket, 'but to be honest I don't give a fuck of what people think; I'm here because there's a chance. A chance that our guys are still alive. Mason's let them down. He's not coming back. That's for sure. But if there's a glimmer of hope that they're alive, I want to at least try. We owe them that, yeah?'

Tonka looked at the man standing before him. He

had been his friend once, their camaraderie forged in the intense heat of combat - a place where few men had been, and from which even fewer had returned. Then, he had trusted him with his life - as was the way in the SAS - but over time, their friendship had ebbed, fading each year from lack of contact. When they became reunited, his comrade had become his boss, a rich, successful man, one who used his position to bully and intimidate. The fraternal feelings had been replaced with distrust, jealousy, even hatred. In an instant, all that negativity disappeared; the man standing before him JJ O'Hare of old - a youthful man, in his prime, afraid of nothing. His old friend was back.

'Just tell me the plans, mate. We can do it. If they're out there, we'll find them. Just like old times, yeah?' Tonka said.

'Yep. Just like old times,' answered JJ, with a smile.

River Euphrates, Iraq,
19.31hrs, 24 May 2007.

It was sunset as Mason stood at the bow of the boat. He was captivated by the dying sun as it sank over the western horizon, mesmerised by the translucent beams emitting from it that struck the murky water, their iridescence changing in an instant to dark ochre and rich gold. As he watched the light dancing on the water's surface, his eyes grew heavy. The combination of the setting sun, summer heat, drum of the diesel engine and his recently eaten dinner all contriving to send him to sleep.

Hollywood, and one of the crew members, were sleeping on sacks at the base of the wheelhouse, their Captain Mahmood at his usual post - the helm. Now he came to think of it, Mason had rarely seen Mahmood out of the wheelhouse since they'd started their journey. He'd not seen him sleep either. And yet the captain still had the energy to smile whenever any of his passengers caught his eye. Mitch was sitting on a sack opposite the Professor, their conversation interrupted as each man took it in turns to take a slug from the bottle of whisky.

'To travel properly, you have to ignore external inconvenience and surrender yourself entirely to the experience. You must blend into your surroundings and accept what comes,' said the Professor, with a drunken slur. 'I forget who said that. It might have been Gertrude Bell, or... wait a minute... I know, I know... it was... Freya Stark.'

'Never heard of them,' said Mitch as he took another large slug from the bottle.

'They were both famous explorers who loved Arabia. A bit like me, really'.

'I've got a love of whisky, beer and hot, hot women,' said Mitch, wiping the whisky off his lips with the back of his hand.

'I thought you said that you only had one bottle left,' said Mason as he sat on the sack next to Mitch.

'I lied,' replied Mitch, with a big grin.

'So, who were these women, Prof?' asked Mason.

'They were both women fascinated by the Middle East. Gertrude was an amazing character; she had a big influence in Arabia after the First World War. T E Lawrence - you know, Lawrence of Arabia - was one of her protégés.'

'And the other one?'

'Freya Stark. She was another fascinating Arabist. She came up with one of my favourite quotes: *Risk is the salt and sugar of life*. Bloody marvellous,' said the Professor as he stared into space, thinking of a bygone age. 'It seems that this place – Mesopotamia - the land of the two rivers, has a special appeal for adventurers. Its draws them in like a magnet.'

'You're right, Prof. I love it here,' said Mitch, as he took another swig.

'How can you blame them, though? This place is where it all began: religion, Adam and Eve, the Garden of Eden, writing, hanging gardens of Babylon, the list goes on and on,' continued the Professor.

'Do you think that's why Sir John stayed?' asked Mason.

'We'll never know for certain. And that's one of the most frustrating things with historical investigations. We can never interact with the subjects we are investigating because – by definition – our enquiry always takes place after the fact. Most of it's conjecture, of course. We join the dots; we fill in the gaps we find with the most logical explanation we can imagine, and we try to back it up with evidence. But something we can rely on is that Sir John never returned to the West. Something kept him here. I'd like to think that he fell in love with the place.'

'Probably fell in love with a hot, hot Arab chick, more like,' pitched in Mitch.

Mason got up and walked back to his earlier vantage point. Just as the sun disappeared below the horizon, he caught sight of a group of children who'd taken a herd of water buffalo down to the water's edge, deciding to finish off their day with a dip in the cool water. As the boat passed, they stopped their horseplay and waved at the passing vessel, their efforts rewarded when Mason waved back, making them wave even more. *I suppose, in another life, and with no pressure, this trip down the Euphrates would be magnificent,* he thought to himself. But the reality rushed back to him. This was no pleasure cruise; the consequence of failure would be death for the prisoners - maybe all of them.

His eyes were growing heavy again. He pushed his back up against a hessian cloth sack, its contents giving easily, and listened to the drone of the engine, the vibration running through his entire body. His last thought before he went to sleep was of a Sunday morning in bed with Katie next to him, Izzy bouncing on his chest, her auburn curls and laughter cascading down onto him, showering him with love.

Hereford,
Five Years Earlier.

The excitement had started to grow as the bread that had been accumulated all week was broken into pieces and put back into the plastic wrapper. The ritual had started. It was time to feed the ducks. As soon as the car had stopped moving, Izzy popped the release button on her harness, and was out of the child safety seat, scrabbling across the back of the car, ready for the door's opening. She knew it was naughty, her actions resulting in a telling-off from her mother. But the cross words were worth it; this was one punishment that she was willing to accept; after all there were hungry ducks to feed, and that was the end of it! Soon, all three were walking down to the jetty wrapped in their winter coats, Izzy between her parents them, her hands gripped tightly as she swung back and forth, her laughter growing louder and louder as they approached the all-important feeding session.

Katie had hold of Izzy, sitting in the back of the small rowing boat, as her daddy pulled on the oars. Within moments, his powerful strokes had them in the middle of the small lake, a trail of ducks in the boats' wake, quacking in anticipation of the feed. Izzy had named them all: Donald, Blacky, Browny, Whitey, her favourite being Minnie Mouse - the name bestowed on the prettiest and most girly-looking of her flock of ravenous, web-footed friends.

Izzy, spurred by her excitement stood on the seat. 'Careful. You'll fall in,' Mason said as he pulled the oars in.

'I'm OK, Daddy. Minnie is hungry; she needs more food,' Izzy replied, her movements becoming more and more animated.

'Izzy. Stop it. You're rocking the boat. Stop her, Katie, she's going to fall in,' Mason shouted as the rowing boat rolled from side to side as its three occupants began to move around.

'No, Daddy. Minnie needs more. She's hungry,' Izzy

shouted, as she threw a handful of crumbs overboard, her voice turning into a scream as she lost her balance and fell into the water.

Katie reached out to grab Izzy. But, as she stood, the boat rocked and unbalanced her, she too falling into the lake. Mason, frantic, threw himself to the back of the boat and thrust his arm into the water. He could see them both submerged, just under the surface, their eyes wide in horror as they began to sink into the cold icy water.

He stretched as much as he could but couldn't grasp Katie's extended fingers. The stiffness in his shoulder was stopping him. *Why is my shoulder stiff? Why does it hurt so*, he'd said to himself, as he screamed at Katie, 'NOOOOO.'

River Euphrates, Iraq,
00.05hrs, 25 May 2007.

He was drenched in sweat. His shoulder on fire with pain. He was on a boat. Where were Katie and Izzy? He looked around. There were two men sleeping close beside him, on sacks. It came rushing back. He was on a boat sailing down the Euphrates. He breathed again, and wiped the sweat from his face. Another nightmare.

He got up and stretched his aching, knotted limbs, the pain in his muscles easing as his cramped legs came back to life. But the ache in his stomach remained. It was always there, gnawing away at him from waking until his last thoughts at night, a constant reminder that his family were gone.

He picked up a plastic bottle of water, tilted his head and emptied the contents into his parched mouth. The overflow from this hurried action ran down his chin and onto his chest. As he wiped off the residue, his eyes fell on the two sleeping men. Both had passed out on the sacks where he had left them earlier. The reason for their condition evident, the empty bottle of whisky at the Professor's feet, and the part-filled bottle being cradled by Mitch.

He sat opposite his two travelling companions and picked up the walking stick that had been leant to him by John, the Village Elder. In the darkness, the intricate carvings were hidden from him, so he ran his fingertips over the wood, made smooth by centuries, trying to decipher from memory the contours whilst watching the two sleeping men. He'd gone to Iraq with his head full of thoughts of death. His life - like a cheap trinket – to be discarded when the fancy took him. But it hadn't worked out the way. There were other people involved now, people who relied on him to be the best he could.

Mitch, the snoring man cradling the bottle of whisky - a man so full of life - was dying. But he was doing so with dignity, hanging on to every precious moment, living it to the full, without any remorse or complaint. Mason knew that his friend would trade places with him in an instant. Mitch, he imagined, would gladly master the pain and sorrow that came with Mason's life in exchange for the gift of being alive. But Mason was prepared to throw it away - discard the most precious thing he owned, like a piece of tatty old clothing. He felt ashamed of such thoughts, but couldn't deny them to himself.

He stared at the Professor, his thoughts wandering to the plight of Thor, Dusty, John and Rachel. They all needed him. He was the adhesive that bonded them all together. His actions, whether he liked it of not, impacting on them all. His new friends had given him a reason to carry on - a reason to survive, a reason to live.

After the accident he'd acted like a child who was lost, angry and frustrated. Thrashing around in the dark, looking for answers, bitter when they hadn't come. But as his fingers brushed against the smooth wood of the stick, the haze of self-pity began to lift. His thoughts clearer and clearer, as the night breeze wicked the moisture from his clammy skin. The answers to his painful questions once so elusive, now plain, unable to hide in their dark recesses. The illumination was complete, as if a light had been switched on. He wasn't there when the truck had jumped the central reservation and hit the car. Moreover, if he had been, he also would have been killed. He finally accepted something he had formerly only understood intellectually; he couldn't have done anything. It was an accident. He wasn't to blame.

As he smoothed the cane, calmness washed over his body, building with every stroke, granting him something that he had not experienced since before the accident: peace. As he breathed, it spread through his body, running through the veins and arteries like a tonic, his whole body relaxing. Even his shoulder had stopped hurting, and so had the gnawing, empty sensation in the pit of his stomach.

He closed his eyes and breathed deeply. Memories of Katie came flooding back. He could remember what her skin felt like, the smell of her hair, the excitement of her passion; he could feel her warmth and her love. Yes, her love: he could feel it. She was with him, and so was Isabella. He remembered the joy of seeing his beautiful baby for the first time, of experiencing a bond that only parents can know. He recalled the feelings of pride as she grew, and repaid his love - with snuggles and the words 'I love you daddy.' He'd had all this. It had been short - too short - but he was richer for it.

He lay back on the sack and stretched out. He couldn't remember the last time he had felt so relaxed. It was as if the dark cloud that had surrounded him had lifted. He closed his eyes and welcomed them into his sleepy thoughts. *Tonight, I will sleep with my girls*, he said to himself. *And tomorrow... I will be ready.*

CHAPTER FOURTEEN

Target HQ, Basrah,
07.55hrs, 25 May 2007.

The Target security team stood around their three neatly-parked Toyota Land Cruisers, awaiting the emergence of their CEO from the operations room. Rumours had quickly spread that the reason JJ was in town was to launch a rescue mission for their two captured comrades. The Target men, dejected from the recent losses, had taken it upon themselves to lend their support, and had organised a team to go on the daring raid.

'Strange,' Tonka said as both men stepped into the brilliant sunlight. 'There are no moves planned for this morning. What's this team doing here?

As JJ walked towards his vehicle, he was approached by one of the waiting men. 'Mornin', boss,' said the man as he walked towards the Target CEO. 'Sir... Could I have a quick word?'

JJ looked at the advancing man. He was a big guy, with a shaved head and a trimmed goatee. 'Dan, isn't it?' he replied, remembering him from a previous interview.

'That's right, boss,' said Dan as both men shook hands.

'What can I do for you?'

'Me and the lads want to volunteer for the rescue mission,' said Dan enthusiastically.

'And what rescue mission would that be?' answered JJ, trying to control his anger.

'We thought... We thought you and Tonka were going to rescue Dusty and Thor?'

'Ahh, I see. *That* rescue mission,' JJ answered. 'I tell you what,' he said, raising his voice loud enough for the other waiting men to hear. 'Let's all gather round, shall we?'

The six-man security team fanned out in a semi circle in front of their employer. 'Dan, what's your military background?' asked JJ.

'Uh.. ummm, what do you mean?' answered the team leader, taken aback by the direct question.

'I want to know what regiment you were in.' probed JJ.

'Royal Logistics,' the man answered, looking at the floor.

'What about you?' asked JJ, as he pointed at the other assembled men.

'Artillery.'

'Green Jackets.'

'Grenadier Guards.'

'Light Infantry.'

'You're quiet?' said JJ, pointing at the last man. 'What were you, in your other life?'

'I was a Royal Navy diver. I'm medical qualified, and I have done a close protection course,' blurted out the man, in an attempt to justify his existence.

'Okay, okay. I get it,' said JJ, cutting him off. 'So now what I want you to do is to raise your hand if you have any hostage rescue experience.'

There was silence as the team looked around at each other, waiting for the first one to raise their hand.

Dan scratched his shaven head. *I could have sworn that two of my guys said they were Special Forces*, he thought. *And the diver definitely told me he had done the underwater knife-fighting course.*

The team's heads had dropped, their earlier swagger and bravado now as abundant as rocking horse shit.

Dan stared at the diver, willing him to raise his hand, but the former frogman looked away, his arms firmly by his sides.

'No... I thought not,' continued JJ. 'I tell you what, gentlemen. If - and that's a big if - there was a hostage rescue happening, I think it would be better if we left it to the professionals, eh?' he said, turning his back and storming off towards the waiting vehicle.

The team walked back to their vehicles in silence. 'We could have done it, Dan,' said the diver. 'Yeah,' said the Green Jacket. 'I thought that was he was a bit harsh. He could at least given us a chance... Wanker.'

'All we need is to get proof that our men are still alive. With that evidence, Brit Mil is duty-bound to sort it. Turn it over to the professionals. Can you imagine what would happen if those bunch of lunatics got involved,' JJ said, nodding in the direction of the sullen team. 'It would be utter carnage.'

'So what have you got in mind, then?' asked Tonka as they got into the vehicle and closed the armoured doors.

'I want to find the place where the text was sent from, and set up an O.P., scope it out.'

'Covertly?'

'Yeah... can you get something low profile like an old BMW or something?'

'Shouldn't be a problem,' Tonka replied as he started up the engine.

'Sounds like a plan. We'll go first thing tomorrow.'

River Euphrates, Iraq,
08.01hrs, 25 May 2007.

He looked at the sack of grain, his mattress and the rolled up piece of canvas functioning as his pillow and yawned. Despite the makeshift nature of this bed, he'd just had the best night's sleep he could remember, the nightmares that usually stalked him during the dark emptiness absent. As he sipped the hot sweet tea - supplied to him by the helpful crew member - he watched the same companion trying to wake the two drunken travellers. Mitch, after a few shakes, was respons-

-ive. But there was still no movement from the Professor.

Mitch took off his shirt, and as he stood up grabbed hold of the bucket that the crew used to gather water from the river. He threw it overboard while still holding the rope that was attached to its handle, and watched as it sank into the murky water. With a heavy jerk, he pulled it clear, the water sloshing around the plastic interior as it cleared the gunnel, landing on the deck with a thud. Readying himself, Mitch took hold of the handle and poured the contents of the whole bucket over his own head. His whoops were loud, the bracing affects of the cold water tightening his every muscle. He repeated the process again. But this second bucket was not for him; when he was sure he had an audience, he emptied the contents all over the Professor.

The gallons of cold water hit the Professor like a sledgehammer, the whole crew laughing as the poor man's body came to terms with the impromptu shower. As the drenched man struggled to his feet, Mitch collapsed back onto the sacks of grain, his arms wrapped around his sides as if to stop them from splitting, his legs buckled with merriment.

'Come on, Mitch,' said Mason, as the laughter died down. 'We've got work to do. I need to speak to the Captain.'

Both men made their way to the stern of the boat, and climbed up the small ladder that led to the platform where the wheelhouse stood. Inside were the ever-present Captain and his relative - of dubious connection - Hollywood. 'Where are we?' asked Mason over the drone of the engines.

'We're about six hours away from our destination. Let me show you,' said Hollywood as he motioned towards the screen of the GPS. 'This is where we are now,' he said, pointing at a small triangle lit well against the grey of the translucent screen. 'And this is our destination,' he continued, simultaneously pressing a button that allowed the screen to zoom out. The screen showed the black outline of the meandering river, its dark silhouette thickening into a larger water feature. 'This is the lake of Al Qurna,' pointed out Hollywood, the blackness almost engulfing the entire screen. 'Look at this,' he said with his customary smile, pointing at another black feature - a river that joined the lake from the north. 'This is the Tigris. Al Qurna is where they meet.'

'Is this where we're headed?' asked Mason, placing his finger over a small square with a dot at its centre at the easternmost edge of the vast lake.

'Yep... That's the port,' Hollywood said as he slapped the Captain on the back.

The Captain nodded and pointed at the square. 'This good. This Al Qurna,' he said with his broken English, before continuing the conversation with Hollywood in his native tongue.

'He said that he has to drop us off at Al Qurna,' translated Hollywood. 'If he goes any further, we will run into British river patrol boats.'

Mason got out his small notebook and opened it at the page where he had written Rachel's position. 'Plot this on the GPS, Hollywood,' he said, as he read out the coordinates. Hollywood pressed the digits on the keypad, and then hit the 'mark' button. Immediately, another black square with a dot in the middle appeared on the screen - just below and to the right of their destination.

'How far is that from Al Qurna?' asked Mason.

'It's about... twenty kilometres.'

Mason looked at his watch. *08:45,* he thought, *I will call her at 12:00. That should give her enough time to get there before last light.* 'Right, come on, Mitch. We'd better make ourselves busy.'

They had already checked and cleaned the weapons on the first day. In ordinary military units, that would have been enough. But the two men were ex-Special Forces; their regime was more rigorous; nothing was left to chance. The Professor watched on as the two men stripped and assembled their weapons again and again. But Mason was slowing, the strain evident. It was etched across the man's face, the pain clearly searing through his injured shoulder.

'He won't give in, Prof,' shouted Mitch, as he cocked the reassembled AK three times before firing off the action. 'He is as stubborn as an old goat. He's always been the same.'

Hollywood could see Mason struggling with the heavy AK47. 'Hey, Mason… do ya wanna use this?' he called from the wheelhouse, pulling up his shirt to reveal a gold enamelled Beretta M9 pistol that was tucked into the waist belt of his jeans.

Both men stopped and looked at each other with big grins

'Hey, that looks awesome,' said Mitch, immediately taking hold of the pistol. 'Where did you get it from?'

'It's real gold,' replied Hollywood, basking in the attention. 'One of Saddam's Generals gave it to me. We smuggled him out a couple of years ago. He didn't have enough money, so I took this in payment.'

'No shit. It looks really expensive,' said Mitch appreciating the weight of the garish weapon.

'Let's have a look,' said Mason. The pain in his shoulder forgotten as the two men played like kids with this pistol that wouldn't have looked out of place in an American rapper video.

'So it's gold then?' asked Mason.

'Yes. real gold,' replied the proud owner. 'Your shoulder is sick. Please use it. It is much lighter than the AKs.'

'Only slightly,' answered Mason as the weapon sunk into his hand. 'I tell you what,' he said, with a look of concern. 'Best keep this safe…eh,' he said with a wink, 'we wouldn't want you to lose it.'

'It is magnificent… no?' Hollywood stated as Mason handed him back the pistol. 'Truly magnificent,' he continued as - in true gangster fashion - he thrust it back into the waistband of his jeans.

'What about me? What gun do I get?' asked the Professor as he stood up. 'I'll have the gold one if no one wants it?'

'Steady, Tiger,' said Mitch. 'No guns for you.'

'What do you mean? I have to protect myself.'

'No you don't,' added Mason.

'Why not?'

'Because you're staying here,' answered Mason.

The Professor's face dropped. 'That wasn't the deal.'

'What deal?' said Mason. 'There was never a deal. The only reason you are here is because you got caught up in this. And it was too dangerous to leave you behind in Syria. Look, the Captain will drop you off with the first Brit Mil patrol that he sees. You'll be back in the UK before you know it.'

'But... but, I don't want to go back to the UK. I want to stay here. I've spent my whole life waiting for this and you... you are going to send me back?' he said, shaking his head.

'Look, Prof. I'm going to try to rescue my guys from a gang who only a short time ago killed four of them. This is going to get hairy. There is a very real chance that some of us will get hurt. It's no place for you; you're a civilian.' Professor Cornelius Gregory sat down on his sack, his face like thunder, totally dejected. Once again, he thought, he'd come *so* close - only to fall at the last hurdle.

'It's 1157 hrs,' said Mitch handing Mason the phone. 'Best make that call.' Mason nodded, pulled out the aerial and pressed the button. He heard Rachel answer before it had even rung. 'Mason... Mason... Is that you?' said the excited voice at the other end. 'They released my father! I have my father.'

'That's great news,' answered Mason.

'Yes. But I have more for you. Your men are being picked up tomorrow. My father told me. You must hurry.'

'Do you know Al Qurna?' asked Mason.

'Yes, of course. Why?'

'Do you know the harbour?'

'Yes, yes. I know that too. Why do you ask?'

'Because we will be there at 6 o'clock.'

There was a pause as the information sank in. 'Really?...
You mean I will see you today?'

'Can you get there? By 6 o'clock?'

'Yes... I can.'

'Good… then it's today.'

IPS Station, Al Amarah,
07.57hrs, 25 May 2007.

They had been woken by the call to prayer, as was their
usual routine, both men lying on their backs, watching as the
first rays of the morning sun creep across the cell wall, a
primitive sun dial, marking the first highlight of the day:
breakfast.

'Who do you think that man was the other day, Thor?'
asked Dusty, as he propped himself up against the cool wall.

'Not sure. But whoever he was, he made things happen.
That meal they gave us last night was outstanding.'

'Yeah. And John's gone. Poor old sod. Do you think they
released him?'

'Don't know, mate. I like to think they did,' said Thor,
giving a big yawn.

'Me too,' replied Dusty, his bottom lip beginning to
shake with emotion. 'I hope he's safe - safe with his family,'
he added, before breaking down in tears once more. 'I don't
know how much more I can stand,' he said sobbing.

'You need to keep it together,' replied Thor, 'If John got
away then there's hope for us, yeah? I've got a feeling that
guy is going to make things happen. Things are looking up.'

The door at the top of the concrete steps opened.
'Breakfast,' said Thor, giving Dusty a fake punch in the arm.
'That's got to cheer you up?'

'Yeah,' grunted Thor with a fake laugh, wiping the tears away with his sleeve. 'Who would have thought I would get excited about the slop they serve for breakfast.'

Al Qurna, Iraq,
18.20hrs, 25 May 2007.

The sun was low in the west as the river dhow entered the final stages of its journey. The mood on the boat tense, the frivolity of the morning long gone as the unsleeping Captain monitored every movement of his hard working crew. Mason and Mitch were also busy with preparation for the dangerous task ahead of them. The only one on board with no sense of urgency the Professor, who was sat on his sack, his despondency clear to all.

'Al Qurna,' shouted Mahmood as he stepped out from the wheel house for the first time during their voyage and pointed at a line of bright shapes on the horizon. The distant flotilla of boats marked the location of the small harbour, the smile on the Captain's weather-beaten face bigger that at any other time on the voyage.

'He's happy,' said Mitch. 'He gets his bonus now.'

'How much did you offer him?' asked Mason.

'His normal rate was $25,000. The deal was $40,000 if he got us here in two days.'

'Forty grand?'

'Yep. But don't worry about it,' answered Mitch, with a wink. 'I withdrew the cash on my American Express card before we left.'

Mason took the sat phone out of his pocket and pressed the call button. There was delay as the signal punched its way through the ionosphere, bounced off the unseen spacecraft, and was directed back to terra firma. A click, and then a familiar voice. 'Mason, is that you?'

'Yes, Rachel. It's me.'

'Where are you, Mason?'

'We are just arriving at the jetty,' he replied.

'I am at jetty also. Can you see me?'

Mason turned to Mitch. 'She's on the jetty. Can you see her?'

'Tell her to wave,' said Mitch as he looked through his binos.

'Wave, Rachel,' asked Mason.

'What is 'wave'?' she answered.

'You know. Hold up your arms and move them about.'

'Ahhh... yes, yes... wave... I understand.'

Mitch scanned back and forth along the jetty, until he found what he was looking for: standing in between two moored cargo vessels was the figure of a black-robed woman, her arms raised skyward, gesturing as if her life depended on it.

'We cannot stay here,' said Hollywood, as they watched the crew attach the mooring ropes to the wooden jetty. 'The Captain says that this is not a good place. The police here are bad.'

'Roger that,' answered Mitch as he jumped onto the wooden planks, landing right in front of the woman that he had been watching through his binoculars. 'Hi. Rachel, right?' he said as he righted himself. The young woman looked curiously at the man wearing the eye patch, 'Yes, how did you know that?' she answered.

'Lucky guess I suppose,' he teased.

'Where is Mason?'

'I'm here,' Mason answered, climbing off the boat - far less energetically than his friend.

Rachel rushed at him, her arms thrown around his thick torso, her face buried deep into his chest. 'I told you I'd come back,' he said, as he placed his finger under her chin, raising up her face.

'Thank you. I was so frightened and lonely,' she said as her deep green eyes began to mist up. 'I believed in you. The thought of you coming back made me strong.'

'That's Mason all over, baby,' interrupted Mitch. 'Say what you mean, and mean what you say.'

Rachel turned to Mitch. 'And who is this?' she asked, with disdain, furious at the man who had just ruined the reunion she had dreamt about.

'Sorry. I should have introduced you straight away. This is an old friend of mine: Mitch.'

'Pleased to meet you, Mitch,' she said, politely, her anger in check.

'We must hurry, Mason. There is little time,' she continued, 'I have boats waiting to take us to the village. Grab your things. We must set off before dark.'

'Hollywood,' shouted Mason. 'We need our things. Can you pass them over the side?'

As the bags were offloaded, the Professor scrambled on to the jetty. 'I need to stretch my legs,' he said, in answer to Mason's enquiring look.

'Okay. But don't go far,' Mason replied. 'I think the Captain wants to make a quick turnaround.'

'Let me help you,' offered Hollywood, as he picked up the last of the heavy holdalls that contained the weapons. 'Is it far to the boats?' he asked Rachel.

'They are at the end of the jetty. Not far,' she answered. 'Follow me.'

The small group set off in single file down the wooden jetty, the planks of wood that served as the walkway creaking under their footfall, whilst the waves lapped against the thick, worn, tree trunks that had supported the heavy structure for centuries. When they got to the end, Rachel pointed at two boats that were tied alongside each other. The nearest boat fastened to the jetty's supports fore and aft. They were slim craft, four metres long, their outboard engines raised clear of the water, bobbing as the wake of a departing boat washed into them.

'These are my cousins: Joshua and Jacob,' Rachel said, pointing to the two men, who were steadying themselves against the waves.

Mason turned to the Professor. But, before he could say anything, he was interrupted by the ringtone on Hollywood's phone. Hollywood put down the heavy bag, searching in his pocket for the electronic device that was merrily playing 'whistle while you work'. *Very apt*, Mason thought, as the young Syrian stopped the melody with a succinct 'Hello.' As Hollywood continued in Arabic, Mason turned to Cornelius. 'Okay, Professor. This is as far as you go. You and Hollywood had best get back to the boat.'

'No, no,' interrupted Hollywood, as he finished the call. 'The boat is going. There are police on the jetty. They always try to get money from the captains. Mahmood has cast off. Look…' he said, pointing at the boat that had just passed them.

'Shit. Shouldn't have paid him so quick,' said Mitch, as the group turned to see their boat heading back off into the vastness of the lake, the waves crashing into the hull evidence of its speed.

'It's not a problem,' said Hollywood with his usual smile. 'He will be back at dawn to pick us up.'

'But we can't stay here until dawn; we have to go now,' said Rachel. 'And, if you two are left here,' she said, pointing at Hollywood and the Professor, 'you'll be arrested.' She looked at Mason. 'They will have to come with us.'

They quickly climbed off the jetty and into the boats. As Mitch helped the Professor climb on, he slapped him on the back. 'Be careful what you wish for, Prof,' he said with a wink.

The two cousins were experienced from a lifetime spent in the wetlands, their skill evident from the effortless way in which they manoeuvred the flat bottomed boats through the dense undergrowth. Mitch, Hollywood and the Professor were in the second boat, which was being handled by Joshua.

Meanwhile, Jacob led the way, carrying Rachel and Mason. Each boat had an outboard motor, but they had to get well clear of the dense mass of reeds before they could risk the propeller turning. So, until it was safe, they had to make do with poles, just as their ancestors had done.

The Marshes at one time had been almost impenetrable to outsiders. But, over the years, a network of channels had been established. Just as well-worn tracks change eventually into lanes and then roads, so too had these marshes yielded to use, the characteristic dense reeds absent in these passageways that criss-crossed the wetlands. When the boats reached one of the thoroughfares, they were able to lower their engines into the water and make real progress.

'This journey would have taken days using the old method,' said Rachel, over the whine of the outboard engines. 'Now, it will take just a few hours,' she said, shielding herself from the cooling spray.

Masahuin Village,
23.30hrs, 25 May 2007.

'Where is your father, Rachel?' asked Mason as he quenched his thirst with another cup of apple juice.

'Miriam said that he is sleeping. But he wants to speak to you after you have eaten.'

'Food can wait. Can I see him now?'

Rachel got up from her seat next to her aunt, and went into the bedroom. She returned minutes later. 'He is awake,' she said, holding open the drape that separated the two rooms.

Mason knew the room only too well, for it was here that he had been brought by John after being found injured – a lifetime ago. 'I knew you would come back,' said John, trying to sit up as Mason entered while his loving daughter placed pillows behind the injured man to support him.

'It was always my intention,' answered Mason. 'I am sorry that I have brought so much trouble to you and your village.'

'It is no matter,' replied John, as Rachel made him comfortable. 'We had to help you. It is what we do; it is what Sir John de Guise would have wanted.'

'So, it is true, then,' Mason said, sitting himself on the small stool next to the bed. 'Sir John ended up here after Palmyra?'

'Yes, he did. He found peace here. He took a wife, and taught the people the ways - his ways: the ways of chivalry. That's why we had to help you. It is our creed to help travellers in distress; it is what he gave us, and it is the code we live our lives by.'

'And the ossuary?'

'Jesus,' he smiled. 'The body of Jesus. Sir John couldn't take it back to Jerusalem. To do so would have unleashed terrible consequences. He'd had his fill of death; enough blood had soaked his hands. So he brought Jesus here. And we have kept the treasure a secret ever since.' John coughed uncontrollably, the red spots appearing on his lips quickly wiped away by his daughter.

'Has he seen a doctor, Rachel?' Mason asked.

'Yes,' she nodded, as her eyes filled with tears.

'She treats me like a child,' said John. 'I know that I am not long for this world. My insides are broken. But enough of this talk. I want something from you, Mason. Will you grant a dying man a last request?'

'If it's in my power, I will gladly give it to you,' answered Mason.

'Take my hand,' John asked. 'I want you to promise me that you will look after Rachel when I'm gone. I want her to experience the outside world. Her mother Fatima longed for it. She thought that she'd hidden it from me. But I knew all along what was going on. There is no one left here now. She has cousins, yes, but they all live in the city. She has only stayed here in the village to look after me, and I fear for her after I have gone.' Mason looked at Rachel, the young woman covering her face as the tears ran down her cheeks.

'Sir John said that it was inevitable that one day someone would come and discover our secret. We did not know when, or whom. But we prayed that the man would be just and righteous, and indeed he is. Our prayers have been answered, my son,' he said, tightening his grip on Mason's hand.

'I will look after her, I promise,' Mason said, placing his free hand over John's.

'Good... Good. I knew you would,' John said, wincing as a spasm of pain shot through his body. 'There is one more thing,' John said, through gritted teeth, as the pain subsided. 'Our belongings - the things that we have revered for centuries: Sir John's sword and shield and of course the body of Jesus. All were taken by those vile creatures. When you rescue your men tomorrow, you must somehow get them back.'

'I will try my best,' nodded Mason.

John smiled. 'Your best is good enough for me my son.'

'But what of my men? Have you seen them?'

'Yes... Thor and Dusty...they helped me to survive in that wretched place. But you must hurry. There is no time to waste. They're being taken tomorrow by the Iranians. I fear for their safety.

Mason placed John's hand back on the bed. 'What shall I do with Sir John's things?' he asked. 'If I bring them back here, the police will take them again.'

'You are correct. The police will not let any intrusion go unpunished. I cannot tell you the correct course of action; you must listen to your heart, the heart of a righteous man,' whispered John.

'Father, you must rest now,' said Rachel, helping him to lie back down.

'Yes. I am tired and must sleep. And you must plan your day, Mason. We have Joshua and Jacob - as well as a few other men who have come from the city to help you. They are good boys. Please take care of them.'

Mason walked out into the kitchen, unaware that the conversation had traveled this short distance for all to hear it. The first thing he saw was the face of Professor Cornelius Gregory. He sat speechless, as though he had just seen a ghost.

Target HQ, Basrah,
06.10hrs, 26 May 2007.

'Mr JJ,' Ronda interrupted, opening the door to Tonka's small office, 'there are some gentlemen here wishing to speak to you.'

'If it's that bloody team from yesterday, tell them they'll all get the sack if they don't sod off.'

'No, sir. It's not the team.'

That will be them, JJ thought as he looked at his watch, 'You'd better come with me, Tonka. I need to introduce you to some people.'

In the middle of the operations room stood two Iraqis. 'Ahh, my friends have arrived,' said JJ, shaking their hands enthusiastically. 'Tonka, let me introduce you to Firas and Ata.' The men were brothers, their bushy moustaches, wavy dark hair and deep piercing brown eyes adding to their shared resemblance. 'They are old friends; we've worked together before,' JJ explained. 'They're going to be joining us today.'

Tonka looked at JJ with surprise. 'You didn't mention any of this yesterday,' he said with concern.

'Firas, Ata, please go outside. We will join you shortly,' said JJ to the two men, before escorting them to the door. 'Is there a problem, Tonka?' he said as he re-entered the operations room.

'Damn right there is.'

'We'd better talk about it in the office then,' answered JJ.

'So what's going on?' demanded Tonka as he closed the door.

'Okay, okay... Look. I should have told you that I changed the plan. But there was no time. I thought of it late last night. I knew I could do it better. I called Firas and Ata, and they said they would help. It will be far better with them. Safer. Easier to get through the checkpoints. They have brought their own transport: two local cars; we will blend in far better if we have them on board. It's a much better solution.'

'I'm not happy with this.'

'So I changed the fucking plan and didn't tell you. I've got a lot on my mind. I'm sorry I didn't tell you, okay?' answered JJ in a tone to match Tonka's. 'If you're not happy, no problem. Stay here. I will do it on my own,' he said, getting up and walking out of the office.

There was silence. And then JJ heard the noise he wanted to hear.

'Wait, wait,' shouted Tonka after him.

JJ turned. 'Yeah?'

'Okay, I'm in.'

JJ turned and carried on walking. He had played him again. *This is getting too easy,* he thought, as he opened the door to the car park.

The door was ajar, Ronda couldn't help but overhear. 'Don't do it, Tonka. Please. It doesn't sound good,' she said as Tonka stepped into the operations room.

'You're right, Ronda. I have a bad feeling about this one too. But I owe it to Dusty and Thor to have a go.'

Ronda nodded. 'I know, those poor men. What they must be going through...'

'Listen... if it goes wrong, you make sure you give all the information to Brit Mil.'

'I thought that JJ said no Brit Mil involvement,'

'I know, but if it goes bad, we will need them. I will be in contact with you via phone.'

'Stay safe, Tonka,' Ronda replied, with a nervous smile.

JJ stood in the middle of the car park at the front of the Target office. He had time to watch as the early morning light began to chase away the evening's blackness. Holding his phone to his ear, he waited for the connection.

'Good morning, John,' said the sleepy voice on the other end.

'Sorry James. Were you sleeping?' asked JJ, with a hollow grin.

'Considering that there's a two hour time difference, what do you think?'

'I wanted to let you know that all is going to plan. My Iraqis have just turned up. The four of us will be setting off shortly.'

'Splendid. So that's you, the Iraqis and...?'

'Tonka.'

'Ahh, yes. Tonka. Isn't he going to complicate the matter? Witnesses and all that?'

'Yeah. I know what you are saying. But he's a good operator, and I need his skills and experience... just in case... you know what I mean?'

'Well, it is your show, John. Do what you think is best. Just make sure that the solution is clean and there are no loose ends.'

'Yes, I will. Don't worry. There'll only be three of us on the return journey.'

Masahuin Village,
06.11hrs, 26 May 2007.

Rachel shook Mason's shoulder. The injured one. He'd fallen asleep, exhausted, alongside his three other comrades, but was soon awake as the pain shot through his body.

He shot up with a start, grabbing hold of the Kalashnikov, the adrenalin pumping through his body. His senses, dulled by sleep, were now working overtime, trying to analyse his surroundings as quickly as possible. When he was in the SAS, he could survive on hardly anything. He could go for weeks on the smallest amounts of food, sleep and even water, his extreme fitness sufficient to compensate for the toughest of terrain and the most demanding conditions, enabling him to make accurate, snap decisions, no matter how tired or hungry he was. But that was then, and this was now.

'Rachel... What time is it?'

'It's dawn.'

'Yes, yes. Of course. I'll wake the others,' he said, his senses returning. 'Can you make some coffee?'

'It is already done. Come to the house when you are ready.'

The smell of coffee overwhelmed Mason, Mitch, the Professor and Hollywood as they entered into the compact cooking area. As they sipped at the piping hot beverage, they were joined by Jacob and Joshua, and another five Masahuin men, all of whom jostled for space in the small kitchen.

'Is this everyone?' asked Mason, as he studied the faces of the new arrivals.

'Yes,' replied Rachel. 'Jacob and Joshua you've already met. These are my other cousins: Baldwin, Frances, Louis, Nathanial and Philip,' continued Rachel. Each man nodded his head as his name was spoken. 'We could have got more but time was short.'

'The numbers are good,' said Mason as he took another sip of the thick, black liquid.

Whilst Hollywood and Gregory had slept, Mason and Mitch had talked to Rachel at length, quizzing her about the area of the police station, painting a mental picture of their target. They had even woken her father to check the internal layout of the police station, not wanting to leave anything to chance. They had to try to control as many aspects of the mission as possible, their confidence in their ability to pull it off being the key to the whole operation. They had run through all the scenarios they could think of, exhaustively working through them one by one. At 03:00, they had boiled it all down to one simple-but-effective plan of action.

Mason picked up a piece of chalk and drew a rudimentary diagram on the kitchen table. 'This is the police station,' he said, pointing at the white rectangle etched on the dark wood. 'There is the only one way in and one way out of the compound,' he said, looking at the assembled men, '... and it sits on this road that runs north to south. This feature,' he added, pointing at a wavy line close to the road, 'is the canal where the boats will drop us off and wait.'

'Rachel, you are to stay with the boats, okay?' ordered Mason as he looked at the young woman who was busy filling the men's coffee cups.

'NO,' was her emphatic answer. 'I know the area, and I need to show you where the men are kept. I must come with you.'

'She has a point,' said Mitch, with a smile, before Mason could reply.

Unphased, Mason carried on. 'Professor, Jacob and Joshua, you will stay with the boats,' he said, pointing at the drop off location. The three men nodded.

'Rachel, you will come forward with the main party, identify the target location, and then...' he paused, looking directly at Rachel. 'You WILL retire back to the boats in support of Joshua and Jacob. Is that understood?'

Rachel looked directly at him, but couldn't hold his stare. She put the pot of coffee back onto the fire while desperately trying to hide her flushing red cheeks.

'Do any of you have weapons?' Mason asked the other five men. There was silence. Hollywood came to the rescue with a quick burst of Arabic. 'Each man has an AK47,' he answered on their behalf.

'Good,' Mason continued, as he spoke directly to them. 'You will provide fire support. You are to stop anything that moves on the road once Mitch and I have entered into the compound. Hollywood, you will be in charge and coordinate

390

from the tree that overlooks the police station.

Hollywood quickly translated the information, and gave a quick explanation on the tabletop map, the five men gesturing their approval with large grins. 'Mitch and I will enter into the building and rescue the hostages. Are there any questions?' Mason asked the silent men.

'What time have you got, Mitch?' Mason asked.

'I've got 06:25.'

'It's going to take an hour to get there,' said Mason, addressing the whole group. 'We need to leave in ten minutes.'

'Is that it?' said Gregory to Mitch on the way out.

'What were you expecting? D DAY?' was the sarcastic reply. 'Listen, most plans don't survive the initial contact. When it goes loud, the complicated ones go to rat shit very easily. It's not like the films; you can forget all that mission impossible bullshit.'

The Professor scratched his chin. 'Yes. I can see that,' he said, as he tried to evaluate all of this new information using his usual academic rationality.

'But it's okay, Prof,' Mitch said, patting the man on his back. 'Mason and I know what we're doing. And we are relying on three simple words.'

The Professor looked surprised. 'Three words?'

'Yeah. Three simple words. They're Mason's favourites: Speed. Aggression. And... Surprise: S-A-S!'

Road North of Basrah, Iraq,
06.40hrs, 26 May 2007.

JJ was in the lead vehicle - an old battered series seven
BMW, riding with Firas. Tonka and Ata were in the rear in
an anonymous, old, dark red sedan, the name plate of which
had disappeared a long time ago, making the make and
model much harder to define.

Saddam's roads were as straight as the Romans had built,
lending them perfectly to speed. 'These guys are crazy,' said
Tonka into the microphone of the Motorola handheld radio
as both vehicles shot north at a breakneck pace, 'Why didn't
you warn me about this? Over.'

'They were never this bad,' answered JJ. 'But at least
we'll be there in no time. Over.' he added, trying be positive.

Tonka watched as JJ's BMWs brake lights flashed on.
'Problem? Over,' he asked Tonka.

'There's is a bridge ahead. Traffic is slowing. Stand by
for police checkpoint,' JJ warned.

In its approach to the bridge, JJ's car overtook a panelled
van, its darkened windows distinctive against its white
paintwork. Ata tried to follow his brother, but there wasn't
enough room. Instead, he pulled in behind it. 'Stay here,'
ordered Tonka. 'It's okay. We can still see the lead car,' he
assured the impatient driver. Ata nodded in agreement. And,
as the wide road gave way to the narrow lanes of the bridge,
he took his foot off the accelerator. The speed reducing
much to the relief of Tonka, who released his grip on the
car's tired upholstery.

As the lead car approached the police checkpoint, JJ
turned off his radio and put it under his seat. Tonka did the
same, leaving nothing to chance, both ex-SAS men carrying
out a routine drilled in to them in the Regiment.

The old BMW slowed and stopped, reacting to the
policemen's hand signal. The faces of the Europeans covered
by shemaghs warranted only a cursory glance by the bored
officer, the inspection lasting no more seconds. Then, as

quickly as they had stopped, they were off again, sent on their way by a nonchalant flick of the officer's hand. JJ looked in the rearview mirror as the white van cleared the checkpoint. Seconds later, he caught a glimpse of red as the rear car came into view, it too free of the Hesco chicane. He picked up his radio and turned it on.

'All good?' he asked.

'Yeah. Clear' was the reply, as Tonka grabbed the upholstery in readiness for lift off.

'JJ. STOP, STOP, STOP!' came another message within seconds.

'What's the problem?' asked JJ.

'He's hit the white van. Pull over. Pull over.'

JJ watched in the rear view mirror as the van and the red sedan parked up on the dirt shoulder of the road.

'The driver is out,' JJ said, offering a running commentary. 'He looks pissed. Stay in the car. Let Atar do the talking.'

'Roger that,' replied Tonka. 'Ata's out. They're having a big argument.'

'There's another guy getting out of the van. He's heading towards you,' advised JJ.

'Yeah. Eyes on. Tall, thin. Nice suit. He looks Iranian,' said Tonka, holding up a newspaper to hide his radio. 'It looks like the Iranian is calming it down... Yep. The van driver is heading back.'

'Good... Good. Roger that... I can see them,' observed JJ. 'The Iranian has just lit a cigarette and is pointing to his driver to get back in the van. Looks good. Can you move yet?'

'Yeah. We're good to go. Moving now,' replied Tonka.

JJ watched as the red car emerged from behind the van.

'Let's go,' he said to Firas. 'But no more accidents, okay?'

The Iraqi pressed the accelerator all the way down to the floor with his right foot. 'Okay, boss,' he answered.

The Marshes,
07.10hrs, 26 May 2007.

'Can he fix it, Mitch?' shouted Mason to his friend in the other boat.

'He doesn't think so,' replied Mitch as he passed Jacob a spanner. 'He reckons the propeller is bent. It must have hit a submerged log. He hasn't got the tools to straighten it. And, even if he did, it would take hours,' he translated for the man who was chest deep in water, inspecting his damaged outboard engine.

'We can leave this boat and get in yours,' Mitch suggested.

'We can't all fit in one,' protested Rachel. 'Too many people... too dangerous.'

'She's right,' replied Mason. 'We daren't risk the boat capsizing.'

Mason's mind was racing. The clock was ticking. He needed a solution, and fast. He looked at his watch. They were already twenty minutes late. 'How far have we got to go, Mitch?' he asked.

Mitch pulled out the GPS from his bag. 'We've got another eight kilometres,' he answered. 'It would have taken us about half an hour at our previous speed.'

'We could tow it,' said Rachel.

'Of course we bloody can,' said Mason, much to the delight of Rachel. 'Get as many people into the front boat as possible,' he ordered as they pulled alongside the stricken craft.

IPS Station, Al Amarah,
08.05hrs, 26 May 2007.

The crash had taken the sting out of their drivers' enthusiasm - much to the delight of the passengers. With the remainder of the journey relatively uneventful, JJ sat with his map on his lap, concentrating on the screen of his GPS, the device counting down the distance to the exact position from which the text from the satellite phone had been sent.

'Two hundred metres,' JJ called out over the radio, instructing Firas to slow his speed. 'One hundred. Okay. This is it. Pull off the road.'

Tonka got out of the red sedan and walked towards the stationary black BMW. JJ was sat with his finger on the map, marking their current position. 'This is it,' he said, as he got out of the car. 'Follow me.' JJ crossed over the road and walked towards a large tree on the left hand side of the road. He opened his black moleskin notebook, and compared the location with the digits on the GPS screen. 'The person who sent the text was stood right here,' he said, showing Tonka the evidence.

Tonka looked around, studying the terrain with his expert eye. 'Whoever sent the message was looking at what was going on in the location on the opposite side of the road,' he said, gesturing with his head towards the entrance to the compound. 'And, if I'm not mistaken, it looks very much like a police station.'

'You're right. Whoever sent it was standing right here, watching. 'But if Dusty and Thor are being held captive, it couldn't have been them.'

'Correct.'

'Mason. Could he have sent it?'

'I doubt it. There's no way he could have got here in time.'

'Then who?'

'I've no idea,' replied JJ, staring at the red and white boom gate that guarded the compound's entrance. 'But, if was I a betting man, I would say that Dusty and Thor were brought here. It all fits. The witness said that the men were taken prisoner by the IPS. And here's the evidence.'

'Do you think they're still in there?' Tonka asked.

'There's a possibility,' replied JJ. 'But the only way to

find out would be to get in there and take a look.'

'I reckon that's what the texter was doing,' replied Tonka. 'Waiting and watching. For all we know, they might be watching us right now.'

'I think you're right,' said JJ as he walked behind the tree, in an attempt to conceal himself.

'So what's next?'

'I think I will call the texter,' said JJ, taking his phone out of his pocket, scrolling through the menu to find the number of the satellite phone. He hit the 'send' button. There was a delay. And then it began to ring.

'Shit. It's the van,' said Tonka as he too hid behind the tree. Both men watching as the van that Ata had crashed into earlier drove slowly past their two parked cars.

The vehicle turned into the entrance of the police compound and stopped at the boom gate. Tonka and JJ watched as the driver's window lowered, the sentry quickly coming to attention and saluting, before raising the red and white metal pole.

The van pulled up right outside the front of the building, the doors opening quickly, as the occupants spilled out into the dusty courtyard. The two onlookers recognised the driver and the tall, well dressed Iranian. But what they hadn't seen was the additional two men that were in the back, the thickset duo cradling AK-47s in their arms as they stretched their legs in the morning sun. The Iranian carrying a briefcase was greeted by a man dressed in a police uniform. The visitor ushered them into the building, leaving the driver and his armed escort outside.

'Something is going down,' said JJ.

'No shit, Sherlock,' replied Tonka. 'Looks like we've hit the jackpot.'

CHAPTER FIFTEEN

The Marshes,
08.06hrs, 26 May 2007.

Their speed was painfully slow, but they were making progress. 'How far now?' shouted Mason, as he saw Mitch glance down once more at the screen of his GPS.

'Under two kilometres.'

Mason looked at his watch. It was nearly an hour since they had stopped. 'That's ten minutes at this rate,' he shouted over the drone of the outboard motor - the comment more for his own reassurance than anything else. And then it hit him: silence. He looked around to see the one remaining engine engulfed in a cloud of smoke.

'What the fuck?' he shouted, as flames began to erupt from the casing of the only serviceable engine, Joshua trying desperately to quell the growing blaze.

IPS Station, Al Amarah,
08.15hrs, 26 May 2007.

The briefcase was laid open on the Commander's desk. The bundles of hundred-dollar bills checked thoroughly by the Sergeant, while the Iranian and the Commander enjoyed a cigarette.

'Would you like some shay?' asked the Commander.

'No, thank you. I have a very busy day ahead of me,' said the Iranian, blowing a long train of smoke through his nostrils. 'I have to be back in Basrah. I will have to pass on your very kind offer.'

'Of course,' replied the Commander. 'Excuse me while I give instructions to get the prisoners ready,' he said, as he stood up and walked into the other office to pass the order.

As he came back in, he caught the eye of the Sergeant, who was stood to attention at the side of his desk. There was no need to talk; he knew from the modest nod given by his trusty assistant that the money was good.

'It will take a short while to ready the prisoners. Are you sure you don't want shay?' the Commander said, glancing at the pile of dollars that the Sergeant had stacked neatly on his desk.

'Ahh... why not,' the Iranian said, looking at his wristwatch. 'We can use it to cement our transaction.'

The morning routine was well established. They would have their breakfast of goat's cheese, boiled eggs and flat bread on metal plates. No cutlery. Everyone ate with their hands. An hour or so after being dropped off, one of the guards would come back for the empty plates, which the prisoners would stack by the cell door.

'This isn't right,' whispered Thor, as they watched four policemen descend the concrete steps. 'There's something going on.'

The first policeman waved his arm, a signal for the two prisoners to assume the usual position - on their feet, facing the far wall, hands behind their backs - that was demanded of them whenever the cell door was opened. With the prisoners ready, the jailers poured into the small room, their heavy boots kicking the empty plates, betraying their eagerness to reach the two prisoners.

Dusty was the first to be manhandled, his arms held behind him, secured with plastic handcuffs. Then it was Thor's turn. But the big man was having none of it. Thor struggled with his two assailants as they pinned him against the wall, his strength surging, the adrenalin rushing through his huge body.

As he turned his head, he could see Dusty being taken up the steps, handcuffed, with a hessian sack over his head. In a rage, he pulled his arms from behind his back with such force that the two policemen holding each limb were wrenched off their feet, the stone wall bringing their forward momentum to a painful halt. Free of his antagonists, he spun around - just in time to see silver plate of the rifle butt close on his face. The blow connected with his forehead, just above his nose. There was a delay for a split second as the nerve endings transmitted their signal to the brain. The result; disconnection, as his whole body shut down, his impressive limbs dangling without function. He fell to the floor in a heap, the disgruntled guards setting about him with their truncheons, their blows un-noticed as he passed into unconsciousness.

'There's movement,' said Tonka, as he peered around the tree, compact binoculars raised to his eyes.

'What's going on?' asked JJ, trying to manoeuvre himself into a better position.

'It looks like they're getting ready to move. The guy with the nice suit is on the steps, shaking hands with the Police Commander. They all look very pleased with themselves.'

'The guards are getting very excited... someone is coming out... FUCK ME!'

'What is it?'

'It looks like our guys.'

JJ ripped the binoculars out of Tonka's hands, and watched as a hooded man was thrown into the back of the van.

'OK. We've got to do something. We have to stop the van,' said Tonka.

'There's a second guy... They're dragging him... he looks unconscious.'

'That has to be Thor; look at the size on him. We have to

stop the van.'

Tonka looked at JJ. 'Come on, man. We have to do something. We can't just let them drive off,' he hissed at his boss.

Everything was in slow motion. He tried to get his arms and legs to move, but they wouldn't; he'd lost control of them. *I am paralysed*, he thought. *This is a nightmare.* He tried to shout, scream at his attackers. But he'd even lost control of his voice. *I have to wake up... I have to move*, he screamed at himself.

His head swung like a pendulum back and forth, chin bouncing on his chest, his muscles unable to offer any support. The heavy blow had also rendered most of his senses inoperable. He was deaf, and his one eye had swollen so badly that he couldn't see from it. It made for a very surreal, out–of-body type experience. He felt remote, like a spectator watching himself.

They hadn't hooded him after the scuffle, the guards wanting to stay away from his powerful limbs. So he was able to notice as the concrete floor of the police station give way to the dust and sand of the bare courtyard. *Ahh yes*, he thought to himself, *the courtyard; they have brought me outside to shoot me.* The idea of his imminent death presented itself to him with no fear. Instead, it washed over him almost soothingly. *It will all be over soon*, he thought.

In the corner of his eye, he could see a white van with blacked-out windows, its back doors open in readiness to receive him. *They aren't going to shoot me; they're going to put me in the van. Why would they want to do that?* he asked himself.

The idea of being taken somewhere else - to start this captivity all over again - sent a pang of terror through his body. His damaged nerve endings reacted in an instant to this new revelation, his hearing returning, his limbs coming back to life.

'NOOO,' he screamed, as the policemen attempted to throw him into the back of the van. The plastic handcuffs - that were poorly secured on his wrists by his frightened jailers - gave way. His massive hands released, he set about making them into clubs of flesh and bone, which he flailed at his jailers – his antagonists.

His blows began to rain down on them, fists finding vulnerable points that only experienced fighters know about. He had downed three in a matter of seconds. But his main weapon as a fighter - the element of surprise - had now been expended. The guards moved back out of range of his accurate punching combos, and readied themselves for the counter attack. Their weapons didn't require as much skill or energy as those of their British opponent. As they withdrew to safety, each man readied his pistol or rifle at the prisoner's large body.

Devoid of accessible targets for his fists, Thor began to run towards the compound exit, his stiff legs – aching from the lack of exercise – struggling to keep up with the brain's unequivocal demand to *get the fuck out.*

'He's making a run for it,' shouted Tonka, reaching for his pistol.

'What the fuck are you doing?' shouted JJ, grabbing hold of Tonka's hand, long before it could make contact with the concealed weapon.

'We've got to help. Look, they're going to catch him,' Tonka screamed as he tried to break free of JJ's grip.

Both men watched as Thor's lumbering figure came running towards them - hotly pursued by the guards, who had been ordered by the Iranians not to shoot at their lucrative prisoner.

'You'll kill us all!' said JJ, as he pulled Tonka behind the tree.

They both watched as Thor was beaten to the ground in a vengeful orgy of violence. Blows raining down on the man's exhausted body.

'If you go out there, you're on your own,' said JJ, looking directly at Tonka, the distance between them close enough to feel the breath on each other's skin.

'What do you expect me to do? Just stand here?'

'Yes,' said JJ, finally letting go of him. 'We will follow the van, and see where it goes.'

'Is that it? Is that the plan? We follow them?'

JJ ignored him. Instead, he returned his gaze to the pitiable sight of their comrade being dragged back to the van. *This is perfect*, he thought. *Dusty and Thor are about to disappear. Problem solved.*

Tonka was silent, rage bubbling within him as he watched the van approach the boom gate.

'That's them leaving,' said JJ. 'We'll give them a couple of minutes and follow on behind, Okay?' He looked over at Tonka. 'Okay?' he repeated.

Tonka looked directly at JJ. 'Naah, fuck it,' he said as he started to run towards the parked cars. As he reached the BMW, he pressed speed dial on his cell phone. 'Ronda,' he shouted into the Nokia handset, '... this is Tonka. CONTACT, CONTACT, NOW! At the police station in Al Amarah. Two hostages out in the open, in white van, send help. OUT,' he rattled off, not even waiting to hear her reply.

'Come back, you idiot,' shouted JJ from behind the tree. But it was no good; Tonka, the ex-SAS soldier, had decided on his course of action; there was no turning back now.

He reached the parked BMW, and jumped in the passenger's seat just as the nose of the white van emerged from the compound. 'CRASH,' he shouted to Firas, pointing at the white van. The Iraqi looked at him and shrugged his shoulders. Tonka drew his pistol, pulled back the slide, and pointed at the driver. 'CRASH,' he repeated, as the van turned onto the road and headed towards them.

The spinning tyres found traction on the hot tarmacked

surface, and the car shot forward. Firas was heading towards the van, but had no intention of crashing his beautiful car. As the van approached, he tried to swerve in the opposite direction. But Tonka was one step ahead. As he tried to push the steering wheel away, Tonka grabbed it, veering the speeding car directly into the path of the accelerating van.

They hit head-on. Firas was saved by the steering wheel, but Tonka wasn't so lucky. The combined closing momentum of the two vehicles shot him through the windscreen and onto the bonnet.

The driver of the van opened the door and staggered into the road - his fake Gucci sunglasses dislodged from the sudden impact, sitting awkwardly on his face. He pushed the glasses back up onto his head, and took in the scene of devastation in front of him.

The two vehicles were entwined, the ruptured radiator of the BMW pumping out steam with a violent hiss, the engine still revving uncontrollably, the noise hideous, like the screeches of a dying animal. Firas was unconscious, slumped behind the wheel. Tonka lay motionless on the crumpled bonnet, the lacerations on his swollen face oozing blood.

The van driver took his pistol from its holder on his belt and with the heel of the pistol grip smashed the driver's window. He reached inside and turned the key instantly killing the ignition and the power to the engine.

Silence returned, offering the van driver the space to think about his next move. He looked at Firas slumped in front of him and then at the two vehicles in their tangled embrace, aimed his pistol and shot the man three times in the head. Stepping back, he moved to the front of the bonnet and studied the unconscious passenger, whose head was becoming engulfed with steam from the ruptured radiator. Raising the weapon, he poised himself to deliver another coup de gras.

'Did you see that, Mason?' shouted Mitch, as the men scrambled up the bank towards the large tree. 'That car just drove straight into the van.'

Mitch hid behind the tree and watched as the van driver got out and assessed the crash scene. 'The driver's just smashed the car window,' he commentated for Mason and Rachel, who were crouched a metre or so from the lip of the ditch. 'Fuck me,' he exclaimed excitedly as three sharp cracks rang out, 'He's just shot the driver.'

'Was the guy in the car armed?' asked Mason.

'Naaah… he was unconscious. Can't see any weapons. The bastard just executed him.'

Mitch had the driver in the sights of his AK47, the man's body framed in the black metal circle, the focal point aimed directly at the centre of the man's head. He watched him walk to the front of the vehicle and raised his pistol at the man lying motionless on the bonnet.

'Not today, matey,' he said under his breath. 'Uncle Mitch has decided to be a guardian angel.'

He squeezed the trigger, enjoying the jolt in his shoulder as the rifle kicked back, the bullet leaving the AK47 at supersonic speed. As he controlled his weapon, bringing it back down on the target, he saw that first bullet impact the driver's head. Ruptured blood vessels spraying a pink mist into the hot morning air as the bullet ripped through the man's brain, killing him instantly.

Seconds later, the back doors of the van burst open, the two-armed guards exiting with haste, spurred on by the sound of gunfire.

'That's two out of the back of the van, both armed,' came the commentary from Mitch.

'What's in the van?' asked Mason.

'Can't see. Give me the binos,' he said, holding out his hand for the high resolution binoculars being offered from Mason. He held it to his good eye and adjusted.

'You're not going to believe this, but it looks like our

boys.'

'Confirm that,' said Mason with a calm, clear voice.

'Two men, on the floor, tied. Can't see their faces; they're wearing hoods.'

'What are the guards doing?'

'Checking out their buddy - and the new hole in the back of his head.'

'There's no time to lose,' said Mason as he climbed up from the ditch, taking up a crouching position beside Mitch. 'We need to get Dusty and Thor out of harm's way. We need to move now. Get the rest of the guys up here, and cover the entrance to the police compound. They'll want to come out soon and see what's going on. You need to stop them, okay?' he added, patting Mitch on the back. 'Rachel,' he said, taking hold of the girl's hand and pulling her up from the ditch, 'get the guys up here. Nothing comes out of the compound. Make sure they understand.'

'What's our next move, Mason?' asked Mitch, without taking his eyes off the crash scene.

'I'm going to rush the van.'

'I will come with you,' answered Mitch.

'NO,' replied Mason, readying his AK47. 'Cover me.'

'Roger that,' said Mitch, standing up to get a better view. 'But you need to get going. The two guards looked pissed, and they're heading back to the van.'

'Okay. LET'S DO IT. GO, GO, GO!' shouted Mason as he broke cover and dashed forward.

He had already covered a good ten metres before the two guards were aware that he was running towards them. But, now alert, they both brought their weapons to bear on the charging man. Mitch had targeted the man on his left first. He flicked the safety catch of his AK down another notch - to the automatic fire position, aimed at the centre of the body mass and squeezed the trigger. The powerful three-round burst of bullets sent the barrel of the weapon upwards as it thudded back into his shoulder. But the recoil response was expected; the rifle was in the hands of a professional who had practiced this very task over and over again, honing it to perfection.

The first bullet caught the man in the stomach, the second in the chest. The killer blow entered through his throat, shattering his spine as it exited through the back of his neck. In a fraction of a second, Mitch adjusted his position for his second target. He repeated the procedure. By the time Mason had reached the van, both guards had been released from their mortal coil.

'Dusty... Thor. It's Mason,' he shouted as he jumped into the van. 'We have to get you out of here,' he continued, pulling off their hoods and cutting through their plastic cuffs. 'Can you walk?'

Both men were stunned. But the smiles on their faces said it all. 'No time to talk; just follow me, and do as you're told,' he shouted over the noise of the gunfire erupting from beside the tree.

As Mason got out of the van, he waved frantically for Mitch and Rachel to join him. 'Rachel, take these two to the boats and wait there,' he said, helping the men out of the back of the van.

'Why?... What are you going to do?' Rachel questioned. 'We have the hostages; we can leave.'

'No,' said Mason, as he jumped onto the tarmac, 'I gave your father my word... remember? The artefacts... I'm going into the compound.'

'You can't. It's too dangerous,' she added.

'Mitch, make sure she gets back to the boats,' Mason shouted.

'Naah... can't do that, mate,' was the reply. 'I'm coming with you.'

Five Minutes Earlier.

JJ had watched the violent scene unfold before him, aware that Tonka's crash would soon have the entire location crawling with police. Slowly and without noise he'd begun to extract himself. But just as he'd started to climb down the ditch, he'd noticed movement. Climbing into a nearby clump of reeds, he'd watched Mason's party pass mere metres in front of him. He'd had heard the sickening report of the pistol as it dispatched the driver and the burst of gunfire from Mitch, but he was blind, his sight blocked by the thick vegetation. Crawling on his stomach, he finally got into a position where he was able to observe.

You bastard, he said to himself as he watched Mason help the two hostages from the back of the van. *The hero again… Not if I can help it.*

IPS Station, Al Amarah,
08.21hrs, 26 May 2007.

'So, what next?' asked Mitch.

'That's easy,' replied Mason. 'The police can't see the road. They don't know what's going on. We'll drive the van into the compound.'

'Are you sure?'

'They probably think that the van's been ambushed. So, if we just drive back in, chances are they will think that the Iranians have fought our way out of it.'

'And that's your plan?'

'Yeah. Can you think of anything better?'

There was a pause. 'No.'

They went to the front of the van, both men looking at the body that lay on top of the bonnet of the crashed BMW. The blood from the head lacerations and the steam from the

407

radiator had turned Tonka's head into an unrecognisable mass of swollen flesh. 'Poor sod,' said Mason, as he went to open the vans front door. 'We'd best check to see if he's dead. What do you think?'

'I'll do it,' replied Mitch.

While Mitch searched for a pulse in the casualty's carotid artery, Mason took hold of the van door and gave it a good yank.

'Hold it right there,' said the figure crouched in the foot well, his pistol pointing at Mason's face - at point blank range. 'Back away. Slowly. Very slowly.' Mason took several deliberate paces backwards, his assailant unflinching, rising up from his hiding place as the duel unfolded, the man's collarless shirt and crisp suit evident as more was unveiled.

They weren't hard to follow, their progress through the thick undergrowth painfully slow, their injuries clearly getting the better of them. He could have stopped them at any time. Killed them. They were easy prey. But not yet; he wanted to do it all in one go.

Ahead, the thick vegetation peeled back, allowing him to see a large expanse of water and two moored boats. There were three men - two Marsh Arabs in one of the boats, preoccupied with fixing their engine. And, as he peered through his compact binoculars, he could see that the third man was European.

He wasn't going to wait on the track; that would have been amateurish. His training wouldn't allow that. Instead, he stepped off the pathway of recently trodden reeds crushed by the rescue party, and circled around. He soon found what he was looking for - a location within striking distance where he could lie in wait.

'You have rescued your men,' said the Iranian, in flawless English, as he pointed the gun through the 'V' made by the open passenger door. 'Well done. You have achieved your objective. But I am afraid that you will now have to take their place.'

Mason looked at the man, and then his weapon. The safety catch was off, the hammer was back and the man's finger lay poised on the trigger.

'You speak English well,' Mason said, trying to keep the man occupied.

'Thank you. I lived in London for many years. But now is not the time for polite conversation. Put down your weapons. And, if your friend makes another move, I will shoot you in the face.'

Both men slowly placed their heavy rifles on the floor and stood up.

'Back away from the weapon, and get on your knees. Hands behind your heads,' he shouted as they slowly obeyed his orders. 'My business transaction has not gone well this morning,' he said, stepping out of the van and surveying the crash scene. 'You have taken something I have paid generously for. You have killed my men. And - what is more disturbing - you have seen my face.'

Mitch looked up. 'Yes. That's right. I will never forget seeing a nose like that. Fuck me. It's huge.'

The Iranian looked on in disbelief. 'There is a gun pointed at your heads. I have your life in my hands, and you mock me? What craziness is this? Do you have a death wish?'

'You don't know the half of it,' said Mason, glancing over at Mitch.

They had rehearsed scenario after scenario during their time together in the military. Discussing the 'what if' factor was a constant feature in their planning. Years before, whilst working in Beirut, they had trained for capture; they had spent days working out what to do if that fateful event ever occurred. Today, many years later, it had. And, as they knelt in front of their captor, both their minds raced, searching for the game-changing idea that could save their lives. Their eyes met fleetingly, the idea passing between them in an instant. There was no talk; there was no need; they both knew exactly what to do next.

'Does your finger get lost when you pick it?' asked Mitch. The Iranian didn't answer, the window for conversation expired.

Mason dived right and Mitch left, the pistol cracking into life as Mason rolled across the floor, wriggling like a snake to avoid the deadly lumps of lead as they contacted with the hot tarmac.

The Iranian had fired four shots at the moving target before his perspective changed from black tarmac to blue sky. The fifth shot arced harmlessly into the wide blue yonder. Both his legs had been taken from beneath him in an instant with a powerful foot sweep that had flipped him onto his back. Mitch followed this up with an open right hand, the heel of his palm smashing into the Iranian's nose, spreading the appendage across his face, while his other hand ripped the pistol from a lacklustre grip.

'I can't remember,' said Mitch, breathless, pointing the pistol at the bleeding man, 'how many times out of ten it is that the right handed shooter follows the target to his right.'

'It was something like seven or eight,' replied Mason, rubbing his painful shoulder. 'Next time, you can be the bloody target. I'm getting too old for this shit.'

'Yeah, whatever,' answered Mitch as he grabbed hold of the Iranian, pulling him to his feet. 'Welcome aboard, mate. You're coming with us.'

Mitch got the van started on the fourth attempt, slowly reversing to disengage the twisted metal still coupling the two damaged vehicles. The bloodied Iranian sat between them, the muzzle of his own pistol jabbed into his ribs. 'Just sit quiet,' Mason said as the van lurched backwards. 'Or I'll get him to finish the job. Understood?' he said, nodding towards the ex-Legionnaire.

Mitch turned the vehicle around and crept forward, giving the thumbs up to Hollywood and the Mesahuin men who still behind the tree firing randomly into the police compound as they drove past. The young Syrian acknowledged the signal with a return gesture, just as Mitch stamped on the accelerator, the tyres struggling to find grip on the hot surface, but finally shooting the crumpled van forward towards the compound.

'The Iranians have been ambushed, Sahib,' the Sergeant briefed his Commander, as both men took cover on the ground floor of the main building. 'We can't see what's happening outside. But there are men behind the large tree opposite the entrance. They have us pinned down.'

'How many men do we have?' shouted the Commander over the noise of the gunfire.

'There are two on the roof, and four here,' said the Sergeant, pointing at the men who were also crouched behind the low wall, trying to make themselves as small as possible, too nervous to peer out of the windows that rested on the metre–or-so of bricks. 'The rest are out on patrol. I have radioed them to return.'

The Commander nodded his concurrence. 'We're not the target, Sergeant; they have come for the hostages. If it was the military, they would have overwhelmed us by now. There is something not right.'

The Commander's answer was cut short by the noise of the speeding van as it hurtled back into the compound, the red and white barrier no match against the speeding vehicle.

'Hold your fire,' shouted the Commander to his men, as they raised their weapons to engage the slowing van. 'It's the Iranians.'

'So far so good,' said Mitch, taking his foot off the brake. 'They're not shooting at us. Now what?'

411

'Follow me,' said Mason, pushing the Iranian out of the van door. 'Start shouting 'AMBUSH', you fucker,' he said, digging the pistol hard into the man's back.' The three men burst into the building, the Iranian – as ordered – shouting 'AMBUSH,' as the door gave way. They were in. They had achieved 'surprise'; now it was the turn of 'aggression'.

The Sergeant wasn't sure. It didn't look right. But by the time he had made his mind up, it was too late. He aimed his pistol towards Mason, but never got to pull the trigger, falling back as two bullets slammed into his chest. The technique was tried and tested - the two-bullet combination, aimed at centre of mass, developed by the SAS to dispatch a deadly combination of 9mm projectiles. Mastered properly, the 'double tap' - as it was called - could be delivered with fatal consequences.

'The rest of you get to live...' shouted Mason, approaching the officer with the large moustache, pointing his pistol directly at the man's head. '... so long as you put down your weapons and give us what we want.'

'And what might that be?' asked the Commander, motioning his men to put down their weapons as he stared down the barrel of Mason's handgun.

'We have come for John's belongings,' Mason said as he drew up alongside the Commander. 'We know you have them. Get them NOW, or I will kill you.'

The Commander looked bemused as the request slowly sunk home. 'John's... belongings?' he answered. 'Ah. You mean the Marsh Arab, he said, all the while focused on the barrel of the gun. 'Yes, yes, of course. They are in the storeroom,' he replied, matter-of-factly. 'My men will get them for you.'

'Mitch, go with them,' replied Mason. 'And explain that if there is any nonsense I will kill their boss.'

'They must be very precious to you,' continued the Commander, as his men filed into the room that led off the main corridor. 'To risk so much, that is...'

This man killed my teammates, Mason thought, choosing

to ignore the question, *and he took the others hostage.* He looked at his face, and then directly into his eyes - dark, unforgiving, murderous eyes. *How many men has he sent to their death?* he wondered. He looked down the top slide of his weapon, and lined the sights up directly on the man's forehead.

'Why do you want to kill me?' the Commander answered calmly, seeing the turmoil building in Mason's eyes. 'I have done nothing to you... I'm cooperating, aren't I?' he queried.

'You killed my men,' replied Mason, with a clenched jaw, as he took up the first pressure on the pistol's trigger. 'You killed four, and would have killed the rest if we'd not come back for them.'

'This is a war, we both have killed,' replied the Commander as he stared back at Mason, his eyes unblinking, his voice exuding authority. 'What I did, I would do again. You know that... for we are the same...'

'Okay, that's it,' shouted Mitch, as he re-entered the corridor. 'All the stuff is in the back of the van, along with all these guys' weapons. Let's get the fuck out of Dodge.'

Mason lowered his gun. The moment of retribution had passed.

The young policeman, from his position on the roof, had seen the van enter the compound, and he had heard his Commander shout 'Don't shoot'. But then it had all gone quiet. The more experienced policeman that was with him told him to go and investigate. And so, with great trepidation, he had started to descend the concrete staircase. As he'd passed the Commander's office, he checked. It was empty, the whole building shrouded in an uneasy silence.

He went to the top of the internal staircase, his heart beating so hard that he thought this noise alone would give him away. He took several deep breaths, and counted to three, before plucking up enough courage to look over the iron balustrade. The sight that met his eyes made him recoil. At the bottom of the staircase stood a man pointing a gun directly at his Commander.

This young policeman was a new recruit - the son of one of the Commander's favourite old soldiers, who'd been killed in the war with Bush. He had never fired a weapon in anger until that morning, his first action not going well; when the rounds had started to come in, he'd hidden behind the small wall that ran around the edge of the flat roof, merely listening as bullets thumped overhead and crashed into the masonry. Finally, he picked up enough courage to return fire. His several badly aimed shots made at the behest of his fellow policeman, who had threatened to shoot him for being a coward.

I must go and get help, he thought, hiding himself for the second time that morning. '*NO*,' a voice inside him said. *If you go up to the roof, you will be called a coward again. Save the Commander. Do it NOW*. He made sure the safety catch on his Kalashnikov was set to automatic fire, and took several deep breaths before counting to three.

Mason was caught in the open, with no cover from the bullets that raced past him. The heavy brass heads exploded into the concrete, sending shards of lethal shrapnel whizzing around the ground-floor corridor. He dropped to one knee. Instinctively, aimed his pistol at the source of the threat: the silhouetted target at the top of the staircase, and fired. The two rounds left the muzzle of the pistol within a split second of each other, hurtling towards the faceless figure. But Mason was out of practice, his first bullet hitting the shooter in the leg, the second one missing completely.

Galvanised by his luck, the young policeman aimed again. Lining Mason up, he pulled the trigger. The metal 'CLICK' - even through ringing ears – was audible to everyone in the police station. In his haste, the young recruit had forgotten to change the magazine on his weapon, and had run out of bullets. The 'dead man's click' - as it was called during training – usually rewarded with a smack around the head by instructors, on this occasion drawing a far more austere punishment. The first blow was received in the sternum, the second entering his lungs just below the collar bone, the impact knocking the young policeman onto his back. As he lay prostrate, looking at the ceiling, he began gasping for air.

It would take a further five minutes for him to die, his ruptured lungs filling with more and more blood with every snatched breath. His brain slowly being starved of oxygen. Cause of death: drowning.

His target dispatched, Mason stood up, his pistol still pointed at the downed man. His ears were buzzing, and his body ached like hell. It had been close... very close. Rising to his full height, he arched his shoulders forward, both hands gripping the pistol, arms locked at the elbows, as he scanned the building for other shooters.

He looked first at the Commander, who had taken cover on the ground next to him, and then at the four policemen and the Iranian. They were all cowering away from the aim of his gun.

'Are you okay, Mitch?' he shouted.

'Fuck' was the reply as the man slid down the wall, a large crimson stain growing on the front of his shirt. '...I've been hit.

Mason moved over to Mitch's crumpled body and opened the injured man's shirt.

'It's only a scratch,' he said, glancing over the wound with an expert eye. 'Stop messing around. Let's get going.'

'It was a ricochet,' grunted Mitch, as Mason helped him up. '... A fucking ricochet. Can you believe it?'

Mason stopped the beaten up white van alongside the crashed BMW – as an improvised roadblock to cover their retreat. 'Out you get,' he said to Mitch as he jumped from the stationary vehicle. 'We've got to do the rest on foot.'

Hollywood and the Marsh Arabs came running up to the van and started to unload the precious cargo. 'Get back to the boats,' said Mason to the young Syrian, pointing towards the crushed reeds at the side of the road that led down the embankment. 'I will meet you there.'

'Okay, boss,' answered Hollywood, looking on with concern at the wounded man still sitting in the van. 'What about Mitch? Shall we carry him?' he asked.

'I'm not going anywhere,' Mitch replied, as he laboured out of the open door.

'Look... will you stop fucking about,' replied Mason. 'They're going to be all over us in minutes. We need to get going.'

'No can do, boogaloo,' answered Mitch as he leaned against the van, patches of crimson from his drenched shirt leaving streaks against the white paint. 'You knew this was a one way trip for me. This is where I check out. Just leave me a few AKs, and get on your way. I will cover your ass,' he said, as his legs buckled under the strain of his injury.

'It's no problem, boss,' said Hollywood, as he moved towards the injured man. 'We can carry you. There are enough of us.'

Mason shook his head. 'He doesn't want to be carried, Hollywood.'

'But boss?' Hollywood pleaded, 'Let me carry you... Please!'

'Hollywood, get the fuck out of here,' shouted Mitch. 'NOW.'

'Best go...' Mason said to Hollywood, placing a hand on his shoulder, as he watched the tears form in the young man's eyes. 'I will take care of him.'

'He's a good man,' said Mitch, nodding towards the dejected figure of Hollywood as he walked to the back of the

416

van and to the throng of Masahuin who were busy unloading their priceless cargo. 'Make sure he gets back okay, will you,' he asked.

Mason nodded as he reached for the two AKs that were sitting on the passenger seat. Quickly checking them to see that they were loaded, he made sure the safety catches were off, and handed them one by one to his old friend.

Mitch grabbed Mason's right hand as he squatted down, holding it tight between his blood stained fingers. 'Better this way, amigo'.

Mason gripped back, pausing to search his friend's face for a change of heart. There was nothing. The only perceptible emotion in Mitch was a steely determination, his jaw clenched against the pain.

'So, this is it, then?'

'Yeah... like a Viking,' Mitch said, with a broad grin, as he released his grip and took hold of the rifle.

Mason stood. 'Don't drink it all. Leave some of that Valhalla beer for me, eh.'

'One last thing,' shouted Mitch, as Mason began to descend down the embankment. 'The Commander... Why didn't you kill him when you had the chance?'

Mason stopped, reliving the scene from the police station from only minutes earlier, 'When I looked at him,' he said, pausing, 'I saw something in his eyes. I saw hatred. But there was something else... that scared me.'

'What?'

Mason rubbed his bristled chin. 'He said that we are the same... He was right. When I looked at him, I saw myself looking back.'

Mitch nodded. 'Stay low and move fast, brother.'

From his lair, JJ watched his prey. The two Arabs were still in the boat, fixing their engine, just twenty metres from his position. Meanwhile, the ex-prisoners sat on a tree stump in the middle of the small clearing of reeds close to the two grounded vessels, tended by the woman and the European-looking man. He'd listened intently to the shots being fired at the police compound, counting the distinctive 'cracks' from the automatic weapons. He'd strained to build a mental picture of the gun battle in his mind. Guessing, of course. But he had been in so many gunfights that his trained ear gave him a good indication of what was happening. It had all gone quiet. *It can't be over yet? That's too quick. Surely the police reinforcements should have arrived by now?* The firing started again, but this time it was closer. *That sounds like they're on the road*, he thought. *Withdrawing back to the boats...* He flicked the safety catch off his pistol with his thumb. Now's the time!

He charged out of the reeds like a wild boar. Body crouched, shoulders hunched, both hands firmly gripping his pistol, eyes staring down the short barrel.

Joshua, who was stretching out his aching back from the work on the engine, was the first to see him. He went to shout, but the two bullets fired in quick succession from JJ's Beretta pistol ended the young Marsh Arab's life in an instant, his limp body toppling over the side of the boat and into the water.

Jacob looked up just in time to see JJ adjust his aim. The first bullet missed. But the second and third found their mark. Jacob slumped back onto the engine.

'STOP,' shouted Thor. 'They're with us. Stop shooting.'

JJ kept moving towards the group, checking his handiwork with a sideways glance as he drew level with the boat.

'They were on our side you, fucking idiot,' shouted Thor, as JJ walked towards them.

'Sorry. I thought they were the bad guys,' answered JJ as he tucked the pistol into the holster on the belt of his trousers.

'They were the rescue party,' shouted Dusty.

JJ closed on the three men and picked up an AK47 that was resting against a nearby log. 'How was I to know?' he continued. 'They all look the same to me.'

Rachel let out a piecing scream. 'You have killed them both,' she shouted, holding up her blood-stained hands for them all to see. 'They were unarmed. Why did you shoot them?'

'I suggest you get that bitch over here now,' he said, as he levelled the rifle at Dusty. 'RIGHT NOW.... if you don't want to end up like them.'

Hollywood was the first to emerge from the small track that opened into the clearing, the crowd of Marsh Arabs close behind him reverently carrying the vessel containing the holy relics. Mason brought up the rear, making sure they were not being followed.

Thor, Dusty, Rachel and the Professor sat in front of JJ, with their backs towards the emerging party. The Glaswegian had dropped the AK down to his hip, his finger caressing the trigger. He'd told his prisoners that any sudden movement or noise would result not only in their deaths but also in the deaths of the others. They had no reason to doubt him; his recent handiwork remained close by, still warm and oozing blood.

Hollywood was the first to notice Jacob's bloody body in the boat. He stopped and stared at it, and then at JJ. 'What's gone on? Who killed him?' he shouted, levelling his golden pistol at JJ. 'Who is this man?'

JJ was swift. He pointed the barrel of the rifle at the man in the mirrored sunglasses and squeezed the trigger. The hip shot was accurate. Hollywood's chest, ripped apart as the burst of automatic gunfire slammed into his body. The kinetic energy punched the young man's body backwards, his arms flailing, his hand abandoning the tight grip on his pistol, sending it skywards. As the garish weapon somersaulted through the morning sky, it reflected the sun's rays, the glinting only ceasing when it found a clump of mud a short distance from the Professor.

JJ had his weapon in the shoulder. 'Mason, get over here,' he shouted, aiming the rifle directly at his former comrade in arms. 'NOW. Or I start killing them,' he continued. 'Drop your weapon. Raise your hands, and tell those bloody rag heads to start running - before I change my mind.'

The Marsh Arabs grounded the relics as quickly as they could. JJ's language needed little interpretation, their respect for the items only tempered by their eagerness to flee the killing field. They soon disappeared down the path on which they had arrived. JJ's prisoner count now stood at five.

'Don't try anything stupid, or I will waste this pretty little thing,' JJ said, as he motioned Mason to get in line and copy the other prisoners: necks bowed, eyes looking at the ground, hands tightly clasped behind their heads.

'What now?' asked Mason, raising his head in defiance.

'Don't you look at me, you cunt!' shouted JJ in answer. 'Get on your stomachs, all of you!'

'Let these go. It's me you want. They have done nothing,' answered Mason as he slowly grounded himself.

'Don't you tell me what to do. It's your fault that we're here. If you had just left things alone, none of this would have happened.'

Mason's mind was working overtime. But he couldn't see a way out. JJ held all the cards. The ex-SAS man knew never to get too close to his prisoners. His training had taught him that the captor must always keep a buffer zone between himself and his captives.

Mason knew exactly how JJ's mind was working. He was reluctant to try anything hasty, knowing that JJ needed only the slightest excuse to shoot all of them. *Keep him talking*, he thought to himself. 'So what's the plan after you have killed us?' he asked.

'That's none of your fucking business,' shouted JJ, white specks of spittle beginning to form in the corner of his mouth.

'What... so there's *no* plan?'

'The plan is to sell the company for more money than you could ever dream of,' JJ bragged with a sneer.

'So, it's *all* about money, then?'

'Of course it's all about money. What is more important than money?'

'There is no amount of money I wouldn't give to have my family back,' said Mason, looking up once more at his captor.

'Yes. Your precious family. You had it all, didn't you? The perfect family. The golden boy of the Special Air Service... the decorations for bravery, the best of the best. But what have you got now, eh? You're lying face-down in a bog. You have nothing. You make me fucking sick.'

'I would rather have nothing than be you,' Mason said, trying to goad his captor. 'I mean... look at the state of you... you fat bastard.'

Mason fancied that his taunts were starting to have an effect. JJ was red in the face with anger, and was moving closer towards him, the gap closing. *Another metre*, Mason thought, as JJ took another pace closer. *Come on, just one more step*. He readied himself like a sprinter in the blocks. *If I can just hit him hard enough, I have a chance. Yes, he will probably shoot me. But at least it will give the others enough time to overpower him.*

'You think you're so fucking good, don't you?' answered JJ, the anger in his voice subsiding. 'Ha fucking ha, Mason. I can see what you're trying to do. But it's not going to work. Your time is up. I've actually had enough of this shit.'

JJ stepped back out of the danger zone. He raised his weapon and took aim. 'I'm going to empty the whole magazine into the lot of you,' he shouted. 'And then, if you're still alive, I will finish you off with my pistol,' JJ screamed insanely. 'You're all dead!'

'Is this a private party?' shouted a voice behind him, 'or can anyone join in?'

JJ looked up. What he saw was Mitch and Tonka, the two men hanging off each other for support, their bodies exhausted from their injuries. It was the break Mason had been waiting for. He launched his body at JJ, his shoulder contacting with his adversary's thigh in a classic rugby tackle. As JJ fell, his finger instinctively snatched at the trigger, sowing a hail of bullets harmlessly into the ground.

JJ's composure recovered quickly. As he hit the floor, his hand started to reach for the pistol tucked away in the holster on his belt. He grabbed it and lashed out, the bottom of the pistol grip hitting Mason squarely in the temple, knocking him out in an instant.

'Help him,' yelled Rachel, as she bolted towards JJ.

'How?' shouted back the Professor, jumping to his feet.

Thor pointed at the golden pistol. 'Get the gun. Shoot him.'

The dead weight of Mason's body fell forward onto JJ's legs, Mason's muscular mass pinning the Scotsman to the floor. As he struggled to shake free of Mason's dead weight, Rachel fell on him, her nails targeting the white flesh around his eyes with a ferocity that surprised all that watched. But, even as they wrestled, it was evident that Rachel's slim mass was no match for JJ's brute strength. It was clearly only a matter time before her victim would get the better of her.

With a final kick, JJ rolled free of Mason's unconscious body, grabbing hold of the loose clothing around Rachel's chest as he did so. With his newfound ability to manoeuvre, he pushed his assailant away from him while his other hand brought his pistol up, level to her heaving chest. He should have shot straight away, but he didn't. He hesitated, staring at the mask of beauty and scar tissue.

The only gun the Professor had ever held was his cousin's airpistol when he was a boy. He had tried all summer to hit the tin cans that had been placed in front of him but had failed miserably at every attempt. In the end, he had just given up, unwilling to weather the teasing over his ineptitude.

As he picked it up Hollywood's pistol, he was surprised at its weight. *Much heavier than the air gun*, he thought as he held it with both hands, pointing it at JJ.

'Shoot him!' shouted Thor, as the Professor stretched his arms out, assuming the stance that he had seen so many times on TV.

He brought the gun upwards and stared down the barrel, lining up the sight on the body of the man on the ground in front of him. He pulled the trigger. The weapon kicked back in his hands, the deafening crack taking him by surprise.

The Professor had aimed at JJ's body. But the weapon had moved too far as his inexperienced finger had snatched at the trigger, sending the bullet off target. Instead of the hot metal projectile hitting JJ's torso, it had impacted on the gun that was pointed at Rachel. With a piercing 'thwack', it sent JJ's pistol spinning off into the undergrowth.

'Good shot, mate,' shouted Thor.

'Couldn't have done better myself,' added Dusty. 'Where did you learn to shoot like that?'

The Professor looked over at the two bruised and battered men lavishing praise on his marksmanship. 'Norwich,' he answered. 'When I was ten.'

'I hate to break this up,' said Tonka, the words spilling out from a set of blistered lips. 'But the police are right behind us. We've to get out of here right now.'

The Commander's men, bolstered by the arrival of their reinforcements, edged forward down the track that the two wounded men had used to escape. *They covered the withdrawal of their comrades well*, thought the Commander as they inched forward. *Using the crashed vehicles as a roadblock. Hmmmm. Keeping my men at bay. Professional. Very professional.* But the Commander knew that the tide would turn against these foreigners; they would be overwhelmed by his superior resources.

The column of IPS pushed on down the track, the policeman scouting ahead, stopping every few minutes, cautiously taking a knee, listening for movement, wary of

423

the wounded–but-still-deadly adversary ahead of them.

'They are escaping. They will have boats waiting. You must stop them,' whispered the Iranian to the Commander as they paused.

The Commander nodded in acknowledgement. 'You are correct. They have their escape already planned, but we cannot go any quicker. Our opponents are professional. I will not have my men walk into a trap.'

The police crept forward in silence, the only noise that of the reeds swaying en masse, buffeted by the breeze from the Marshes.

The scout fell back and approached the Commander. 'Sahib, they are just ahead of us,' he said with hushed tones. 'I saw the two prisoners as well as another six, including a woman. They have two boats. It looks like they are getting ready to leave.'

'Have they placed any guards along the trail?' asked the Commander.

'I have not seen any, Sahib,' replied the man.

'Could it be a trap?' asked the Iranian.

'Quite possibly,' replied the Commander. 'Did you see the two men that were firing from the van?' asked the Commander of his scout.

'Yes, Sahib. They are both there. I think we must have shot them, for they seem wounded,' replied the scout.

'Excellent,' said the Iranian. 'We must attack immediately, before they escape.'

'Did your cousins manage to fix the engine?' Mason said, his senses beginning to drift back.

'I don't know,' she replied. 'They were working on the one nearest to us when they were killed.'

'There's no time to try it out. If it doesn't work, we will just have to paddle. Get everyone on board. I will make sure that we're not being followed.'

'Prof, if he looks like he's going to present the slightest

trouble, just let him have it,' said Mason, pointing at JJ, whilst rubbing his temple in a vain attempt to take away the pain. The Professor gave a confident nod in reply. 'No problems,' he answered, as Mason set off on wobbly legs towards the track.

'We're bugging out,' said Mason to Mitch and Tonka. 'Can you get into the boat?' He looked at the two men. They were both in a sorry state. Tonka's face was badly swollen and covered in blood from the lacerations. His eyes were puffed up - to the extent that he could just about see. Mitch, from the loss of blood, was lapsing into and out of consciousness.

'Yeah. We can do it,' replied Tonka. 'We've got this far, haven't we? Come on, mate. One more effort,' he said to Mitch, holding out his hand.

'I thought you wanted to stay?' said Mason with a smile.

'Didn't have much choice,' replied Mitch as he hung on to Tonka. 'This guy dragged me out of there. Wouldn't take no for an answer.'

Mason looked at the large claret coloured patch which had now taken over the whole of Mitch's shirt. *He needs medical attention soon,* he thought. *If he doesn't get it, he's going to bleed out. He'll be dead within the hour.*

It took all of Mitch's energy to get to his feet, the pain writ large across his face, every sinew of his body protesting. 'Just hang in there. We'll get you out of here,' said Mason. 'I'm just going to check that you weren't followed.

The Commander delivered a quick instruction, his men fanning out in a line either side of the track before beginning their short advance towards the unsuspecting group.

They were less than twenty metres from the small clearing when the lead scout raised his hand in a signal to stop. He'd noticed movement and had stepped off the track and gone to ground. As the solitary figure approached, he raised his weapon and aligned the target in to his sights. He slipped off the safety catch, and looked over at the Commander, who was directly behind him.

'Wait until he gets closer,' whispered the Commander. 'You cannot miss. Do you understand?'

The scout nodded, and began to breathe deeply. When he was ready to take the shot, he took one big breath and held it, his body still, ready to squeeze the trigger.

Mason was breaking all the rules that had been drummed into him in the SAS. He was advancing - unsupported - down a track towards the enemy. It was only a matter of time before he came upon his adversaries. He knew that, when he did, it would be survival of the quickest.

He pushed ten metres on, and then stopped. *Not good.* He couldn't see them, but he knew they were there. He was being watched. He stopped and went down on one knee, looking desperately for movement to identify a target. And then he heard it. Distant, faint but distinctive nonetheless. It was the rhythmic judder of blades cutting through air. It was a helicopter - every soldier's friend - and it was heading their way.

'What are you waiting for?' said the Iranian. 'You must attack immediately.'

The Commander, his ears pricked at the sound of the aircraft, held up his hand to stop the Iranian's demands. 'It is one thing to attack security men. But to attack the British army...'

'You must get my prisoners back. We had a deal.'

'Yes, we did,' the Commander agreed. 'And the deal was complete when you left my compound.'

'But you must help me; you must attack.'

'There is a time and a place for fighting the British. And this is not it,' replied the Commander, motioning to his men to take cover from the approaching aircraft.

'But they will know that you abducted the men and held them hostage. They will come looking for you.'

'No. You are wrong,' replied the Commander. 'The police that captured the two men were a 'rogue element.''

'What do you mean? You held them in your police station.'

'Is this what the British want to believe? I will be questioned, yes. But eventually the whole matter will be forgotten,' he said, taking the packet of Marlboros from his pale blue shirt, the dark patches under the arms testament to the heat. 'Because, if they admit that the police are fighting against them,' he said, lighting up, 'they are resigned to the fact that all the billions they've spent have been wasted. They know that such a theory is far too *controversial*,' he said, two long streams of smoke pouring from his nostrils. 'The politicians will never allow it.'

Tonka had pulled the pin on the smoke grenade when he'd heard the chopper. The bright yellow smoke pumped out of the cylindrical device, offering a clear signal to the pilot as he skimmed across the reeds. As the aircraft came closer, the downwash from the rotor blades squeezed the smoke into vortices, pushing them skyward like harmless tornadoes.

The air gunner of the small Lynx helicopter hung out of the open door. One foot on the skid, his hand gripped the doorframe as he talked the pilot in. Speed, height and direction offered to the pilot through his helmet microphone.

The clearing was small. It was going to be a tight fit, but the crew's drills were good. They were up to the task. And in only a matter of minutes after first seeing the smoke, the aircraft touched down - just a handful of metres from the grounded boats.

Mason ran over to the aircraft. He knew that they would only stay on the ground for as long as they had to - and not a second longer. He had to get his injured men on board.

'I have four casualties,' he shouted at the air gunner over

427

the noise of the downwash, holding up his fingers as further indication.

'Four is good,' shouted the air gunner in return. 'That's all I have space for. Load them on. I will send another helo to pick you up… In the meantime, stay here.'

'NEGATIVE… We're surrounded. We'll use the boats.'

The air gunner nodded, and gave a thumbs up. 'Get your men on.'

Dusty was the first, followed by Thor. The relief on both their faces was evident as they scrambled into the confined space. 'He said he would come back,' shouted Thor, a massive grin on his face. Dusty nodded, the relief spreading through his body, the tears rolling down his cheeks.

'Where's Mitch?' shouted Mason, as he pushed Tonka into the aircraft. They both looked round to see Mitch on the floor. He'd tripped over the stone coffin in his effort to reach the helicopter, spilling its contents onto the floor, and was now frantically battling against the intense wind in an effort to put them all back in.

Mason got to Mitch as he placed the final bone into its stone container. 'Let's go,' he shouted, as he pulled the injured man to his feet and threw him over his shoulder. The ancient dust launching into a cloud as Mason smacked him on the backside. 'Fuck me, man,' he shouted. 'Take it easy. What are you trying to do, kill me?'

Mason unceremoniously dumped his friend's body into the helicopter. 'He is wounded,' he shouted, pointing at the damp patch of blood on Mitch's shirt. 'He needs to go straight to the hospital.'

'We will give you covering fire for your escape,' shouted the air gunner.

'NEGATIVE. Take him straight to the hospital. He's lost too much blood,' said Mason, grabbing the air gunner's shoulder to emphasise his point.

'ROGER THAT,' replied the airman as he clambered back on board.

Mason stood back from the aircraft, steadying himself

against the deluge of wind as the rotor blades began to pick up speed for the ensuing take-off that would mark the aircraft's departure.

But just as he stood back, JJ barged past. The escape of the target's CEO from the Professor's custody made possible with the confusion of the landing aircraft.

'There's no room,' shouted the air gunner, as JJ tried to climb into the already-crowded aircraft.

'I own the company,' JJ shouted back, in a vain attempt to justify his actions.

'I don't care what you own,' shouted back the gunner. This aircraft won't get off the ground with you on board.'

'Get rid of one of *them*,' said JJ, pointing at the four men huddled into the cramped interior.

'But they're all wounded,' replied the gunner, with a clear look of disgust.

'I don't care,' replied JJ. 'I want a place.' Thor was sitting closest to the door and turned. 'The only thing you deserve right now is this, mate,' he said as he unleashed a mighty right hook with his huge fist.

The blow caught JJ clean on the chin, sending him reeling backwards.

The air gunner looked back at Thor, his face lighting up with a huge grin. 'Nice one,' he shouted, as the heavily laden aircraft began to climb into the sky.

'We need to get going,' shouted Mason, over the waning noise of the departing aircraft. 'Rachel, get into the boat with JJ, and cover him. Prof, you and I will load the stuff and push off.'

Rachel sat opposite JJ in the boat, Hollywood's golden gun grasped firmly by her two hands. 'I will take great pleasure in shooting you,' she said, as JJ rubbed his chin. 'Just give me a reason.'

'That's it,' said the Professor, as the edge of the coffin cleared the side of the boat.

429

'Right. We're off,' shouted Mason. 'Two. Three. HEAVE.' The two men timed their efforts to move the long narrow craft from the beach. 'Two. Three. HEAVE,' he shouted again. The boat began to move - slowly at first - but quickening as the craft - weighted by the artefacts, Rachel and JJ – finally became supported by the water. When it was clear of the sand and mud, the two men jumped in, Mason using the pole to push it further into the channel of water.

The Professor couldn't help himself. He was sitting amongst the artefacts like a child surrounded by toys on Christmas morning. 'There'll be plenty of time for that later,' Mason said to the academic as he pulled on the engine's starting cord. 'Let's get this engine running first.'

The Professor nodded and made his way to the back of the boat. 'Let's hope they had time to fix it,' he said as Mason gave another powerful pull on the cord. The engine spluttered. It was weak at first, but, as Mason adjusted the throttle, it became stronger. Mason slapped the Professor on the back. 'Brilliant,' he shouted. 'Brilliant!'

Rachel, her back to the engine, glanced around momentarily. It was the opportunity JJ was waiting for. He reached forward and tried to grab the gun. She pushed him back, her finger snagging on the trigger. The gun exploded, but the only thing that hit JJ was a cloud of splinters as the bullet drilled itself into the thick wooden planks. As he tried to grab the gun for a second time, she fought back, only too aware that JJ's brute force would again overcome her. As their bodies wrestled in the confined space, and with the boat rocking violently beneath them, she made one last effort.

Mason picked up his rifle, but they were too close for a shot; Rachel's back was shielding JJ. He watched for what seemed an age as the struggle ensued, impressed by the girl's tenacity – especially by her final act of defiance: sinking her teeth deep into the Scotsman's white flesh.

The gun dropped into the water, sinking instantly, its bright exterior catching the sun's rays before it tumbled out of sight. JJ stood up and hit Rachel across the face with the back of his hand, the blow knocking her backwards. His shield was gone.

'Sit down, or I will kill you right now,' Mason said, his rifle levelled at JJ's centre of mass.

'Fuck you, Mason. I would rather take my chance with the Iraqis.'

'Don't be so stupid. The whole place is crawling with IPS. Just sit down and behave.'

'BEHAVE? Who the fuck do you think you are talking to?'

'I don't care who or what you are. But I do know something: you're going to prison for a long, long time, and your money is not going to save you.'

JJ was furious, his face filling with blood as he clenched his jaw. His cheeks crimson from anger, he eyed Mason, his weight shifting as he turned to look at the water.

'Don't do anything stupid,' said Mason, anticipating JJ's escape bid.

JJ looked at the water and then back at Mason. He took a large breath and dived over the side.

'Shoot him,' shouted Rachel. 'He's getting away.'

'Getting away? There's no escape,' said Mason as he lowered his AK.

The Commander had told his men not to move, happy to watch the scene unfold before him from behind the cover of the tightly knit reeds. But, as JJ emerged from the water, he signalled his men to advance. Mason was right; there was no escape. They watched from the boat as JJ was surrounded, brought to his knees by a series of blows that thumped into his drenched body.

The Commander pulled on his cigarette as he looked at Mason from over the expanse of water. Around him, his men took up fire positions, ready to engage the boat. It was well within range. The Commander stared at the man who had spared his life earlier that morning, both men's eyes locked in a long distance duel.

'Hold your fire,' ordered the Commander. 'There has been enough killing here for one day.'

CHAPTER SIXTEEN

The journey back to the village was long and laborious. They could have relaxed as the risk of attack had rescinded, the dense reeds negating any chance of assault from outside. But the feelings of concern that Rachel had pushed into the distance now rushed back to engulf her. *Father?*

Mason knew what was racing through her mind. The outboard engine - which had passed its prime some years previously - had spluttered to a halt on several occasions during the journey, each time, Rachel anxiously exchanging glances with Mason. For his part, he worked furiously to create harmony between the well-worn engine parts.

The Professor, on the other hand, was totally enthralled. All his attention given to the recovered artefacts which he lovingly inspected, completely oblivious to the blanket of apprehension enveloping the craft.

'Professor,' shouted Mason, for the third time, his previous calls having fallen on deaf, preoccupied ears. 'Professor. I need your help. Pass me the wrench.'

'Ummm? Yes, of course... Where is it?' he answered, oblivious to the urgency in the request.

Rachel eased her way alongside him and picked up the tool, answering his question by thrusting it in his face. 'At your feet,' she hissed, handing it over to Mason.

'How much longer, do you think?' the Professor asked, hoping his query would help redeem his disgrace.

Mason and Rachel both looked at him with contempt, his question too tactless to warrant a polite reply. 'Ah,' he answered for himself, and went back to examining the sword.

It was late afternoon when the boat finally drew up

alongside the jetty. Rachel was out before the boat had stopped moving, her feet hardly touching the ground as she ran up the hill, the burning need to learn of her father's condition driving her forward. She headed off up the hill towards her house, leaving her two companions to secure and unload the troublesome vessel.

The boat's contents were placed into a nearby cart. The absence of a beast of burden meant that both men had to push the wagon up the slight gradient towards the village square.

'It's very quiet,' remarked the Professor, between laboured breaths.

'Quiet?' answered Mason. 'It's more like a ghost town.'

They were met by Miriam at the threshold of John's house, the old woman offering both of the thirsty men a beaker of water to quench their thirst. It took several fills for the dryness of their mouths to be satisfied, Mason finally turning to Miriam, with a thankful smile. 'How is John?' he asked, before returning the earthenware cup to the water pot. She looked away, unable to conceal her distress. 'Can I see him?' he continued. Miriam nodded, holding back the cover that hung in the door as a gesture for him to enter. As Mason passed John's sister-in-law, she held up her veil in a vain attempt to hide her tears.

John lay on his bed, above him a small window - the only source of light - the aperture capturing the last rays of the waning sun.

Rachel sat on a small stool next to him, her hand holding his tightly, her grip like that of a child frightened at being lost in the crowd.

'Ah, Mason,' he murmured, trying to get up.

'Rest, father,' said Rachel as she tried to stop him.

'Quiet, child. I will not greet my guest lying down like some sick old woman. Prop me up with pillows. Come closer, Mason, so I can see you.'

Mason moved closer to the bed. 'I am so sorry that I have brought this on you,' he said, taking John's hand.

'Do not apologise. You did what you had to do, as did I. Please sit. I would talk. Are your friends with you?'

'Only one. The others were taken in the helicopter.'

'Yes, yes. Rachel mentioned this.'

'Would you like to see my friend?' asked Mason.

'Maybe later,' replied John, as he started to cough, the heavy rasp from his chest turning into a wheeze, leaving blood on his lips. 'What I have to say is for your ears only,' he said, recovering his breath. 'Our master - Sir John de Guise - said that one day a man would come that would relieve us of our charge. I believe that you are that man.'

'No, John. You are mistaken. I can't be. How could I...?' John held up his hand, 'I know not of your world. But I know of you. You are a good man. You have proven this through your actions. You told Rachel and your men that you would not leave them, and you kept your word. Such honour and integrity are lacking in these times. Men are prepared to sell out their friends and brothers for coin and advancement. But not you,' he said, looking deep into Mason's eyes. 'Not you, Mason. You possess something that few men have. In the time of our master Sir John, you would have been given a title that would have set you apart from other men. They would have called you 'knight'. You possess the qualities of a true Chevalier, my son.'

Mason looked deep into the piercing blue eyes of the Elder, as they attracted the last rays of the ageing sun.

'My village is deserted. They have all run away in fear that they too will be gunned down like Joshua and Jacob. Our time has come to an end,' said John as he held Mason's stare.

'I have no son to pass this on to. And our code does not me allow to pass it to Rachel - although she is more than worthy. I have thought long and hard over this, Mason. And I have decided that the Secret must pass to you. It will be your duty to guard it. You will relieve my people of their charge was the first to break the glance, looking at

Rachel in an attempt to gather his thoughts.

'It is a lot to ask, I know. But you must decide, as I am not long for this world,' he said, his cough rising once more.

'Please, father. Do not speak so... You will get better. We have the coffin. We can open it, and perform the healing ceremony.'

'True, child. The bones of Our Lord have great power. And they have healed many of our tribe. But I would not have it. I'm tired. I want to be with your mother once more. I crave her embrace. We have been parted for too long. I want to go to her.'

'Please don't leave me, Daddy. I will be on my own. I am frightened,' pleaded Rachel, as tears flowed down her cheeks.

'You are not on your own; you have this man. He will help and protect you. Of that I am sure. Do you accept the charge, Mason?'

Mason looked at Rachel and then John. 'Yes. I accept.'

'Do you promise to keep the Secret from the weak minds of all men. And will you protect my daughter as though she was yours?'

'Yes, I will,' replied Mason.

'I feel a great sadness within you, my son. You carry a heavy burden. Come closer. Let me place my hand upon you.'

Mason knelt down, John's hands embracing his head. 'I absolve you of all that you carry. I shall take it from you. You are to start your life afresh and make the most of this great gift of life that has been bestowed upon you.'

John began to cough again, a convulsion now spreading through his entire body.

'Come, Father. You must rest.'

'You are right, child. I am tired. Lay me down. I will sleep awhile.'

Mason had tried to keep vigil with the two women. But his eyelids had grown heavy, and he had finally succumbed to

436

his exhaustion in the middle of the night. Rachel woke him just before dawn, with a gentle shake on his shoulder.

'Mason,' she whispered to him gently. 'Please wake up.'

'John?' Mason asked as he stretched off his tiredness.

Rachel shook her head. 'He has passed,' she said, looking at the body of her father - which the two women had wrapped in a shroud.

'I am so sorry,' said Mason as he stood and held her as she wept. 'He was a good man.'

'Will you help us bury him?' Rachel asked, between wrenching sobs.

Mason picked up John's body, carefully placing it into the cart that they had used the night before to unload the boat, whilst Miriam went to fetch tools from one of the outhouses to help them with their task.

'Can we go now?' asked Rachel, as Miriam placed the shovels and some rope alongside the body.

'Wait,' said Mason as he went back into the house, emerging seconds later with the stone coffin.

Rachel looked at him. 'I thought you were going to get the Professor,' she said as he loaded the heavy object into the cart.

'No. He can sleep,' replied Mason, readying the cart for the journey to the cemetery. 'This is our business.'

The bright red disk rising in the east had broken free of its earthly tethers by the time the burial party reached the cemetery.

'There is a place set aside for him,' Rachel said, pointing in the direction of a large sandstone slab in the middle of the burial ground.

The slab marked the grave of Sir John de Guise. All around him were buried the prior Village Elders - John's ancestors - who through the centuries had upheld his traditions.

'Why is there an empty space to the right of Sir John's tomb?' asked Mason.

'No Elder thought himself worthy to be buried at the right hand of our master. So it was always left empty.'

Mason took a shovel from the cart and broke ground next to the stone slab marking the final resting place of Sir John de Guise.

'I think that we have someone with us who is worthy, don't you?' he said, looking at Rachel with a persuasive smile.

Rachel smiled back. 'Yes,' said Miriam, her arm around Rachel, nodding in agreement.

The loose earth and sand gave way to the powerful blows from Mason's shovel. And it wasn't long before he had dug a hole big enough to receive the body of the last Elder.

Mason went to the cart and picked up the ossuary, placing it carefully at the graveside before jumping into the chest-deep hole. 'Help me,' he said to Rachel as he manoeuvred the stone box to the lip of the opening. Rachel pushed. The earth, dislodged by their efforts, falling in on him, surrounding him in a cloud of dust. When it was close enough, he took its weight and lowered it gently. 'It will be safe here,' he said, as he scrambled out of the hole, the dust from his efforts clinging to his sweat. With the ossuary lovingly installed, it was time for John.

They placed the rope under the shrouded remains. And, with Mason on one end and the two women on the other, they lowered John into his final resting space.

'What better honour for the last of the Elders than to be buried with Jesus?' Mason said as the two women wept. 'He can carry on with his vigil. Jesus will be safe with him,' he said, as he picked up the shovel and scooped the loose earth into the grave, each load carefully placed, the shroud gradually disappearing.

The sun was well clear of the horizon by the time Mason had finished his solemn task. The birds singing their morning song, greeting the life-giving rays of the sun, oblivious to the sorrow that filled the hearts of their audience.

'My father loved the mornings,' said Rachel, as Mason

438

put his powerful arms around each of the crying women.

Mason nodded, 'no one must know of this,' he whispered while holding them tight. 'We must never tell. Mankind is not ready for this Secret... not yet...'

EPILOGUE

Head of the River Public House, Oxford,
May 24 2008 - a year later.

The pub on the river Thames – or the Isis as the river is called in Oxford – is at bursting point, the students in their brightly striped blazers and summer dresses creating a sea of colour as they bask in the English sunshine. They are clearly glad to be free of the academic pressures of Trinity term – well at least for the weekend – as they celebrate the finale of Summer Eights. This is the intercollegiate rowing regatta that takes place every year, and has been the main topic of conversation since the start of term, the excitement growing as the crews have taken every opportunity to hone their skills on the meandering river, the honour of the ancient colleges - as always - resting on the shoulders of its scholars.

For Rachel, this is another thing to learn about: Oxford and its traditions. They seem to be never ending. It virtually has its own language - or 'lexicon' as Cornelius calls it. But he's promised that if she works hard, he will arrange a treat. So, as she walks down the busy road towards the pub on the river, she too becomes excited – but not because of Summer Eights, oh no. *How could people get excited about rowing? That was something she had to do nearly every day.* She is excited because Cornelius has arranged for the whole group to be together again.

She breaks through the noisy throng.

'There she is! How's my girl?' says Mitch, rising from his chair and kissing Rachel on both cheeks.

'I am well, thank you, Mitch. How is your health?'

'Wow, you say it just like a real English lady. You're doing a great job, Prof.'

'And Mason?' Rachel asks as they all sit.

'Right behind you. He's getting the drinks,' Cornelius says, pointing.

'My, my. Look at you,' says Mason as he places the tray of drinks on the worn picnic table. 'Do I get a hug?'

'So, what you been up to, Mason?' Mitch says, reaching for a glass of Pimms and lemonade.

'I've just got back from the Oman. Doing some anti-piracy work. I took a leaf out of JJ's book. Set up my own company. It was hard going at first, but - after the retraction was printed in the newspapers, clearing my name and all that - things started to move. We're doing okay.'

'Good for you,' Cornelius says, taking a sip from his glass. 'Did you ever find out what happened to JJ?'

'He got what he deserved,' Mitch says, taking a large gulp.

'Yeah, last I heard he was being held by one of the Shia militias. They'd asked for a few million for his release. But we've not seen his pretty face on TV yet, so who knows what they're gonna do with him,' replies Mason. 'Six is dealing with it.'

'And what of Target?' Cornelius inquires.

'From what Tonka tells me, the deal with the oil company fell through. The hostage scandal made sure of that. In the end, some American company came along and snapped it up for peanuts. Most of the guys are still out there. Same job. Just changed T-shirts.'

'But enough of that prick and his company,' Mitch says, taking a cigar pouch from the inner pocket of his jacket. 'Smoke?' he says, offering the expensive contents.

'How's things with you, Prof? Rachel tells me you're doing great.'

'Truly, I am flat out. I'm booked on the lecture circuit for months in advance. The Dean of the college is over the moon. Sir John De Guise's artefacts are on display in the V&A Museum in London. And my book - 'The Jesus Effigy' is reaching higher in the bestseller chart every week.'

Mitch draws on the cigar, 'Splendid,' he says, exhaling.

'There is one nagging thing, though,' says Cornelius. 'I would love to find out what happened to the ossuary. But when I try to ask my beautiful new assistant here, she cuts me off with a frosty stare.'

'Some things are just not meant to be,' Mason says, puffing on his cigar, adding to the cloud of smoke.

'Perhaps,' says Cornelius, disappointed by another rebuttal.

'Anyway, Mitch? What you been up to? A little bird tells me you've been a busy boy,' asks Mason.

'Not much. Just taking it easy.'

'Setting up an orphanage in Basrah doesn't sound like *taking it easy* to me,' Rachel says, to a round of laughter.

'Hey, look, I don't know what happened to my body back there in Iraq, but it was obviously some crazy shit,' Mitch says, shooting a glance at Rachel, before demolishing more of his glass.

'When they cut me open, looking for the shrapnel from the ricochet, they found that the cancer had gone. Said they'd seen nothing like it. Doctors called it a *remarkable manifestation*. I call it a *bloody miracle*, he said, trying to imitate Mason's accent. 'An orphanage was the least I could do. Let's call it payback.'

'Tell them the name, Mitch.' Rachel says as she and Mason exchange a knowing glance. 'I love the name,'

'Lost Kids…' Mitch mumbles with embarrassment. 'You know… like the lost boys in Peter Pan.'

'Yeah, yeah, we get it,' answers Mason. 'Wow - two orphanages and counting. You're getting to be quite the philanthropist. Should be pretty close to cancelling out all of the bad stuff soon, eh?'

'Anyway,' Mitch continues, apparently desperate for the last word, 'it's no big deal. I made so much money on oil shares - even after paying back the Amex bill, there was loads left over.'

'Insider trading?' suggests Cornelius.

'I couldn't help but take advantage. I bought low and sold... well, you know. If it was back in the States, yeah... but Lebanese law is a lot more... accommodating. Anyhow, it gives Miriam something to do. She's the matron ...she's loving it. Taking in the Mesahuin kids, teaching them their heritage and that. Keeping it alive. 'Ain't that right, Rach?'

'Yes Mitch,' she says. 'You've made quite an impression on my aunt. I think she likes you very much.'

'Hey, Prof. What's going on now?' Mitch says, standing to get a better look at the crowd coming from the river. 'They're carrying one guy on a boat?'

'Oh, that will be the cox,' replies Cornelius focusing on the triumphal procession.

'There was no need for that, Prof; there are ladies present,' Mitch says, looking at Cornelius with disgust.

'Oh no, no! The 'cox' is short for 'coxswain'; he's the steersman of the rowing boat.'

Mitch looks over at Mason, the grin and then the nod confirmation enough to pacify the American.

'That team has won the competition; they are *Head of the River*,' explains Cornelius.

'Ahh... hence the name of the pub,' says Mason. 'Correct. The winning team carries the boat - with the coxswain on top - back to their college, where naturally they Seems like a waste,' says Mitch.

'It's tradition' adds Rachel.

'Wow. She's only been here a year and she knows it all. Typical woman,' Mitch says to Mason - in a hushed tone, loud enough for everyone to hear.

'So how's it with you, Rachel?' asks Mason.

'Well... Cornelius says that he couldn't do without me. But I think he is just saying that. He says that my English is improving so quickly that I should be able to sit the Oxford entrance exam next year. But, until then, he will have to put up with me as his assistant.'

'That's wonderful. And the operation?'

'It has been over a month now since I had the skin graft. The doctors say that it will take another five or six operations before it will be gone. But I do not want any more.'

'Why? Was it painful?' Mason asks.

'It's not that. I just feel that covering over my scars would be forsaking my heritage. When I look at myself in the mirror, they are a reminder of my family, my friends, of all the suffering that my people went through. When people ask me how I got them, I tell them the story. I tell them of the courage of my people. It is my badge - a badge I wear with honour. I am proud of my scars.'

ACKNOWLEDGEMENTS

I gratefully acknowledge the assistance of the following people: Dr Gary Hunter, Matthew Stedman, Alexander Pendry, Frank Vassallo, John Saddler, Gareth Green, Alex Mills and the team at Burning Red, Tony Horn, Clare McNaughton.

Lightning Source UK Ltd.
Milton Keynes UK
UKHW02f0719070618
323877UK00012B/1818/P